the
one
that
got
away

the
one
that
got
away

CHARLOTTE RIXON

An Aria Book

First published in the United Kingdom in 2023 by Head of Zeus Ltd,
part of Bloomsbury Publishing Plc

9 7 5 3 1 2 4 6 8

A CIP catalogue record for this book is available from the British Library.

ISBN (HB): 9781803289984
ISBN (XTPB): 9781803289991
ISBN (E): 9781803289960

Printed and bound by CPI Group (UK) Ltd, Croydon, CR0 4YY

Head of Zeus
First Floor East
5–8 Hardwick Street
London EC1R 4RG

WWW.HEADOFZEUS.COM

For anyone who ever looked back and wondered: 'what if?'

'I am glad it cannot happen twice, the fever of first love. For it is a fever, and a burden, too, whatever the poets may say. They are not brave, the days when we are twenty-one. They are full of little cowardices, little fears without foundation, and one is so easily bruised, so swiftly wounded, one falls to the first barbed word.'

Daphne du Maurier | *Rebecca*

April 2022

It's a hotter day than anyone anticipated for April and he's sweating, but not just because of the heat.

The backpack, so carefully laden with its components just a few hours ago, is sticky against his back. He's wary of the crowds jostling him as he strides towards the stadium. He has been here so many times before, he knows the place as intimately as he knows his own home.

Today he has feigned illness and, for the first time in years, missed the game.

They are spilling out now, a swarm of ants in red and white striped vests, buoyed by their unexpected win; 3–2 at home to a worthy opponent. Collective euphoria electrifies the air.

It's a sickness. An epidemic. And soon they'll be cured of it.

His face burns red with the effort, the weight of the bag, the internal countdown in his mind.

Not too much longer. Seconds, literally seconds before it will all end.

His heart is hammering; he realises he has been holding his breath. A hand flies to his forehead as if to steady himself, and the sea of people – mostly men, mostly three pints or more down – coming towards him, those red and white worker bees, starts to blur and merge. Homogenous people, almost indistinguishable from one another: 52,000 of them. It's impossible to see them as anything but one mass, a moving entity. Nothing individual about them at all.

Collateral damage.

But then, one stands out to him; a girl, no more than six, held high on her father's shoulders, waving a scarf. Hair in bunches. Grinning from ear to ear.

It's almost too much. He sucks air into his lungs, turns away, head down, keeps walking. Bigger strides, to put distance between himself and the girl.

He mustn't think of them as individuals.

The stadium is just a few feet away now. Security on the doors, making sure everyone gets out safely. This is the side where the VIPs go after the game. He knows he'll be in there, celebrating.

He has planned it all so carefully.

His fingers fumble for the detonator. He says a short prayer to no one in particular that he has got it right.

And then: a second's pause.

He looks down at his free hand, turning it over and marvelling at his skin. The lines across his palm. The blue-green of his veins.

Someone bumps against his shoulder as they pass. He is at the entrance now. As close as it's possible to get.

It's time.

In the end, it's no more difficult than letting go of the string of a balloon.

He presses the button, and then he is gone.

part one

April 2022

Clara

The woman next to her in the ladies' loo is staring down at the row of handbasins in confusion.

'It's on a sensor,' Clara says, smiling. 'Just wave your hands underneath, see?'

She flicks her own hand back and forth underneath the tap spout until the water begins to spurt. For some reason, it's too hot – always has been – but there's no way to control the temperature.

'Thank you,' says the woman. 'And the soap?'

Clara gestures to the underside of the mirrored wall in front of them.

'Under here,' she says. 'Also automated. And the hand towels are here too. *Not* automated.'

The woman smiles at her again. She looks familiar, but Clara can't think why.

'First day?' Clara says. She's been away from her desk for more than fifteen minutes now, but sod it. It's a Saturday afternoon. Slow news day.

'I'm freelance,' the woman says, holding out her hand. 'Holiday cover. I'm a sub. Nice to meet you. I'm Natasha.'

'Clara,' Clara says, shaking her hand. 'I'm...'

There's a beat, where she remembers that she's not the social media editor any more. Not since she gave it up to go part-time, to focus on her novel after she was signed by a literary agent.

'I work in the Audience team.'

'Oh wow,' Natasha says. 'That must be interesting.'

God no, it's duller than dull, Clara thinks, but instead of saying so narrows her eyes to examine this Natasha, her deep brown eyes and neat frame. Where has she seen her before? Clara wonders how old she is. Impossible to tell.

'I love your ring,' Natasha says, and Clara realises she has let the silence stretch for too long.

'Oh,' she says, bringing her hand up slightly towards her chest. The large purple sapphire sparkles under the soft toilet lighting. 'Thanks. I've always thought it was a bit big, to be honest. My husband's a jeweller.'

'It's amazing,' Natasha says, taking a step closer and peering down. 'The setting is so unusual.'

Clara holds out her hand obligingly, moving her hand this way and that so Natasha can see all its various angles. She is well-practised at this now. The ring is beautiful but the stone is huge and heavy against her skinny, inadequate fingers, and every morning when she puts it on a phrase floats into her mind that she can't quite get rid of: 'You're not wearing it, it's wearing you.'

'How many carats?'

Clara's eyes widen. A bit bold of her. She looks at Natasha's hands, but there's nothing on either ring finger, just a gold signet on her thumb.

'Four,' Clara says, embarrassed now. 'But sapphires are heavier than diamonds, so it's not as impressive as it sounds.'

'It's magnificent,' Natasha says. 'Your husband must love you very much.'

'It's our tenth anniversary in a month's time,' Clara says, pointlessly. Ten years of this ring sitting heavy on her finger. Neither of them have planned anything. These days, it's as though they live entirely separate lives.

'Oh, goodness, well, I expect you'll get an eternity ring to go alongside that then.'

'Perhaps.'

'I got divorced last year,' Natasha says. She looks down at her own naked left hand. 'Sometimes I think I miss my ring more than I miss my ex.'

The laugh that follows sounds forced. Almost a sob.

Clara doesn't want to tell her the truth; that she thinks engagement rings are patriarchal relics, and that if it weren't for Thom's job, she wouldn't even wear one.

'You can buy yourself a ring,' she says, instead.

'Not one like that. Not on a sub-editor's salary.'

Clara nods, offers her a sympathetic smile. They leave the toilet together, their feet in step.

Clara has worked for the newspaper for nearly twenty years, and she still hasn't got used to the shiny office building that now houses it.

After the paper was acquired last year by one of the biggest media organisations in the UK, they moved into the seventh floor of the tall glass column. It's like working in a very echoey airport – complete with security guards on the entrance, who search your bags for bombs, and a tenth-floor restaurant with a roof garden that's bigger than her house and offers views stretching across the city.

'Subs desk is over there,' Clara says, smiling at Natasha,

who has paused next to the bank of desks where Clara sits, as though she's forgotten where she's meant to be sitting.

At the far corner of the room, there's a commotion. Several of the reporters are gathered around a screen.

'Jesus Christ!' one declares.

Clara frowns.

'Oh, yes. I know,' Natasha says. 'Thanks. It was nice to meet you. Bit weird, but if you fancy lunch sometime – I'm here for a month. I don't really know anyone. It's the first time I've worked for a newspaper.'

'Really?'

'Yes, I've always been on magazines. Weeklies, of course. But still. The whole newsroom thing...' Natasha glances over at the huddle in the far end of the office. 'It's quite intimidating.'

All the men, Clara thinks. That's what she means.

'Here,' Clara says, scribbling her name and extension on a Post-it. 'I only work part-time, but I'm in Tuesday, Thursday, Friday and Saturday. Give me a shout sometime.'

Natasha clutches the Post-it note.

'I will, thanks.'

Clara sits down at her desk and taps the space bar of her keyboard. The screen lights up, and she obediently types in her password.

She frowns at the spreadsheet in front of her; this week's lifestyle stories which need scheduling across all their platforms. It is mundane, this work. Beneath her.

But that's OK. Or at least, it would be, if she was actually working on her novel on her days off, as she's meant to be.

She stares at the spreadsheet, the URLs blurring before her eyes.

Then she flicks onto her Twitter account. She uses the

newspaper's scheduling platform for its accounts, but for her personal account she prefers the native browser version.

As always, her eyes land on the trending bar to the right. The words are like fireworks.

Bomb

Explosion

VintagePark

She clicks on the final hashtag, staring at the screen as it refreshes. Memories swim into her mind.

So many memories.

A blurry video is the first to load. People screaming, running towards the person with the camera.

'Holy fuck, holy fuck!' the person behind the camera shouts.

She clicks off the video, clicks back to the hashtag, scanning the tweets.

Oh my god, something just blew up outside Vintage Park. I swear.

Stay away from Vintage Park guys. Some serious shit is going down.

I think a bomb just went off a few streets away. I'm not joking. The whole building shook. Fucking terrified.

Someone just blew up the football stadium! Fucking hell!

Clara looks over at the news guys. They are on their phones already, one grabbing his jacket and heading out.

She clicks on another video, but it buffers, the small white circle spinning before her eyes.

Vintage Park. Saturday afternoon.

Perhaps it was an away game this week. Perhaps the stadium was empty.

Her hands are shaking as she googles the fixtures list. And there it is, in black and white. Newcastle City against Norwich. A home game. He taught her that all those years ago. The team mentioned first is the one playing at home.

Which means he was there.

Of course, he was there. August to May, every Saturday afternoon for their entire relationship. Without fail.

He was there when the bomb went off, but where is he now?

March 2000

Benjamin

It was Tina who persuaded him to come out tonight. He wasn't keen, but she had no one else to go with and he likes doing things for people. He likes making them happy.

Having said that, he has a shift in the department store tomorrow. He's tired. As he stands there, he wonders whether university life is all he hoped it would be, or whether it's all simply too much for him.

Since his mam got sick, life has often felt too much.

But Tina's here, and life's not enough for her.

He likes the way she finds everything fun, and when she hands him a pint – his fourth of the night – he smiles gratefully and takes a deep swig.

'This place only opened a few months ago,' she says, nudging him in the ribs, yelling over the thump-thump-thump of the music. 'That's why the carpet isn't sticky yet.'

He looks down at the carpet. It's red and white, a swirly pattern, something like he imagines a far-off galaxy looking, streaking the night sky. It makes his eyes hurt.

He takes another sip of beer. He doesn't 'do' dancing. Not in a nightclub, not at a wedding, not even when he's home alone. He isn't built for it. He read an article about it once. Tall people can't dance – it takes too long for the messages to travel from their brains to their limbs... or something. Good dancers are always short, like jockeys.

Tina is swaying slightly beside him, her eyes fixed over the rim of her JD-and-Coke, surveying the dance floor. In a minute she'll be off, once she spots someone she's interested in. She's a tiger on the prowl.

And that will leave him standing here, by the bar, alone. But that's OK. He's out, he's socialising, he's anaesthetising his feelings with pint after pint after pint. He's living the university experience. So long as he stands here, in this nightclub, drinking Stella, he is doing what he's supposed to be doing, and eventually it will start to make sense. Surely.

'Oh my god,' Tina says, slapping him on the arm. 'Is that Marcus Forbes?'

He looks across to where she's pointing.

Marcus Forbes is Newcastle City's newest signing. A nineteen-year-old striker who hasn't proved to be worth a penny of the insane amount of money they spent on him.

What a life Marcus must lead. One Benjamin might have had, if his life had gone differently.

'Nah. Too tall.'

'Yeah, you're probably right. Shame. I'd always fancied dating a footballer.'

She winks.

'Anyone you like the look of?' Tina says, her eyes sparkling as she looks up at him.

He likes Tina's company. He likes the uncomplicated way she views him. They met at the department store. She's blonde, pretty, his 'type' on paper and yet...

They went out after work a couple of times – just the two

of them – and he couldn't work out if they were meant to be 'dates' or not.

She treated him like a mate, but at the end of one of those evenings, after many drinks in the Hand and Spear, she reached up and stuck her tongue down his throat outside her house, before stumbling down the front path and coyly waving goodbye at her door, lingering for a little too long.

He didn't do anything about it and they never mentioned it again. He found her attractive and fun, but something told him that they weren't right for each other.

He wanted to be fun, but he found it eluded him.

'Earth to Benjamin!' she says, tugging his arm. 'Anyone here for you?' She's leaning close to him. He can smell her perfume – something floral and sweet. Forgettable and indistinct. 'I quite like the look of him.'

She points at a guy standing in a group of blokes who are all dressed the same. Hair parted neatly in the middle, baggy shirts over their jeans. The one she's pointing at is the tallest and has the biggest shoulders, of course. Benjamin has learnt that about her. She likes them big.

Perhaps that's why she wasn't disappointed he didn't take their relationship any further. He's tall, but he's slight.

'Go and talk to him then,' he says, swigging his pint. He's not in the mood tonight. The whole purpose of these evenings out – a kind of strange fishing expedition – leaves him cold. He doesn't want to meet girls on a dark dance floor. It feels too forced, too unnatural. How can you get to know someone properly when you can barely even hear or see them?

Still, he can't get that girl from last week out of his mind. It was at a different nightclub when he was out with his housemates – a motley crew if ever there was one – and their eyes had locked across the dance floor. At first, he thought it was just a mistake and looked away, but every time he glanced in her direction, she would stare directly at him, and he realised she was trying to tell him something. To signal her interest.

But by the time he had plucked up the courage to walk over to her, there was another boy by her side, his arm around her waist, his lips at her ear.

Later that night, when he lay in his uncomfortable single in the box room of the three-bed student terrace, he turned over the memory of her in his mind. He thought afterwards that she was perhaps the most attractive girl he had ever seen.

But it could have been the lighting, or the beer.

Just at that moment, as if on cue, the DJ changes the track. A whoop fills the air before being drowned out by the sound of a deep trance beat, and the lasers come on. The group of boys Tina has been staring at turn into black silhouettes as the lasers scan their bodies in time to the music.

It's disorientating. It's loud.

It's the reason people come to this club.

He looks around as a laser lights up the space around him but Tina has vanished into the dark of the dance floor. He takes another sip of his pint. He tries to enjoy it.

The song seems to last for an eternity, but when it ends and the lasers stop, Tina is in the middle of the dance floor, her arms wrapped around the boy's broad shoulders, her head tilted up towards his, their faces blending in the darkness.

That's it, then. He's lost his wing-woman for the night. He finishes his pint and then leaves it on the bar. A voice rings in his ear: his father's, during half-time at the match last week.

You're not to spend your whole time at university drinking and having sex, do you hear me? This is an opportunity you've been given. Make the most of it.

Well, he is not drunk – not tonight anyway.

And he is not having sex. It bothers him sometimes, that he is nineteen and pretty much a virgin – that time with Kat from the year above didn't end well – when demonstrably everyone around him is very much *not*.

They are having sex all the time. So much sex. Tina will go home with this man probably, and he won't linger by the end of her front path, hoping to be let off the hook.

He has been in the city for nearly six months now, and Tina is the only girl he has kissed. He feels under pressure, and under pressure, he is at his worst.

He'll go to the toilet, then tell Tina that he's leaving. He doesn't like leaving girls alone in nightclubs with strangers but the last time he expressed concern about this she told him he was being sexist, that she could take care of herself and, then eventually, she told him to 'get to fuck'.

She was drunk when she said it though, so he's not quite sure if she meant it.

He makes it to the other side of the dance floor before the DJ puts another trance song on and plunges the place into darkness again.

He takes a deep breath in the corridor. It's brighter here, strip lighting flickering above his head. The toilets are opposite, but as he heads towards the men's, he notices something out of the corner of his eye.

A girl is sitting on the floor, slumped over her own knees. The foyer is busy with people, drunk and oblivious, chatting or making their way from the toilets. A couple are snogging aggressively up against the entrance to the cloakroom.

A chain of girls holds hands as they writhe their way towards the laser show, mouths wide with laughter.

The girl on the floor isn't moving.

He pushes past some lads who have had too many and they

gesticulate in his face but he ignores them. He crouches down to the girl. Her hair is the brightest yellow, spilling across her shoulders, and her arms are bare and slender, resting on her jeans.

He hesitates for a second but then he touches her lightly on the arm and leans down towards her ear.

'Are you OK?' he says. 'Can I get you some water?'

She looks up, her eyes wide and tear-stained, and he sees, before she looks directly at him, that it is her.

The girl from the other club.

She smiles at him. And in that moment, he feels a shift, and the strange, thudding realisation that his university life will make sense after all.

March 2000

Clara

She cannot believe it is him. That she has seen him again.

'Are you OK?' he is saying, but she can only stare at his beautiful face. His pleasing nose. His immaculate forehead, the curls of hair carefully framing it.

'Can I get you anything?' he says, and she notices he looks worried now. As though he feels some sense of responsibility for her – for her wellbeing – already.

'I'm…' she says, wiping her eyes, realising what a state she must look. 'I'm sorry, I lost my friends…'

He helps her to her feet and she smooths down her tiny black top, brushes the dust from her jeans, and wrenches her handbag back over her shoulder.

'I can help you look for them?' he says, and she registers for the first time an accent.

Northern, but not Manchester or Leeds. He sounds local. She's surprised.

'No, it's fine,' she says, smiling at his offer. He's still holding her arm, ever so gently, and she hopes he will never let go. 'I was just… it's fine.'

He pauses, waiting for her to continue. But she doesn't say anything. She only stares at him.

'Listen,' he says. He blinks at her. 'This might sound crazy, but by any chance were you in Sound Barrier last Tuesday? I thought...'

'YES!' she says, her voice coming out louder than intended. So he had seen her, he had noticed her. She wasn't imagining it.

'Why do you say it like that?' he asks, letting go of her arm.

'Because... I was waiting,' she says, looking down. She swallows. 'I was waiting for you to come over, but you never did.'

'I thought you were with someone... there was a lad with you...'

'No,' she says. 'I... he was no one. I was hoping... for you.'

As soon as she says the words, she prays they will be lost to the shrieking in the background coming from a bunch of girls outside the ladies'. But he smiles and so she leans forward and puts her arms around his neck.

The last rush of vodka courses through her bloodstream.

'Better late than never,' she says, and before she has the chance to chicken out, she closes her eyes, reaches up and kisses him.

March 2000

Benjamin

He's so taken aback by the kiss that at first, he fails to respond. But then his body overtakes his brain and he finds himself lost in the sensation of her lips on his.

He feels he could kiss her forever but after an indeterminable amount of time, they break apart and she looks up at him.

'Shall we go?' she says. 'Are you with someone?'

He's momentarily stunned.

He thinks about Tina, about the fact that he was heading for the toilet, about the fact that he doesn't even know this girl's name yet, and how none of it seems to matter.

'I...' he says. 'I was about to leave myself.'

'Great,' she says and she takes his hand and slots hers into it and tugs him slightly towards the door.

Before he has fully assimilated what has happened, they are standing on the pavement outside the nightclub.

'Who were you out with?' she is saying. 'Those guys from last week?'

He swallows, thinks of Tina.

The girl starts to walk away from the club, up towards the high street and the bus stop. Pressure bears down on him.

'Hang on,' he says. 'Sorry. It's just, I should...'

'I cannot believe my flatmates. Bitches,' she says, staring down at the ground.

He notices that she's wearing tiny strappy sandals, that her toes are white with cold. She's smaller and slighter than he thought, standing next to him. He feels an overwhelming urge to take off his coat and put it around her shoulders.

'I just need to tell my friend,' he says, feeling already like he has failed her. He's not cool nor impressive nor any of the things he so wants to be. But it's the right thing to do. 'Tell her that I'm leaving.'

'Her?' The girl's blue eyes widen. 'You were out with a girl?'

'Yes, Tina,' he says. 'We work together at Gordon's. The department store. But she just met a lad... she'll not be bothered I'm leaving. Will you wait here?'

'OK.'

'My friend left her jacket,' he says to the bouncer who nods and lets him back inside.

Once in, he scans the dance floor until he spots Tina, her arms still wrapped around the muscular boy.

He swallows, then thinks of the girl, hopes she's still waiting for him outside.

He still doesn't know her name.

'I'm off,' he says into Tina's ear as loudly as possible. She pulls her head away from the lad's shoulder, looks up at him puzzled. He makes a gesture with his thumb.

'I'm leaving,' he says, louder this time. 'Is that OK?'

Tina nods.

'See you,' she says and she folds back into the boy's shoulder.

He hurries back outside, sick to his stomach. But the girl is still there. She stamps her feet up and down and pulls her arms around herself as she waits.

'Sorry about that,' he says. Tina will be fine. She wasn't even that drunk.

The girl smiles at him and loops her arm through his.

'What's your name?' he says.

'Clara,' she says, not missing a beat. 'What's yours?'

'Benjamin.'

'Benjamin? Not Ben?'

'I don't really mind,' he lies. 'But my friends call me Benjamin.'

And with that sentence he realises he has done it again. He is dull. The spark has gone. They are standing in the cold grey evening on a cold grey pavement in a cold grey northern city and he is not sparky or fun or interesting and this girl will soon realise and leave.

'So, Benjamin,' she says. 'What are you doing in this awful city?'

'Getting a degree?'

'Funny,' she says, and he thinks, *was it? Oh, good.* His throat is dry. 'What are you studying?'

'Computing for Business.'

'At Northumbria?'

He nods. She wrinkles her nose. Unimpressed.

'How about you?'

'Guess.'

He pauses on the pavement and looks at her.

'English,' he says. 'I think you're studying English.'

She starts, opening her eyes wide and stepping back slightly.

'Wow, that's impressive,' she says. 'Unless... you're some terrifying stalker. Now listen, Benjamin, if we go back to my place now you have to promise not to kill me. I mean, I do have a rape alarm and I'm not afraid to use it.'

She fumbles around in the tiny handbag hanging from her shoulder and pulls out a small black keyring.

'See!'

He frowns.

'I...' he says, but she doesn't seem to want him to reply, because she shoves it back in her handbag and continues trudging up the street.

He supposes she's a little bit drunk, and that she's nervous too, and he decides not to read much into what she's saying. She's chatting now, about her flatmates and whether she should ask for a transfer because they all take too many drugs and she has nothing in common with them, and none of them are on her course, so she doesn't understand how she got placed with them anyway, and she wonders what kind of weird criteria must they use to decide who gets to live with who in the self-catering places, and how, if she's honest, she wishes she hadn't even come to this uni because all her school friends went to Exeter or Oxbridge or LSE, and she only came here because her sixth-form boyfriend came up the year before and she thought they'd be together forever. But then when she arrived she found out that he'd been cheating on her throughout the entire first year, *can you believe that?!*, and so they broke up and she feels stupid now, both that she wasted that opportunity and disappointed her parents, especially her father, who hasn't really forgiven her for not trying for Oxbridge, so now she feels she can't possibly tell them that she's not happy here after all.

He walks alongside her, strangely comforted by the fact this girl he has just met is treating him like an old friend, telling him all her thoughts and feelings without stopping to consider whether it's appropriate. She's filling the silence he hates and not in an obnoxious way. In an entertaining way. He can see she's nervous, but he admires how she's trying to cover it up.

She's an open book. One he wants to read.

'Listen,' he says, as they sit side by side at the bus stop. Her eye make-up has smudged under her eyes but he likes it. She looks unruffled, relaxed. 'Can I get your number?'

She blinks twice, tucking her hair behind her ear.

'Aren't you...' she says. 'Coming back to mine?'

'I have to work in the morning,' he says, looking down at his feet. 'I think I should get home.'

'Oh,' she says. 'Right. It's because... of what I said about my ex, isn't it? I don't see him any more. I'm over him, honestly. It's just embarrassing, that I could have been such a fool. I mean, following him up here like some lovesick teenager! Humiliating. But there's nothing...'

'No,' he says, feeling his neck redden. 'It's not that. I just have to get up early, and all my stuff is in my room...'

'Your stuff?'

'My uniform.'

'You have a uniform?'

'It's not a uniform exactly,' he says, feeling stupid. 'It's just a top. A polo shirt that Gordon's makes us wear.'

She nods.

'So, can I have your number?'

'Sure,' she says, sniffing slightly.

'Do you have a pen?' he asks.

'What? Does it look like I have a pen? Put my number in your phone.'

'I don't have one.'

'What?'

'A mobile phone.'

She stares at him.

'Why not?'

He shrugs.

'I just haven't felt the need.'

'Bloody hell, you really are some kind of psycho.'

He laughs, running his hand through his hair.

'There's a landline in my house share. I just use that if I need to call someone.'

He hasn't needed to call many people since he got here.

'Give me that then,' she says. 'I guess... I guess I'll have to call you.'

He notices her wince as she says it. He's picked up enough since he started at university to know that this is not the way it goes. He's meant to take her number, he's meant to call her, he's meant to do the chasing, the wooing... the making of the effort. She's the prey and he's the predator, except in this case it doesn't feel that way at all.

'I can go back in and ask at the bar for some paper and a pen if you like?' he says.

That sounded desperate.

'No, it's fine,' she says. 'I'm a feminist. Why shouldn't I call you?'

'Right.'

He dictates the number and watches as she types it into her black Nokia.

A bus pulls up alongside them and she stands.

'I'm gonna walk back,' he says. 'Will you get home all right?'

'This bus goes straight to my halls,' she says. 'I think I can manage.'

'Great. So, I'll see you then,' he says. 'If you want to call me... and we can... we can go out properly sometime.'

'All right Benjamin,' she says, reaching out and squeezing his hand. 'I will.'

April 2022

Clara

Her shift ends at 5.30 p.m., by which time news of the bomb is everywhere. She's constantly being fed updates by the News team, which she duly shares to their feeds, adding the required BREAKING NEWS tag to the beginning.

It might be one of the most exciting days she has ever had since she joined the paper but she can't find any thrill in it. All she feels is fear.

The early accounts of casualties are confusing. The newspaper won't report any numbers until the police release a statement. The journalists are all over social media too, replying to witnesses' tweets, asking for permission to use their photographs. It's frantic, and she doesn't have time to pause for breath.

No word yet on who is responsible but, of course, it's already assumed: an act of terrorism.

She's relieved when her boss comes on-shift to take over, supported by the night team.

'I can stay if you need me,' she says, praying that he won't.

'You're all right. Get home and watch a romcom or something. Just dreadful,' Barney says, patting her on the shoulder as she gathers up her things. He sighs. 'Fucking awful day.'

'There are some very graphic images of the aftermath,' she says. 'The guys have been trying to get permission to use them but...' She tails off. It's not for her to decide what's appropriate.

Clara realises her eyes are damp.

'Hope you're OK,' Barney says.

'Sorry,' she says. She covers shocking and depressing news stories every day. But not on this scale. 'This one has got to me a bit.'

'Just senseless,' he says, with a shrug.

No that's not it, Clara thinks.

'See you Tuesday,' she says instead, and she heads towards the lifts.

On the Tube home, everyone is glued to their phones. The woman next to her is scrolling Twitter – waiting for the new tweets to load as she connects to the wifi in each station, her tongue ticking with frustration. It's like she's watching a live-action movie. All that's missing is some popcorn in her lap.

One video, in particular, has been shared multiple times. Clara saw it pop up over and over and the woman is watching it now. She turns and nudges her friend, presses play on the clip again and they both stare in horror.

A man, his north-eastern accent thick with his tears, holding a makeshift bandage to his face, describing the moment the bomb went off. *Just a normal game, you know. We were all made up.* He's explaining how right after he couldn't hear anything but ringing, couldn't understand what had happened. But then he realised he'd been hit by shrapnel.

At one point he holds up his forearm to the camera. It's torn to shreds, the skin blackened and bloody.

Who would do something like this? We were just watching the game, man. It was all peaceful. There were kids there... families... Just enjoying the game.

And then he bursts into sobs.

She has scanned all the footage she has seen this afternoon relentlessly, her eyes sore from looking, looking, looking. But she hasn't seen him. Maybe he wasn't there?

Hopefully, he wasn't there.

By the time she's reached her Tube station, she's absolutely exhausted. Thom should be home from the workshop by now and he'll want to talk about it all, of course. He'll want to know what she's seen, whether or not she'll have any insider information.

But these days, that's not how it works. The real journalists are the people on the ground, the witnesses to the events. They're the ones who break the story. They're the ones who truly create the news.

The media are losing their power. Their ability to control the narrative.

Still, he will ask. He finds her job much more interesting than her novel.

She pauses on the path up to her front door, pushing the thought further.

He finds her job much more interesting than he finds her.

She pushes open the front door to their small Victorian terrace and stands still in the hallway for a few seconds, staring at herself in the mirror. Before she knows what's happening, she starts to cry.

She can't do this. She can't come back here and have a normal evening with Thom. Not now. Not while she has no idea if he's alive or dead.

Twenty years of pain, bubbling to the surface.

It doesn't feel like a choice. Her keys are still clutched in her hand. She turns and walks back through the front door, closing it behind her before Thom has the chance to say hello.

She walks back to Turnham Green Tube, wondering how long it will take her to get to King's Cross. It's a long journey, comparatively, and she'll have to change at Hammersmith for the Piccadilly line. She clutches her phone in her hand, knowing that what she is doing is illogical, nonsensical. But the alternative is impossible.

There is no way she can walk back into their house and sit down and choose what takeaway to order and then anaesthetise herself in front of the television with a bottle of wine.

The bomb is the final straw. But Thom won't understand, and she can't contemplate the idea of explaining it to him, so she lies instead, tapping out a message to him that she knows he won't suspect.

> Been an intense day, going for a drink after work with Lauren to unwind. Hope that's okay? Please don't wait up x

She sends the message just as the Tube travels underground after Barons Court, knowing that it won't resurface for twenty minutes or so, by which time she will be nearly there.

The further she ventures with her mad plan, the better. The more physical distance she puts between herself and her home – that safe, stultifying cocoon she's been hiding in for four years now, ever since she gave up the thought of motherhood and accepted that this life was her lot – the better.

At King's Cross she surfaces, following the signs for the mainline station. Her phone has buzzed in her hand but she doesn't look at it yet. She buys her ticket and walks to the concourse, staring up at the departures board.

The trains to Newcastle are all delayed.

Of course, she thinks. Stupid of her to not think of this. They don't want people travelling up there at the moment. There will be police all over the place, blocking off the city.

And then she notices that there are police here, too. Patrolling the station in pairs, wearing neat baseball caps. They have guns, walkie-talkies strapped to their thighs.

A huge TV billboard above her flashes up telling her the prime minister has raised the terror threat level to 'Severe', a move that seems rather too little, too late.

She sighs.

She *is* stupid. Because even if she got there, what could she do? Wander the streets hoping to catch a glimpse of him? It's been twenty years since she last saw him. How many since they last had contact?

Either way, he might not even still be living in the city.

And even if he is, what are the chances that he will have been involved in the blast? That he will be one of the injured or dying?

Back when she knew him, his father was a season ticket holder – and they always went together. Every other Saturday, throughout the whole season. It was like church to them. A religion. She can't remember him ever missing a home game.

He will have been there today, she is sure of it.

She finally looks down at the reply from Thom on her phone.

Oh, sure. Can't imagine it was much fun at work today.
Have a good time x

He doesn't care. That's good. He's been distracted for the

past six months or so, different somehow. Ever since he saw that controversial osteopath, who he claims worked some kind of miracle on his back.

Thom won't suspect that her anguished heart might have brought her here, to this crowded concourse, to crane her neck up at the board, waiting for one of the 'Delayed' signs to start flashing 'Boarding' instead.

No, Thom will settle in for the evening with that takeaway and that bottle of red and he'll be quite happy. Knowing this alleviates some of her guilt.

She heads for the coffee shop at the corner of the station and orders a cappuccino, sipping it slowly as she watches all the people coming and going.

At one point, she googles him, but she has done this hundreds of times – monthly if not weekly – and there's never been anything of interest out there except an out-of-date LinkedIn page, and a handful of news stories from 2002, which she has read over many times. None of them sounded like they were talking about Benjamin, her beloved boy.

He vanished into the ether when he vanished from her life.

It seems cruel that so many people she'd rather forget pop up all over her social media feeds, yet the one person she knows never will remains elusive.

She doesn't look at the news. She ignores Twitter completely. She doesn't want to hear any more details now. Not until she gets there and sees for herself.

When she finishes her coffee, she gets up and orders another one. And then she waits, watching the minutes on the large station clock tick by until eventually, what seems like hours later, the departures board changes and there, finally, it is. What she came here for.

A train to Newcastle, leaving in twenty minutes.

April 2022

Clara

She's lucky to have got a seat on the train but it's not a good one. She's right by the luggage rack, the waft of toilet passing every time someone opens the vacuum-operated doors. In the space between the carriages, there are people sitting on the floor, complaining about the ticket prices.

Nothing has changed.

She remembers this journey so well. The excitement she used to feel as she left her family home in Hampstead, wheeling her bag up the street to the Tube. Then at the station, she'd buy herself a bottle of water and a banana – because she didn't eat much as a teenager, she was shamefully terrified of putting on weight – and then she'd settle down with her magazine or book and gaze out of the window, nap or read the whole way there.

Back then her mobile phone could only text or make calls, so it spent most of the time in her bag. She'd text him, though, when the train pulled into Darlington. So he knew to come and meet her.

And then, he'd wait on the platform for her. She always told him which coach she was in, and there he'd be as the train drew in and quite often she'd be tearful as she climbed off and their bodies collided.

Those moments of reconnection were the closest to euphoric she has ever felt.

Now, she can't remember when she last visited Newcastle. She wonders how things have changed.

The train is full of people gossiping about the explosion and she wishes she had her headphones with her, so she didn't have to hear them.

One older woman with cropped, streaky hair is frantic, telling the man sitting next to her that her daughter works next to the stadium, that she hasn't managed to speak to her yet.

'Her phone's off. I've been trying the information line, but I can't get through,' she says, staring down at her phone. 'And now my battery's nearly gone.'

The man next to her gazes at her sympathetically but doesn't speak. She wonders what he's on the train for. Where he's going.

Clara closes her eyes and thinks again of Natasha, wondering if she has gone home for the day, too. She isn't sure what kind of shift patterns the subs work. They seem to be all over the place. Redundancies mean they're using freelancers more and more and there are always new faces at the desks.

Why did she seem so familiar? She's sure she hasn't seen her in the office before, but she also feels certain this wasn't the first time their paths crossed. Perhaps she's a friend of Lauren's?

She takes her phone out of her bag and taps out a message. Lauren is the only person who knows the whole story. The only one who understands even five per cent of what this day will mean to her.

Don't judge me but I'm on the train to Newcastle. I've told Thom I'm out with you. Sorry.

She waits for Lauren to connect to WhatsApp and for the tick against her message to turn blue. And then – the inevitable.

Clara's phone begins to ring in her hand.

'Hi,' she says, quietly. No one likes speaking on trains.

'What the... are you OK?' Lauren says. She sounds out of breath. Perhaps she's going out. It is Saturday night after all.

'Yes, I'm fine. I know it's stupid but...'

Lauren makes a noise like steam coming off a kettle.

'Are you seriously... seriously, on a fucking train to Newcastle?'

'I don't know what I'm doing,' Clara says, and then she begins to cry. 'Oh god.'

She wipes at her eyes with the back of her hand.

'I'm sorry.'

'Fuck, I'm meant to be... we've got tickets for the cinema tonight. The babysitter just got here. I'm already late. Where are you? Can you get off? This is madness, you know that.'

'It's fast to York. We've just gone through Peterborough.'

'Jesus. What are you going to... where will you stay?'

'I've got my credit card. I'll get a hotel.'

'And then what? What are you going to do? Comb the streets looking for him?'

'I had...' She doesn't know how to explain this visceral urge she felt. This pull. She had to get on the train. 'I have to make sure he's OK. You know he always went to every match.'

'How are you going to do that exactly?' Lauren says. 'Clara...'

'I'll... I'll go to his work, ask them.'

'How do you know where he works?'

'He told me,' she says. 'When we last emailed.'

'Clara, babe, that was, what, ten years ago?'

'I know, but...'

How can she explain this to Lauren? That she knows him. She knows him deep down, in a way no one else ever can.

Even if he's not still at that job, there will be people who know where he is now.

'Lauren, what if he...' she whispers, holding the phone so tightly that her fingertips ache. 'What if he's injured? Or hurt? What if he's dead?'

She squeezes her eyes shut, as though to block out the possibility.

'Listen. I want you to promise me you'll get off at York and get on the first train back. I'll look up the times for you... Hang on, I'm putting you on speaker.'

'I...'

'Shit!'

'What?'

There's a silence on the line. Clara can't tell if it's the signal cutting out, or Lauren thinking what to do with her crazy friend.

'Shit shit shit,' Lauren says again. 'You'll be too late. You won't be able to get a train back tonight.'

Clara opens her eyes, her lips rearranging themselves into something like a smile.

Leap and the net will appear, as her gran used to say.

'Well, then,' she says. 'I might as well stay on until Newcastle.'

Lauren pauses again. The train lurches to the side as it picks up speed.

'Call me when you get there,' Lauren says. 'Promise me. The second you get off the train, you call me. And don't go anywhere near the bloody stadium. Do you hear me? Just call me. I'll look up some hotels near the station now, see if I can book you a room.'

Clara smiles, properly this time. She is grateful for Lauren's attempts to take care of her, but she doesn't need it. She'll be fine.

'It's OK,' she says. 'I'm forty-one years old. It's a long time since... I'm fine now. I've got my head screwed on.'

'Clara, I love you, but if you had your head screwed on, you wouldn't have just got on a three-hour train to Newcastle on a whim.'

'I'm sorry to have worried you,' she says, her voice gaining confidence. 'But I mean it. I'll be OK. I know it sounds insane but for some reason, I'm just sure...' She pauses, gazes out at the blur of greenery rushing past the window. More space. More distance. 'I'm sure this is the right thing to do.'

March 2000

Benjamin

He's waiting on the platform for her to arrive.

It has been a week since she first called him, and he was out, so she left a message with his flatmate Donny.

Donny thought it was hilarious.

Some lass rang for you. She said could you ring her back and here's her number. Eh-up everyone, Benjamin's finally pulled!

'Shut up,' Benjamin had said, snatching the takeaway menu Donny had written her number on from him.

'She sounded posh,' Donny said, and then he walked away whistling 'Uptown Girl'.

His heart pounded as he dialled her number but she answered straight away.

He suggested Friday night. Newcastle City were playing at home on Saturday, which ruled that out.

'I'm going to visit my parents on Friday,' she said. 'They live in London. Can you do Sunday night? Perhaps meet me off the train? It gets in at 18.07.'

It seemed weird to start a date by meeting someone off the train but, little did he know, this would become their thing, their ritual.

He tried to get onto the platform then realised you needed a ticket to get through the barriers. He explained his predicament to the guy working them, who said if he got a permit to travel, he could wait on the platform.

He located the little red machine. Someone had scraped off the 't' and the 'l' so it said 'Permit to rave'.

He put 10p in, and grabbed the ticket that came out.

And now he's waiting, and feeling a bit like a prat, and wondering if he should have brought her a flower or something, a rose perhaps, or whether that would have been too over-the-top. But somehow it feels wrong to be standing here, empty-handed.

He always takes flowers when he goes to see his mam.

But that's different, of course.

He sees her train coming from the distance, a speck at first, that grows larger and larger as it rounds the bend, grating against the rails. It's enormous, this train, and it seems to be full of people.

He has never been to London.

Eventually, the train spews its occupants out onto the broad platform, and he tries to stand still, confident, scanning the crowds.

How will he spot her? Her bright yellow hair. He will never forget her face, but there are so many faces here. What if she forgets his?

He's so desperate to see her before she sees him. Somehow the thought of her surprising him makes him want to run away.

He's tall though. Six foot two. And that gives him an advantage.

Eventually, he spots a shiny blonde head making its way down the platform. She's wearing a denim jacket, jeans that are slightly flared at the bottom and brown boots. His fingers reach up to his own hair, checking the wax is keeping his curls in place.

She looks up and sees him, and her face splits again into that smile.

Briefly, he thinks that he would like that smile to be the last thing he sees before he dies, then wonders what on earth is wrong with him.

'Hi,' he says, as she draws nearer.

'Hi,' she says, and she seems shy. Of course, this time she isn't drunk. He swallows. It's relatively dark on the platform – the sun went in an hour ago, but even so. Is he a disappointment? 'Hope you weren't waiting long.'

'No,' he says. 'Let me take that for you.'

His hand rests on hers as he takes her bag from her. It's heavier than he expected.

'Good weekend?' he asks.

'Oh,' she says, wrinkling her nose. 'It was all right.'

He nods. He doesn't much enjoy visits home at the moment either.

She takes a deep breath.

'So, Benjamin. Where are we going?' she says as they leave the station.

His cheeks redden.

'I thought... The Elbow Room?'

She frowns.

'It's a pool bar. They sometimes have live music too.'

'Pool?'

His stomach churns.

'It's not far. I thought you might want to go somewhere close. I thought you might be tired after the journey... Plus you live near the Infirmary, don't you? So, it's kind of on the way home for you...'

'It sounds great,' she says. 'I've never played pool before. Well, no, actually that's not true. I have. But only once, in a pub. But perhaps that was snooker. What's the difference?'

'It probably wasn't snooker if it was in a pub,' he says, smiling.

'What's the difference?'

'You really want to know?'

'I really want to know.'

'Snooker has more balls, bigger tables, different rules. It's harder.'

'Are you good?'

'At snooker?'

'At pool?'

He stops outside The Elbow Room. She looks up at the neon sign above the door.

'It looks... quite blokey.'

'I thought you were a feminist.'

She whacks the back of her hand against his chest and grins at him and he feels a surge of longing that brings the redness back to his cheeks.

'After you,' he says, and she trots past him.

They abandon the game after twenty minutes. She won't stick to the rules – continually trying to pot his stripes – and although it would normally annoy him, because deep down he finds rule-breaking difficult to cope with, he finds he doesn't mind. Not when it's her.

'I'm shit at this,' she says, sinking down onto the leatherette bench behind the table. There are still seven balls left to go, but he sits next to her anyway, cue in hand.

'You're not, you know,' he says, smiling. 'If you'd just stop trying to get my balls. You did really well with your number 2.'

She rolls her eyes and sucks her drink through the straw.

'Do you want another? My round.'

'No,' he says, putting his hand over hers and taking the glass from her. 'It's on me.'

'Oh. Thanks. I'll have a gin and tonic then, please.'

At the bar, he scratches his neck as he waits to be served, trying not to look back at her. He has the probably-not-irrational fear that she might run off, leave him there. Or phone a friend and joke about what a loser she's on a date with.

His palms are sweaty as he carries their drinks back.

She's still there.

'Can I tell you something, Benjamin?' she says, as she takes her drink from him.

He sips. Nods.

'I think you have the best face I've ever seen. Is that weird? Like, it's just... perfect.'

He nearly chokes on his drink. He opens his mouth but nothing comes out.

How in the world should he respond? Why aren't there rules for this stuff? Why does everyone else seem to instinctively know what to say, what to do, in these situations?

'Will you come home with me?' she says. 'I'm really tired, but I don't want this to... end. Not yet anyway. And I'm shit at pool and to be honest it's quite... loud in here and I'd rather just sit on my bed with a cup of tea and talk to you properly...'

Talk to you properly.

'I...' For some reason his dad pops into his mind again. What would he say? He would say go for it. Probably. But what does she really mean? He stares at her. Her lip folds in, and she chews it. She is waiting for him to reply.

She also has the most perfect face he has ever seen, but he can't imagine just saying that out loud.

'Sure,' he says, pulling some courage from somewhere.

He looks over at his pint. Barely touched. Would it be rude to ask if he could finish it? He knows he needs it. The alcohol does something to him. Makes him different from who he is; paints him in a better, more socially acceptable light. People like him more, when he's drunk. And he likes people more too.

'Do you want to finish your drink first?' he says, and she widens her eyes as though challenged, puts the straw back in her mouth and sucks and sucks until the glass is empty.

'There,' she says, slamming it down on the table. He looks at his pint glass. He has downed many a pint in the past of course – a rite of passage for any northern lad. But he can't do it here. Not in front of her.

'Aren't you going to do the same?' she says, poking him.

Is it a test? It feels like a test. A test that she doesn't even know she's putting him up to.

He reaches forward and picks up the glass. He takes a large gulp, then puts it back down.

Suddenly he realises he doesn't want to be that pissed, numb version of himself in front of her. He wants her to like him as he really is.

'You win,' he says. 'Let's go.'

April 2022

Clara

The train pulls in at Newcastle. It is late now, nearly 11 p.m. The train still has further to go, all the way to Edinburgh. The people she leaves behind in the carriage are all yawning, heads lolling onto their neighbours' shoulders.

She hasn't texted Thom to tell him she isn't coming home. He'll go to bed and probably won't notice until the morning. He sleeps well these days, now that his back is better.

The thought of it lifts her. It's a kind of freedom.

She should have done this before. Snuck out. Put herself first.

It strikes her that he has been doing the same recently. She thought it was just work – he decided to open a second boutique last year and has been hugely busy ever since. But there's more to it. He started going to the gym again and even signed up for a cookery course.

Textbook midlife crisis, her mother said. But Clara ignored it. Pushed away the questions. There is something going on with Thom, but she hasn't found the energy to care. And that makes her sad but in a resigned way, like the sadness you feel when an elderly, distant relative dies.

And now it's as though a switch has gone off in her brain, a kind of amnesia for her current life. All she can think about is him. About the past she never truly left behind.

She steps off onto the platform and it hits her – the chill in the air that tells her she's back in the north. She'd forgotten just how much cooler it can be up here – especially in the evenings.

She pulls her thin jacket around her, wishing she'd thought to bring a coat. Or a bag with some things in. Like a toothbrush.

Lauren has texted her the details of a Travelodge by the Quayside, telling her that she's reserved a room under her name.

Promise me you'll use it. Promise me you won't spend the whole fucking night wandering around the streets.

PS This Marvel film is shit.

And she'd replied.

I promise. Thank you x

PS sorry to hear that.

It was comforting to know that she wasn't completely free-floating. That someone from her real life was grounding her.

She pushes her ticket into the slot and walks through the barrier. The station is quiet but one thing stands out. The police. Many more than in London, patrolling and huddled in pairs, watching and waiting for anything suspicious.

She takes her phone out of her pocket and taps on the map. Her eyes scan the threads of the city, the intricate, interwoven pattern that the roads and buildings make. A whole universe held in her hand, like some kind of magic.

She used to know this city so well, but it's changed. She can see that even as she leaves the station. Everything is shinier, brighter, as though it's been given a coat of varnish.

She turns left out of the station. His bar is a ten-minute walk from here. She tries not to think about the fact that she is walking in the direction of the stadium.

The pubs are quiet as she passes and there's an eerie atmosphere, as though the city has been tranquillised. But this sedation is punctuated with the occasional shriek of sirens, somewhere off in the distance.

As she walks, she passes more police. They all have guns, held close to their chests, and they all ignore her.

She remembers then. Being here before, doing this same walk. But with him, of course.

All her memories of this city are with him. Except for one.

It has changed, but not so much that the faded memories – of being a different person, a different version of herself – don't creep behind her as she walks.

And then, as though the city is reading her mind, she looks up and sees she's at The Elbow Room.

March 2000

Clara

She's more nervous than she looks as she reaches over and takes his hand, walking away from the bar.

He must think she's an idiot. Totally hopeless, not to have a clue how to play pool.

Or worse, that she's a spoilt brat not to continue playing, when he was so patiently trying to teach her.

But what he hadn't realised – or noticed – was that the pool tables next to theirs were being played on by men. Just men. And that they were looking over at her, that same sideways glance she's so used to, and that at one point one of them nudged his mate and snickered, and she knew it was at her crap shot.

She couldn't face the humiliation. Or the leering.

But now she's terrified. She's taking it to a whole new level and, despite her bravado, she's sick to her stomach that she'll mess things up with him. This perfect, enigmatic creature.

It wasn't like this with Daniel.

She was pushed into that relationship by her friends, by her desperation, by the fact that he was the only vaguely attractive boy she knew who had ever expressed an interest in her.

And she was held in by the intensity of his feelings for her.

By the fact that she was seventeen and so desperately wanted to be in love. By the praise he heaped on her, by the fact he once handed her an envelope with £50 in it, telling her that she made him so happy he wanted to thank her.

It hadn't occurred to him that paying her might make her feel like a prostitute. He was so upset by his misfire when she raged at him, throwing the notes in his face.

How dare you! What the hell!

But still, he was an eighteen-year-old boy, with no clue how to express his love. She realised that he thought this was the most powerful way. And despite her indignation, the gesture did resonate with her, and she did think: *wow, this is something real.*

She thought they would last forever. How awful that he's the reason she's here now, at this university.

She went against her parents and followed him up to this cold northern city, so far from home.

Even her school friend Melissa told her she was making a mistake, but she believed the relationship was worth it. But when she finally arrived last term, everything felt wrong. Daniel was different with her. Awkward and dismissive.

It only took a few days to find out about his cheating, when they ran into one of his conquests in a bar. The girl had flung her arms around Daniel, then looked Clara up and down and said, 'This must be the girlfriend?'

Even more galling was that he was so casual about it, as though she was a fool to have expected him to stay loyal.

She'd followed what she thought was her heart. But it wasn't. It was a fantasy of her own creation. And when they split up, she wasn't even heartbroken. It was worse: she was ashamed, her pride in tatters.

But what they had wasn't love. Of course, it wasn't. Because standing here on the street with this person – this *dream* – she already realises what love truly is. Something intangible. A feeling that has taken hold of her entire being, both physically and mentally.

He's quiet though. She can't tell what he's thinking. So she keeps talking, to fill the void. About her weekend, about her mother, with whom she has an uncomfortable, judgemental relationship; about her younger sister, Cecily, who had to be taken to hospital last night to have her stomach pumped after drinking too much at a house party.

'She's an idiot,' she says, glancing sideways at him. His mouth is set still, she can't tell what he's thinking. 'She's only sixteen. It's the second time it's happened. If she wants to down six vodka Red Bulls then she should eat something first.'

'Well, she's a teenager, I guess.'

'Yes but...' she pauses. 'She was really sick when she was little. She had leukaemia. It really pisses me off that she doesn't take better care of herself.'

He stops on the pavement, looks deep into her eyes.

'But she's OK?' he says, sounding concerned. 'Now?'

'She's OK,' she says. 'Completely cured. I mean, she has check-ups every year, but she's been in remission for nearly a decade. But... everyone forgets about how ill she was. No one ever really talks about it. It's like some weird family secret. Sometimes it feels as though I'm the only person who remembers. And I was only six! I was terrified she was going to die.'

'That must have been very hard.'

'It was horrendous. I had nightmares for years.' Her voice drops. 'I guess the anxiety has never really left me.'

'She probably misses you,' he says, thoughtfully. 'I guess. Now you're gone.'

Clara hasn't considered that.

'Well, it feels like I'm back every bloody weekend. My parents are *so* pissed off with me for not going to Oxford or Cambridge. My dad insisted that I do Economics A level, even though I'm rubbish at maths.'

Is it her imagination or does he squeeze her hand ever so slightly? She's not sure, but she likes it. Likes the feel of his skin against hers, the way their palms fit together. She never wants to let his hand go.

'What are your parents like?' she asks.

'Not like that,' he says. 'Although I certainly disappointed my dad when I gave up football.'

She frowns, wondering if it's a joke.

'Football?'

'Yes. He had high hopes for me when I was young. I was... decent. Who do you support?'

'Oh,' she says. He's serious! 'No one. Sorry.'

'Southerners,' he says, rolling his eyes.

'You?'

'Cut me open and I bleed Newcastle City. Of course.'

She nods, bemused.

'Here I am,' she says, pausing outside her halls of residence. 'I'm in the self-catering bit, thank god. Get my own ensuite as well. Although when I moved in, the sink wouldn't drain and so Lauren unscrewed the U-bend and...' She pulls a face. 'You don't want to know what she found down there. Students are disgusting.'

He laughs.

'Are you coming up then?' she says, tugging on his hand. She's suddenly struck by a pounding fear that he has changed his mind, that her non-stop chatter has put him off, that he wants to make a quick escape.

'Sure,' he says, and she breathes out. 'Lead the way.'

They climb the concrete staircase in sync, still holding hands, which is a bit awkward when a lad from one of the upper floors tries to get past them on his way down.

She prays her flatmates will all be in their rooms.

'I was a bit drunk the other night,' she says, swallowing. 'When I called my flatmates bitches. They're all right, really. They just... they're not like me. I mean, I guess they are in lots of ways, and I suppose I can be a bitch sometimes. I was just really drunk and upset because one of them was taking the piss out of me because I refused to take E... They don't seem bothered by that poor girl, the one in the news? Her brain swelled up when she drank too much water after taking ecstasy and then she died. Do you remember that story? What was her name? It's just, stuff like that, you know. It really affects me.'

He smiles at her. And without thinking, she leans forward to kiss him. It's like a hundred sparks going off all over her body, and she feels faint with it.

'I...' she says, but what can she say? She wants them to be alone, right now, in her bed.

She pushes open the door of the flat. It stinks, as it always does, because someone has left a binbag full of rubbish in the recess behind the door.

'Sorry about the smell,' she says. 'It's Jo's turn to take it out but she can't be bothered so she always leaves it there until she next leaves.'

'You're all right,' he says. 'I live with three lads.'

She wrinkles her nose, imagining it.

They are still holding hands.

'This is my room,' she says, shoving open the heavy door with her shoulder. It's got a fire-hinge fitted so it weighs a ton.

She switches on the light. She tidied it before she left on

Friday, and thanks her past-self for this foresight. He sets her bag down by the bed.

'Do you want a drink?' she says, taking off her jacket and laying it over the back of the small desk chair. 'I can offer you water or neat vodka? Tea?'

'Tempting but... no ta,' he says, pulling her down to sit next to him on the bed.

She closes her eyes briefly, thinking that this might be the happiest she has ever felt. Or the most alive, at the very least. She loves it all. The smell of him; some kind of hair product or aftershave tinged with an earthy, clean feel. His eyes, which, as she looks into them now under the harsh strip lighting, she can see are tinged with flecks of gold. She pushes her hands against his jumper, feeling the shape of his chest.

He reaches up and brushes the hair back from her face. But he doesn't say anything.

She's so consumed by the moment she finds herself pulling away from it. Overthinking it. Imagining if it were Daniel here, telling her that she looked beautiful, that her eyes were like ponds, or something else utterly banal.

But Benjamin doesn't speak. He just looks at her. Really looks at her, as though she's some kind of curious creature he has never encountered before.

'I...' she says, because it's too much this silence, this unbearable loaded silence. Her voice drops. 'I really, really fancy you, Benjamin.'

She closes her eyes at the horror of it. She is the Daniel now, in contrast to his purity, his silent confidence in the moment. She is the one spoiling it all.

It's enough to make her want to cry, but instead she hears him say:

'That's good. I really fancy you, too.'

And then they are kissing, hungrily, and she pushes him back against the bed and flails at his clothes, tugging off his jacket and fiddling with the belt of his trousers and for a second they break away and he's just in his T-shirt, and then she's down to her bra, which thankfully is one of the good ones, and they are kissing again and she wonders briefly whether or not the condoms they handed out in the first week of term are in the bedside table, because she thinks she put them there but she's not sure and so she reaches again for his belt, and he helps her undo it and then...

He puts his hand over her hand as she reaches inside his trousers.

'No,' he says. 'Not...'

She keeps kissing him, ignoring him because surely he doesn't mean No, she's heard him wrong, or he's trying to be sensitive to her, as a girl, but he takes her hand again and moves it, more forcibly this time, away from his crotch.

'No,' he says, gently.

She pulls away and looks at him.

He kisses her again.

'This is enough,' he whispers in between each kiss.

She sits back, wounded, staring down at his legs.

'But, I could feel... you were...'

His cheeks redden. She has embarrassed him somehow. What has she done wrong?

Her head pounds as she thinks of all the other boys she has been in this situation with, how they were the ones coaxing her hand down to their boxer shorts, how they kept putting theirs up her skirt and into her knickers.

'I can... I can give you a handjob if you like?' she blurts. 'We don't have to...'

He looks away.

The spell she has been under since she first held his hand outside the pool bar finally breaks.

'Listen. I think I better go,' he says, shortly, pulling his jumper back over his head. 'Is there a bus stop near?'

Tears spring to her eyes, burning them.

'Don't go,' she says. 'I'm sorry.'

'You have nothing to be sorry about,' he says. 'I just think it's late... early lecture tomorrow.'

She frowns. They are both first years. Early lectures are missable, if something is worth it.

'Oh, right,' she says, sniffing.

She's misread the situation, clearly. It feels like the whole world is collapsing around her but it's fine. She's stronger than this. 'Sure. There's a bus stop just on the corner, if you turn left outside and then walk to the end of the street.'

'Great,' he says. 'Thanks.'

She follows him downstairs to the entrance of her halls. They are no longer holding hands. He's practically running down the stairs now, his feet tapping out a frantic rhythm as he escapes her.

It's excruciating.

She hates him.

'I'll see you then,' he says, pausing with his hand on the door. She looks at it, wonders how it can be that just ten minutes ago his hand felt like it fitted hers perfectly.

'Yeah, sure,' she says, blinking away her feelings. 'Hope you get home safe.'

'Bye, Clara,' he says, and she turns and walks up the stairs without looking back.

March 2000

Benjamin

He has probably messed everything up, but that's no great surprise. What was he thinking anyway? She wouldn't be interested in someone like him.

He pulls the collar of his jacket up around his neck and stomps down the street, nausea swirling.

He wishes he could cry.

And she looked so upset as he left. Crushed. Like he'd slapped her.

He doesn't even know what he was afraid of, only that he didn't want it to be like that. Not his first time. Not with her.

He decides to skip the bus and walk all the way home. Some kind of stupid penance, though not even, because he doesn't mind walking. He was built for it; long legs and large lungs making it feel as though he's doing what he was designed to do. Stride.

Walk away from his mistakes.

But he can't shake the image of her face. That sweet face.

When he finally gets back to his house, it's nearly midnight. Donny is in the living room, watching something that looks like porn but that he'll insist isn't. He has a blanket over his lap, his hands underneath it. It makes Benjamin's stomach turn over again, and he skips saying hello or goodnight, mounting the stairs to his tiny bedroom two at a time instead.

The bulb went in the bathroom three weeks ago and no one has bothered to replace it, so he washes his face and brushes his teeth in the dark, and then crawls into his bed, turning over and over the evening in his mind, wondering why and how he is so incompetent at everything.

He leaves it three days before he calls her. Three days of torture. Of self-flagellation, of wondering how she is feeling, what she's saying about him – because surely, she will be telling everyone. She's an open book, remember, and now he's stupidly slammed the cover shut by mistake.

As he walks around the city, he imagines bumping into her, what he would say.

When Tina invites him to go out that night after work, he agrees, but only because he can't be alone with his thoughts for much longer before going completely insane, and he hopes that the beer and the boom-boom-boom of the house music will drown out the riot in his head.

But it doesn't work. She is still there, Clara. In his brain. Following him around with her big bloodshot eyes.

You're a sensitive lad, his mam always says. *Never lose that.*

Why didn't she beat it out of him, like other parents must have with their kids?

On the third day he concedes he has nothing to lose. He takes the phone up to his room and sits on his bed and dials her number without pausing.

It rings four times and then she answers.

'Hello?'

He can't read her tone. Perhaps she deleted his number and has no idea that it's him.

'Hi,' he says, his voice strangled. 'How are you doing? How's your sister?'

He thumps himself on the side of the head with his free hand.

'My sister?' she says, but she's not angry. Her voice is light. Bemused.

'I mean... er, after her...'

'She's fine,' she replies. 'I think. I mean, I'm sure. She's fine. I spoke to her this morning and she was busy moaning about her GCSE revision.'

'That's good,' he says. *Keep talking keep talking.* 'So, I was wondering if you wanted to go for another drink? Maybe you can choose this time? Somewhere in town? I mean, wherever you like... the pool place wasn't up to much, was it? I'm sure you know some better places than me.'

This is it, he thinks. The verdict. She leaves him hanging, like a contestant on a game show.

He hears her take a deep breath. 'Yes, sure. How about this Saturday?'

A second chance. He can't believe it.

But... Saturday.

'Oh, Saturday. I have... football.'

He could miss it, for her, but what would he tell his dad?

'I thought you said you didn't play any more?'

'No,' he says. 'I don't, not properly anyway. I was in the county youth team, when I was younger.'

'Oh, wow,' she says. 'So you were really good then?'

I could have been.

'I was all right,' he concedes.

'So why did you quit?'

He pauses. They're meant to be arranging their date. How come they're talking about this? He *hates* talking about this.

But he should tell her the truth: he couldn't hack it.

The pressure was too much for him and he started getting panic attacks before he was due to go on the pitch. All those faces, looking at him. The weight of expectation. It felt as though his throat was closing up, as though he was dying. And there was nothing he could do about it.

His coach said he didn't have the head game for it.

He didn't quit. He was dropped.

'I guess I just didn't want it enough.'

'But you're still a fan? You actually go and watch Newcastle City's games?'

He shakes his head into the phone, as though she's said something insane.

'Well, yes, all the home ones. My dad and I have a season ticket. And I go to the away games when I can, too. But they're at home this weekend. Vintage Park stadium.'

'Oh,' she says, silent for a while.

'I mean, I guess I could miss it? It's just...'

'No, it's fine. I didn't realise. My dad doesn't really watch sport.' She pauses. 'I mean, he'd watch England play, I guess.'

'Well, obviously.'

'Forget Saturday then. How about Thursday?'

'Thursday's good,' he says, relieved. 'I have a shift at the store in the day but I'll be done by six. Where?'

'How about I come to you?'

He looks around at his tiny bedroom, horrified.

'Oh,' he says. 'It's...'

'Please,' she says. 'I'd like to see where you live.'

It's both worse and better.

'OK,' he says. 'But why don't we go for a drink nearby first? My place is pretty small and my flatmates are always in.'

'Don't you live in halls?'

'No,' he says. How can he begin to explain the ignominy of the situation?

He'd done badly in his A levels and hadn't got the grades he'd needed. His teacher tried to get special dispensation for him, given the fact his mam was poorly, but it didn't make enough difference.

In the end, he had to go through the Clearing process to secure his place at Northumbria, considered by many as the inferior of the city's two universities. And by the time he'd done so, there was no space left in their own housing for him.

His dad had suggested staying at home and commuting in every day, but his mam had, mercifully, vetoed this.

'I'm not in university accommodation. My place is privately rented,' he says, finally.

'Oh, that's cool,' she says, sounding, somewhat shockingly, like she really does think so.

'The nearest pub is the Hand and Spear,' he says. 'We could meet there. Say, eight p.m.?'

'Great,' she says. 'See you then.'

He lets out the breath he didn't know he was holding, stares at the ceiling and smiles.

March 2000

Clara

'You're giving him another chance?' Lauren says, staring at her as she applies more eyeliner. 'He's a total flake.'

'He's shy,' Clara says, narrowing her eyes. 'That's all.'

She hopes that is all.

'Well, if he resists you tonight then there's something wrong with him,' Lauren says. 'Because you look hot.'

Clara turns and smiles. She is wearing a pink denim mini skirt and has a ton of hairspray in her hair to try to add some volume.

'Thanks,' she says. 'I'm gonna have to take a cardigan though, aren't I? It's freezing.'

'You are,' Lauren says. 'But you probably won't need your rape alarm with this one.'

It's a joke but neither of them laughs.

'Have fun,' Lauren says. 'Text me later if I've gone to bed by the time you get back.'

The stupid thing is she's shy too, she thinks, as she boards the bus, flashing her student travel pass at the driver. She's always known it, but others have never seen it in her. Never appreciated that her talking, her nervous chatter, is her way of covering up the feeling that she doesn't understand other people. That they are different from her.

It was worse in the first term. When she arrived at this ginormous university and realised that somehow everyone else understood how to make friends from nothing. To create conversation from silence.

She had been so sheltered before she came here. The same exclusive girls' school right through from four to eighteen. The same group of friends. The smallest, safest of worlds.

A world that taught you nothing about what was outside it.

Thankfully she has Lauren, who is also from London, and has more patience than the other five girls in her flat. They regard her as an oddball, one they don't have time to coach. Even though they are all the same age, the others seem to have experienced so much more than her already.

University is nothing like she'd imagined. For one, no one seems to take their work seriously at all. But it's been bearable, just about, thanks to alcohol.

And that's what she will use tonight.

Perhaps it was stupid to ask to go to his house, but she wants to understand him better. He gives away so little of himself and it puts them on an uneven playing field.

Her bus gets stuck in traffic so she arrives late and flustered, pushing the door of the pub open and trying to ignore the churning in her guts.

Where would he be? Scanning a pub to find a familiar face is something normal people find easy, but she feels like an exhibit as she lingers on the large internal doormat, like everyone in the pub is secretly judging her.

But then she spots him – the back of his head, those perfect dark curls. She swallows and walks towards him.

'Hi,' she says, and he looks up at her. He stands and smiles and pulls out a stool for her.

'Thanks,' she says, taking a seat, pulling down her skirt and folding her arms over her handbag in her lap.

'Gin and tonic?' he says, still standing.

'Oh,' she replies. 'You remembered.'

'It's what my mam drinks,' he says, winking. 'Old lady.'

They talk until the bell rings for last orders. She hasn't eaten anything apart from the bag of crisps they shared on their third round, and when she stands up she feels light-headed.

'Back to yours then?' she says, her eyes crinkling at the corners.

'Sure,' he says, and takes her hand.

Please, she thinks, as they walk along. Please let it go well this time.

'I wanted to talk to you,' she says, the words tumbling out. 'About the other night. What happened? What went wrong?'

She glances sideways at him.

'Nothing went wrong,' he says. 'Are you cold?'

She is, but she shakes her head and presses on.

'No, but you practically ran away. I thought I would never hear from you again.'

'I just didn't see the rush,' he says, quietly. 'I don't know. I really like you. I wanted to get to know you a bit. Is that bad?'

'No.'

'Well then.'

'And now?'

'And now what?' he says, playfully.

She nudges him. Takes a deep breath.

'And now, I think if I go back to your house and you don't agree to sleep with me I will be quite... distraught.'

'Distraught?!' He whistles through his teeth. 'Clara, man... if a lad said something like that.'

'I know,' she says, blushing. 'I'm sorry.'

He sighs.

'Look, can't we just see what happens?'

'Are you nervous?' she says, her mouth open. 'Do I scare you, Benjamin... what's your surname?'

'Edwards. See, that's my point. You don't even know my surname yet.'

'Edwards.' She turns the name over in her mind, to see if it fits him. It is smart, clean, attractive, so she decides it does. 'Do I scare you, Benjamin Edwards?'

He stops in the street and turns to look at her, taking her other hand.

'No,' he says, quietly. 'Clara Davies-Clark. You don't scare me.'

She smiles in bemusement. 'How did you know my surname?'

'It was on your bus pass. You were holding it the other night.'

She pauses.

'Well, there you are then,' she says. 'We both know each other's surnames now.'

She leans up towards him and they kiss, gently to start, but then greedily, frantically, and he wraps his arms around her and pulls her in tight so that her whole body is pressed against him. She wants to meld them together. The cold air whips around her legs, as though urging her to push herself even closer to him. His warmth, his stability. She closes her eyes, wishing the moment could last forever.

She can't tell who breaks away first but, when they part, she finds herself overcome with something she can't describe. She looks down, buries her face in his chest again, breathing in his smell.

'I'm drunk,' she says. 'I feel dizzy.'

He strokes the top of her head.

'Come on you,' he says. 'I'll make you a cup of char.'

'Char?'

He rolls his eyes.

'Tea,' he says. 'Donny's right – you are posh.'

That's what her flatmates said about her, too. She has no clue who Donny is, but being branded as posh makes her uncomfortable, although, of course, there's no denying she is posh. Her family are loaded. They have a big house in Hampstead. Her father is a barrister, her mother is the niece of a baron, although no one really talks about that. It'd be vulgar to bring it up.

But it's there, like some hereditary stamp of superiority her mother carries with her at all times.

She knows that Benjamin is from the north, but this is the first time their different backgrounds have occurred to her. And he has noticed it before she has. He has thought about it, clearly, and she can't put her finger on why this bothers her.

But they both drink tea.

'I would love a cup of... char,' she says, smiling and taking his hand again.

His house is an unremarkable Victorian terrace, like so many around here, the front garden an overgrown tangle of weeds. There are crisp packets and beer cans sprinkled on top of the vegetation, like some kind of decorative coating.

'Your garden is a tip,' she says, neutrally.

'Aye,' he says. 'But it's not us. When I first moved in I cleared it away but it just keeps coming back. Pissed people chucking stuff in as they walk home.'

Aye. Is it her imagination or is his northernness somehow more apparent this evening? She doesn't remember these little sparks of dialect the last time they met but she likes them. She seizes on them as evidence that he is relaxing in her company.

There's a tingle of excitement in her stomach as he pushes open the front door.

'Come straight up,' he says, as she peers through the hallway to what looks like a conservatory at the back of the tiny house. Someone is watching television, something to do with football.

She pauses at the bottom of the stairs.

'What about my cup of char?'

'I'll make it and bring it up to you,' he says, flushing slightly. She likes this, the way he wears his emotions on his face, the damp red tinge that appears whenever he feels a little stressed.

'Don't you want to introduce me? How many girls have you brought back here exactly?' she teases, even though she knows she's being a twat now.

'None,' he says, simply. 'You're the first. And they're likely getting stoned in there, so their conversation will be shite, and I just didn't think you'd want to be put through it.'

'Oh,' she says. 'Right. Thanks.'

She follows him up to his room, which is small but tidy, the blue checked bedlinen faded from washing. It smells clean, and his desk is empty except for a neat stack of exercise books and some pencils in a tray.

Underneath there's a pile of magazines. She cocks her head sideways to read the spines.

Empire.

FourFourTwo.

A football magazine.

On the wall next to the wardrobe is a calendar called '90s

63

Pin-Ups'. She looks at this month's specimen. Miss March. A blonde named Caprice is naked except for some strategically placed duct tape, her hair tousled across her shoulders. Her face looks vacant as she pouts in the photograph.

'Oh,' she says, but somehow, it's a relief to see this here. 'Classy calendar.'

He doesn't acknowledge her comment, but interestingly doesn't blush this time.

'Tea then?' he says.

'Strong please,' she says, sitting down on the bed, still looking at Caprice. 'Tiny bit of milk, no sugar.'

They lie in bed talking until the sun comes up. They discuss it all – her course, his course, her family, the fact that for the two years of her sister's illness, Clara felt as though she didn't really exist.

'Sometimes I wondered if I was invisible,' she says. 'Like, I *really* thought I might be. Or that I could only be seen at certain times. Some kind of twisted magic power. It felt as though my parents had forgotten I even existed. And then she got better and everyone was happy and that was it. We all just had to pretend it never happened. It was so confusing.'

They talk about her flatmates, what she thinks of the city, his preconceptions about London and how much he wants to visit. He's from a village about forty minutes away from Newcastle, he says at one point, and then changes the subject. He has no siblings but always wanted a sister.

Shyly, she tells him what she's never told anyone. That one day, she wants to have a novel published.

'Writing helps me make sense of things. And reading is the most magical thing in the world, don't you think?' she says.

'Storytelling is the most powerful way of communicating with others. I want to leave my mark on the world, leave something behind. Otherwise, what's the point?'

From time to time, they kiss, but she makes no further attempt to undress him, and her disappointment that he doesn't try to undress her eventually disappears.

Her curiosity, however, doesn't.

At 4 a.m., when they have almost drifted off to sleep, she can't contain it any longer.

'Are you a virgin?'

She can hardly believe that someone like him, someone so utterly handsome and charming and kind and funny, could be, but at the same time it would make sense. It would make his reluctance make sense.

He shifts beside her, turning away slightly to look up at the ceiling. He is still stroking her hand as he answers.

'Not exactly,' he says.

'What?' she replies. 'What does that mean?'

He turns back and kisses her again.

'It means... I've done some things. But I've never... not in a long-term relationship.'

'Done some things?'

There's a beat before he answers.

'You are a sex pest,' he says. 'Obsessed. I know I'm really handsome and irresistible, but still...'

The laughter feels forced.

'But you've slept with someone?' she presses. 'Before?'

He nods. But doesn't elaborate.

She bites her lip. It's the answer she wanted but also didn't want.

'How about you?' he says. He blinks multiple times. She knows him well enough now, just from this one night of lying together and talking, to know that this shows he is nervous. That, like her, he both wants to know and doesn't.

'I've slept with three people,' she says, honestly. 'My first proper boyfriend – the one who's at uni here too – and then two guys last term. One of whom lives in the flat above me. I was quite obsessed with him for a bit, but then… well, anyway he's a dick. And it's annoying because I keep seeing him in the laundry room.'

He stiffens beside her.

'Right,' he says. 'Don't tell me any more about him, then. If I'm likely to bump into the lad.'

She frowns again. She can't take this any longer. This awkwardness.

She wants him to have more of her than anyone else has ever had.

'Benjamin?'

'Yes?'

A split of sunrise streams through the curtains they didn't bother to draw when they lay down hours ago.

'Will you sleep with me? Now?'

April 2022

Clara

She stares up at what remains of the pool bar. It's boarded-up, the shuttered windows covered with flyers, but the original sign is still there, its neons no longer illuminated.

She feels winded. It's insanity, of course. How can a place she visited only once have such a profound effect on her?

She has to get a grip. She takes a deep breath and continues trudging up the street. His bar – the Ocean Bar – is about a five-minute walk.

It seems crazy to her that he ended up running a bar. Of all the things he could have done with his life, it seemed the least likely.

But then again, there was so much she didn't understand about him. So much that frustrated her. Sometimes she found herself wishing she could take over his body for a month or something, to help put him on the right path. To get him set up for a job that was worthy of him.

You have so much potential! she had once shouted at him. *If only you had a bit more faith in yourself!*

She had shouted at him a lot.

Has she ever shouted at Thom? If she has, she can't remember it.

There are more blue flashing lights up here and she starts to panic that the police won't let her through, but thankfully after a few more paces she spots the Ocean Bar, on the corner.

She has never been inside but she has stalked it online in the past and it looks agreeable enough. Bland but safe. The place to go for a few cheap drinks before heading on to somewhere edgier.

Beneath him.

She closes her eyes at a memory that strikes her without warning.

You've put me on a pedestal that I don't deserve.

She bites her lip and fights back the tears.

The bar is open, amazingly. People are huddled around tables, heads bent low together, sombrely discussing the day's events.

It's a long shot, but it's her first step towards finding him. Of resolving what has been left unresolved for so long.

She takes a deep breath and steps inside.

March 2000

Benjamin

When he wakes later that morning she is still there.

Her eye make-up – which he thought she was wearing too much of yesterday although he would never have told her so – is smudged and her nose is pink, but she is still as beautiful as he remembers her.

'Morning,' he says as she shifts beside him.

'God, what time is it?'

Her voice is croaky and he leans down beside the bed and passes her the bottle of water he keeps there.

She sits up and takes a glug.

'Ugh,' she says, wiping her mouth with the back of her hand. 'Thanks.'

She hands it back to him and he drinks some too.

'I have a lecture at eleven,' she says, dolefully staring at his tiny bedside clock. 'Shit.'

'You'll make it if you hurry?' he says.

'Are you kidding me?' she replies. 'Look at me! No chance.'

She settles back down next to him and rests her head against his shoulder. He kisses the top of her head and thinks about last night. It wasn't a disaster, but it could have gone better.

It was difficult to get the thought of the three other lads she mentioned out of his mind. But at the same time, he is so attracted to her that he didn't stand a chance of doing anything impressive.

She didn't seem to mind. Afterwards she held him, a hot sticky sweaty mess, and told him that she couldn't wait to do it again. So they did, about an hour later, and it was better that time. Perhaps he has passed that test. And she is still here, after all.

Her eyes are still closed but her hand starts snaking its way down his chest. He put his boxers back on last night afterwards, but she is still naked, seemingly unbothered. Her hand reaches the top of his shorts and he feels her fingers slip underneath the waistband.

'No,' he says, stopping her. 'I need the loo. Sorry.'

She smiles sleepily at him.

'So do I, but I can't be bothered to move.'

'You go first,' he says, sitting up. He reaches over to the small bedside table and pulls some toilet roll out of the drawer. 'You'll need this.'

'Oh,' she says. 'Nice.'

She climbs out of bed and he tries not to watch, even though he really wants to, as she unselfconsciously puts her knickers back on. She looks around for her skirt and top.

'Here,' he says, throwing her his T-shirt. 'You can borrow it if you like.'

She smiles and pulls it over her head, standing there in front of him. It just about covers her pants.

He wants to tell her to never take it off.

'It's the door opposite.'

'Thanks,' she replies.

While she's gone he sits up in bed and drinks some more

water. He has a lecture at twelve, one he really doesn't want to miss, and then he needs to go to the library. And then he needs to call his mam.

She's seeing her oncologist this morning, and he always rings after to find out how it went. There's not too much hope left, at this stage, but there's a glimmer – a final clinical trial was mentioned last time he spoke to her, the last-chance saloon – and he clings to it like an ant clings to a fingertip. She will *have* to be eligible, and it will *have* to work, because the alternative is impossible.

And she has been in this situation so many times – so close to the end and yet something has always been promised: a new treatment, something else they can try – to buy her just that little bit longer.

He has so much to do before he speaks to his mam. But he can't kick Clara out. Not after last time. He'll have to miss the lecture then. That's OK. It's just one.

He scratches the back of his neck.

She's back sooner than expected, standing there in his T-shirt, her hair tucked behind her ears, some of the eye make-up now rubbed away. She looks tired but even more beautiful than last night, when she was dressed up like a doll.

'Your bathroom is gross,' she says.

He nods.

'I know, sorry,' he says.

'I have to go,' she says, folding in her top lip.

'Because of the bathroom?'

'No, don't be silly. I've got stuff to do. I don't want to go but I also...' She gestures at herself. 'I look a mess.'

He smiles.

'OK then, but you really don't. Look a mess.'

'Can I see you again soon?' she says. 'Like tonight?'

He pulls her back towards the bed and she falls on top of him.

'Tonight's good for me,' he says, and he kisses her.

It takes him all morning to come down from the high. He waved her off at the front door – she insisted on walking to the bus stop alone – but he watched her from the front room window and made sure she got on safely.

Then he went back in the house and lay on his bed, staring up at the ceiling, thinking it might have all been a dream, until his stomach started growling.

Of course, he missed his lecture. He tried not to think about his father's words.

He has disappointed his father for seven years now, ever since he was thrown off the football team. The sad fact is, he is incapable of performing under pressure, no matter what the circumstances. But his degree is his chance to prove that he can do something with his life. That he can escape the small-town fate that others saw as inevitable.

Bright lights, big city.

Don't throw it all away over a girl.

He makes his way down to the kitchen slowly, in search of food.

Later, he takes the cordless landline telephone up to his room and calls home.

His mam answers after three rings. It is her job to pick up in their house. His father is a sociable man, but he hates speaking on the phone, and anyway, they get to catch up at the game every fortnight.

'How did your appointment go today?' he says.

'It was all right,' his mam replies. Her voice is quieter than usual. 'Now, tell me about you. How's the course going? Are you warm enough? Are you eating enough fruit?'

He feels the nausea rising.

'Mam,' he says, frustrated. 'Tell me the truth.'

April 2000

Clara

They have been dating for a month now. They have seen each other almost every day since, and they have slept together at least twice each time.

He has become part of her routine, her life here at university. As essential as breathing.

But still, they haven't made it official.

'You can't get a proper boyfriend in first year,' Lauren complains as they sit in the refectory, their lunches on trays. 'It's so lame.'

Clara is grateful for Lauren. Her only real friend. She's sensitive and wise like Clara, but more relaxed and sociable.

Lauren is Clara without her stupid anxiety.

'But I think… I love him,' Clara says.

Lauren rolls her eyes.

'But think about how we met! It was literally fate. I saw him in that other club and he never came over, but what are the chances of us being in Options at the exact same time a week later?'

'Pretty high given that we're all students at the same university.'

Clara bites her tongue. He's not at her university, he's at the other one, but she hasn't told Lauren that yet. She can't bear the thought of anyone judging him.

Her perfect, perfect Benjamin.

'There are, I don't know, thirty thousand students in this city! I reckon the chances were pretty low, actually.'

'You need to sleep with someone else,' Lauren says. 'Because you're getting in way too deep. Remember what happened with Daniel?'

Clara remembers all too well what happened with Daniel, which is exactly why she knows that Benjamin is special. Everything about him feels different.

But Lauren is still talking. 'What about Richard? He really fancies you.'

Clara frowns.

Richard is part of a group of guys that the other girls in her flat hang around with. He's been in their kitchen a few times, and last term, before they left for Christmas, he cooked a turkey roast for them all.

'Richard? You're not listening to me. I don't want to sleep with anyone else. I'm... I'm in love with Benjamin.'

'Clara... I don't want to sound like your mum but you're eighteen and you've known him five minutes.'

Clara looks down at the sandwich in front of her.

'A month actually...'

'Come out with us tonight. Come on, you haven't had a night out with us for ages – we've hardly seen you. You're getting way too intense with this bloke. You'll only end up getting hurt.'

She inhales sharply. Because Lauren is right. She suddenly has tunnel vision, a premonition of the future. A certainty that yes, this boy will break her heart.

If Daniel could hurt her the way he did, then how could

Benjamin possibly *not* hurt her, when he already means so much more to her than Daniel ever did?

Going out tonight will be a tactical move, a game-play that she doesn't want to engage in, but at the same time she knows she has to. It's a protective measure. That's all.

'OK,' she says. 'I will.'

As he promised he would, Benjamin phones her as she's walking home from her last lecture.

'How was it?' he says. 'Narratives of witchcraft and magic?'

She laughs.

'How do you remember this stuff?' she says. 'And it was good thanks. We're looking at the relationship between the prosecution of witchcraft and xenophobia.'

There's a pause. She laughs again.

'Yeah, I have no clue either. Anyway, how's your day going? Has Donny cleaned the kitchen yet?'

She hasn't been over to his house since that first night. She saw enough on that visit to understand that he is staying there because it's cheap. Besides, her flat is so much nearer campus, plus she has her own bathroom.

'What do you think?' he says. 'Listen, I have to… I have to go home tonight. Home, home, I mean.'

'Oh,' she says, and a sudden panic strikes her. 'Right.'

She wants to ask why, but her voice is frozen in her throat.

'I might be a few days,' he is saying. 'But I'm not sure yet.'

'Right.'

She can almost hear him stiffening up at the tone of her voice.

'I'll call you when I'm back. Is that OK?'

Is that OK? It sounds passive-aggressive. It doesn't sound like him. What is he hiding?

Don't they have phones at your house? she wants to scream.

She thinks of Lauren, her warning earlier. She thinks how glad she is that she has already started to build that tiny wall around her heart, that she has plans for tonight, that she won't be spending it alone in her room, thinking of him.

'Yeah, sure,' she says, eventually, but the voice doesn't sound like hers. She realises with alarm that she is on the verge of tears. It's ridiculous – an overreaction – but she can't seem to stop it.

He doesn't reply. Her fingers are sweaty against the warm plastic of her phone. She presses it to her ear.

'Are you still there?' she says, when the silence has become unbearable.

'Yes,' he says, softly. 'I'll miss you Clara Davies-Clark.'

She almost sobs, her hand clamping over her nose to muffle the sound.

'Yes,' she says. 'I'll miss you too. But...'

The words hang in her mind, unspoken. *When will you be back?* She can't even force them out. No one wants to sound needy. Desperate.

'I'll call you as soon as I can,' he says. 'Bye CDC. Good luck with those witches.'

That night she goes out with Lauren and Jo and Sinead and Rebecca, and she gets blind drunk.

So drunk that at 1 a.m. she finds herself outside the club in the street, vomiting into the gutter while Lauren rubs her back, smokes and chats to some boy she's picked up.

'There, there,' Lauren says, every now and then. 'Get it all out.'

'I want to go home,' Clara says, when the vomit has turned to acid and she feels utterly hollow. 'Can you get me a cab?'

'Of course, sweetie. If you're sure,' Lauren nods.

And then, he appears.

Richard.

'I'm leaving anyway. I can take her,' he says. 'I'll make sure she gets back OK.'

Lauren looks him up and down.

Clara leans against a lamppost, wishing her brain wasn't pickled, so that she could assess the situation. Make the right decision.

'OK,' Lauren says. 'But just put her to bed with some water. Lying on her side. I don't want her puking in her sleep.'

'I'm not going to puke any more,' Clara says, indignantly.

'She'll be fine with me,' Richard says, and Clara screws her eyes up and looks at him. 'I'll take care of her.'

'I should go with you,' Lauren says, glancing back. The boy she was talking to before has wandered off to get a light. 'Shit.'

'No, it's OK,' Clara says. Her stomach aches. 'Go and enjoy the rest of your night. I'm sorry. Richard can… he can take me.'

They clamber into the back of a cab and she lays her head down on the middle seat, groaning.

She wants to ring Benjamin, of course. But how can she? He hasn't got a phone.

After their third date she thought about buying him one. But she worried it would look too possessive. Now she wishes she had.

When will he call?

Richard puts his arm around her and helps her up the stairs

to her flat. He smells of strong aftershave. The one they all wear. Polo by Ralph Lauren. Artificially masculine.

She turns her head towards him and spots a row of acne along his jawline, mixed in with pock-mark scars.

But he is good-looking, she knows. Her flatmate Sinead had a crush on him last term, but he turned her down. Sinead is unusual-looking. Distinctive. Not like Clara. Clara is a blonde, petite, the sort of girl that most men find both acceptable and forgettable. She knows that. She knows her place.

'Here we go,' he says now, kicking open the front door to her flat. She realises then that he has her handbag hooked over his arm. Her head is pounding, her limbs like spaghetti.

'My room is number 4,' she moans, and he unlocks it and lays her on the bed as delicately as possible.

'Silly sausage. Let me get you some water,' he says, stroking her hair. She turns away and faces the wall but he is back before she knows it, a pint glass in hand.

'Here,' he says and with effort she sits up and takes a deep drink.

He takes her shoes off, his hands resting on her ankles a little too long.

She thinks of Benjamin, his phone call earlier. The way he holds so much of himself back from her all the time. When she has been so open with him. So giving.

What the fuck is his problem?

'Do you want me to, uh, help you get into your PJs?' Richard asks. She can see the hope in his eyes.

She closes her own. It would be easier, she thinks. To give him what he wants.

And he's not so bad. And Lauren would be pleased with her. She would think it was the right thing to do.

And it would keep her heart just a little bit safer. A strange kind of ammunition against the future hurt that the boy she loves will surely inflict on her.

They haven't made any kind of commitment, after all.

She sits up and strokes Richard's face. He really is quite attractive. His eyes are a little close together, but his nose is neat and slim, and he has beautiful teeth. He's studying Economics. He's clever.

Her mother would love him.

'You're so beautiful Clara,' he says, staring into her eyes. It's too much. It's the way that *they* look at each other, as though there is nothing else in the world to see. She can't take it. Not from this boy, this pale imitation, so she leans forwards and kisses him because that's the easy thing to do, and that will make his stare go away.

He responds immediately, a match thrown on petrol, his hands suddenly everywhere and that strong sickly scent of his aftershave filling the air around her. She tries to numb herself to it, closing her eyes tight and letting him climb on top of her.

He thinks she's easy, he probably knows about the boy in the flat above that she slept with in the first term, when she thought somehow it might help her to fit in.

Before she really processes what is happening, he has pulled out a condom and he is inside her, and she thinks about yesterday, when Benjamin was inside her, in the same place this boy is now, and she thinks that makes her disgusting, actually, and she's glad of the condom because they have never used one. She's on the pill and she didn't feel the need, before, with him.

But she's grateful for the condom now, that at least there's some kind of tangible barrier between herself and him. He's still trying to kiss her, telling her how much he likes her, how wonderful and beautiful she is, how he has been desperate to do this since he met her. All things that Benjamin has never said directly, but that, somehow, he has never needed to say.

She pulls her mouth away from Richard's, squeezing the tears from her eyes but groaning appreciably, a finely tuned act she perfected in her relationship with Daniel. The way to make it end sooner was to pretend that you were enjoying it a disproportionate amount and so she tells him how big he is and how hard he is and before she knows it he has collapsed on top of her, his shirt sweaty and sticking to them both.

His mouth is close to her ear as he tells her again how fucking hot she is, how happy this has made him, and she turns her head away and looks at the wall, suddenly completely sober, and all she can think as she lies there is that she hates Benjamin for leaving.

April 2000

Benjamin

There's nothing more they can do for her.

His father George is drinking in the living room when he arrives home. He doesn't get up from his armchair but he nods a greeting as Benjamin lays his bag down by the door.

'She's upstairs,' he says, turning away.

Surely his dad hasn't been crying? That's not the sort of thing he does. Benjamin notices the bottle of Scotch on the table beside him.

They ought to have been more prepared for this day, this day that feels as though it has been years in the making. And yet, Benjamin has never allowed himself to imagine it.

The news she couldn't tell him on the telephone last week was that she was too sick for the clinical trial. Her consultant said she would get the *very best palliative care*, trying to make it sound like something special, rather than the very worst news possible. She was offered a place in a hospice, but she turned it down, saying she didn't want to take up a bed when she had a perfectly good one at home.

'How much longer?' Benjamin says, the words practically choking him. 'How much longer do they think?'

'Hours,' George replies. 'She wants to see you.'

He washes his hands in the kitchen sink – a force of habit, she has been susceptible to any passing infection for as long as he can remember and he's become obsessed with personal hygiene – and takes a deep breath.

He squeezes the banister tightly as he climbs upstairs to his parents' bedroom.

There's an end-of-life nurse sitting in the corner of the room. She smiles at him as he comes in. He hasn't seen her before, but she has a kind face and bright red hair.

'How is she?' he whispers, afraid to look at his mother.

'Peaceful,' the nurse says, smiling. 'I can leave you with her for a while, if you'd like.'

Benjamin swallows. He nods.

'Hi Mam,' he says, sitting beside her bed and taking her hand. He looks up at her face and swallows. She's asleep, he thinks, but her breathing is noisy. He squeezes her hand, noticing how cold it is. The skin is like crêpe paper. She seems so much older than when he last saw her.

'It's a lovely day,' he says. 'I wish you could see it. Your favourite kind. You know, when it's sunny but not too hot. The air has that smell of spring.'

He looks at his mother's face, for any sign that she's listening. Her chest continues to rise and fall, the pattern of her breathing irregular and stilted. Like an engine that can't start properly.

He blinks, raises his eyes to the ceiling. His leg is jiggling. He puts his left hand on his knee to stop it, but it just quivers under his grip.

'I met a girl,' he says. He leans in closer, even though he knows his dad won't be listening. 'You'd like her. She has these eyes. I know it sounds soft. But they're almost purple. Violet, I guess? And she's smart too. She's studying English. She's from London.'

He pauses, waiting for a reaction. Is it a trick of the light, or did her eyelids flicker?

'Her family are pretty successful, I think,' he says. 'She makes me nervous. But in a good way. She's... what would you say, Mam? Sparky. She talks non-stop, but – it's weird, but underneath, I think she's more like me, really. I hope Dad will like her. I guess he will, she looks a bit like that actress he likes... what's her name? Jodie Foster.'

Nothing. He wishes the nurse was in here. It's too immense, this moment.

Then, as though he's missed a step on a steep staircase, suddenly he is free-falling. He lets out a giant sob, brings his forehead to their entwined hands.

'Oh god, Mam,' he says. 'I don't want you to go.'

She makes a sound, a rattle, and he stares up at her. Her eyes open, momentarily.

'Mam,' he says. 'It's me. Benjamin.'

'Ssssh,' she says, and then she closes her eyes and lets out a slow, final breath. 'Don't cry, love. She sounds... she sounds perfect.'

He has to stay for more than a fortnight afterwards, even though every minute he spends there is excruciating.

His mam, he realises, was not just the heart of his family, she was its brain and limbs and arms too. She was what made it work properly. And without her, there is nothing but disconnect.

After a day of drinking and falling asleep in his armchair, George changes into someone Benjamin doesn't recognise. Someone cold and practical.

He doesn't say her name, refuses to talk about her directly.

Instead, he organises the funeral, spends hours phoning relatives to tell them the news in a short, staccato way, brushing off their condolences. *Well, yes as you can imagine I'm very busy. Better be getting on.*

They miss the football that weekend for the first time he can remember.

George rejects Benjamin's offers of assistance with the preparations, even though, actually, Benjamin would have liked to have been involved. He thinks – even though he had known his mother for only nineteen years, whereas his father knew her for twenty-three – that he knows her better. They had a closeness, an understanding that, despite his father having met her first, he can't see in the way George is organising the funeral.

But then, perhaps there were things about their relationship he didn't understand.

He knows one thing though. His mam would not want them to fight. She would want them to co-operate. To be gentle with one another.

And so, Benjamin lets his father choose the music and arrange the readings, and he decides to make himself useful in another way. He shops and cooks, he takes down his mam's old Delia recipe book and looks up the simplest things that he knows his father would like and that he knows he has little chance of ruining completely.

When he looks back he realises that, within a fortnight, he has learnt to cook.

He thinks of Clara, of course, all the time, but he can't bring himself to phone her. He doesn't want to bring her into this. This time, which is unique, something to be borne. To live through and to never speak of again.

He imagines how deeply she would feel his loss, especially

given her sister's cancer battle. How much the news would upset her. She feels everything so intensely, he already knows that. How could he cope with her feelings alongside his own, which are almost enough to drown him?

No, it is better all round not to involve her.

When she asks him, as she surely will, eventually, he will say that his mother died after a long illness.

His mother's death is the end of one thing, and his life with Clara is the start of another. And even though they overlapped for a short time, they are distinct. Two halves of his life that don't need to mix.

It feels safer that way.

April 2022

Clara

There's a television hanging from the corner of the bar and everyone is huddled around it, their necks bent at awkward angles as they listen to the breaking news report.

It seems unbelievable that the drama they are watching on screen is unfolding just a mile or so away.

No evidence of any further security risk.

At least twenty fatalities, with more wounded.

The youngest confirmed dead believed to be just twelve years old.

The newsreader interrupts the looping footage of people being loaded into ambulances.

And now for an update from the city's chief constable of police.

You could hear a pin drop in the bar, it's so quiet. She stands behind the crowd gathered around the television and listens to the policeman, dressed all in black, on the screen.

I can confirm details of this afternoon's incident as we currently know them. That at around 5.04 p.m. we received reports of an explosion at Vintage Park stadium in the city centre. This was at the conclusion of the Newcastle City vs Norwich Park football match. Currently we have twenty people confirmed to have lost their lives in the explosion, and around fifty casualties that are being treated at five hospitals across the city. We are currently treating this as a terrorist incident until we have further information. We are working closely with National Counter-Terrorism Policing Network and UK Intelligence Partners. This is clearly a very distressing time for everyone. We are doing all that we can to support those that are affected as we gather information about what happened this afternoon. We are still receiving information and updates so will provide further detail when we have a clearer picture.

'Fuck me. Twenty dead,' one of the barmaids says. She's holding a glass in one hand, her thick brown hair scraped into a messy bun on top of her head.

Clara looks at her and their eyes meet.

'Sorry love,' she says. 'We're closed.' She turns and shouts to the other bartender. 'Owen, did I tell you to lock the door or what?! Jesus Mother of Christ!'

'Oh,' she says, gesturing towards the people gathered under the television. 'Sorry. I thought...'

The barmaid's nose wrinkles.

'Our neighbours,' she says. 'I invited them in earlier. We're all a bit in shock. But it's locals only tonight, I'm afraid.'

'Right,' she says. 'Of course, I understand. It's just...'

She takes a deep breath, tries to find some courage. The barmaid stares at her, irritation creeping across her face.

Twenty dead.

How many people attend a football match? Thousands upon thousands. It'll be OK. The likelihood is so small. Surely.

He can't be dead. She feels sure that if he were, she would know somehow. She would feel it.

'I'm looking for someone,' she says, and tears spring to her eyes. 'I think he might have been involved, and he works here,

I think. Or at least, he used to... he was the manager once. We haven't spoken for a while but I heard about the bomb and I was so worried and I just thought I would come here to check if he was OK. He was a big football fan. Huge. Never missed a game.'

The barmaid softens slightly, puts the pint glass down on the bar.

'You look like you need a drink,' she says, and she turns and pours Clara a measure of whisky. 'Here.'

Clara takes it from her gratefully. It burns her throat.

'So, this guy you're looking for,' she says. 'What was his name?'

April 2000

Benjamin

He is back in Newcastle within three weeks. His village is only forty minutes away from the city centre, but it feels like returning to an entirely different country.

His father has hardly spoken since his mam died. After the funeral, all he did was grunt whenever Benjamin tried to strike up a conversation, spending long evenings down the Comrades Club instead.

Benjamin wanted to reassure him that it wasn't his fault Mam had died. But it was too obvious a thing to say, out loud, and he knew George would find it offensive, and say something like, *Of course it's not my fault*. Even though Benjamin could tell that his father blamed himself.

They had all tried their hardest. But her cancer – stage III, ovarian – was aggressive and determined; just when they thought they'd won a small victory over it, it would return with a vengeance. She had been sick since Benjamin turned thirteen, and despite the brief periods of hope, it felt as though she got sicker each year. Her oncologist was determined, deeply involved. But ultimately, there was nothing anyone could do. No one could fix her.

In the days after the funeral, it was clear that George didn't want him there to witness his grief, and Benjamin didn't want to be there either, so it seemed to be best if he just left.

'All right twat,' Donny says, slapping him on the back by way of greeting when he returns. 'We nearly let your room go. Where the hell have you been?'

'My mam died,' he says, quietly, putting his bag down at the bottom of the stairs.

Donny's face fell.

'Shit, man,' Donny says. 'I'm sorry, I had no idea.'

'It's OK,' he says. 'She was sick for a long time.'

'Right.' Donny shifts on his feet. 'Shit. Sorry. Shall I make you a cuppa then?'

'Yeah,' he says, smiling. 'Ta.'

He traipses up to his room, throwing back the curtains and opening the window. It's as tidy as he left it, his pile of magazines still stacked under the desk, the calendar still showing March. He squints at Caprice and flips it over to April.

Jordan.

He's unpacking his bag when Donny comes in and puts the huge Sports Direct mug down on his desk. He smiles at the gesture – the mug they all fight over.

'That lass rang for you,' Donny says, folding his arms. 'Twice. I said I didn't know when you'd be back.'

He swallows.

'Right,' he says. 'Ta. I'll call her.'

'You going off her?' he says. 'She seemed quite intense, like.'

Benjamin doesn't reply.

'Thanks for the tea,' he says. 'And listen, please don't tell anyone about my mam.'

★ ★ ★

He leaves it until the evening to call. He doesn't want to interrupt her if she's at lectures, and in the heartache of the last few weeks he's forgotten her timetable, which days she has to be in, which days she's meant to be doing independent study.

He dreads to think what reception will await him at his own university, even though he told them his situation and that he had to go home for a bit. His tutor seemed sympathetic but the last time he checked his email he could see the work was stacking up and, rather than try to tackle any of it, he ignored the problem.

At 6 p.m. he takes the landline up to his room again and dials her number. She answers straight away.

'Hi,' she says. 'Stranger.'

He swallows. It's fair enough, he deserves it. But she'll forgive him. Because they are meant to be. He is her person, and she is his, and that's just the way it is. Ever since he told his mam about her, he's felt this certainty in his bones. She is the one for him.

'Hey,' he says. 'How are you?'

Never apologise to nobody.

That's what his football coach used to say.

Don't let them see your weakness. No one respects the weak.

'I'm good,' she says, her voice squeaky. 'Lots going on, you know. Too many nights out, too many essays. I thought the whole point about first year is that you could get away with not doing much, but I swear Dr Goodman is a psycho. He sets us so much additional reading.'

'I'm sorry,' he blurts. His coach was wrong; sometimes apologies are necessary. 'That I haven't been in touch.'

She pauses, sniffs.

'Yeah, well, my flatmates all think you're an arsehole now.'

'Do you?'

'What?'

'Think I'm an arsehole.'

She sighs.

'I don't know what to think. Why did you go away for so long? And why didn't you call me? Don't they have phones at your house?'

'It was… family stuff,' he says. No, he has to resist. He can't – he won't – let these two things mix. He's at university to make a better life than the one he'd have at home in his village, isn't he? Besides, he doesn't want her pity. He doesn't want to break down now, and cry the tears he's mostly managed to suppress so far. 'I'm sorry I didn't call. I just… had a lot going on. But it's all sorted now.'

'What about your course?'

'Yeah, I have to see… I'll talk to my tutor tomorrow about catching up what I missed.'

'So, you're back?' she says. 'In the city?'

'I'm lying on my bed right now,' he says.

She breathes out.

'Are you busy tonight?' he asks. 'Shall I come over?'

'I'm going out with some of the boys in the flat opposite tonight. And Lauren and Sinead.'

'Right,' he says. Has he got it all wrong? He was so confident that it would be fine, that they would pick up where they left off.

'I'm sorry, it's just you didn't call…'

'I know,' he says. 'I should have done. I wish I had. I missed you though. I really want to see you again.'

'Well come out tonight then,' she says. 'We're going to

McCluskey's. Do you know it? Right by our flats. See you there at eight.'

She isn't giving him a choice.

'Great,' he lies. 'See you there.'

April 2000

Clara

She knows it might be a disaster, but there is something coursing through her veins: self-destructive poison. Or is it just her way of testing him?

Anyway, he deserves it.

They are sitting in the corner of the bar, jugs of cocktails covering the table in front of them. It's happy hour and they've stocked up in advance. Strawberry daiquiris and Sex on the Beach. The boys from flat P3 are drinking snakebites.

Under the table, Richard keeps nudging her leg with his.

They haven't slept together again. It's been easier than she thought to avoid being alone with him and she was careful not to drink too much the couple of times they did go out in a big group, feigning tiredness and slinking off early before he had the chance to try anything on.

He has taken the rejection as she expected him to, sleeping with a frizzy-haired girl from Ricky Road halls and then telling Lauren about it, in order to ensure it gets back to Clara.

She feels nothing about this attempt to make her jealous. If anything, she feels relieved.

She looks at him and he flushes, moving his leg away. It's not his fault. After all, she encouraged him. He's a nice boy really, and if she was being objective about it, *she* used *him*.

She has one eye on the door and only half an ear on the conversation around the table, which seems to revolve around whose parents still buy them Easter eggs. It's juvenile, harmless chat, and she zones out as she sips her drink, waiting for him to arrive.

And then, there he is.

Her first thought as she sees him walk into the bar is that she loves him. She feels an innate understanding that he is her soulmate, the one she should be with.

But then her second thought is that she hates him because he left her and didn't seem to feel the need to contact her for nearly three weeks, and because he has never told her how he really feels about her, and because he leaves her completely unsettled.

She stands up and waves, and he comes over.

'Hi,' he says. 'You look… amazing.'

So do you, she thinks, but she doesn't say anything. What can she do with him? Why does he constantly leave her feeling like she wants to cry?

Her heart is actually fluttering. A bird trapped in her ribcage.

'Are you OK for drinks?' he says, somewhat pointlessly given the jugs of orange and pink liquid on the table, and she nods and he ambles off to the bar.

She wishes he had a ticker tape running on his beautiful forehead, telling her everything that was going on in his mind. She has no idea how to read him or what he is thinking.

She sits heavily back down, making Lauren squeak, '*Steady on!*' and she risks a glance at Richard. He is glaring at Benjamin's back.

When Benjamin returns, everyone budges up and he squishes

in beside her and they drink and chat about everything that doesn't matter and nothing that does, but after an hour or so he puts his arm around her shoulders while they're speaking and so she puts her hand on his leg and then when she comes back from the toilet she sits on his lap and they kiss in front of everyone and she doesn't care.

'I love you,' she whispers, into his ear. 'But I hate you too.'

He pulls back at this, frowning at her.

'What?'

His eyes widen.

'I love you too.'

She's walking on air when they leave the bar, oblivious to her friends, to the code of conduct she has just flouted. They won't care, they are as wrapped up in their own lives as she is in hers.

'I'm starving,' he says and so they join the queue for fried chicken, kissing and laughing, and she tries to squash the tiny voice inside her telling her that he can't be as incredible as he seems, that her hormones are betraying her, because deep down she suspects he's not being straight with her and she deserves more.

But she ignores that voice because he's told her that he loves her, and what else matters really? Everything else can be worked out.

They are nearly at the front of the queue when they hear a voice shout her name.

'Clara!'

She turns her head away, her hands still clutched to Benjamin, trying to work out who is calling her. And then she sees him, a few paces away in the street.

Arms outstretched, bottle of Corona dangling from one hand.

Richard.

She bites her lip.

'We're in the queue,' she calls, as though this might let her off the hook, but he's walking towards them both now. In seconds he will be in front of them. She looks up at Benjamin but his face is neutral, unreadable as always.

'All right mate,' Richard says, stopping right next to them. 'I don't think Clara's introduced us properly. Rude.'

She suddenly feels very sober.

'This is Benjamin,' she says. 'Benjamin, Richard.'

Benjamin nods at him.

'All right.'

'You two are together now, is it?'

'Looks like it. Want us to get you some chicken?' Benjamin replies smoothly, and Clara sees a new side of him. He's cleverer than she's given him credit for.

Richard pauses, squinting at them both. His eyes roll back in his head slightly and he stumbles and drops his empty bottle of beer to the floor.

'Nah, I'm going to a club. See you later, Clara.' He pauses, his shoulders rising slightly. 'Benjamin.'

When they are back at her flat, they make love twice, the second time almost immediately after the first, and she is overwhelmed by the feeling that she could just do this thing, this physical act, over and over again with him and somehow it would never be enough.

But he falls asleep after the second time and so she rests her head on his chest and strokes his arm and tries to sleep too.

In the morning, he pulls his T-shirt back on, and then turns to her and asks:

'What's the deal with the Richard guy?'

She sits up in bed, pulling the duvet cover up and tucking it under her armpits.

'Oh,' she says. 'Him.'

'He has a crush on you?'

It's not a question, but he's made it sound like one.

She bites her lip. For some reason, he finds it so easy to hide things from her, but she can't hide anything from him.

'I guess so,' she says, eventually. 'He was pretty pissed last night.'

'Territorial,' he says, meaningfully.

She shrugs.

'I suppose a lot of his friends have got together with girls from my flat and... perhaps he thought I was going to be his conquest. Although, Sinead had a massive crush on him last term and practically threw herself at him... so maybe something will happen there.'

'Did you sleep with him?' he says. He shifts away from her. Just a tiny amount, but enough that she spots it. 'Is he one of the three?'

'What? No. No...'

It's a lie and it's not a lie.

'No, he's not one of the three.'

'I wouldn't mind,' he says. 'I just... it would be interesting to know.'

'He wasn't... one of the three.'

He kisses her.

'Right,' he says. 'I can't blame him for fancying you, of course.'

'Is that all... is that all this is?' she squeaks, suddenly

frustrated. 'I mean, we fancy each other, a lot, clearly, because we can't seem to stop having sex and it's the best sex of my life, and basically I feel like bursting into tears every time but in a nice way. But is this just sex? Because last night you said you loved me and... Jesus. Benjamin, you went away and ignored me for three weeks, and I went out of my mind. Like, literally out of my mind wondering what was happening with us, and now you're back and I still don't have any answers, and I want to know if you're... if you're going to make some kind of commitment to me because it's so confusing and exhausting and I don't want to be some needy whining pathetic *girl* about it but I don't understand you. I don't understand what you want from me.'

She lets out a great gasp.

He stares at her. His cheeks redden, just a tinge.

'Oh. Well, I thought we were dating,' he says, his eyebrows twitching. 'I mean... if that's what you want. That's what I want. I want us to be dating. Do we need to say it? I thought you just knew...'

'No!' she shouts. 'You don't just *know*! You have to say it. You have to ask me.'

'What, like proposing?' His eyes twinkle now.

'Yes! Bloody yes!'

'OK, then, shall I get on one knee, is that what you want?'

She laughs. He crouches beside her bed.

'Will you be my girlfriend, Miss CDC?'

She closes her eyes, inhales deeply. The clouds have parted.

'Yes,' she says. 'I will. On one condition.'

'What's that?'

'You get a bloody mobile phone.'

May 2000

Benjamin

He settles easily into a routine in the week. University in the day, meeting Clara after their lectures and going back to her flat to cook something together, then chatting and making love until they fall asleep around midnight.

But the weekends are different, of course.

'You're going to watch the football again?' she says, watching him from her usual spot in the bed as he gets dressed. 'When you said you were busy, I thought you meant you were working today.'

'Newsflash CDC, there are matches every week. So, you know, it's kind of consistent, this football thing. That's the reason I don't work Saturdays. Anyway, what's the difference?'

'Well, work's work. Football is different. Not mandatory. Can't you just miss it? For once?'

'Can't you just miss me?'

She throws a pillow at him.

'I won't miss you at all. You can sod right off.'

He leans down to kiss her, and she turns her face so that it lands on her cheek.

'Have a nice day, my little charmer,' he says. 'I'll call you later.'

★ ★ ★

When Newcastle City aren't playing at home, Benjamin and his three flatmates go to the pub on the corner to watch games. It's possibly the only thing they really have in common. The only time he feels like one of the lads. Football is a universal language. His safety net.

If he ever examined it closely, he would say that football was his therapy. A chance to reset after a busy week, alongside people just like him. It grounds him. But he doesn't know how to explain this to Clara.

There's a group of them now. Not just lads. Tina supports Leeds, and then there's a few of her friends who have joined the group, plus one of their next-door neighbours, who's older than them, City born and bred.

He sits back in the pub with his pint, feeling, for the first time since his mam died, content. He thinks of Clara, his girlfriend and now, he realises, his best friend too, and he smiles. He hopes she's having a nice afternoon.

It's a good match. Donny leaps up in his chair as Leeds' striker approaches the goal. But a successful tackle by Leicester's defensive midfielder means he slumps back down, thumping his hand on the table.

There's the sound of a phone pinging. Benjamin ignores it at first but then he realises that it's his. He still hasn't quite got used to having one.

He pulls it out. It's a text message from her.

Hi BE, OK you win. I do miss u. I miss u all the time and always. What r u up to? XXXXXXXX

He twitches in his seat.

He understands her now, can sense when things are heading in the wrong direction. This is a warning shot across the bow.

She *knows* what he is up to. He sucks on his lip before slowly – because he still hasn't completely got the hang of using number keys to make letters – typing a reply.

In the pub. Leicester r up 2-1. Miss u2 x

He considers it for a second. She taught him about using short versions of words to save character space. She'll like that he has listened.

He sends the message and puts the phone back in his pocket.

It's a bit of a fib, because he's not really missing her. Not right now. Right now, he's happy where he is. But that's OK, isn't it? They can't be together all the time.

Leicester scores and Donny bangs his fist on the table again. He's four pints down already – it'll be ten before the day is out. It's something they have in common. The ability to drink and drink and drink. Benjamin is tall. He can easily drink six pints in an afternoon.

'Fucking ref is a fucking eejit.' Donny stomps off to the bar.

'To be fair to them, Leicester have played well,' Tina says, edging closer to him. 'Three minutes left of injury time. No chance.'

'Second half, they played too slow in the midfield,' Benjamin says, his eyes fixed to the screen. 'Go on man! Give some fuel to the ball for Christ's sake!'

Tina moves even closer, so that their legs are touching.

'So, International Man of Mystery, how's things with the new lady? What's her name? Claire?'

Benjamin frowns. He has told Tina her name on several occasions.

'Clara.'

'Clara.'

'Good,' he says, taking a swig from his glass. 'She's...' He tails off. He can't describe her in a word. He probably couldn't describe her in a hundred because she is different things every day. But what she is, and what he feels most strongly of all, is *his*.

But he can't say that. *She's mine.* It would make him sound like a psycho.

'Benjamin's in love!' she sing-songs, pinching his arm.

'Shut up,' he says, looking down.

'When do I get to meet her?'

'Oh,' he says. 'Whenever.'

'Tuesday? We're going to Planet Earth after work. Bring her!'

'I'll ask her if she's free.'

'Excellent. I can't wait to cross-examine her. See if she's good enough.'

The full-time whistle blows.

'Don't be daft,' he says, wrinkling his nose. 'Of course she is.'

May 2000

Clara

Something is prickling her.

The feeling that she has been prioritised, and she's come out below football. That he hasn't asked her if she wanted to do something this afternoon. That he's just decided, he's going to watch football again, and she can fit in around that.

It's been the same every week. At first, she didn't mind – or even notice really, because she liked to spend Saturday afternoons cleaning her room and doing her washing, and at the beginning of the second term her flatmates started 'Saturday pizza night' where they all crowded into Sinead's room to watch romcoms on her fancy telly with the built-in video player. But that isn't mandatory. It isn't *set in stone*. For some reason, she and Benjamin have fallen into this pattern of parting just before lunch on Saturday, and not meeting up again until Sunday afternoon.

But that's OK, isn't it? That's reasonable enough.

But today it niggled at her.

He has never even asked her to join him.

Is it because he doesn't want her to meet his father?

She looked up today's matches – the football fixtures were so complicated, seemingly endless matches and endless different tournaments – and it turned out his team weren't even playing. So what football match is he actually watching? And why couldn't he have just spent the day with her?

They could have gone shopping together.

Instead, she's walking around town alone. She had the vague idea of buying something new – a nice dress perhaps, or a top to go with her favourite black trousers. She's barely spent any of the allowance her parents gave her for expenses and it's just sitting there in her account.

She wanders through Topshop and Dorothy Perkins and Oasis and Warehouse but she's restless, unable to find anything she likes.

Outside Blimpie, she bumps into Lauren and James, Richard's friend. They've been seeing each other officially for a few weeks now.

It feels pointed. So, Lauren and James get to spend Saturday afternoons together, then.

She leaves them to their romantic afternoon and pulls her phone out of her bag to read Benjamin's last message. It's 5.10 p.m., so the game must be over by now. He'll still be in the pub probably.

Sometimes he calls her on Saturday evenings, late, and she can tell he's drunk because he slurs a bit and doesn't really listen to her. She always hangs up from these calls feeling itchy and annoyed.

Well, sod it. She will call him now and they can do something together.

He's saved as Mr BE, at the top of her Contacts list, just above Home. She presses down hard on the green rubber button and puts the phone to her ear.

It rings. And it rings. And it rings. Eventually, the generic voicemail clicks in.

'*The person you are calling is unable to take your call. Please leave a message after the tone.*'

'Hi, it's me. Can you ring me back?'

She hangs up, her heart suddenly pounding.

She has done this to herself, she knows. She has worked herself up into *a state*.

The kind of state that when she was in her early teens would find her locked in the downstairs loo, crying and knocking her head against the wall, as if trying to rid her mind of all the bad thoughts. Her parents were terrified – they took her to see a psychologist who told her that she was a perfectionist and that they needed to ease back the pressure they put on her.

So they started being extra nice, praising her when her marks weren't even that good. She could see right through it, and all it did was drive her behaviour underground.

When things got very difficult, she would take the razor from the bathroom and sit on the toilet and gently slice away at the skin of her thigh, until the bright red sprang up and the sight of it shocked her into stopping.

Most of her friends had eating disorders. There were assemblies at school about bulimia and Abigail, whose weight dropped to five stone at one point, was eventually sectioned.

But no one talked about how to cope with the need to physically hurt yourself, and she was too ashamed to tell anyone that physical pain made her emotions somehow easier to bear. That self-harm was actually a way to remind herself that she was alive, that she was real, that she existed. That she mattered.

No one understood that all those years ago when Cecily got sick, something fundamental shattered in Clara: the ability to trust, to feel safe in the world. The innocent, deep-seated faith that all things would ultimately be OK was gone, forever. And what was left in its place was a gaping fear that the worst things could happen when you least expected them.

Before she knows what she's doing, she's boarded a bus to Jesmond.

She hasn't been here since their second date, when they slept together for the first time, in his tiny bedroom. They're coming up for three months together, yet it feels so much longer. It already feels like a proper relationship. Anything over three months at their age is a big deal.

The pub is busy, people spilling out onto the pavement. They are ninety per cent men, but she can't see Benjamin anywhere.

She swallows. She's nervous now, her anger turned sour, into something like self-loathing.

As she walks into the pub one of the twats on the pavement wolf-whistles at her. Her cheeks burn as she scans the crowds, looking for Benjamin's familiar shape. And then, there he is, at the bar, paying, a round of drinks in front of him.

He's told her before that he doesn't have much money. That's why he has to work at the department store, because otherwise he'd really struggle to pay his rent and bills. She printed out some stuff about hardship grants for him but he never mentioned it again.

The anger rises once more. How can he afford this, then? She watches as he takes a £20 note from his wallet and hands it to the barman.

She's about to march up to him and ask him what the hell he's doing when something else happens. A blonde girl, plumper than her and with a friendly, open face, picks up two of Benjamin's drinks and carries them over to a table in the corner. There are a couple of boys there, one of whom she recognises as his housemate, Donny. Benjamin and the girl sit down and they sip their drinks and carry on chatting. He looks happy.

She's tactile, this blonde, resting her arm on Benjamin's shoulder and smiling at him as he talks.

Clara knows some girls would cry. But she's too angry, and instead she marches right up to the table and stands there, arms folded at her waist, until he looks up and sees her.

His head jerks backwards slightly and he puts down his pint. 'What... hey!' he says. He blinks slowly. He's drunk. 'Baby.'

'What the hell... who... who is she?' she spits, without daring to look anywhere but directly in his eyes.

'What? This is...'

'How could you do this to me!'

He stands up and pulls her by the arm.

'Let's go outside,' he says, quietly. So, she's an embarrassment to him.

'No!' she shouts. The madness is upon her, there's no point trying to fight it any longer. 'I won't! I hate you! You... you arsehole!'

She starts to claw at him, grabbing his jumper and pulling it away from his chest – his perfect chest that she has slept against so many times. That felt like the safest place in the world.

'Stop!' he splutters, trying to contain her frantic arms. 'What are you... what are you doing? Are you mental? Jesus.'

'How dare you! How dare you do this to me!' she screams and then before she knows what she's doing she's grabbed the pint glass from the table and she sloshes it – trying to hit him in the face but missing woefully, so that all that happens is her own arm is now soaked, and some of his trousers and his trainers too. The pint glass drops to the floor.

She lets out a great sob and turns, running out of the pub and back onto the street, the disgusting smell of Guinness in her nostrils, her hands dripping and sticky.

He's there, of course, right behind her.

'What the hell,' he says, pulling on her arm again and she turns to look at him, tears blurring the image of his perfect face.

His perfect, awful face.

'I hate you!' she screams and then as he tries to follow her again she pushes him away, hard, so that he stumbles backwards. 'Don't you dare try to follow me! Leave me alone!'

April 2022

Clara

The television continues blaring out the same rolling footage of people being loaded into ambulances. The barmaid is staring at Clara.

'What's the name of the guy you are looking for?' she says, again.

'His name is Benjamin Edwards,' Clara replies.

Her heart is pounding. If this woman doesn't know where he is then that's it. Game over. It's futile. She should go home. Really, she should.

'Benjamin?' the barmaid says.

'Yes, does he still work here?'

The barmaid's eyebrows furrow. She looks at Clara again, as though trying to work her out.

'You're not Zoe, are you?'

'What?' Clara says. *Who's Zoe?* 'No. No, my name's Clara.'

'Right, OK,' she says.

'So, you know him then? You know Benjamin?'

'Yeah, course. He left a few months ago, though. To concentrate on his film work.'

His film work? Clara flushes with warmth at the thought of this. She knew it. She knew one day…

'But Jonno will have a number for him, I'm sure. If that's any use to you.'

Clara beams.

'Yes,' she says, trying to keep herself together. 'Please. That would be amazing. If you don't mind. I just want to know he's OK.'

'Sure, let me just ask.'

She disappears through a door behind the bar and leaves Clara standing there, still clutching the empty whisky glass.

A number. A phone number. She could actually phone him and he might answer. And then what? What the hell would she say?

Hello-how-are-you-I-know-it's-been-years-but-I've-thought-of-you-every-day-and-I-wanted-to-say-sorry-for-everything...

Even the thought of it has her on the verge of sobs.

'Here you go,' the barmaid says, returning with a slip of paper.

'Thank you,' Clara says, staring down at it. 'I... just... do you know how he is? It's been a while since we saw each other.'

'I only worked with him for a month or so before he left,' she says. 'Sorry. Didn't get to know him that well. Nice guy, though. Quiet. But funny.'

Clara nods, recognising this description. The barmaid stares at her, expectantly.

'Right, well, then. I'll leave you to it,' Clara says. 'Just one more question... if you don't mind?'

'Sure.'

'You asked if I was Zoe. Who is she?'

'Oh god,' she says, rolling her eyes. 'His ex. I never met her but I heard a lot about her. Had a lot of issues, Jonno said.

Drink, I think.' The barmaid pauses, staring at Clara, her head cocked on one side. Her eyes widen. 'You promise you're not...'

She looks down at the piece of paper in Clara's hand. Clara's fingers tighten around it. It's hers now, and she's not giving it back.

'No,' Clara says, smiling what she hopes is a reassuring smile. 'I'm not Zoe. I promise.'

June 2000

Benjamin

He stands on the platform with her, saying their goodbyes.

It's been two weeks since their big fight. And finally, he feels things are on an even keel again. He explained about Tina. That she was a friend from his work, nothing more. He didn't tell her about their drunken kiss, which feels like forever ago now anyway. Clara apologised. They made up, and they made love and it was more passionate than it had ever been before. She stared at him throughout, right in the eyes, and he told her that he loved her and that he would never hurt her, and she started to cry.

Afterwards, he felt drained for days.

He tried to persuade her to meet Tina, but she refused. In a way, he was relieved. After the pint-throwing incident, Tina labelled Clara a psycho. It seems better if they never mix.

And now, Clara is going home for the weekend. Back to her London life.

'I don't want to go,' she says, hugging him, her voice small.

'It's only two nights,' he says, kissing her forehead. 'And it will be so nice for your mam to see you. I bet your parents and Cecily have missed you. It's been forever since you last went back.'

'Yes but I wish I had asked you to come with me now.'

'Next time,' he says. He can't imagine meeting them. The family. It's a terrifying prospect.

She kneels on her train seat waving at him through the window of the carriage, and he jogs down the platform until the train picks up too much speed and she is lost to him.

And then he turns around and makes for home.

He goes out that night with Tina and they get more drunk than he has been for ages. So drunk that, by the time they leave the nightclub, he's barely able to walk. He stumbles home, Tina beside him, picking chips out of a polystyrene box, and they practically fall through his front door.

'Fuck me,' he says, his hand landing heavy on the newel post in front of him. 'You are a bad influence, Tina Bryan. Never again. Never again.'

'Lightweight,' she says, kicking off her shoes. She dissolves into a fit of giggles. 'Jesus Christ almighty! I am fucking wasted!'

He rolls his eyes at her and switches on the kettle. She goes through to the conservatory, collapsing on the sagging sofa. Her skirt rides up and he sees a flash of her knickers. Red.

He looks away, pulling his phone from his back pocket: 3.20 a.m. No new text messages.

Clara will be in bed now, of course. In her big family mansion.

He splashes boiling water on the teabag.

'Do you know Jimmy from menswear?' Tina says, yanking off her cardigan.

'Uh-huh,' he replies, handing her a cup of tea and taking a seat next to her on the sofa.

'He's been sacked.'

Benjamin pictures Jimmy: slicked-back hair, prone to winking.

'Eh, what for?'

'Caught with his hand in the till,' she says, forking another chip. 'Barbara literally saw him. Stuffing twenties into his trousers. Idiot.'

He nods, feeling suddenly sober. Jimmy reminds him of the guys he left behind at home: scraping by from payday to payday, choosing between heating and food. It's not Jimmy's fault he's never caught a break.

'Well, I guess if he was desperate?'

'Not right though, is it? Stealing. Anyway. How's Little Miss Psycho? Bet she's tried to call you a million times tonight, knowing you're out with me.'

He doesn't like being faced with this. His own guilt.

'I haven't told her we're meeting up,' he says, quietly.

'Tut-tut,' she says, waggling a finger in his face. 'Benjamin's a naughty boy. She'll skin you alive when she finds out.'

He shifts away from her.

'It's cool,' he says. His head starts to pound. 'We're just friends, aren't we? Nothing more.'

'Not since you broke my heart,' she says, laughing.

He sits up.

'No, Tina I...'

'Oh forget it,' she says. 'It's fine. I've moved on. I'm clearly not psycho enough for you.'

'She's not a psycho,' he says, but Tina ignores him. 'She's just... passionate.'

'Damaged.'

He stares at her.

'What?' he says.

'She's damaged,' Tina says. 'You can see it. I feel... a bit sorry for her, really. Goes to show, money can't buy you mental stability.'

'She's not damaged,' he says, defensively. He's tired now. Wishes he had never invited Tina to come back with him. He can't tell how much of what she's saying is because he rejected her, and how much is what she really believes.

'Oh god, don't get weird about it,' Tina says. 'We're all damaged in one way or another. You're... I dunno.'

'I'm what?' he says.

'Impotent,' she says, and then she cackles, leaning back in the sofa and nearly spilling tea down herself.

'Impotent?'

'Backwards at coming forwards.'

He feels as though she's punched him. Is this what she thinks of him? And if so, why the hell does she want to spend any time with him?

'Just because I don't like getting involved in other people's business,' he mutters, frowning. His headache has taken grip now. 'It's not a bad thing.'

'Oh god, cheer up grumpy,' she says, putting a hand on his leg. He wants to flick it off. That would shut her up. *Impotent.* 'I just mean you're sweet. Nice. You're a nice guy, that's all, Edwards. Now get over yourself, for god's sake.'

He thinks of what his football coach used to shout at him. *Nice guys finish last.*

So what would a not-nice guy do now? Tell Tina to get out?

He turns his head away from her. He should have gone to London with Clara after all.

June 2000

Clara

She's sitting on the train as it waits at Darlington, carefully applying make-up, when she feels someone tap her on the shoulder. She turns, annoyed, but then she sees that it's him.

Benjamin.

'Oh my god,' she says.

'Surprise.'

He leans down and kisses her. Properly. The woman in the aisle behind him tuts.

'Let's go,' Clara says, stroking his face. 'Let's go out there.'

She gathers her stuff together and follows him through to the vestibule at the end of the carriage.

'I can't believe you... how...'

'I wanted to surprise you. So I got the earlier train out to Darlington so that I could get on yours and travel the last bit back to the city with you. Is that a bit creepy? I was trying to be romantic.'

'Shut up and kiss me again,' she says.

When they get back to the city, they walk hand in hand, Benjamin carrying her weekend bag. She is happier than she has ever thought it possible to be. Being here, being reunited with him – it makes her feel whole again.

'I have some exciting news,' she says as they round the street outside the station. 'I was going to save it until... but fuck it!'

She never swears. His eyebrows rise.

'It's my dad. He's got you... he's got you an internship in the technology department at his firm. Eight weeks. The whole summer. And get this – they're going to pay you two hundred pounds per week!'

'Wha...'

'I know! It's amazing, isn't it? It was his idea. I told him that you were studying computer stuff, and that you'd never even been to London, and he said they were looking for interns for the summer and... well, it's sorted. Daddy has quite a lot of sway at his firm. He's pretty senior. Anyway, I'm jealous. Wouldn't mind earning that kind of money myself. It's going to be brilliant. You can stay with us, Mum said. She wants you to have your own bedroom, but the house is so big, they'll never notice, you can sneak back into your room in the morning and they'll be none the wiser. Just imagine it! The whole summer – together! I can show you London, take you to all the best places... if that's not too patronising. I mean, it's just, you said you'd never been and I thought perhaps...'

'Wow,' he says. 'I don't know what to say.'

'Say you'll do it?'

'Well, yes, of course. Of course, I will.'

She squeezes his arm.

'It's going to be brilliant.'

They stop off at McDonald's on the way back.

'High-class celebration,' she says, as she tucks into her cheeseburger. 'So, tell me, what did you get up to this weekend? I mean, I know you probably spent most of the day alone in your room missing me, right?'

She's teasing, but she does worry about him. He's so pale that the skin under his eyes is almost purple.

Despite his height, he looks so fragile sometimes. She knows that he doesn't sleep particularly well. The opposite of her. She has always slept like the dead.

'Nothing much,' he says.

'Computer games then?' It sounds more judgemental than she meant. But she doesn't understand the obsession with Championship Manager, the way his flatmates seem so consumed by it. They take it so seriously. It's actually quite pathetic, but she's trying to view it as sweet.

He nods. 'Well, and I watched the Liverpool game in the pub.'

'I really don't get it,' she says, shaking her head. 'How you can care so much about...'

'Football?'

She swallows.

'You don't even know these men. Like, you've never met them. Half of the Newcastle City team aren't even from Newcastle. So why does whether or not they manage to kick a stupid ball into a net have such an impact on you?'

She hates it, the way his mood will darken if his team loses a match. The fact that alcohol seems to be the only cure for these post-match blues. It makes no sense to her.

He smiles and shrugs.

'Ah, it's not for me to explain the unexplainable,' he says, winking. 'Let's talk about something else.'

But it's buzzing at her again. What is wrong with her? Why must she keep trying to pick this scab? What's she trying to prove?

'But...'

'I didn't just watch the match. I actually went out last night,' he says.

Her stomach plummets. Who did he go out with? Tina?

'What? Where?'

'That new club in town. The one with the revolving dance floor.'

'You didn't tell me you were going out.'

He takes a bite of his burger.

'It was a last-minute thing,' he says.

'Who did you go with?'

His eyes widen.

'Oh, you know. The usual suspects.'

'Donny?'

He nods.

'You look knackered,' she says, sitting back in her chair. 'Like, properly rough.'

He laughs.

'I knew that was why I loved you, CDC. Because you make me feel so good about myself. Thanks.'

They finish their meals in silence. What is wrong with her? Why is she so angry?

So, he went out to a club. So what?

He's a student. That's what students do. They drink too much and experiment with drugs and sleep around and it's all totally normal.

But why didn't he tell her? Why not this morning, when they were texting? Why didn't he mention it before?

Why does it feel like he's hiding things from her?

Like a slap to the face, she realises there's a reason for these feelings.

It's not just because of Daniel, and his betrayal. Not just

because Benjamin disappeared for nearly three weeks in the early days of their relationship, and never explained why.

It's also her own guilt. It's because of what she did with Richard. Because she has never told him.

Her own guilt is keeping her from trusting Benjamin.

'I'm sorry,' she says. 'I didn't mean to be mean.'

'You're all right, CDC,' he says, squeezing her hand across the table. 'If it helps, I had a shit night anyway. It's always shit without you. Now listen, please give me your address so that I can write to your dad. I want to say thank you for the internship.'

July 2000

Benjamin

He feels sick to his stomach when they arrive at King's Cross station. She lives just a few miles away apparently. They'll be getting on the Tube.

'It's busy,' he says, as they make their way down the escalator.

Cities make him nervous. And this is the biggest of them all. She squeezes his hand.

'London's not that much busier than Newcastle.'

She's said it to make him feel better, but they both know it's a lie.

He hasn't told her much about where he's from. A small village just outside Newcastle, with unremarkable views, where the weather and the architecture are predominantly grey. The people are cheerful though, friendly. They are generous despite having very little, and a sense of humour is valued above all else.

His mam barely ever left the county, but used to wrinkle her nose at the mention of southerners. *Selfish, driven people,* she'd say. *Superior.*

But he had told his mam about Clara right before she died and she had approved, and that meant a lot to him. He likes to think the two of them would have got on. Clara isn't selfish, she's not superior. She's driven, though. She seems to possess an energy that's overwhelming at times, despite being, well, quite shy. He admires the combination.

They step outside Highgate Tube station into bright sunshine. The main road is busy, congested with traffic, and he wonders why people would choose to live somewhere so overwhelming.

But Clara's family home is on a quiet, tree-lined street, the detached houses set back from the road. Red-brick and grand. Traditional, as he imagines Clara's family to be. She has warned him several times that the house is big. She spoke about their wealth in a detached, factual way. She wasn't trying to show off, he realised, but arm him.

His own home is a semi-detached cottage, set on the edge of the village. The garden was his mam's pride and joy, and he dreads to think what state it's in now. He hasn't been back since Easter.

His father was unexpectedly emotional when Benjamin told him about the internship. Proud and encouraging. Benjamin saw then that George really did have his best interests at heart, always. George wants Benjamin to fulfil his potential, in the same way Clara does.

'Here we are,' she says, pushing open the enormous front door. Inside, the temperature is remarkably cooler, and the wood-panelled hallway is dark. A large grandfather clock ticks peacefully in the corner.

'Wow, it's nice. A bit like a museum,' he says.

'Obviously Daddy's at work, and Mum will be out playing golf or something,' she says. 'Which is good cos it means I can show you everything. And we can have sex.'

He flushes. It's not that he doesn't want to, of course. He is fairly sure he would never not want to have sex with her. But it's more the idea of doing it here, in her parents' house. It feels disrespectful.

'What about your sister?'

'I told you,' she says, tugging his hand. 'She won't be back for ages. Come through, let's get a drink then we can go up to my room.'

Her bedroom is huge. Bigger than the living room in his house. The walls are papered with a floral pattern that seems quaintly old-fashioned, and the curtains at the nine-paned window have fancy tassels on them. She yanks them across, throwing them into darkness, then sits down on her bed.

'Come here,' she says, and he joins her on the bed. She tugs at his clothes wordlessly, pulling his T-shirt over his head and kissing him.

She reaches for his belt buckle.

'It doesn't feel right somehow,' he stammers.

'Oh, shut up,' she says. She's wearing a strappy vest top and she pulls it off and unhooks her bra. He looks away. He realised early on in their relationship that just the sight of her topless was enough. She didn't even have to touch him.

'Stop CDC,' he says. 'You know I can't...' but she silences him with a kiss, and before he knows it, it's game over.

Afterwards, she goes to the toilet and he gets dressed quickly, still paranoid at the thought of her mother coming home unexpectedly and finding them. He wouldn't have been able to bear that shame.

He sits on her bed, looking around at the curious combination of childhood and teenage things in her room. There's a small heart-shaped photo frame by her bed, inside which is a picture of her and another girl – her best friend from school, Melissa, who went to Oxford.

'I don't think Melissa or my parents will ever forgive me for not doing the same,' Clara says later, when she finds Benjamin examining the photo.

He didn't say it, but he thought it was more important for Clara to forgive herself.

There are also posters of actors, ripped from magazines and stuck up in a collage behind the headboard. Mostly Leonardo DiCaprio.

He understands the appeal, and jealousy is not one of his traits. She has made him watch *Titanic* three times since they got together.

He can't quite believe he's here. In London. That in two days' time he's going to start working in the technology department of a leading law firm.

It blows his mind. And it's all thanks to her.

Tina hadn't been a fan of his news. She thought it was controlling of Clara to arrange his entire summer for him.

'Fuck. She just doesn't want to let you out of her sight,' Tina said, on their final shift at the department store, when they had a quiet moment at the tills. 'Does she?'

He'd frowned at that and gone home afterwards feeling concerned that Tina might have a point. But now he's actually here, everything feels right.

He knows they're too young for it, but he thinks, idly, that if someone suggested they got married he would be completely up for the idea. It seems inevitable that one day they will be, and living in London with their children. How many will they have? Three? Four? He's not sure. It'll be up to her. As, he presumes, most of their life will be.

She comes back in from the bathroom and smiles at him. She's wearing just her knickers and her bra, and he tries to ignore the effect this has on him.

'I'm tired,' she says, stretching her arms above her head. 'Shall we have a nap?'

She pushes him backwards on the bed, curls up beside him.

'Clara, man,' he says. 'You can't do that to me. Your mam will be back soon. Get some clothes on.'

'Oh shush, you prude. My mum won't care.'

There's an awkward silence then, as he remembers her three-before-him, and the long-term boyfriend from sixth form, who's now at university in Newcastle, too. She will have slept with that lad here, of course. In the very spot they're lying on now.

He pushes the vision away. Perhaps jealousy is one of his traits after all.

Dating Clara is such a disorientating experience. It's like every day she pulls more and more feelings out of him. Feelings he had no idea he was capable of having.

'I'm nervous about Monday,' he says, trying to ignore the softness of her stomach under his fingertips. 'Is that pathetic?'

'No,' she says. 'But you'll be fine. Daddy will look after you. He said the team you're working in are really nice. They're mostly in their twenties.'

He takes a deep breath.

'I get really nervous, sometimes,' he says. 'Like, so nervous I can't eat.'

'Everyone gets nervous sometimes. You don't see how brilliant you are. How everyone else sees you. How I see you. Literally, when you walk in a room, I think: this man is magnificent. How can anybody do anything but adore him?'

He rolls his eyes at her. But she's not teasing. She means it.

His heart swells.

'It's not just nerves though. It's a physical thing. I get dizzy, it makes me feel like I'm going to pass out. It's the reason I couldn't make it as a footballer. Even though I was good. I was...' He pauses, uncomfortable at the thought of showing off. 'Well, I was really good, you know. But it was paralysing. I couldn't hack it. It's a mental game, as well as a physical game. I could never get over the mistakes I made. They haunted me, man. You don't understand. I mean, you only see part of me.'

She traces her finger up and down his arm.

'I know you're shy,' she says. 'That's one of the things I love about you.'

'It's pathetic.'

She hoists herself up onto her elbows and looks at him. Her eyes are bright sparks. Sea glass.

'You're not pathetic,' she says, softly. 'You're amazing. And this isn't bloody football, and there won't be any pressure on you to be anything more than what you already are. And what you already are is brilliant.'

July 2000

Clara

She couldn't stand the thought of Benjamin working all summer while she lay around doing nothing. She'd had grand ideas about starting to write her novel, but when her dad offered the job to Benjamin, she asked if perhaps there was something in the firm that she could do, too, so they could travel in together. And her dad said she could do work experience in the HR department.

She's only going to be paid £150 per week, but that's OK. She suspects it's better for his self-esteem that Benjamin earns more.

They get the Tube to the office hand in hand, Benjamin's eyes marvelling at the new Jubilee line extension, with its anti-suicide doors. She loves how impressed he is with London, how he sees everything through fresh eyes.

They settle into a routine; leaving the house together in the morning, separating in the cool marble lobby of the office, then meeting up again for lunch. She's amused by his enthusiasm for the Boots Meal Deal, and teases him about it daily.

They abuse the work email accounts they are given, sending stream-of-consciousness emails to each other all day long.

At the end of the first month, they decide to go to one of the bars by the river Thames after work. It's a beautiful, warm July evening, and they sit watching the water, sipping their drinks.

She's so happy. Life is perfect.

'We've spent every day together for forty days now,' she says. 'I don't want to go back to uni. I don't want to deal with everyone else.'

He doesn't say anything, but shifts around in his pocket, pulling out a small box.

'I got you something,' he says, pushing it across the table towards her. 'To say thank you.'

She's so surprised she doesn't know what to say, so she picks up the box and opens it. Inside is a bracelet, with a tiny diamond star in the centre of the chain.

'It's white gold,' he says, quickly. 'I kept the receipt if you don't like it...'

She takes the bracelet out of the box and fastens it around her wrist, stroking it.

'I love it,' she squeaks. 'Thank you. I... I don't know what to say. I haven't got you anything.'

And it's true. She's never bought him anything proper. His birthday isn't until January, and she was thinking of just getting him some new trainers or something. Nothing romantic like this.

'I thought it was just right,' he says, quietly, sipping his pint.

'I love you,' she says. 'I wish we were thirty so we could get married already.'

'Ahh, don't wish your life away,' he says.

'No, I know, it's just... don't you feel like you're just waiting for it to start? Like, properly start? This uni business. I'm studying all these books and it's interesting and great but I feel like I'm treading water, until the real business of being a grown-up starts and I can actually achieve something.'

'What about your novel?'

She feels shy talking about it with him. He once asked, 'How do you plan to write a novel, then?' and she felt odd, as though perhaps he didn't understand her after all. How could she explain to him what writing meant to her? It felt as natural as breathing. She didn't like the feeling of distance that opened between them in that moment, so she changed the subject.

'I've been making some notes,' she says. 'When things are quiet. Which is, like, ninety-nine per cent of the time. I swear they have nothing for me to do. They must have been really pissed off when Daddy forced me upon them.'

'What's it about? Your novel? Tell me again.'

'It's about the pressure to conform. When you're a teenage girl. And why teenage girls put more pressure on themselves than teenage boys.'

'Is that true?'

She stares at him.

'Of course it is! Why do you think girls out-achieve boys in practically every subject at A level? Women carry the weight of the world on our shoulders.'

He frowns, gives a slight shrug.

'Perhaps you need to spice it up a bit,' he says. 'I mean, think about the stuff that gets published. What was that book that was huge recently? The one about the wizard kid?'

'*Harry Potter*?'

'Yeah,' he says, nodding. 'Write something like that.'

She rolls her eyes.

'Idiot,' she says. 'That's a children's book. I want to write about the human condition. I have things to say.'

'Oh yes,' he says, his eyes twinkling. 'You always have things to say.'

★ ★ ★

One evening, Clara leaves Benjamin to call his father while she goes downstairs to help her mum Eleanor prepare the dinner.

Cecily is sitting in the corner of the kitchen, painting her toenails pink.

'You could help with dinner too, you know,' Clara says, glancing over at her.

'Leave her be, Clara,' Eleanor says. 'She's had a long week. She's very tired.'

'A long week of what exactly?' Clara snaps. 'Pouting at herself in the mirror?'

'Fuck off, Clar.'

'It was a joke,' Clara says.

'Please, girls,' Eleanor says. 'Not tonight. You'll give me a headache.'

Clara pulls a face at her sister. When Eleanor's back is turned, Cecily sticks her tongue out at Clara, as though she's a little kid.

Clara's phone buzzes in the back pocket of her jeans. She pulls it out, reads the message.

It's from Richard. She doesn't know how he got her number, but suspects Lauren.

Hey Clara, I'm having birthday drinks in Covent Garden this Friday. 8pm at The Coal Hole. Would be great to see you. Richard x

She swallows, forcing the phone back into her pocket. He has invited her to things a few times over the summer. She supposes he's just being friendly but she doesn't believe in being friends with people you've slept with. And she can hardly imagine telling Benjamin that she's abandoning him for the evening to hang out with Richard and his rugby mates.

She turns to her mother, tries to forget about the text.

'So. Tell me. What do you think of Benjamin?' Clara asks.

She hardly ever speaks to her mum about, well, anything in her life, and as soon as the question is out, she regrets it.

Especially as Cecily is still in the room. Albeit with her Walkman on now, blasting out tinny Eurodance.

'Oh, he's adorable,' her mum says, pouring herself another glass of wine. 'Very handsome.'

Clara smiles.

'I think maybe we'll be one of those university couples that lasts, you know.'

Her mum sniffs, her eyebrows rising. She gives a knowing smile.

'What?'

'Oh! Nothing, darling. He's a really lovely boy.'

'He's not a boy! Why did you smirk?'

'I didn't smirk, Clara. Have you finished with the potatoes?'

'You did,' Clara says, handing her mother the bowl. 'I saw it. You think we won't last.'

'I didn't say that.'

'You don't have a clue. You don't understand how much we love each other. We really love each other.'

'I'm sure.'

'Well, what then? Why the face?'

'Nothing, sweetheart. I'm glad you're happy. We were so worried about you after that first term, when you came home looking dreadful. Nothing but skin and bone. And all that drama with Daniel, so upsetting. I saw his mother on the high street a few weeks ago, did I tell you? She kept her head down and kept walking. She must be ashamed. I, for one, will never forgive him. If it wasn't for him, you could be at Oxford now, with Melissa.'

'Mum, I don't care about Daniel! I'm embarrassed that I ever did. I was just a kid. And if I hadn't gone to Newcastle, then I would never have met Benjamin. So it all worked out for the best.'

'Your dad didn't want you to go back to Newcastle in the new year, you know. I had to persuade him to let you.'

Clara doesn't hear her.

'Besides, what Benjamin and I have is *nothing* like me and Daniel. I can't believe you'd even mention him in the same conversation.'

Her mum pauses.

'I'm glad you've found someone who makes you happy. Someone to have a bit of fun with.'

'What does that mean? Tell me,' Clara says, fiercely. 'Tell me what you really think of him. What you and Daddy think.'

'I just told you,' she says, waving a hand in the air. 'He's lovely. Very handsome. Just...'

'What?'

'Well, I'm sure you know this, but... he's not... enough for you. Is he?'

Clara's face burns.

'He's not on your level,' her mum is saying, and now Clara wishes she could tape over her mother's mouth, to shut her up. 'You'll outpace him, and he'll end up resentful and insecure, and you'll end up bored. You're a complicated girl, Clara. You need someone like Daddy. Someone strong, someone with their own ambitions. But that's OK. Your university love is special, and Benjamin is too. You'll always remember him. And this wonderful summer you're having together.'

'You're wrong,' Clara says, biting her lip. 'You're completely wrong about everything.'

'Well,' says her mother, smiling, giving a slight shake of her head that makes Clara want to slap her. 'Let's see. Hopefully I am.'

August 2000

Benjamin

'I don't want to go back, Mr BE,' Clara says, her summer refrain. 'Let's just quit.'

It's Saturday afternoon. Their last Saturday afternoon in London and they have had a picnic on the Heath, then walked across to get ice creams from the tiny gelato shop that's been there since the 1950s. And now they are lying on her bed in their underwear, staring up at the ceiling.

'We can get a flat together in London,' she says.

He can't tell if she's joking.

'It'll be different this year,' he says, into her hair. 'You'll have me.'

'I know, but... the place I'm going to be living...'

He's staying in the same house share as last year, with the same people. It hadn't occurred to him to find somewhere else to live. But she's moving into a small terrace, with Lauren and Sinead.

'It's a shithole,' she says. 'All because Sinead was too hungover to come with us to see the nice one I found.'

'I'm sure we can make it nice. At least you have a big room.'

'I wish we had got somewhere together,' she says. He shifts away from her slightly. What is it about this idea that alarms him? He isn't sure exactly. He loves her, he knows that much. He can't picture his life without her. And yet, she always wants to rush everything.

'You're only young once, CDC,' he says, but the words sound borrowed. 'You have to make the most of your university experience.'

It's what he tells himself, frequently. He had to grow up so quickly thanks to his mam's illness. Now she's gone, he wants to savour this time of being young and free of responsibility.

'I don't like it,' she says, her voice small. 'The only thing that's good about university is you. I don't like my course, I don't have any friends. It's just not... me.'

'You do have friends. And you do like your course,' he says, pleasantly. 'I've never heard anyone talk so animatedly about *The Bell Jar* before.'

'Idiot,' she says, sitting up and throwing a cushion at him. 'You've never heard anyone talk about any sort of literature before.'

He considers this for a moment. It's true, of course. His mam liked Agatha Christies, but they didn't talk about them together, and does that even count as literature? He isn't sure.

'Lauren's nice,' he says, changing the subject. 'I like her.'

She frowns.

'Do you fancy her?'

'What? No, what are you on? I just mean, she's a nice girl. I think you should give her more credit.'

She makes a non-committal noise and rests her head back on his shoulder again.

'The football season is starting again next week, isn't it?'

He's surprised.

'It is,' he says. 'Well done, my clever little piglet. Are you going to start coming to matches with me?'

'You've never even asked me! I thought it was boys only?' she says. 'Oh, and Tina, of course.'

'Don't be stupid. You're welcome any time.'

This is a lie, he realises. She would be a distraction. She would get angry with him over – he's not sure what exactly, but she would.

Again, he's aware that for some reason, the different parts of his life don't mix. Is that bad? He hasn't been home all summer. Clara couldn't understand why he didn't want to go home for the bank holiday weekend at least. He could tell she was angling for an invite.

But the train fare home is expensive, and he's been saving every penny he's earnt this summer to help him get through next year at uni.

'It's just so boring,' she's saying – something he's heard her say so many times now. It seems odd that he can love someone who hates football so much, but then again, opposites attract.

'I don't find it boring,' he says.

'Oh god, I know, you're obsessed with it. You love it more than you love me!'

She pouts like a five-year-old.

He inhales deeply, his jaw tensing. It's never enough. Whatever he says to her – however much love he shows her – it won't fill the hole she has inside her. She is a chasm of need. It makes him sad. It makes him feel he is failing her.

'You're ridiculous,' he says, quietly, kissing her forehead. 'It's just a game. Come with me to a match, when we're back in Newcastle. You might even enjoy it.'

It consoles her for now, but he can feel the sense of something unravelling.

A catch of thread on a seam, growing longer by the day.

April 2022

11.17 p.m.

Clara

She stands outside the bar, holding the number in her hand. It's still noisy out here, the sound of sirens wailing in the not-so-far-off distance.

She takes her phone out and looks at the screen. Thirty-seven per cent battery left. Enough then. If she's really going to do this.

She reads the WhatsApp message from Lauren again, taking in the details of the hotel she has booked.

It makes sense to go there, to make the call from somewhere warm and private. It's not putting it off. It's just being sensible.

She texts Thom to tell him that she's decided to stay over at Lauren's, making up some excuse about a last-minute trip to a karaoke bar. He doesn't read the message, but she doesn't care.

She's fairly sure she knows what has been different about Thom, anyway.

There's another woman.

She doesn't think Thom will have done anything physical, anything that would constitute a black and white betrayal. But she reckons he's been having an emotional affair, and that it has been going on for a while.

Is she betraying him? By coming here?

She feels guilty, suddenly. He's a good man. A kind man. He's been patient with her for ten years.

She sniffs. She can't think about Thom, not right now, nor the life she's left behind that she's not sure she will ever return to. She quickens her step.

The streets are full of memories, some so faint she has to tug at them to see them clearly. At one point, she remembers the scene of one of their most ferocious rows, and she closes her eyes at the recollection.

Rose-tinted glasses. That's what Lauren always says about her feelings for Benjamin. That she's making their relationship into something that it's not. *You need to look forward, not back.*

But in a life that has always felt so uncertain, she is sure of one thing: that their feelings for one another were real. The most authentic emotions she has ever felt. So powerful that they have shaped her soul. Her very being.

She is breathless by the time she reaches the hotel. It looks new – she's sure it wasn't here when she was at university. She squints as she walks into the bright lights of the shiny lobby.

There's no queue at the reception desk, and she's checked in by a woman with her hair pinned back into a French knot.

'Is there a mobile phone charger I could borrow?' Clara asks, as the receptionist hands her back her credit card. 'And toothpaste and a toothbrush maybe?'

The receptionist gives her a puzzled look.

'I'm sorry, I'm stranded here because of... after the...'

She feels ashamed for lying about something that will have wrecked so many people's lives. She has read about people who do this – people who pretend to have been caught up in horrific events in order to elicit money or sympathy or just plain old attention. The thought makes her want to twist the soft skin of her forearm with her fingernails until it bruises.

'Of course, pet,' the receptionist replies. Clara loves her accent – that soothing northern lilt. So much friendlier, so much warmer. Why did she ever want to leave this city?

The woman reaches down and hands Clara a small white paper bag.

'It's our comfort pack. And there are Bluetooth chargers in the rooms, built into the bedside tables. If your phone needs a cable charger, just call down and we'll send one up to you.'

'Thanks,' Clara replies. The thoughtfulness leaves her on the verge of tears. 'Thanks so much.'

The room is small but immaculate, with a floor-to-ceiling window at one end, looking out at the city. She can't see the stadium from here, but the sky lights up with flashes of blue every few seconds, a reminder of the horror that's still unfolding.

Can they still be removing casualties from the scene? How many lives have been destroyed this evening?

After making herself a cup of tea, she sits on the bed and stares at the phone number in her hand, trying to work out what she will say to him.

What she is trying to achieve.

Is it closure, as she keeps telling herself? Or something more?

Over the years, she has fantasised about a different life. The one she thought she would have. The one she was supposed to have, with him.

That summer after the second year of university, they rented a place in a student halls of residence so they didn't have to stay at her parents' house. He was working as an intern for her dad's law firm again, she got a summer job in a bookshop.

She had grown up a lot in the second year of university. There was less going out, less getting drunk, more hard work, which she found a comfort. Benjamin practically lived in her house, and things were peaceful and for the most part harmonious.

But they still fought, and she still found it difficult when he went out every weekend and came back slurring. She tried her best to ignore this behaviour. She knew it wouldn't last forever. Eventually, they would grow up and things would be different.

She was finally starting to understand what she wanted from life. It seemed very simple, and the certainty of knowing what was in store for her – of having created her own sense of destiny – was incredibly reassuring. She would write novels and marry Benjamin. He would get a job in IT somewhere in the city, and they would live happily ever after.

And then it all went wrong.

The tears stream down her face, catching her by surprise, and she grabs the tissue box from beside the bed and lets them come, noisily.

And then she is sobbing, properly sobbing, for the first time in years, alone in this hotel room. It's a release she needs.

She switches the television on. The BBC is running continuous news coverage of the bomb. The same police chief statement that she heard earlier. And then, something else.

A serious-faced reporter – the type she could never have become – is standing outside the stadium talking into a handheld microphone. Clara puts the tissues in the bin, turning away from the screen.

'And now we're going to talk to a gentleman who's missing a child in the incident,' the reporter says.

Something makes her look back up.

Her hand flies to her face.

And there he is.

Alive.

The same face, the same forehead, the same curls.

But thinner, his once-plump cheeks sunken.

The same and not the same.

'Benjamin Edwards,' the reporter says. 'Please, tell us who it is you're looking for.'

'It's my son,' this older, different-but-the-same Benjamin says. 'My son Aiden. He was at the match and he's missing.'

April 2022

Benjamin

He is still in shock as he turns away from the cameraman and looks over at the stadium just a few streets away. They won't let him get any closer.

His son. His son might be in there, right now, lying injured or dying, and they won't let him anywhere near.

Benjamin was working in Whitley Bay when one of the assistants, Guy, told them what had happened.

'Someone's bombed Vintage Park!' Guy shouted. 'My girlfriend was working a shift in her bar round the corner and heard it happen.'

He'd heard the expression 'his blood ran cold' before but until that moment had never truly appreciated that that was exactly what it felt like.

Someone looked on social media, shouted, 'It's true, fucking hell!' and then everything around him faded to black.

He couldn't hear or see, he could only shake his head, yanking out his phone so hard he nearly ripped a hole in his pocket, fingers trembling as he tapped viciously at the screen to call his son.

But it went straight to voicemail.

He left the set without saying a word to anyone and got in

his car and drove as fast as he could to the city. There were already police cordons in place around the stadium, and so he abandoned his car outside his old student house in Jesmond and finished the journey on foot.

But when he arrived no one could tell him anything. It was just confusion, chaos.

In desperation, he agreed to speak to the reporter, but even as he gave his short interview, deep down he knew it was futile.

It feels like that other terrible night all over again. He's at fate's mercy. Whatever has happened cannot be undone.

Why is Aiden's phone switched off?

He slams his fist against a lamppost, barely feeling the ricochet of pain shooting up his arm, and then he begins to cry.

part two

November 2012

Clara

Her wedding is running two hours late. It hasn't stopped raining all morning.

Agathe, the hotel's wedding co-ordinator, tells her that this is good luck.

'It means you'll have lots of babies,' she says, winking. 'But, oh, it is annoying. I'll just go check with the officiant. She might have a few people after you, and we don't want you getting married in the dark! Oh Lord, this weather.'

Clara stares at herself in the mirror. Her hair is elaborately braided on the top of her head, but the humidity of the Caribbean island is making the thin hairs that frame her face go wispy.

She sprays more hairspray on them, trying to stick the flyaways to the rest of her hair, and fans herself with her bouquet.

It was Thom's idea to do this. To elope.

How about the Bahamas? I've never been there.

He loved to travel. To escape.

Thom's parents had died in a car accident when he was young, and she suspects this is another reason he didn't want a big wedding, which would only highlight the enormity of what he had lost.

But now that she's here, she feels guilty to have cut her own parents out of her big day.

'It'll be more romantic, this way,' Thom had said. 'Just us. More meaningful. Can't stand those big weddings. All that fuss for one day. Then they break up a year later. It's not about the wedding anyway. The marriage is what's important.'

She had murmured and agreed.

Because the truth is, ever since he went down on one knee and offered her the most magnificent sapphire she had ever seen – 'Violet, like your eyes' – she has been struggling.

Four words torment her, day and night.

Square peg, round hole.

She's not entirely sure where those words came from, but if she was feeling sentimental or fanciful she would say that they came from her psyche. From somewhere deep within her. From a place she didn't truly understand.

A little voice. The voice of truth telling her that this marriage is wrong. A misfit.

But how do you say 'No' to someone who proposes, without ending the relationship completely?

And she doesn't want to do that.

They met at her colleague Chad's birthday party. Thom and Chad had been at school together, and Chad worked at the same newspaper group as Clara.

Clara noticed Thom out of the corner of her eye, as she stood at the bar with her long-drained G&T, wondering how long until she could make a subtle exit.

The first thing she noticed was his smile – his neat white teeth – then his smart clothing, and lastly the ease with which he carried himself across the groups of friends and towards her.

'You look like you'd rather be anywhere else than here,' he said, when he was finally standing beside her. He leant an elbow on the bar. 'It's making me sad.'

She was amused by his unconventional – if perceptive – chat-up line.

'I'm not good with big crowds,' she said. 'Not a huge fan of shouting over music either.'

'Me neither,' he said, even though she could tell it was a lie. He seemed comfortable in his skin, and she envied him. Perhaps if she stood next to him for long enough, some of it would rub off on her. 'Shall we get out of here? It's awful. I mean literally, this is the worst night out I've ever had in my whole life. Look at all these happy, young people having fun. Hideous. How dare they! I'm never speaking to Chad again.'

She laughed, and allowed him to lead her out of the nightclub.

Out in the open air, they sat on a bench in the small square just past Carnaby Street and he told her that the site used to be a plague pit. She was impressed with both his knowledge of London history and the way she felt so relaxed in his company. She asked if he was a banker because she assumed someone so self-assured must do something like that for a living, and he got up in disgust as if to leave. She felt her heart trip for a moment when she thought he was serious, then soar when he turned back around and smiled at her.

It was a whirlwind romance, and she didn't let herself examine it in much detail. Thom was a force of nature, determined and strong, and she allowed herself to be swept up by the courage of his convictions.

He had enough confidence for them both, and she found his certainty took away some of her anxiety. She thought that they made sense: he was the yin to her yang.

As the months passed, she realised that she loved him, in a way that wasn't particularly bone-shaking but grounded in the knowledge that he was a good and kind man, that he would provide a good and kind life for her. Deep down, that was all she had ever wanted.

And it was the most she could hope for, after everything with Benjamin.

Thom was ambitious, creative, passionate about his work. He was generous and popular, too. He had a network of friends who relied on him and, although at first she found it annoying, she had come to admire this. The way he treated his friends like family.

He didn't watch football.

He had a *good soul*. He was a better person than her.

And he loved her. He loved her in a way she sometimes didn't understand. He loved her with a simplicity that left no time for game playing or drama.

He made her feel safe.

And yet, a voice of doubt persisted.

It's louder than ever, today, as she stands here in ivory silk.

You can't put a square peg into a round hole.

She closes her eyes. She learnt long ago to ignore the voice of her intuition. It had proved to be untrustworthy too many times.

She stares out of the small wooden bungalow at the sugar-white sand. Whatever she is feeling, she can't deny that it's paradise here. Thom is in the bar, having a pre-wedding drink. But it feels faintly absurd that they are getting married today.

Was agreeing to this elopement her way of pretending it wasn't really happening?

Is this just a fantasy wedding? Is she living a fantasy life?

It feels like it sometimes. Like she's checked out of the game, and is letting someone else control her moves.

Agathe returns, flashing her a huge smile.

'Come, my beautiful bride,' she says. 'We've got the golf cart up here and we'll drive you to the pagoda. It's not looking like this weather's stopping any time soon, and we want to get you married before sunset!'

Her last chance gone, then.

Clara nods. Her fate is sealed, and it's OK. It's not a bad fate. She's just being silly.

'Your problem with life is that you expect too much from it,' Benjamin once said to her. 'Why isn't it enough to be safe and fed and warm?'

'Not loved?' she had asked.

'And loved, yes, of course, loved. But you *are* loved, Clara. By so many people.'

Square peg, round hole.

Shut up.

She smiles at Agathe.

'Great,' she says. 'Let's go.'

November 2012

Benjamin

His car starts making a weird stuttering noise before the engine cuts out completely.

'Fuck fuck fuck,' he shouts, as he steers it to the side of the road.

He gets out and stands staring at the empty stretch of concrete ahead. It's a B road through the countryside and there's no one else around.

He sits down on the verge, pulling his phone out of his pocket, and texts Zoe.

My car's broken down. I'll be there asap.

He lifts up the bonnet and frowns. The fuel pump has cut out. That's the problem with a fifteen-year-old rust bucket of a car. The parts keep seizing up.

His dad would say to give it a whack with a hammer, but he doesn't have any tools to hand.

His phone pings with a reply.

Great.

He takes a deep breath and slams his fist on the fuel pump to try to get it running again. It takes six goes, and one sore fist, but eventually the fan kicks in again and the pump starts working. God knows if it will hold out all the way to Zoe's house, but it's better than nothing.

He needs a new car, he knows, but he can barely afford the child maintenance for Aiden. His boots have holes in and leak water when it rains. The lining of his coat is ripped and his jeans are wearing thin at the knees.

He just needs to get this job. Just something. A glimmer of hope on the horizon – it's all he can ask for.

Thankfully, the car judders its way through the rest of the journey and in the end he's only about twenty minutes late. Zoe is sitting outside her block of flats, sucking on a cigarette, Aiden by her side, holding a football.

'Daddy!' Aiden squeaks as he waves from the car. Benjamin takes a deep breath and plasters on a smile.

'Hello mate,' he says, slamming the car door shut and looking at his son.

Seven years old. It's gone so fast.

Aiden runs towards him, grinning.

'Can we go to the park first? Daddy? For a kick about?'

'If we have time. Let me just have a word with your mam,' Benjamin says. 'Go sit in the car.'

He looks up at Zoe. She looks pale, dark circles ringing her eyes. Her hair is greasy and pulled back in a ponytail.

'All right?'

'I'm meant to be somewhere,' she says, turning away. He notices her stumble slightly as she walks back to the front door of the block.

'I'm sorry. My car...'

'Seriously, I'm not interested, Benjamin. Get a better car.'

He sighs. He can't plead poverty with Zoe, because she will say what she always says – that it's his fault he's broke. That it's his fault because if they lived together as a family then they'd have more money.

Everything is his fault. Even her drinking, no matter that it started long before they even met.

'What time do you want him back tomorrow?' he says.

She looks back at him, screwing up her face.

'Not too early,' she says. 'After tea or something. I'll text you.'

He nods. Will he have news by then? Hopefully. Hopefully they'll ring and offer him the job, and everything will get better.

He just needs a break. Ever since the call centre let him go in the last round of redundancies, it feels as though life has been an uphill struggle.

'Right,' he says. He turns to walk to the car but then pauses and looks back at her.

'Look after yourself, Zo,' he says, but she just blinks at him and turns on her heel.

Aiden is sitting in the front seat of the car, spinning the football between his hands.

'Not a chance,' Benjamin says. 'Get on your booster seat.'

'Dad!'

That cheeky smile. It's the best thing about his son.

'In the back,' he says. 'Now.'

Aiden sighs and squeezes himself through the gap in the front seats.

'Strap yourself in,' Benjamin says. 'God knows how far we're going to get.'

'Why?'

Benjamin looks at his son in the rear-view mirror. Takes him all in, as he does every time he picks him up. The sandy curls, the smattering of freckles across his nose. The wide-open optimism in his eyes.

He deserves a better life than this.

'Never mind,' he says, feeling like his heart could break in two. 'Now, who wants McDonald's for lunch before the match?'

No matter how hard up they have been as a family, somehow, George has always found the money for season tickets. They meet him at the stadium, taking their seats in the east stand for the home game.

As matches go, it's pretty boring – a goalless draw – but Aiden watches the players transfixed, analysing their every move.

'Curtis Wilson was awesome!' he squeaks as they queue to leave the stadium. 'Did you see that free kick?'

George smiles.

'I did,' he says, ruffling his hair.

'Grandad?'

'Aye?'

'One day I'm going to play for Newcastle City. You wait and see.'

'Your dad nearly did.' He glances over at Benjamin, but Benjamin looks down at his feet. 'Football runs in your veins, you know. My dad was a county player too.'

'Why did you give it up, Daddy?' Aiden says, tugging Benjamin's sleeve.

'Oh well… you know. It's a tough world. It's no good just being good. You have to be really, really good. The best.'

'I'm going to practise and practise until I'm the best,' Aiden says, to no one in particular.

Benjamin smiles, but then thinks about what this means. The kit. The boots. Driving him to training.

One word. Money.

He takes his phone out of his pocket but he hasn't missed any calls.

'Problem?' George asks.

'No, just waiting on some news.'

They are sitting down to supper in the small kitchen when Benjamin's phone rings.

He snatches it up from the counter and pushes open the back door into the November chill.

Two minutes later he's back.

'I got the job,' he says. 'I start on Monday.'

'That's great!' Aiden says. He puts down his knife and fork, very carefully, and claps. 'Go Dad!'

Benjamin smiles and strokes Aiden's head, looking over at George.

'Dad?' he says. 'I got it. The bar job.'

'I heard,' he replies, without looking up from his food.

'It's great, Grandad!' Aiden says, nudging him. 'Daddy said if he got that job he could get me some new boots.'

'I would have got you boots if you'd asked.'

'Dad,' Benjamin says. 'Please.'

George puts his fork down and looks up. Benjamin wishes, pointlessly and with familiarity, that his mother was here. Although he knows how disappointed she would be in him. Perhaps it's for the best she's not.

'I'm pleased for you,' George says. 'I'm sure it'll be a weight off your mind to have some money coming in again.'

Benjamin smiles his thanks but, inside, he wants to cry.

November 2012

Clara

They are celebrating Lauren's promotion in Claridge's. It's the first time they have met up since Clara got married.

A trip to see the famous Christmas tree first, Lauren had suggested, and then on to the gin bar. Clara can't believe that Christmas is just around the corner. She will be thirty-two next year. People say time is healing but, if anything, her pain seems to grow more acute with each passing year.

She has tried to forget all the dates, the milestones. But her mind won't let her. They play in a loop around her brain. Today she is thinking: it's been eleven years since they enjoyed the run-up to Christmas together. Their second, and their last. Eleven years! She can hardly fathom it.

Lauren brings over the drinks and sets them down alongside the teeny dish of nuts that's already on the table. Clara has managed to restrain herself from eating the whole lot.

'So, how is married life?' Lauren says, as they clink glasses. 'I still can't believe you just ran off and... *did it* like that.'

'Are you telling me you were desperate to be a bridesmaid?' Clara smiles.

'Well, I wouldn't have minded.'

'Sorry.'

'Don't be silly. Show me your rings again.'

Clara holds out her hand and Lauren touches her fingertips. The violet sapphire sparkles under the lights. Beneath it sits a slim band of diamonds.

'It's so gorgeous. That was a very clever move – marrying a jeweller.'

It's a joke, but Clara stares down at her drink and doesn't respond. She thinks about last night. The pain. It's not getting easier. If anything, it's worse.

She bites her lip.

'What's the matter?' Lauren says. 'It's not Benjamin...'

Lauren knows her so well. Has seen her at her worst, can tell when she's trying to cover things up. But this time, her instincts are wrong.

But she has unwittingly given Clara an excuse. Something else to talk about, rather than what's really on her mind.

'I sent him an email,' she says, quietly. 'A week before the wedding. It was stupid...'

'Oh god. What did it say?' Lauren says.

'Nothing really. Just that... just that I still loved him.'

Lauren exhales.

'Jesus. OK.'

'I know. It was stupid. But it felt... honest. I had to do it. In case...'

'What?'

'I don't know. In case I was making a mistake.'

'Clar,' Lauren says, reaching across the table to squeeze her hand. 'Listen to me, it's... normal. To get cold feet. To think about your exes. Of course it is. I was the same, when James and I got married.'

'Really?'

'Of course! I was petrified. And it was extra hard, you know,

161

being the first. Twenty-nine isn't exactly old to get married but I was still worried that I was too young, and that I might be missing out on something by settling down so soon. Especially as most of my friends were still single.'

'It's not that though,' Clara says. 'I just feel sometimes like my life has gone off-track somewhere. That I'm living the wrong life. The wrong version of my life.'

She looks down at her ring again.

'With the wrong person.'

Lauren shrugs.

'Well, if you are, then I guess you can always get divorced.'

Clara laughs. There is both pain and relief in Lauren's brutal, simplistic way of viewing the world.

'I guess.'

'You know this is just your anxiety talking, right?' Lauren asks.

Clara nods. She supposes so. That's what they tell her. The professionals.

She has anxiety, *understandably*, after the *trauma*.

What people conveniently choose to overlook is that she has been like this her whole life, ever since Cecily was sick. At the time, the adults in her life were so worried about her sister, no one seemed to consider that the illness might have affected Clara too. The *trauma* came later. And it might have brought her anxiety to the fore, but it had always been there, colouring everything a muddy shade of purple. Bruising everything that was good.

What people also overlook is that her anxiety is the reason the *trauma* happened in the first place.

'What did he say?' Lauren asks.

'Who?'

'You know who. Benjamin.'

Lauren says his name sadly, as though he's an injured or sick child. Lauren is the only one who was truly on her side afterwards. Who understood the complexity of it all. Clara will always be grateful to Lauren for that.

'He said he wasn't worthy and that I should forget him. And that he hoped I'd be very happy in my marriage. He said he felt a great mixture of emotions, from sadness to guilt to regret, but that I shouldn't waste my time thinking of him or what might have been, that I've mistaken him for something that he's not.'

The words come out in a rush. They are burnt on her brain now; another memory she will never be able to shake off.

Lauren closes her eyes briefly, then smiles.

'Listen Clar, I love you. And I'm saying this nicely, and sincerely. But have you heard that expression – when people show you what they are, believe them?'

She shakes her head.

'Well, I think Benjamin is showing you what he is. And I think you should believe him.'

She was wrong. Lauren doesn't get it; she'll never understand.

'But what he *is*, is my fault. It's all because of me! I'm the reason he ended up in this situation.'

'That's just not true. You're not responsible for what he did, and you had no hand in how things ended. It's just life. You can't control it. You seem to think you can, you seem to think you can make things go the way you want just by willing it, but it doesn't work like that. Life isn't that easy.'

It feels like a criticism, but Clara knows Lauren is saying this to make her feel better. To try to open her eyes.

'I just...' she says, staring down at the bowl of nuts. 'What I can't get past is that I just don't believe it had to be this way.'

'You have to listen to him,' Lauren says. The edge to her

voice tells Clara that she's becoming frustrated now. People are often frustrated with her. They want her to fall in line. To accept the status quo, her diagnosis, *their* version of *her* feelings. 'He's told you he doesn't think that you're right for one another. You have to listen to him.' Lauren pauses. 'And, remember, he won't be the same person you fell in love with when you were just a kid. Clara, he's been to *prison*.'

She says this last sentence slowly and with great emphasis, as if this very fact hasn't haunted Clara every day since.

Clara closes her eyes.

'I know,' she says. 'I know, but I can't help thinking... if I could turn back time...'

'Clara, seriously. Sometimes with you it's like, I don't know. Arrested development or something. You're stuck in the past, circling an event round and round your head, but it's not something you can change. You've got to move on. You've got a wonderful life. You've got Thom now. A good job. A future. Can't you just look back and think it was, I don't know, one of your formative experiences, and that it was good, and it taught you lessons, and move on?'

Clara wants it to be that simple, but it's not.

'But it's my fault,' she says, quietly. 'I think that's the problem. I ruined his life. How can I move past that?'

Lauren sighs.

'Listen, Clara. What he did is not your fault. You need to believe that. You are not responsible for him. You never were. What he did, that was all on him. Not you. Him.'

Clara nods, her bottom lip wobbly. She so wants to believe her. She wants to take the strength of Lauren's conviction and inject it into her uncooperative brain.

'I'm sorry,' she says, after a pause. There's too much tension, now. They were meant to be having a nice evening. Just the two of them. A girls' night out. She's stupid, she should never have brought this subject up. 'We're supposed to be celebrating your promotion, and here I am blathering on about the same ridiculous subject as always.'

She rolls her eyes and then raises her glass.

'To you, Miss Head of Human Resources!'

They clink them together.

Lauren sits back in her chair, staring at her sadly. It's as though she feels as hopeless about Clara's future as Clara does.

'Thank you,' Lauren says, eventually. She plasters a smile on her face. It takes a few seconds to meet her eyes. 'Now for god's sake, Clara Beaumont, tell me about your bloody wedding.'

December 2012

Benjamin

He hurries out of the bar, locking up before racing home. His last shift before three days off for Christmas is over. He's never been so shattered.

When he gets back to the house, he collapses in bed. It's nearly 2 a.m. Ever since he started working again, his sleep has improved. He still wakes up inhumanly early, but he no longer tosses and turns before falling asleep.

The bar job is exhausting but it's better than being stuck in the call centre; in a room with no windows, the buzz of strip lighting above his head giving him a headache as he spent the day being shouted at by disgruntled customers through a headset. And while he has never been good at small talk, being able to observe people in the bar, living through the highs and lows of their lives, is a strange comfort to him.

In the morning, he eats his cereal looking out at the snowy front garden and thinking about the day ahead. Christmas Eve. Of course, he doesn't have Aiden for Christmas Day itself – Zoe wouldn't budge on that, no matter how many times he asked. He has never spent a single Christmas Day with Aiden.

Your choice. You walked out. Made your bed.

It wasn't worth the fight. When she wants to be, Zoe is a

ferocious opponent. It amazes him that someone like Aiden, a kid so sweet and kind, can have come from her.

It scares him, too. He worries there's that seed inside Aiden, that one day might finally sprout, and then where will they be? It terrifies him that one day he might just transform, like a caterpillar to a moth, into something more *Zoe*.

As a teenage boy himself, Benjamin had been pretty quiet and well-behaved, but that's because his mam was sick.

Despite how difficult she makes his life, he can't regret sleeping with Zoe, because if he hadn't, then he wouldn't have his son.

They had met in the pub. When he first got out of prison, he felt lost. Desperate to rebuild his life somehow, but also, clueless as to how to start. And one night after he was released, when he couldn't stand his father's silent looks over the dinner table any longer, he marched out of the house and into the first pub he saw, and did exactly what he shouldn't have done. He drank nine pints in a row.

He woke up the next day in Zoe's bed, with absolutely no memory of how he had got there. There followed the most awkward hour of his life, where he attempted to let her down gently, while navigating his escape.

She insisted he leave his phone number, and so he did, thinking perhaps he could take her for a coffee when he was feeling a bit more together, and explain that he wasn't looking for a relationship right now. He felt consumed with guilt about it for days.

She phoned him six weeks later. It was so long after he'd almost forgotten the incident, but during that phone call she told him she was pregnant. That she wanted to keep the baby and that she thought they should try to make a go of things.

He's ashamed to admit it now, even to himself, but it was

the worst moment of his life. He'd just been getting himself back on track and then... bam! Here's another bomb, just in case the last one didn't blow things up enough!

He tried, he really tried, to make it work. But the two of them had absolutely nothing in common and, after a few weeks, he told Zoe he thought it would be better if they co-parented the baby as friends.

And she had been angry with him ever since.

He looks up as George comes into the kitchen, nods him a greeting and switches on the kettle. At sixty-five, George is not old, but Benjamin has noticed that it takes him longer and longer to get going in the mornings. At some point in the last few years, his hair turned completely white.

Life hasn't been easy for George, and Benjamin has only made it harder. Another thing he feels responsible for.

'Happy Christmas Eve, Dad,' he says.

'And you,' George replies. 'Another cold one, looks like. I thought I'd get the sledge out of the garage. From when you were a kid. We can take Aid up to the Seven Mount. He might enjoy it.'

'That's a great idea,' Benjamin says, smiling his gratitude. 'Thanks. He'd love it, I'm sure.'

Aiden is the one mistake George can forgive Benjamin for. He loves his grandson more than anything.

George nods, stirring sugar into his tea.

'What time are you picking him up from his mam's?'

'Ten.'

'Great, I'll have it ready for when you're back.'

Aiden is waiting outside the block of flats, football tucked under his arm, bag at his feet.

He looks so small, standing there alone.

'Where's your mam?' Benjamin asks as he approaches him.

Aiden shrugs.

'In bed. She has a headache or something.'

Benjamin frowns, glancing up at the window of Zoe's bedroom. The glass is cracked. He's sure it wasn't like that last week.

'I'll go and have a word with her,' he says, but Aiden interrupts.

'No don't, Dad, please. I'm starving. Mam had nothing to eat. Please. Can we go back to Grandad's and get some scran?'

Benjamin rests his arm on his son's shoulder.

'Of course,' he says, ignoring the feeling of unease at the pit of his stomach. 'Of course we can.'

Back at the house, Aiden wolfs down two bowls of cereal and four slices of toast. George is outside, brushing the dirt and cobwebs off the sledge.

'When did you last eat, Aid?' Benjamin asks, watching him shovel his third bowl of Shreddies into his mouth.

Aiden shrugs.

'Yesterday?'

'Did you have tea?'

'I can't remember. Yeah. Maybe. Mam brought something back from the reduced bin at the Co-op. Tuna sandwich or something. She was being weird again. Singing.'

He rolls his eyes.

'She thinks she's good enough to go on *X Factor* but I think she's pretty bad.' He pauses, as though considering it. 'I didn't tell her that though.'

Benjamin takes a deep breath and fills a glass of water from the tap.

'You're looking thin, mate,' he says, as non-judgementally

as possible. 'You need to eat more, to get your strength up. Especially if you're going to be a footballer one day.'

Aiden grins. He wants it so badly. He's only seven, but he already wants it so much more than Benjamin ever did.

Aiden puts the empty cereal bowl down by the sink.

'Can I go and see Grandad and the sledge now, Dad?'

'Of course. I'll clear up here and come out in a bit.'

Once Aiden has left the room, Benjamin slams his fist against the side of the fridge, taking deep breaths, trying to stem the threat of tears. He can't cry. Not today. It's Christmas Eve. But it's all so wrong. He wants more for his son than this.

It's not Zoe's fault, he knows. She had a pretty traumatic childhood herself – a violent father who abandoned her and her four siblings when she was just eight. But her drinking is becoming a problem again. She lost her housekeeping job at the Premier Inn in town two months ago, and now she only has benefit money to live on until she finds something else. And he's not sure she's actually been looking.

Still, she manages to find money for booze. And yet his son hasn't eaten properly for more than twelve hours.

God knows what chaos awaits Aiden tomorrow at Zoe's. He can hardly bear to picture what his son's Christmas Day will look like.

He knows he needs to do something, but what? He wishes she would agree to let Aiden come and live with them, but even if she did, would that be fair? To take a child away from his mother? He misses his own mother so much, even as an adult, that the idea seems positively cruel.

He looks out the window at his father playing with his son, and he knows the answer. It has been there all along.

He knows what he needs to do. He needs to do what he should have done when she was pregnant all those years ago. Move into her flat. Take over. Take care of them both. Persuade her to get some help for her drinking. Support them all, especially now he has some money coming in again.

That would be the right thing to do. That's parenthood. And perhaps they might even find some way to be happy together.

It's not the life he imagined, but his son must come first. His son is the only thing left worth saving. He can't let him down.

There's an ache in his chest. Like someone squeezing the air from his lungs. How has it come to this?

He closes his eyes, resting his head against his hands, and allows himself a moment to think about Clara. The past. The life that never was.

He thinks about the email she sent him a couple of months ago, just before her wedding, the sincerity with which she expressed her love for him.

He remembers how she ended it.

The short version of this email reads: I love you and I'll wait for you.

It upset him so much it took him two days to reply. And when he did, he could only manage a few lines and, like him, they were wholly inadequate.

It was incredible, the way she saw him. The way she always saw him, as something better than he actually was.

There were times at university that he found it, *her*, a bit much. Her belief in him was ardent; her attention manifesting in myriad ways: links to articles she thought might interest him, 'helpful' little to-do lists written on Post-its that he found stuck to his bag each morning, unsolicited and feverish advice on any topic he raised.

When he confessed he was struggling to manage his

final-year workload, it was Clara who persuaded him to give up his job at the department store so he could spend more time on his studies.

She was trying to help him, because she loved him, and most of the time, her help went unacknowledged. He was too lazy to see it, let alone act on it.

But now, he wishes he could be that man. The man she always saw in him. Despite everything. Despite everything he did, and everything he didn't do.

Anyway, she's married now. He's happy for her. It makes him feel less guilty, knowing that she can move on, live a better life. Perhaps she will have a baby. He always thought what a wonderful mother she would make. She would notice *everything*.

And as for him: he already has a family who needs him.

Perhaps he can live up to her expectations of him after all – only, in a different way than she ever imagined.

January 2013

Clara

New year, new start.

Clara sits opposite the therapist. She has a soft pink face, kind and caring. She's the sort of person who would never shout at her children.

Her voice is soft too.

'So, Clara, as you know, I'm a psychosexual therapist, and I'm specially trained in helping people with sexual problems. So, why don't we start with you telling me why you're here?'

'The consultant at the Well Woman clinic referred me,' she says. 'After I got upset.'

The therapist raises her eyebrows. Clara wonders how old she is. Perhaps late forties.

'I was having a smear,' Clara pauses for breath. 'I found it quite difficult...'

'I'm sorry to hear that.'

Clara looks at the therapist. Her name is Sarah. Her eyes are still kind, but now, a little more confused.

'Afterwards, she started asking me questions about my life and I... well, I broke down and told her everything. I don't know where it all came from, but I just started pouring out all the things I've been worried about in my marriage. We've been struggling to...'

'Go on,' Sarah says, taking a sip of water.

Clara twists her hands in her lap. She is so ashamed.

'Have sex. I can't seem... we can't seem to...' She laughs, but the laughter quickly turns to tears. Her cheeks burn. A small voice whispers spitefully in her ear: *failure*. 'I don't know what's wrong with me. It just hurts. So much. And I can't do it. I can't bear it. I hate it.'

Sarah hands her a tissue.

'I feel so guilty. And I feel so sorry for Thom – my husband. He's such a lovely man. He's so patient with me and it's not that I don't love him, because I do, but I just... I just don't want to have sex with him. I don't know why.'

'I see,' Sarah says, but her voice is entirely without judgement. 'And how long have you and Thom been together?'

'Almost two years. He proposed after six months. It was too soon, wasn't it? It was too quick. If I'm honest, I didn't know how to say no. He'd made me the most beautiful ring. He's a jeweller. Everyone was so thrilled for us.'

'Take me back to when you first met,' Sarah asks. 'What first attracted you to him?'

I was lonely, Clara thinks.

'He was so... together,' she says, instead. 'He... well, he sort of picked me, I suppose. He was just confident and relaxed and happy within himself. I'd had a difficult time in my twenties. Someone I knew died while I was at university. It was difficult to come to terms with.'

She pauses. She doesn't want to talk about this. She's done that therapy a million times.

'Anyway, a friend invited me to a birthday party, and Thom

was there, and he just seemed so... into me. But not in a threatening way, in a nice way. He seemed strong, I guess. Like someone I could lean on. And he is. He really is.'

'So when you first got together, how were things then?'

'Good,' she says, feeling her cheeks burn again. But were they ever really good together? She isn't sure now.

'And in the bedroom?'

Clara looks down.

'It was... OK. Not great, I suppose. But it was fine. I mean, normal. We did it, and I guess I didn't expect much. I haven't really slept with that many people... and if I'm honest, I only remember really enjoying it with one of them. But sex itself was fine, I guess. He was always very gentle. I wouldn't say I particularly liked it though.'

She pauses, swallowing.

'He would always wait for me to initiate it, and it felt like so much pressure. I used to see it as a chore. Like doing the washing or cleaning the bathroom. Is that awful? I felt so happy when it was over with, another thing ticked off my list. I'd feel so relieved, like I'd achieved something! But lately, I can't bring myself to do it any longer. I can't bear it. I get so tense and then I can't...'

Clara takes a gulp of air. She feels hot, claustrophobic. She rests her forehead on her palm, an elbow digging into her knee.

'Oh god, this is so embarrassing. I can't believe I'm telling you all this.'

'Trust me when I tell you, I've heard a lot worse. Please. Talking about sex is literally what I do all day long.'

'I know, it's just... I guess it's what I avoid thinking or talking about all day long.'

Sarah smiles.

'Do you find him attractive?'

Clara thinks about Thom.

His wiry frame, his pinched nose and thin lips. The tautness of the muscles across his slim chest. He is lean, like a runner. He's not conventionally handsome, but at the same time he's not ugly either. In fact, when she first introduced him to her friends, they all seemed to think he was good-looking.

'I... I don't know how to answer that really,' she says.

Sarah looks at her, as though she's said the wrong thing.

'I mean, I love him.'

'That's great. What do you love about him?'

Clara takes another deep breath.

'I love his enthusiasm for his work. I love his calm nature. He never gets ruffled or stressed. He's always on an even keel. He's usually cheerful. He's strong. He's just...'.

From nowhere, a word springs into her mind.

Dull.

'He's safe,' she says, eventually. 'Thom's just very safe. And in the past, I was in a different kind of relationship. Not a dangerous one exactly but... one where I felt more vulnerable. But you make yourself vulnerable and what happens? You get hurt.'

'So you were hurt? Once before?'

She nods, biting her lip.

'I don't... I don't think I can talk about that really. I'm sorry.'

'It's fine, Clara. You don't have to tell me anything you don't want to.'

Sarah writes something down in a small notebook. She pushes her glasses back up her nose and looks again at Clara.

'Have you ever had any treatment for any mental health issues? Any past trauma?' she asks, her voice gentle, as though placating a young child.

'Yes,' she says, ignoring the implications of the word *trauma*. 'I've done CBT. In my teens. I had some issues with anxiety. My sister Cecily was very sick when I was little. I thought she was going to die. Ever since then, I guess I've been a worrier. And you know, there's the usual story... I was the oldest child, top of the class at a super-high-pressure school, lots of people telling me how brilliant I was. I mean, none of it is that awful, I don't want to complain. My parents expected a lot from me. They were subtle but the pressure was there. It was always there. To be the strong one. The one who coped, who could fend for herself.'

She pauses, squeezes her eyes shut.

'When I was younger, I felt I couldn't tell anyone how I was feeling, especially my parents. They had been through so much with Cecily, and I didn't want to put any more on their plate. I know it sounds mad, but I've always felt as though the ground is unstable somehow. As though it's constantly shifting beneath my feet. I don't know if that even makes sense.'

Sarah nods. Her eyelids flicker.

'I got some support at school, for my nerves. That's when I had CBT. But I don't think my parents ever really realised how bad it was. They're not the sort of people to put much store by the concept of mental health. It's all a bit stiff upper lip, really. *Lots of people have it worse, count your blessings* – that's my dad's mantra.'

Sarah nods again.

'I'm going to prescribe you something. A local anaesthetic called Lidocaine. I'd like you to apply it to your vulva – that's the external area outside the entrance to your vagina – twenty minutes before you anticipate you might have sex. It should help you to relax a little, and it will remove any discomfort.'

Clara sits up in her chair.

'An *anaesthetic*?'

'It's just a temporary thing,' Sarah says. 'A way of breaking the association of sex with pain. But what's most important here is I want you to try *not* to have sex. You'll need to go home and talk to your husband about this. Explain that Sarah, your bossy counsellor, has told you to promise her that you won't have sex. Hugs, kissing, massages, touching – all of that is fine. But no sex.'

'But if we're not going to have sex, then why do I need the gel?'

'We need to take the fear out of this situation for you. To break that connection. The gel will mean that you don't feel anything physical – no physical discomfort. But more importantly, we need to take the pressure away. That's why I'm telling you now, not to have sex. But I *would* like you to spend some time with your husband. Just relaxing with him, talking to him. Phones off, television off, just the two of you together, wherever you feel most comfortable. Whether that's in bed, or in the bath or even just lying on the sofa together. Now. Tell me about your job.' She looks down at the notebook in front of her. 'You're a journalist. Is it stressful?'

Clara shakes her head, confused by the abrupt topic change. What technique is Sarah using on her? Over the years it feels as though she has experienced them all. She can see right through them.

'No, not particularly. It's busy but not stressful. I enjoy it. I'm really lucky. I've been at the same newspaper ever since I left university. It's a great place to work.'

'Well, that's good. It sounds as though you have a lot of positives in your life, Clara. A great job, a kind and understanding husband. And I'm sure we'll be able to help you overcome this. So, I want you to take this prescription to the chemist, and then remember what I said. And then I want you to come back to me in a month's time, and we can take it from there.'

March 2013

Benjamin

Zoe was less keen on the idea of Benjamin moving in with them than he thought she would be. But she agreed, eventually.

And for the first few months it is actually OK. Zoe signs up to AA – reluctantly – and attends meetings every week. She makes friends with her sponsor Dan, a man in his late forties who lives half a mile away. They take long walks together, and she becomes obsessive about her step count.

Obsession is Zoe's Achilles heel, but better that she's obsessed with walking than obsessed with drink.

And Aiden is happy. Benjamin can see that, in a million small ways. He no longer throws tantrums when asked to get dressed in the morning, he no longer bursts into fake wails whenever he's told off. His nightmares vanish within days of Benjamin moving in.

It's not utopia, but it's a kind of contentment that Benjamin thinks he could settle for. He can't expect much, after all. After what he did.

He's grateful for these crumbs. And actually, are they even crumbs at all? Having a happy, contented, healthy, well-fed son makes him rich beyond measure.

'You look so much like my mam,' he says, one day, as they

brush their teeth, staring at each other's reflections in the small mirror above the basin.

'Your mam?' Aiden says, his mouth full of toothpaste.

'Yes. Your granny, June. Same fair hair.'

'Mam says I get it from her,' Aiden says, wrinkling his nose. Benjamin smiles.

'Maybe.'

Zoe's hair is bleached blonde most of the time. He's not sure he's ever seen it in its natural state.

'My mam would have thought you were champion, Aid,' Benjamin says. 'Now come on, we'll be late for school.'

He gets in late most nights after working at the bar. Zoe is usually already asleep. Since she stopped drinking, she sleeps better, and rarely wakes up when he comes home. He's grateful, coward that he is, that he can creep in beside her most nights, without having to talk to her.

During the day, Zoe often goes out. He's not entirely sure where to, because she doesn't tell him. Certainly not to work. She hasn't made any effort to replace her job at the hotel and he's too cowardly to bring it up.

They are basically flatmates, and even though he tries, he can't seem to create any warmth or spark between them. She doesn't understand him. Doesn't find him interesting in any way. Barely listens on the rare occasions he does try to strike up a conversation.

He supposes that he hurt her, very deeply, when he told her that he didn't think they would work out, and ever since then, she has closed herself off from him. He can't blame her for that, of course.

He should be relieved, but the situation is discomfiting. And he worries that it's not sustainable. Aiden is fine now, while he's still so young, but surely, he will pick up on his parents' awkwardness sooner or later? And then what will Benjamin do?

To avoid these questions circling round and round his head, he tries to keep busy. He offers to do extra shifts at the bar, covering any staff absence gratefully. At the weekends, he ferries Aiden to football training and kids' birthday parties, and he takes care of all the life admin: the washing, shopping and cooking. Then all the extras, like making sure that Aiden has an outfit for World Book Day, helping out at the school fundraiser, creating something that can pass as an Easter bonnet... there is a never-ending list of things that need your attention when you're a parent.

He tries to involve Zoe in the more fun tasks, but she becomes ever more distant and disinterested. As though his moving in has allowed her to move out. Mentally, at least.

'Are you drinking again?' he asks, one Thursday evening when he's off work. Aiden is already asleep.

Zoe is wearing black leggings and a hoodie that drowns her petite frame. Huge gold hoop earrings dangle from her ears. Her neck is craned low over her mobile phone, but snaps up at the accusation.

'What?' she says. 'No, of course not.'

He sits down on the small armchair opposite. The blinds are drawn in the cluttered living room, and it's too dark to see her face in any detail.

'You can tell me,' he says, trying to sound as non-confrontational as possible. 'It's very common, I think. To... relapse.'

'Fuck off,' she bites back, and he closes his eyes.

'OK,' he says. 'But if there's... if there's anything I can do.

You know. I'm always here for you. For you and Aiden. I want to help, if I can.'

'Yes, Saint Benjamin,' she says, rolling her eyes. 'I know.'

He frowns. What does she want from him?

'I'm not a saint,' he mutters, launching himself to his feet and turning to go through to the small kitchen and start on the washing-up.

'I'll say,' she says, under her breath.

He pauses for a split second, but decides he deserves it, and doesn't reply.

The next evening, he is at the bar cashing up when his phone rings, shrill and loud. He answers it, irritated at the interruption, without looking who the caller is.

'Hello?'

'Hi Benjamin,' a woman on the other end says. 'It's Margaret from number 5A. I've got your lad here, he came round because he's worried about his mam. She hasn't come home and he doesn't know where she is. Can you come back? He's pure worn out, wee thing. Shouldn't be on his own, not at his age.'

'Christ,' he replies, looking at his watch. It's 12.34 a.m. 'Of course. I'll be twenty minutes. Thanks.'

He hangs up without waiting for her reply, grabs his jacket and locks up, not even pausing to put the takings away.

Once back, he takes the concrete staircase two steps at a time and before long he is outside 5A, the flat opposite Zoe's. As always at this time of night, the stairwell stinks of urine and his heart breaks all over again that this is where his son is growing up.

He thinks briefly of that summer in London, when the head of IT at Clara's father's firm said he had a unique way of solving problems, and he shakes his head in disgust at himself. It is a sore spot that never heals over. He won't let it.

He knocks quietly on the door of 5A. Somewhere in another flat in the block, a dog barks.

Margaret opens. She's red in the face, wearing a bright pink dressing gown with stained lapels.

'I'm so sorry,' he says, smiling. 'I can't think where Zoe has got to.'

'You're all right,' Margaret says. She pauses, sucking in her lips. 'She's out a lot these days. And her new fella... I'm not sure about him to be honest.'

Benjamin sniffs sharply. What fella? Has Zoe been having Dan round in the evenings when Benjamin is at work?

'I'll have a word with her,' he says, inadequately.

'Aye,' she says, nodding. A cat appears and winds itself around his ankles. 'He's just through here, pet. He fell asleep on the sofa after I gave him a bowl of cereal. Half-starved he was. I remember my boys at that age. Hollow legs, we used to say.'

The living room is crowded with too-big furniture, an ornament on every surface. But it's clean and warm, and curled up in a ball on the saggy leather sofa is his son, a blanket over him. He looks so peaceful, Benjamin can hardly bear to move him.

'Thank you,' he says, to Margaret. 'For looking out for him.'

Margaret almost glows, and Benjamin remembers someone telling him once that there was no such thing as altruism. Was it Clara's dad? It feels like something he might have said. Now that Benjamin looks back, he wishes he'd been able to spend more time with him that summer. He was the kind of man Benjamin hoped to be. Wise, high-achieving, calm.

'It's a pleasure,' she says. 'I don't sleep well these days. He

knows he can come and find me if he's worried. But perhaps…
well, it's not my business, but I don't like the look of that man.'

'He's her AA sponsor,' Benjamin says. 'He's not meant to
come round here, though.'

Margaret shakes her head.

'Her AA sponsor? I didn't think they allowed opposite sex
sponsors.'

'Oh,' he says, and then suddenly it all makes sense. What a
fool he has been.

'Well, like I said, not my business,' Margaret continues, 'but
I've seen him a few times now. And I can't help but feel sorry
for the lad. He's only little. It's confusing for him.'

'I'll sort it,' Benjamin says, leaning down and scooping
Aiden up. 'I'm sorry, and thank you again.'

May 2013

Clara

They're on holiday again. A spring break on the island of Kefalonia.

Thom likes holidays. He likes the good life: working hard and playing hard, too.

But it feels loaded. The pressure mounts the second they board the aeroplane. It's clear what he hopes he'll get out of this holiday, though of course, he hasn't said anything. He has never tried to force her into doing anything she doesn't want to do, and somehow, that makes it worse.

All the impetus is on her.

Clara packed the gel right at the bottom of her suitcase, underneath all her underwear. She can hardly bear to look at the smooth white tube. It seems to taunt her. *Freak.* What kind of freak needs to use an anaesthetic to have sex?

They have used it a few times with some degree of success. But each time afterwards, she had to hide in the bathroom to cry as she wiped it off her body.

She has an official diagnosis now: *vaginismus*. Even the name of it sounds horrible. She tried to explain it all to Thom but her face burnt and her throat tightened and she could hardly get the words out. It was humiliating.

She's not sure he really understands how awful it is for her.

But that's not his fault – she hasn't told him what happened to her. How can she? He'd be devastated if he knew. And she kept hoping, with time, things would get easier.

Four months later, she only has one session with Sarah left, and it doesn't feel as though she's moved forward much at all.

Her suitcase is mostly full of books. They are one of the only things that offer her an uncomplicated kind of pleasure, and her favourite part of the holiday so far was being in WHSmiths at the airport, when she stocked up on the three for two table.

'What the hell have you got in here?' Thom joked, as he picked up her tote bag.

'Sorry,' she said. 'Books.'

'No, don't be silly. It's great. If you want to write a novel, you need to read some.'

'I read loads,' she replied tartly, before realising it wasn't a criticism. Why was she so defensive? 'I should get a Kindle. It's just… there's something about proper pages.'

This morning, they pay 20 euros for their sunbeds and spend ten minutes adjusting the parasol so that they both have the optimum amount of shade. She doesn't like her face to be in the sun. It makes her feel faint.

Thom wanders off for a paddle, and Clara lies there, listening to the sound of waves lapping. Thinking, as she so often does when her mind is allowed to wander, of Benjamin.

Of their one holiday together. They went to Turkey during the Easter holidays of their final year. Marmaris.

They spent most of the week in bed, waking at midday and wandering down to the beach for a couple of hours' sunbathing in the afternoon. They bought doughnuts from the man who strolled along the beach selling them, and slept in the sun all afternoon, and she can't remember a time when she felt more relaxed.

University was almost over. And they made plans. He would move down to London, they would find a place together and they would find jobs and they would start their adult lives. Properly. Together.

And then it all went wrong.

Thom and Clara eat lunch at the beachside restaurant, the seat pad sandy beneath her legs. Clara orders halloumi and flatbreads, with fresh tzatziki. The food is delicious. The temperature perfect.

'So,' Thom says, dipping some of his own bread in the small bowl of olive oil on the table. 'Have you had any more thoughts on your book?'

It was her New Year's Resolution: start writing properly.

And now it's May. She's abandoned everything she's started. It all felt trite, pointless, shallow. And she's been haunted by a little voice in her head that composed whole paragraphs of brilliance when she least expected it, but all on the one topic that she knows she couldn't – or shouldn't – write about: Benjamin.

Thom's showing an interest in her writing and she should be grateful, but again, it feels like a challenge. A criticism.

'Not really,' she says.

'How are the ones you bought in the airport? Any I should read?'

She scoffs a little at that, and then she feels mean. His literary tastes are different from hers, but that doesn't make hers better. She composes her face.

'One of them is brilliant. It's called *After You'd Gone*, by an author called Maggie O'Farrell. I haven't read any of her stuff before.'

'Oh, what's it about?'

'It's... about heartbreak. Family secrets. The main character loses her husband and it's about how she struggles to cope...' She pauses. 'It's about life, really. All of it.'

Her eyes prick with tears.

'God,' she says, sniffing. She uses her napkin to dab them. 'It's really moving.'

'It sounds it,' Thom says.

'Anyway,' she says. 'I wish I could write something... anything like that. But I don't know if I'd ever manage it.'

'Well, you won't know until you try,' he says, easily. 'Will you?'

'Let's change the subject,' she replies. 'You know I hate talking about my writing.'

He smiles sadly and motions to the waiter to bring him another beer.

In the distance, she sees two men in board shorts loading a couple onto a huge inflatable ring. They are laughing with fear and excitement.

Thom follows her gaze.

'We should try that,' he says, nodding at them. 'If you're up for it.'

She watches as the speedboat takes off, dragging the couple behind it. The woman is screaming loudly, the sound carried across the whole beach.

'It looks terrifying,' she says. 'No thanks.'

'Oh Clara,' he says, nudging her. 'It'd be fun. You never know, you might like it.'

He grins at her and she softens slightly. Lately, she feels guilty whenever she's with him. Guilty that she punishes him every day for loving her. It's not his fault, is it, that she's such a mess?

But then again, he picked her. She didn't force him.

What does he like about her? She often wonders this.

Is it her desire to write? Her job, which most people seem to find impressive and interesting? The way she sees him more clearly than he sees himself?

Or is it just down to the fact that she's pretty and from a good family?

Maybe it was as simple for him as seeing someone he found physically attractive, and deciding she was The One, as though choosing a house or a car.

And then, when it started to go wrong – some fault with the electrics, or a leaky roof – he just decided to make the best of it.

'You try it,' she says. 'If you survive, then maybe I'll have a go.'

'You're on.'

He leans back in the chair, takes a sip of his beer.

'It's glorious here, isn't it?' he says, lightly. 'I could live here, I think. Set up a small workshop in the town. Bet I'd make a killing with all the tourists. The cruise ships bring in hundreds of rich Americans every day.'

She smiles and rolls her eyes.

'No, I mean it,' he says, leaning forward across the table. 'What do you think? We could live like kings over here. You could write your books, I could open a shop. Imagine how much we'd get for our London flat! The property here must be dirt cheap.'

She feels a sense of panic creeping over her. Her *anxiety*. She tries to quell it, focuses on her breathing.

She reminds herself: no one can make her do anything she doesn't want to do.

'I love London,' she says, as firmly as she can. 'My family are there… all our friends. I don't want to leave.'

Thom shrugs, takes another sip of beer.

'Just a thought,' he says.

Square peg, round hole.

After lunch, they return to their sunloungers, and she continues to read the next book from the pile she picked up at the airport. This one isn't as good, and her eyes grow heavy as she reads. She's almost asleep when she feels Thom prod her lightly on the shoulder.

'I'm going to do it,' he says. He's caught the sun, and there's a new collection of freckles across his nose. She sees her own face reflected in his sunglasses.

'Do what?'

'Go on the ring thing,' he says.

She sits up on her elbows.

'Oh god, really? Is it safe?'

'Of course,' he says.

He hands her his camera.

'Here, make sure you get some shots.'

She watches as he ambles down to the men by the speedboat. They chat briefly and then Thom puts on a lifejacket, settling himself down into the inflatable ring.

He's mad. But she's glad too, that he's happy. He's enjoying himself. When he's happy she feels more like the wife she should be.

The speedboat starts up and takes off at an incredible pace, dragging the inflatable ring behind it. She sees Thom grip the plastic handles of the inflatable tightly but then he's out of sight, tossed and spun around in the foam of the waves as the speedboat zigzags through the water. It's going so fast that she feels uneasy.

She scans the beach until she spots the girl she heard screaming on the ride earlier. She's sitting up on her lounger, topless, reading a magazine.

Clearly, it's not dangerous. This is just her anxiety, rearing its head again.

Clara lifts the camera and takes a few shots, but the boat and the inflatable are going so fast that everything she captures is just a blur. She uses the lens to zoom in, and she manages to get one of Thom's face; his mouth wide open in that peculiar place between terror and joy, his hair drenched.

A woman selling woven bracelets approaches Clara's sunlounger, blocking her view of the ocean. Clara politely turns her down and when the lady moves on to the next lounger, the sun is right in her eyes.

She hears a yell. It takes a few seconds of squinting before she locates the speedboat again, still spinning the inflatable ring behind it.

But when she looks at it, she realises that the ring is now empty.

And Thom is nowhere to be seen.

May 2013

Benjamin

Zoe doesn't come home that evening. Or the next morning. Or the next evening. She has left her phone, taken a small bag with some of her belongings.

Once she's been gone for more than twenty-four hours, Benjamin calls the police. Without too much difficulty, they track her down to a village the other side of town, but when they question her, she tells them she doesn't have a son.

'I'm sorry sir,' the police officer says, shrugging awkwardly. 'But… we can't force her to come back. She refused to come with us, and became quite agitated when we suggested she might want to speak to you. I'm afraid she was under the influence of alcohol at the time.'

Benjamin is relieved that Aiden is at school.

'Was she alone?'

The officer shakes his head.

'No, there was a gentleman there with her.'

Dan.

'But she can't just… abandon her son? Isn't that… a crime or something?'

'We're happy to refer you to social services, if you're concerned about your ability to care for…'

'Absolutely not,' he snaps. His face is burning with anger. 'He'll be fine with me. I'm his father.'

The police officer opens his mouth as though he's about to comment but instead just gives a short nod. Benjamin shows him out and closes the door behind him.

How can he break this news to Aiden?

Sorry mate, your mam is a selfish bitch who lied about going to AA and has run off with some random fella, and you won't be seeing her again.

Actually, what worries him more is the prospect of her returning in a few weeks, months... years... and then what? Will she just expect to pick up where she left off?

He phones his father.

'They found her,' he says.

'Dead?'

'No,' he says. 'The other side of town. With... Dan. But she doesn't want to come back apparently.'

There's a long pause on the line. Benjamin feels exhausted. It's too much, this life. It's always been too much. He has been failing at it since he was born.

'Well, good riddance,' George says, eventually. 'We'll all be better off without her.'

Benjamin wants to agree, but then he thinks of his own mother. What a seminal, fundamental role in his life she played. It was hard enough losing her at nineteen. He can't imagine what his life might have been like if he'd lost her when he was eight.

But then again, she took to mothering naturally. She loved being a mother, and it's clear to him now that Zoe never has.

Benjamin looks around at Zoe's flat. It has never really felt like his home, and now he can't wait to be out of the place.

'But Dad,' he says. 'I don't know... How can I... how can I look after him and work at the same time?'

George takes a sharp intake of breath.

'You'll have to move back in here,' George says.

'But...'

'But nothing. We're family, we stick together. And I love that boy.'

It's true, Benjamin thinks. Aiden brings George joy, gives him purpose.

'I wish...' he begins, but his father has hung up. He doesn't want to hear Benjamin's wishes. He doesn't want to deal with Benjamin's emotions, or feelings.

Spend too long thinking about your feelings and you'll drown. Life is for living, not bloody ruminating.

It's like telling him to be the very opposite of what he is. And he doesn't know how to do it.

That night, as he tucks Aiden up in the tiny box room back at the family home, Benjamin tells him that his mother will not be coming back.

'But why?'

'Your mam—'

'Had demons,' Aiden finishes Benjamin's sentence for him.

Benjamin smiles sadly, wonders where he has heard that expression.

'It's nothing to do with you,' he says. 'You must always remember that. She's not... well.'

'She's an alco-lick,' Aiden says, knowingly.

'Who told you that?'

'That's what Dan called her,' Aiden says, quietly. 'One night when they were fighting. He called her a fecking alco-lick.'

Benjamin closes his eyes. They sting with tears.

'I'm so sorry that you had to hear stuff like that,' he says. 'I wish... I'm sorry that I've been working so much, and that I left you alone with them. But things will be different now. I promise.'

'It's OK, Dad,' his son says, a faraway look in his eyes. 'Mam always wanted to be somewhere else. She'll be happier now. And I've got you. And Grandad.'

'You have,' he says, gripping him tightly. 'And I will never leave you. Do you understand me? I promise you. I will never leave you.'

Aiden smiles. Benjamin knows the intensity of these feelings are too much for a little boy. That he just wants calm reassurance, promises of Coco Pops tomorrow morning, stability and care.

'Goodnight, Aid,' he says, leaning down and kissing him on the forehead. 'Let's have Coco Pops in the morning, shall we?'

'But it's not Sunday!'

'I won't tell if you don't,' Benjamin smiles.

His son gives a little gasp, then snuggles down under his duvet, murmuring a goodnight.

May 2013

Clara

She is sitting by his hospital bed, holding his hand, when he comes round. Her face is blotchy and swollen from sobbing.

'Thank god,' she whispers, as his eyes flicker open.

'Clara?' he says, but his gaze is unfocused.

'I'm here,' she says, leaning in closer. 'I'm here. You're OK. The doctors have checked you over and you're fine. You bumped your head on some rocks when you came off the stupid ring thing but the lifeguard got you out of the water quickly and you'll be fine.'

He smiles. There's a dark purple bruise covering half of his face.

'My back hurts,' he says, frowning.

'I'm not surprised,' she says. 'You're head to toe in bruises. But you'll recover. As for me. I'm not sure I ever will. I thought I was going to have a heart attack.'

It's meant to be a joke, but she realises she is actually crying again.

'Hey,' he says, his voice croaky. 'I'm sorry.'

'I honestly thought... I thought that was it. That you were gone.'

'And you weren't happy about it? I've got good life insurance, you know.'

'Thom,' she says, warningly. 'Don't. I was so scared...'

'I'm sorry,' he says again, squeezing her hand. 'I promise never to do water sports again.'

She nods, wiping her eyes.

'I should think not.'

He shifts slightly in the bed, sitting up a little.

'Oh well,' he says, 'it's a good story to tell the grandchildren, I guess.'

There are three days left before they have to fly home and she spends them feeling as though she has been let off the hook.

Thom is still very sore and tired after his concussion, and fills most of the time lying in the shade on the beach, fully clothed. She sits on the sunlounger next to him, watching him out of the corner of her eye, thinking about the tube of gel in her suitcase, and the fact she has got away without having to use it again.

For now.

When she thought Thom had drowned she almost vomited with fear. She knows now, with a certainty she hadn't known before, that she loves him. That Thom is important to her, that's it's not that he was the wrong man at the right time. That he matters, even if her feelings for him are completely different from the feelings she had for Benjamin.

She's not dead inside. Just dead below the waist, perhaps, as she once joked to Lauren.

But that's still not fair on him, is it?

She sees the way other women look at her slim, fine-featured husband. The way the other tourists in the hotel have gazed at them both during dinner. Thinking what a picture-perfect couple they are. Her with her neat waist and bright blonde hair. Him with his tanned skin and kind eyes.

People see them and imagine, as he does, the babies they will have. It's all right for now – he's thirty-three, babies are something he wants but has not yet begun to obsess over. But the clock is ticking. And then what? How could she ever conceive with her condition?

On the plane on the way home, he listens to music, his eyes closed, content. She stares out of the window at the earth below. Her eyes hurt as she remembers flying back from Marmaris with Benjamin, all those years ago.

They had sex in the toilet – a stupid dare Lauren had set her: 'Bet you're too chicken to join the Mile High Club!' Benjamin hadn't been particularly keen – he was tall, and the toilets weren't exactly spacious, but she had easily persuaded him.

It blows her mind now she thinks about it – that she was once the one pestering someone to have sex.

The guilty thoughts make her feel sick. She reaches over and squeezes her husband's hand. The hairs on his arm have turned golden in the sun. Despite his accident, he is better for this holiday. He's enjoyed himself, will tell friends how good it was to get away.

But the idea of whispering in his ear now, suggesting he meet her in the toilet, is almost comedic.

She slumps back in her chair and tries to sleep.

They are unpacking later that evening when she brings it up. It's a boiling-over pot of water and she can no longer keep a lid on it.

'I'm sorry,' she says, as he unzips his washbag and takes out the contents.

'What for?' he says, looking up at her with confusion.

She bites down hard on her lip.

'I'm sorry that we didn't have sex on holiday,' she blurts, and then she's noisily crying.

He exhales.

'It's fine, darling,' he says. 'Your counsellor said we shouldn't...'

'That was what she said to start. Months ago! And she was using reverse psychology. She thinks if she tells me not to do something then I'll want to but... it doesn't work. My brain doesn't work like that... I can see through it all... and she said we should do other stuff... you know, with the gel and just cuddling and this holiday would have been the perfect time and... we didn't... We didn't even kiss.'

He looks away. He doesn't want to talk about the elephant in their marriage. He would prefer to go on pretending there isn't a problem. To go on pleasuring himself in the shower instead, to eliminate any physical need that might draw attention to the great gaping hollow in their relationship.

'Clara, I nearly bloody drowned on the beach,' he says. 'I'm still bruised all over. My back is killing me. Sex hasn't exactly been top of my list of priorities either.'

'I'm so sorry,' she repeats, because what else is there to say?

'It's fine,' he says, looking at her with a tenderness that makes her heart want to break. He doesn't understand her, and he doesn't even realise it. 'We're both tired. Let's get some sleep. We can talk about it more tomorrow.'

★ ★ ★

But of course, they don't talk about it more tomorrow. Or the next day.

A week and a half later, Clara is sitting in front of Sarah the therapist, feeling like a failure.

'I suppose I should just leave him,' she says, like a mournful child. 'It's not fair on him, is it?'

Sarah takes a deep breath. She seems distracted this week. In a way, Clara supposes she has failed, too.

'How do you think Thom feels about the situation?'

'He says he doesn't mind, that it's not a big deal. But he's lying, isn't he? He's just being kind because he loves me.'

'Perhaps he's not lying,' Sarah says but as she speaks Clara thinks that this would be a great solution for Sarah – for their sessions to end with Clara being told that her problem is not actually a problem after all. 'Perhaps he honestly doesn't see it as an issue. You know, there are plenty of people in happy, healthy relationships who don't have sexual intercourse. The most important thing is that the people in the relationship are happy about it.'

'But he's not happy about it,' Clara says, feeling even more like a child. 'And neither am I.'

Her own words surprise her. She's concentrated so much on Thom, on what she's depriving him of, that it's only now she realises that *she's* been deprived, too. She used to enjoy sex, with Benjamin. Has it been spoilt for her forever?

Is that her punishment, for her crime?

Sarah nods.

'I think perhaps it would be useful if both you and Thom attended therapy together. To help you work out this issue as a couple, rather than you individually. It sounds as though he's an incredibly supportive man, so do you think this is something he would be prepared to do?'

Clara raises her eyebrows.

'I don't know,' she says, eventually. 'But I suppose I can ask.'

May 2013

Benjamin

He's standing at the side of the pitch, thinking he should have worn a warmer coat. Even though it's nearly June, this is the north east. He's lived here his whole life, he should know better.

He stamps his feet up and down, blows into his hands to warm them up a bit.

Being here takes him back to his own childhood. Memories of his mam and dad watching him play on Sunday mornings. Before she got sick she never missed a game. She was his biggest fan, convinced he would go all the way.

His father was less optimistic, more realistic, but even so, he supported him. He was also the most upset when his coach told him that Benjamin didn't have the mental strength to make it.

But Aiden is different. Aiden is stronger than he ever was. And now Benjamin is here, to support his son. His son's absolute and unwavering love for the beautiful game.

Somehow, he already knows that Aiden will do better than he ever did. He will make sure of it.

He read an article in the *Guardian* last week about intergenerational trauma. The idea that the events you experience actually affect your DNA, and are passed down in your genes to your own children. He got halfway through the piece before closing the webpage.

It might be true, but if there's nothing that can be done, why torture yourself with that kind of knowledge?

'Go on son!' he shouts as Aiden rounds the box towards the goal. 'Go on!'

Aiden's foot moves sharply as he attempts to score, but he's thwarted by the other team's defender, a nimble boy with knees that look too big for his skinny legs.

The huddle of parents lets out a collective groan.

He smiles at his son's face. His dear little face. He doesn't give up, seems oblivious to the crowd. He's frowning, deep in thought, watchful for another opportunity.

And another opportunity comes, just ten minutes before the final whistle. And this time, the ball soars past the keeper and into the back of the net.

The parents erupt. Benjamin finds that his eyes fill with tears.

It is the best feeling in the world; watching your child achieve something.

'Well done,' he says, after the match ends, thumping him on the back then lifting him up for a proper hug. 'That was awesome. Proud of you.'

Aiden smiles; a shy, modest smile, and Benjamin hands him his water bottle. He drinks deeply.

'Are we going back home now?' he asks.

'We can do, but I thought...' Benjamin looks down at his son's boots. They are filthy, clumps of mud stuck to the sides. 'I thought a proper striker needs a proper pair of boots. What do you reckon?'

And then, the grin is huge. From ear to ear.

'Really, Dad? Really?'

'I thought… some Nike Vapors?'

His son's face falls.

'But Dad. They're fifty pounds.'

'I know,' Benjamin says. 'But you deserve it.'

The next day he has a phone call from Aiden's football coach, Kenny.

'I think he's got real skill,' he says. 'You need to take him seriously.'

'He's only eight years old,' Benjamin replies, but his heart is swelling.

'Aye, but I wanted you to have the heads-up,' Kenny says. 'It's important that the parents are on side. I reckon your boy could go far. Just make sure he keeps up the training. He's a bit too in his own head sometimes. Needs to work on his teamwork. But with the right coaching, he'll be in the county youth team before you know it.'

Benjamin thanks him and hangs up, staring out of the window.

Aiden is in the garden, repeatedly heading a ball his grandfather has tied from a tree. The ball swings back and forwards as he punches it with his forehead. He's too young to be heading balls really, but there is no stopping him. And the ball is soft, it's not a real football.

At dinner that evening, Benjamin asks him what it is about football he loves so much.

Aiden shrugs.

'Dunno, I just love it,' he says, shovelling baked beans in his mouth. Benjamin is envious of the simplicity of his answer. He doesn't seem to have inherited his father's neuroticism, and for that Benjamin is grateful. So grateful.

But later that evening, when Benjamin is tucking him up in bed, Aiden pulls him down and softly says:

'When I'm playing football it's the only time I feel like I'm being myself.'

Benjamin nods.

'Does that make sense Dad? Or does that make me weird?'

'It makes total sense,' he replies, brushing Aiden's curls from his forehead with his hand. 'Now get some rest, champion.'

George has gone to bed early. He has been feeling more and more tired lately. Benjamin asked him to go for a check-up at the doctor's, but George dismissed him with a 'pfft' sound.

George has avoided medical professionals ever since Benjamin's mam died.

Benjamin is sitting alone, in the small living room at the back of the cottage, flicking through the channels disinterestedly. There is nothing on that appeals to him.

He wonders where Zoe is, if she even thinks about him and their son. She never expressed much interest in Aiden's passion for football. She never expressed much interest in him at all, really.

He remembers a time, when Aiden was very tiny, when Zoe seemed like she might be the doting mam. She spent a fortune on teeny outfits for him, enjoyed showing him off to people, gushed about him constantly. But Benjamin quickly realised that she was treating him more like a cute accessory than a living, breathing person.

And then, she started complaining that she was missing out on her youth. She was only twenty-three when she had him.

That's when her drinking started to get worse.

He has looked Zoe up online since she left, but she doesn't

use social media, so there is no way of finding out how she is.

After the police left, he drove to the grimy suburb where they said they had found her, but he couldn't track her down. The police had refused to tell him where exactly she was living, which seemed utterly absurd, but was apparently legal, as they weren't married.

He could have taken her to court for maintenance, but there seemed little point, when she clearly couldn't even maintain herself.

He went there on four occasions, each time wandering the streets for hours, to no avail. He wanted Aiden to know he had tried, even though, deep down, he didn't want to find her. Selfishly, he was glad she had left.

Then he went back to her flat, filled two suitcases with the things she had left behind, and handed the keys into the council. He left some chocolates outside 5A, to thank Margaret for looking out for Aiden. He had never officially registered as living at Zoe's flat, so there was no way he could keep it. Not that he would have wanted to, in any case.

But still, tonight he feels downcast that he has no one with whom to share the good news from Aiden's football coach. That he is back here, living with his father.

Back to square one. Perhaps this is his destiny – to live a life that never progresses. Two steps forward, two steps back.

He goes to the fridge and takes out a beer. After it's gone, he gets another. And another, and another, and another.

And then he takes out his phone, and he does something he only allows himself to do occasionally.

He googles Clara.

May 2013

Clara

There's an email in her inbox that makes no sense.

His name. She has to look at it twice. She briefly wonders if it might be spam. Someone spoofing his address, because that happens, doesn't it? People do that.

She's at work, a busy shift on the paper. Three boys were stabbed in the East End overnight. The Mayor of London called the incident 'horrific', but the truth is that these events have become so commonplace, people are becoming almost numb to them.

She wants to write an opinion piece on it, but she's too shy to approach the features editor. It's not really her place.

The night team have just left, looking bleary-eyed.

Matt, her boss, is leaning over the partition between their desks, talking to her, and she flicks her eyes back towards him, trying to focus on what he's saying. But the whole time her stomach is rolling over in something that feels like excitement, but that might actually be terror.

Is this it? The beginning of the end?

Please, let it be the beginning of the end.

Eventually, Matt finishes his list of instructions for the day

– she hasn't absorbed any of it – and looks back down at his own computer screen. Hers has gone to sleep.

Perhaps it's all a dream. She taps the space bar to wake it up. But no, it's still here.

Benjamin Edwards.

From nowhere, tears appear, and, before she knows what's happening, she is crying.

She knew, she just knew, that one day he would come back to her. And here he is.

She rushes to the toilet, because there's nothing more mortifying than the prospect of Matt seeing her cry. Inside the cubicle, she lets the tears flow. She cries for Benjamin, for Thom, for herself, for the wasted years.

She thinks of the reply he sent her when she told him she was getting married – the email she knew had taken him hours to write, telling her that he wasn't good enough, that she deserved better.

She thinks of all the emails she has written him since, trying to persuade him that he was wrong. That she was sorry. That she was an idiot, and she should have trusted him and it was all her fault.

That she loved him.

Dozens of them, but in the end she was too proud – or was it ashamed? – to send them.

She lets herself cry until all the tears dry up and then she wipes her eyes in the mirror and washes her hands, and returns to her desk and looks again at the email.

There's no subject line.

Fingers trembling, she clicks to open it. He sent it late last night. A thought flickers in her mind; he must have been drinking.

Her eyes widen.

Just two words. A tentative step. Cautious even when drunk. That's so him. But also, so surprising.

Just two words, a shaky hand reached out across the divide. Two words, from him to her:

What's new?

May 2013

Benjamin

He shouldn't have sent it.

When he wakes the next morning, he can hear Aiden downstairs with his father, having breakfast. His head is pounding. It's a Saturday and he has to be in work by eleven, but the first thing he thinks of is the email.

What's new?

It was selfish. He's ashamed. But sometimes, he feels so frustrated at the way things have worked out, that he just wishes he could go back and be the person he once was.

Or rather, the person she thought he could be.

The funny, easy-going one. The one without a criminal record.

It's not the first time he has written an email to her. But it's the first time he's actually sent one.

He's tried many times before. Tried to get some of the messy, noisy stuff in his head out onto the page. But writing never came naturally to him – not like it did to her – and when he would read over what he'd written, it never sounded right.

He was angry with her, but he was angrier with himself, for not seeing what should have been so obvious.

He reaches for his phone and, barely daring to breathe,

checks his email. He has no new messages, but the one he sent at 12.04 a.m., having consumed more alcohol than he had in months, is there, in his outbox. So he definitely sent it. It wasn't a bad dream.

Shit.

Well, it could have been worse.

He clicks on the drafts folder.

Here, among the other assorted messages that he's abandoned midway through composing, are all the emails he's written to Clara since he got out of prison, but never sent.

He opens one of the early ones, from 2005. Just after Zoe told him she was pregnant, when it felt like all hope was lost.

His eyes widen as he scans it now. He was so angry when he wrote it. Even back then he knew he would never send it – it would have killed her.

Even now, being reminded of the thoughts that once tormented him is excruciating.

I loved you so much. And now what? I hate this, but it feels as though I'm so angry with you. But how can I deal with being angry with you? With you, my best friend, my **person**?

How could you have not told me about him, Clara? How could you have kept it from me all that time? I can't understand it. It doesn't make sense to me. Not with what we had. You told me everything. That's what I thought. I was an idiot.

And if only I had known, everything would have been different.

God.

That last line alone would have destroyed her.

He opens another draft email.

I don't blame you. It feels as though I do, sometimes, but I know that's not it. Despite everything, I love you. But I wish you could tell me what exactly happened that night. Beforehand, I mean. In the club, and then after. What exactly happened. I mean, exactly. Frame by frame. It would help. I need to get some kind of sense of it, or my head will never be right again.

I'm drowning here CDC. You left me here to drown.

And then, another from a few years later, in a different tone entirely.

Happy Birthday CDC. I don't know where you are right now, or what you're doing, but I hope you are happy.

I dream about us often, the life we might have had. Living in London together in our early twenties: you writing your novel, me hopefully bringing home enough from my job in IT to keep you in the manner to which you have become accustomed. Perhaps I could never have done that. But anyway. Holidays. Dinners out to nice restaurants, meeting up after work. Trying scallops again, and not feeling intimidated this time. Perhaps we would learn about wine together. Or take a long trip to Thailand, living out of backpacks. Perhaps you would learn to love football, and I would start to read novels. I don't know.

I just know that I wake up from these dreams, and you're not beside me and I feel as though someone has punched me in the chest, and it's hard to remember how to breathe.

But if you are happy now, it makes it easier. Are you happy?

There are at least ten more messages. All unsent. Frozen in time.

He is better now. That fierce, guttural anger when he first got out of prison eventually morphed into sadness. Regret. Guilt. Frustration.

And last night, he was drunk, and fed up, and restless.

What's new?

He remembers actually saying 'Fuck it' aloud as he tapped the send button.

But she hasn't replied.

That's OK. Perhaps she won't. Especially after she had told him explicitly, right before she got married, that she still loved him, and he had shut the door in her face.

You should forget me, Clara. I'm not worthy. I feel a great mixture of emotions, from sadness to guilt to regret, but you shouldn't waste your time thinking of me or what might have been. You've mistaken me for something that I'm not. I hope you'll be very happy in your marriage.

He remembers it well. Perhaps after that measly email he sent her, she never wants to speak to him again. It would be easier that way.

It would be so much easier for them both if she just never replied.

He slams his head, once, hard, against the headboard of his bed.

He is an idiot. He fucks everything up. His whole life

is a fuck-up, and it's all his fault, because he had so much potential, so many chances, all the opportunities in the world and yet...

And yet, he's a thirty-two-year-old man still living with his father, in a dead-end job that will go nowhere, raising his son on his own.

His eyes sting.

He sits up, and swings an arm down underneath the bed. There's a shoebox there that he hasn't opened for a long time. He wrenches it out, a cloud of dust following, and lifts the lid.

There they are. The only tangible memories he has. A handful of photographs – real ones, printed on paper, because they are from the days before smartphones.

Clara and him in London, the tower they worked in behind them. He remembers the way she used to tease him when he got excited about his daily Boots Meal Deal. The way they once had sex in a stairwell at the back of the office, so terrified and frantic it was barely enjoyable, really. He had never felt so alive.

There are pictures of them on their one holiday to Turkey – the first and last time he had been on an aeroplane. He had burnt his face so severely that it swelled up, and she called him Hamster Cheeks for weeks, but he didn't care. She had opened so many doors for him; he had experienced so many things for the first time with her.

Then, underneath the photographs, there are the letters she wrote him and cards – so many cards – not just cards for birthdays or Valentine's Day but often for no reason at all because they couldn't stop saying how much they loved one another.

At the bottom of the box is a small woven leather bracelet. He remembers Clara buying it for him in Marmaris, fastening it around his tanned wrist and telling him he mustn't take it off.

'Not until you're wearing our wedding ring instead,' she said, and then they kissed and even though he was only twenty-one and most of the people his age saw marriage as something far, far in the future, if they even saw it there at all, her words didn't make him nervous in the slightest.

But the clasp broke the week before university finished, and he never told her.

This is it. In this box. All that feeling, all those emotions, so consuming and draining. How can they be compressed down to just this? A small box of memories. Young love in all its foolishness. But somehow, so much purer than anything he has felt since.

Last night when he searched her name online, he saw she had been promoted at the newspaper she works for.

He felt a sense of pride and ownership that he knew he didn't deserve to feel. But it was the most he could hope for. To see her achieving her goals. To see her succeeding, making something of herself. Living up to her potential, when he had failed so miserably to live up to his.

It made him feel better too, to know that his stupidity hadn't ruined her life in the way that it ruined his. And though he couldn't bear to think of the man she married in anything more than a nebulous sense, it made him happy to know that she was loved and looked after.

He's a good man, she had written in that email before the wedding. *You would like him, I think. He's uncomplicated and sees life as positive, in the main. But I don't love him. Not in the way that I loved you. Not with any passion or conviction. It's a different kind of love. Perhaps it's safer. Perhaps it will keep me safe.*

He liked that thought. That she was safe. He seized on that paragraph and ignored the one that came after it, when she said that feeling safe was like feeling dead.

She had always been passionate. The fights they'd had! He often had to physically restrain her as she pelted him with her tiny fists, her face transfixed with rage. He thought, perversely, that he loved her the most when she was like that, despite his frustration.

Now, of course, such behaviour would be seen as abusive. Zoe often lost her temper with him too, swearing at him and calling him names. But the difference was that Zoe's anger was directed towards him, whereas he knew, deep down, that Clara's anger was really directed towards herself. That she saw him as an extension of her.

He could never love her enough to make her love herself. Clara had decided that her life would look a certain way, that she would achieve certain things, and therefore any failures on her part were proof that she was worthless.

He puts the lid of the box back on and shoves it under the bed. *Don't look backwards, you're not going that way.* He can't remember who told him that. Someone at the prison probably.

They were right, of course.

But the trouble is, he's not going forward either.

May 2013

Clara

She works hard that day, feeling as though she has a candle alight inside her. The email is a secret, a compliment, it gives her some kind of power or feeling that magic still exists in the world. It's dangerous.

It makes her feel loved.

But still, she doesn't reply.

The truth is, she doesn't reply because somehow, replying would take away some of the power it's given her. But also, she doesn't reply because she doesn't know what to say.

When her shift ends, she meets Lauren outside their favourite Soho restaurant. A tapas bar, where three sharing dishes each is not quite enough but four is too many. She still worries, stupidly, about her weight, even though her attractiveness seems so unimportant when she's married to someone who sees her as a personality rather than a physical person.

Lauren is trying to get pregnant and therefore not drinking.

'I'll just have a carafe of the house red to myself then,' Clara says to the waiter. 'Thanks.'

'I'm sorry to be boring,' Lauren says.

'You know what's boring? Apologising for not drinking.'

'I'm sorry again then.'

'Shut up!'

'How are you? Any progress?'

She means about the sex, of course.

Clara shakes her head. She wishes she had never told Lauren about that. She wishes she had never told anyone.

She's had her last session with Sarah, and has yet to pluck up the courage to suggest to Thom that they go to counselling together. She knows instinctively what his reaction would be. *There's no way I'm talking to a stranger about our private business!*

Since his accident, he hasn't seemed interested in sex anyway. He's recovering well, but the pain in his lower back persists, and doesn't go away even with painkillers.

'No, but... I got an email today. From Benjamin.'

Lauren sits back in her chair, keeping her expression neutral. Clara knows her so well: Lauren will be partly excited by her news, partly annoyed by it, and partly nervous for her.

'What did it say?'

Clara takes a deep breath.

'It said: "What's new?"'

Lauren snorts.

'Is that it?'

The waiter sets down a glass of sparkling water before Lauren and the wine before Clara, and Clara suddenly wishes she wasn't drinking after all. She knows what will happen. She'll get drunk and then later tonight she'll hide in the bathroom with her phone while Thom is in bed and she'll type something stupid in reply and she'll lose this magic gift he's given her – of power and love and knowledge that he is thinking of her.

'Nice of him to make the effort,' Lauren says, glaring at the glass of water. 'That's really fucked up.'

She actually sounds angry. Clara sits up straighter in her chair.

'Oh, do you…'

'What the hell is he playing at? After that bullshit email he sent you last year?'

'I don't think he's playing at anything,' Clara says. Benjamin doesn't play games. 'I think he was probably drunk and sad and…'

'It's selfish. He's not thinking about how it might affect you.'

Clara rubs her hand across her nose.

'It's not affecting me.'

'Of course it is! Look at you – you're all… I dunno… glowy and excited or something.'

Clara looks down at her lap. She can't deny it.

'Well, I just…'

'Well, what? What do you think will happen now? Seriously? You'll reply and then what? Nothing will change. He'll never be that twenty-year-old kid you thought you were in love with again, you do know that?'

'I know…' she says, but her words dry up. 'I can't just ignore his message, can I? That would just be cruel.'

'Well, why haven't you replied already then?'

'Because…'

She pauses, trying to dig out the truth from the tangle of feelings in her head.

'Because I'm scared.'

'You're scared that he'll let you down again. Just like he did all those years ago. And listen to me, Clara. You're right. He will.'

May 2013

Benjamin

Three days go by and she doesn't reply and he's relieved. He can pretend it didn't happen. It's easy enough, if he stays busy, and he is always busy because he has Aiden full-time now, and there's so much to organise.

The school have been great, offering sessions with their in-house counsellor so that Aiden can talk about the fact his mother has left, although he's not sure Aiden actually does much talking in these sessions. Afterwards, when Benjamin asks him how they went, he will shrug and say 'Fine' and then ask if he can go and have a kick about in the park before teatime.

It's both reassuring and disconcerting. Can it be that easy, really, to switch off your feelings about your mother? Even if your mother is as unreliable and inconsistent as Zoe?

He is taking the washing out of the machine when he feels his phone vibrate in his pocket. Instinctively, he knows it is her, that she has replied.

When they were together, he often felt that he and Clara had some kind of psychic connection. He would be walking to a lecture, for example, and he'd suddenly think of her and then she'd text him.

Once, he was killing some time in town during a break in his lectures and took his phone out to call her and ask if she wanted to meet up – and literally bumped into her coming the other way.

So it's not a surprise at all to read the notification on his screen, showing her name as the sender of his new email.

His eyebrows rise involuntarily and he feels that familiar rush of blood to his cheeks. He pulls out a chair from the kitchen table and sits down, tapping the notification to bring the email to the screen.

Hello stranger…

He pauses, relaxing. So, she's not cross.

What's new? Nothing is new. Apart from my new job. I'm now very high up and very important at a very significant newspaper, don't you know.

Still living in the same flat in Shepherd's Bush.

What else?

Well, I still miss you.

CDC XXX

He swallows, leaning an elbow on the table.

He feels hollowed out, exhausted. He should never have sent that email. It was stupid, like scratching open a healed wound.

He notes that she hasn't asked him anything. He knows her – if she doesn't ask him anything, then if he doesn't reply she won't feel rejected. She has closed the door on the conversation, but left a tiny crack, just in case.

She's so smart, he thinks, and he loves her all over again.

He reads the email three more times, closes it and puts his phone back in his pocket. Then he stands, picks up the washing basket and heads to the garden to hang it to dry.

A few years after his mother died, his father got really into watching films. It came out of nowhere – George had never particularly expressed an interest in television or the cinema before. But suddenly, he was signed up to Sky Box Office and paying for all the extra channels. Now, every night after their 6 p.m. supper, he sits in his armchair in the living room and scrolls for a few minutes until he finds something he fancies, and puts it on.

Benjamin is usually at the bar working in the evenings, but he has two nights off a week and rather than attempting any kind of social life, he joins his father in the living room, and they choose something together.

Tonight, they are watching *Shutter Island* – a film about a man investigating a disappearance at a psychiatric facility.

'It's an homage to Hitchcock,' his father says, as the starting credits roll.

Benjamin nods. He doesn't want to laugh at his father's passion for film, but the idea of him saying something like this when his mother was still alive… well, it was unthinkable.

All Benjamin can think about is the fact that the lead actor is Leonardo DiCaprio. He remembers the posters in Clara's bedroom at her parents' house that first time he visited. It's as though everything has some link back to her – as though she, in many ways, was like another mother to him.

After all, she was the one who really introduced him to the world.

But that sounds messed up.

The film is entertaining enough, and he enjoys seeing his dad so relaxed. Sitting back in his chair, taking periodic sips of red wine. It seems as though Zoe's leaving has taken a load off George's shoulders, too.

At the end, Benjamin thinks about what the film is trying to tell him, and he struggles. Is it just a story about one man being slowly destroyed? Is it about a man who cannot live with the guilt of what he's done, and so hands himself over to others to decide his fate?

There's an uncomfortable silence in the living room as the film ends. Benjamin glances over at his father.

'What did you think?' Benjamin asks.

'Bit daft,' George says, getting up and picking up his wine glass. ''Night then.'

Benjamin holds back a laugh.

''Night Dad.'

He stands for a few minutes, staring out of the French doors and into the small garden, which is dominated by football paraphernalia – a small goal at the far end, cones set along the lawn at equal distances, the soft ball hanging from the tree at the back.

He wonders about his son's future, what he will think when he looks back on his childhood. When he meets someone he loves for the first time and tells them that he was raised by his father and grandfather in a small cottage in the middle of a former mining village.

At least he has his football. It seems to Benjamin that you can survive anything life throws at you if you have a passion to pull you through. A reason for being.

As for him, his passion is his son. Aiden is what keeps him from cracking up, from breaking down, from ending it all.

But there is something else, too. A hope, that he pushes away repeatedly, but that keeps bobbing back to the surface. A long-buried desire, that he wishes he didn't have. That he tries so hard not to have.

To see her again.

He takes out his phone, and begins to type.

May 2013

Clara

Hello. Sorry about my late-night message. A moment of nostalgia that I probably shouldn't have acted on. But I am glad to hear things are going well for you with your work, although not surprised at all. But what about your novel? I hope you haven't given up on the idea of writing it. I certainly haven't given up on the idea of walking into a shop one day and seeing your book at the front, with your name on the cover.

What will you write about?

When she first reads his email, she's angry. It feels as though he's shaming her about her writing, even though, of course, he isn't. He's being kind, which he always was. Thinking of her, and not of himself. Remembering her ambition. The one thing she was so passionate about. Other than him.

Where has that passion gone?

Thom comes into the bedroom and places a cup of coffee on her dressing table. He's leaving for the airport in an hour or so – to a jewellery exhibition in Dubai. It's a huge opportunity for him and he's been preparing for months. He will be gone for a week.

The tube of gel gets buried ever more deeply in her knicker drawer each week.

'All packed?' she asks, mildly. 'Thanks for the coffee.'

'Just about,' Thom replies, smiling at her. 'The taxi is here. Early.'

'Oh, right,' she says. She suddenly doesn't want him to go. She doesn't want to be left alone with herself. What if he doesn't come back?

What if he finally realises he deserves better than this? How would she cope? He's her anchor, he makes her life make sense.

'How's your back today?'

His face twists. He takes a deep breath.

'It's all right,' he says, giving an attempt at a smile. 'I've got enough codeine to see me through the trip.'

'You'll be standing a lot at the exhibition,' she says. He tries to hide the pain but she can see that without his drugs, he's in agony. She's heard him talking to his physio on the phone. No one can get to the root of the problem. Back pain is a common condition, they say, as though that makes it any more bearable. 'Make sure you sit down as much as you can.'

He nods.

'Try not to worry about me.'

She stands up and gives him a stiff hug. They so rarely touch each other any longer, it's like hugging a stranger.

'If you... while you're there... if you meet anyone... any glamorous young jewellers and you think perhaps... well, I don't know. If you have one too many drinks after the show and get carried away then...'

'Clara,' he says, his voice sharp.

'I'm serious,' she says. 'Please, don't think of me. Don't think of me at all.'

'I do nothing but think of you,' he says. 'You're my wife and I love you.'

She nods, bites her lip.

'I love you, too.'

'I know you do,' he says, and he kisses her on the forehead. 'I'll see you in a week. And I'll call you when I get there.'

'Bye then,' she says. 'I hope… I hope it goes well.'

Thank god for his job, she thinks, sitting back down at the dressing table, as he closes the bedroom door behind him. *Thank god for his dedication, for his distraction, for his ability to cope with just about anything. Thank god for him.*

She reads Benjamin's email again and, in a fit of something, she taps out a reply and sends it without reading it over.

Novel is a non-starter. What will I write about? I don't know. I haven't written any fiction for ages. I'm so busy with work that I don't have time even if I wanted to write. But you know. One day. It takes time to cultivate genius after all.

What about you? What are you up to these days?

She sounds stupid but she feels safer now. She's ripped up his earnestness and stamped over his attempts to be thoughtful or deep. She's talking to him like he's just an old friend she's lost touch with. Not the most important person she ever met.

But his reply comes sooner than expected this time. Almost as though they are texting not emailing.

You'll get there. I never met anyone as determined as you.

As for me, I'm working in a bar – the Ocean – in the city centre. It's pretty new – it wasn't there when we were at uni. You get to see all sorts on a Saturday night. I have some stories to share that would be very good for a book!

He's responding in kind. Chatty, cheerful, as though the weight of their shared history has disappeared.

Playing it safe.

It's not enough.

Her armpits grow damp as she sits there wondering what the hell she is doing but, even so, her fingers type what she really wants to say before she has a chance to stop them.

I bet! Well, if you ever want to venture south to share them with me, I'd be all ears.

Seriously, Mr BE, I would love to see you again.

Nothing dodgy. No agenda, I promise. I just would. It feels wrong that we are not in each other's lives.

She deliberately uses her nickname for him – a small gesture that shouts of an intimacy she no longer deserves.

She wants to say, *I'M STILL YOURS*, but those initials are the closest she can get.

She sits there, heart pounding, waiting for a reply, fingers reflexively refreshing the email app every few seconds. But nothing comes.

In the end she stays there for an hour, the half-drunk cup of coffee now stone cold, and still nothing comes.

What did she expect? Lauren was right.

In her mind's eye, she imagines a door being slammed shut, plunging her into a room of darkness.

Eventually, she stands up, and, frustration mounting, kicks the small wastepaper basket underneath her dressing table across the room, scattering cotton-wool buds and pads over the polished wooden floors.

part three

April 2022

Benjamin

He has rung Aiden sixty-two times. But his phone is still switched off.

The police have directed him to a hotel around the corner from the stadium to wait for news. The officer called it the Friends and Relatives Reception Centre, as though he was going to a wedding.

As he walks, he passes shell-shocked faces clutching flowers, making their way towards the police cordon. He sees that people have started to lay down bouquets and candles at the top of the road that leads to the stadium.

He shakes his head. Flowers? What use are flowers at a time like this?

In the hotel, he can't sit still, so instead he paces the lobby, refusing multiple offers of drinks from the sympathetic staff.

He's used his phone so much that it's burning up in his hand, the battery nearly dead. It's so hot he's worried it will turn itself off or something.

What would his dad say? He'd say to calm down. To trust that Aiden is a sensible lad. That he will be fine.

But there will be hundreds of sensible people who are caught up in what's happened today.

Hundreds of sensible people who are now probably lying in hospital injured, or worse, while their loved ones wait for news.

It doesn't matter how sensible you are if someone wants to blow you up.

June 2017

Clara

Her hands are shaking as she reads out the first section of her novel to her writing group.

She can't look up at them, even though their tutor said it's important to glance up from time to time, to establish some eye contact with the listeners.

It helps to communicate your message, she said.

But she's scared that if she looks in their eyes, she'll see what they really think of her writing. Once she finishes, she finally risks a look upwards.

It's difficult to read the expressions on their faces. They look so serious she almost wants to laugh.

Thankfully Elaine, their tutor, breaks the silence.

'Thank you, Clara. That was very powerful,' she says. 'Moving, too. Well done. What did everyone else think?'

This is the bit she hates. She hates it even when it's someone else's book they're talking about, and now it's her turn, she wants to run out of the room and hide in the toilets.

'I thought the way the character – Sadie – the guilt she felt, I thought that was very powerful,' Mark, the kindest critic of them all, says. 'Considering of course, it wasn't her fault.

What he did. But it was understandable that she felt guilty, by association.'

'Yes, also the way it was written, and her reaction to it was really beautiful,' Elaine says. 'That decision not to punctuate… to just have that long flowing monologue as she tells her parents what has happened – it was great.'

Clara looks down again, smiles shyly.

It's a cliché but it's true – baring your art to the world is like standing naked in front of strangers and asking them to comment.

'I also thought,' Elaine adds, 'that the sense of self-hatred came across very strongly in this piece. Immediately you hope she'll find some sort of redemption, or, at the very least, be able to forgive herself.'

Clara doesn't know if she should speak, but even if she wanted to, she can't. It's humiliating, the way her cheeks flame and her voice dries up when she tries to talk about her writing. The others seem much more confident discussing their work.

'Now, does anyone have any criticism, anything they'd like to share constructively? Any way we can help Clara make the start of her story stronger?'

Clara swallows. At the back of the room, Marta – the dark-haired former singer who terrifies her – speaks.

'If I'm honest, I thought she needs to give herself a break. All that self-flagellation, it's fair enough, but you know what? Shit happens. She needs to move on. Get over it and stop feeling sorry for herself. And I think if you write a character like that – if you have too much of those traits, then, well, eventually the reader just gets pissed off with them and that's it. You've lost them. I guess, we just need to see a bit more of a proactive attitude maybe, in the next chapter? A whole book from her perspective, in that frame of mind, well... that could get really wearing for the reader.'

She pauses.

'Sorry, Clara, I don't want to be a bitch but, by the end of it, I wanted to give her a good shake. I think with some pruning back though, it could be much more powerful. What's left unsaid is more impactful than spelling it all out, don't you think?'

The room is silent. Marta shrugs.

'Well, that's just what I think,' she says, her voice quieter now.

'That's definitely an interesting consideration,' Elaine says. 'We can discuss the unlikeable narrator in another session, as it's a pretty contentious topic. But, I think we can certainly agree that Clara's use of language in this piece was really powerful, so well done. Let's all have a clap.'

They clap her and she feels juvenile and useless, as though they are all now pretending that they're impressed, when really they think her writing is shit.

When the excruciating clapping ends, Elaine announces that it's time for them to have their break, and that they're due back in an hour.

She lingers behind as the rest of them head off into the Southwark sunshine. Elaine has opened her laptop, is typing something and doesn't seem to realise Clara's still there.

'Can I have a word with you?' Clara asks eventually.

Elaine looks up.

'Of course. Well done for today, there's so much promise in your writing, there really is.'

'Thank you,' she says. Strangely, Clara has always believed this, deep down, despite all those long periods of inactivity. But to hear someone like Elaine – a Booker long-listee no less

– confirm it, is possibly one of the greatest things she has ever experienced. 'I just...'

Elaine smiles at her.

'I'm a bit nervous. About the book I'm writing. It's kind of autobiographical. I mean, the incident in the book – the thing that sends Jonathan to prison – that's something that happened once. To someone I knew.'

Elaine nods.

'And I'm worried. I don't know what the rules are. Obviously, I've changed the names and some of the details. But, I guess, if he read it. This man, whose story I'm telling, in a roundabout way... well, is there any chance I could get into trouble? You know, if one day, it was published or something?'

Elaine takes a deep breath.

'Well, it's definitely something to consider. But many first novels are in some way autobiographical – it's normal. And you might find that this book isn't the one that gets published first anyway. Not to disillusion you, but it's very common that first novels don't get publishing deals.'

Clara feels like crying. Elaine can see the heartbreak on her face.

'That's not to say it won't. What I mean is, don't worry about that now. You can cross that bridge when you come to it. You're a talented writer, but I think you're only just working out what you really want to say. So, keep writing, and tell the story you want to tell. And try not to worry about where that will lead you.'

July 2017

Benjamin

Of course, he never got to graduate the first time. Because of a mistake he made, handing in an incomplete final project, he technically never even finished his degree. And he didn't go back after he left prison. Too much paperwork, and he felt too ashamed.

He doesn't remember feeling particularly sad about it at the time. Of all the things he lost, it seemed the least significant.

But over the years, it started to upset him a bit. He wasn't naturally quick to learn, and he had to try much harder, it seemed, than everyone else. It upset him that he had spent three years working so hard only for all that work to be effectively thrown in the bin.

But when Aiden turned eight, Benjamin made the decision to go back to uni, to start again, and now here he is, in a municipal building just off the town square, with his fellow graduates, celebrating his 2.1 in Digital Film Production.

Not Computing for Business – that woolly subject he studied so long ago, when digital technology was still in its infancy. But Digital Film Production, an actual tangible skill that leads to a real, if competitive, career.

He finds his father in the crowd after the ceremony. George hands him a pint, pats him on the back.

'Well done, Benjamin,' he says. 'I was… well, I was really proud, seeing you up there in your gown. Your mam…'

Benjamin nods. They both know.

George smiles, but his eyes are watery.

'I couldn't have done it without you,' Benjamin says, quietly. 'So, thank you. Seriously, thank you.'

'You did all the work. All I did was sit and watch the films with you. Not exactly a big contribution.'

Words bubble to the surface of his mind but he can't let them out. Everything he wants to say to his father. The thanks and gratitude he knows he will never find a way to express adequately.

George has done so much for him.

Taken him in, forgiven him for what he did, supported him when he had nothing and, most of all, been an incredible grandfather to Aiden.

Benjamin knows he could not, and would not, be standing here now if it wasn't for his father's support.

But they don't talk about such things, so instead Benjamin just smiles and rests a hand on his father's arm. He's wearing a suit, and beneath the thick fabric Benjamin can feel the slightness of George's bones.

After the short official celebration draws to a close, Benjamin turns down his coursemates' offers to go to the pub and instead heads home with his father. His fellow graduates are almost all in their twenties, and he feels even more out of place among them than he did when he was studying the first time around.

But for the first time in a long while, he's excited for the future. He has several projects on the go already, and he can't wait to get his portfolio out there. He knows it will be tough, but when he thinks what he's been through already, he also knows he'll be all right.

Back at the house, his phone rings. It's Emily, the girl he has been seeing.

'Hey baby, how did it go?' she says, her voice typically upbeat.

'Aye it was good thanks,' he says. 'Can't believe I've finished. Do you want to come over tomorrow? Celebrate?'

'You're on. I'll bring cake,' she says. 'I'm so proud of you.'

Aiden chooses the evening's film – *Jurassic Park*, the original – even though they have seen it more times than he can count.

'Epic,' Aiden says, as the raptor devours one of the rangers, and Benjamin smiles.

He thinks, *this life is good*.

For once, he is sure of it.

The next day, Emily brings fizzy wine and cake as promised. The four of them sit in the garden around the metal table George has spray-painted so many times that the surface has bubbled.

'Cheers to you,' she says, raising a glass and smiling. 'From Newcastle to Hollywood.'

He feels his neck flush.

'Not sure about that,' he says, 'but thanks.'

She leans over and kisses him lightly on the mouth.

'Puke,' Aiden snorts behind them.

'Oi you,' Emily says. 'Cheeky.'

Aiden grins. Jam from the cake oozes out, spilling onto his top.

'Aiden!'

'Ugh, it's sticky,' Aiden says, wiping it with his hand.

'God Aid, don't rub it in – you're making it worse!'

Emily laughs.

'I was thinking,' Emily says, glancing sideways at Benjamin. 'Perhaps I could take Aid to the Metrocentre next week? I don't want to be rude, but he could maybe do with some new T-shirts.'

He is, of course, wearing his City top, as always.

'I mean, not that your football gear isn't lovely, Aiden, but perhaps a change of clothes every now and then? My treat.'

Benjamin glances at Aiden.

'Can we get a KFC after?'

'Oh god, yes I guess so.'

'Excellent,' Aiden says, scooping the last bit of cake into his mouth. 'Count me in.'

Benjamin smiles. Emily is so good with him. With them both.

'Dad?' Aiden says, putting his plate down on the table.

'Yes, champ?'

'Coach Kenny's asked me over to his house after training tomorrow. Is that OK?'

'Aid, it's a school night. And I'm not sure…'

'Please! Gary's going, and Jonny too. This is the first time Coach Kenny's asked me – it's a really big deal!'

Benjamin looks at Emily, who raises an amused eyebrow. Benjamin has met these boys, of course, at training drop-offs, and he's met their parents too. He doesn't much like the look of Gary's father, who seems to think it's perfectly acceptable to swear viciously at his thirteen-year-old son in front of everyone.

'Quick with his fists, that one. Poor lad,' one of the other dads said to him as they watched Gary's father berate him, and Benjamin winced. He found that kind of thing very difficult to observe.

At least Gary had football as an escape from his home life.

'No mate, sorry. Not on a school night.'

Aiden exhales dramatically.

'But! But everyone else gets to go! It's not fair.'

'They're all older than you. Another time.'

'For fuck's sake,' Aiden exclaims, springing off the garden chair.

'Language, Aiden!' Benjamin shouts, but his son ignores him, doing keepy-uppys in the middle of the lawn.

Where has his little boy gone? He's still in there, somewhere, underneath the bravado of a man.

Benjamin watches as his son deftly knees the ball in the air, then heads it straight into the goal at the back of the garden.

'He's getting so good,' George says. 'I mean, really. He's better than you ever were, and you were pretty decent. When does he hear whether or not he's made the youth team?'

'Soon, I think,' Benjamin says. 'But I don't know, it's taking a toll on him. He's only twelve. He's always exhausted. And his teacher is concerned that it's affecting his school work.'

'Pfst,' George says, waving a hand in the air. 'He won't need schoolwork if he's going to play for England, will he?'

Benjamin thinks about his father's attitude to education and, not for the first time, wonders where it originated. Is it a chip on his shoulder that came from never having had much of an education himself? His dad is intelligent, in his own way. Practical. But he left school at sixteen to start work as an electrician's apprentice and that was that. Career path chosen, and firmly stuck to.

'Dad,' he says, warily. 'You know as well as I do that he needs something to fall back on. In case football doesn't work out.'

'Of course it will work out, the lad's a genius. Look at his feet. Light as a feather.'

'But what if it's too much for him? What if he gets injured?'

'Well, if he gets injured then he can coach. Like his coach. The boy is happy. He's doing what he loves.' George leans down and lowers his voice. 'Just be grateful. After all he's been through. Just be grateful he's turned out as well as he has.'

That evening, Benjamin watches Emily as she undresses and slips into bed beside him, naked. She's six years younger than him. He has always been self-conscious about the way he looks and he feels ugly and old next to her.

'I had a lovely day,' she says, softly, stroking his chest.

'Me too,' he says. 'Thanks for bringing the cake.'

They make love quietly – he still finds it uncomfortable doing so in his childhood bedroom, knowing that his father and son are just thin walls away. Afterwards, she looks down at him, her forehead damp, her face glowing.

'I love you, Benjamin,' she says.

He is so startled at this that he freezes.

'Oh,' he says. 'Thank you.'

Then, seeing a shadow of hurt pass over her eyes, he pulls her back down towards him and kisses her hard, keeping his own eyes closed.

July 2017

Clara

She has bought Lauren two pink ceramic money boxes from Tiffany's. Thom said it was a little extravagant, but money is the one thing they don't need to worry about, and so she never sees any problem spending it. Thom's jewellery business has become incredibly successful – he's winning awards all over the world for his innovative work, and is planning on opening a new boutique in Mayfair.

He takes care of all the bills, in the same way that he takes care of everything in their life. And so the modest salary she earns at the newspaper is hers to spend as she pleases.

Fun money, Thom once called it. She felt her jaw tense afterwards. When was the last time she had any fun?

She presses down hard on the doorbell outside Lauren and James's terraced house in Wimbledon. There are some expensive-looking balloons tied to the pillar outside the porch. Clara reads the words emblazoned on them.

It's a girl!

Baby shower!

She swallows. Lauren has waited so long for this. Five years, in fact. And now: twins.

Lauren's sister, Elizabeth, opens the door and Clara can't be sure if it's her imagination or whether her smile momentarily slips. Either way, she welcomes Clara in with a stiff smile.

'They're all in the front room. Lauren's the size of a house, poor thing!'

Twins. Clara can't imagine it. She hasn't provided Thom with so much as an orgasm for the past four years.

'Hello,' Clara says, as Lauren sees her and tries to stand up. She really is the size of a house. 'Don't get up you idiot! I'll come down to you.'

She leans over and kisses Lauren on both cheeks. There are three other women in the room – women she recognises vaguely from the wedding and Lauren's previous birthday parties.

'Hi, hi,' she says, smiling at them all. Already, she is wondering how long it will be before she can leave.

'Champagne,' Elizabeth says, holding out a glass.

'Oh wow, thank you,' Clara says. She puts the two carefully wrapped boxes on the buttoned footstool in front of them.

'I think that's all of us then,' Elizabeth says, beaming at them all. 'Let the games commence!'

The games, it transpires, involve racing to see who can change a nappy on a doll the fastest, and also an excruciating game of He Said/She Said, in which they discover that Lauren and James had completely different ideas about parenting their upcoming newborns.

But still, the alcohol helps. And Lauren looks as though she is enjoying herself. After the first few games, Elizabeth brings out delicately cut sandwiches on a tray and afterwards they tuck into a giant croquembouche.

It's all very Nappy Valley, but Clara is so pleased for her friend. Lauren has endometriosis and has endured years of treatment and two painful operations to get to this point. They have been through so much together, both struggling in their own ways, but finally, there's an end to the pain for one of them.

Clara is spooning croquembouche into her mouth when one of Lauren's friends, Sadie, sidles up to her.

'Clara, how are you?' she asks. 'Haven't seen you for ages.'

Clara nods, her mouth full of pastry.

'Good, good,' she says.

'Am I right in thinking you've had a baby too?' Sadie asks.

Clara swallows the last of the bun.

'Oh, no… no, sorry, not me.'

Why is she apologising? She kicks herself.

'Oh.' She notices Sadie staring at her ring. Sometimes, she hates the ring. It's an attention-seeker, not like her. 'Not keen?'

Clara glares at her. The temptation to answer *Yes, I would love to have a child but I'm unable to because I can't physically have sex and, even if I could, my husband is in chronic pain and doesn't much fancy it either* is so strong that she has to feign a coughing fit and leave the room instead.

Eventually everyone leaves – it turns out they all have their own babies waiting for them at home – and there's just Lauren and Clara left in the living room, surrounded by wrapping paper and crumbs.

'Thank god. That was fucking exhausting,' Lauren says, leaning back. She has three new chins since the last time Clara saw her, and she looks so uncomfortable in her own skin. Literally.

Clara laughs.

'I'm glad you enjoyed it. Not long now, eh!'

'Nope, the C-section is booked for the twenty-first. I can't really believe it. But I guess people have survived worse. It's just hard, you know. Everyone expects me to be so grateful all the time – the miracle pregnancy and all that. I wouldn't say this to anyone else but... the thing is, I didn't actually want twins.'

Clara smiles again and squeezes her friend's hand.

'Are you nervous?'

Lauren pauses, takes a shallow breath, which seems to be the only type of breath she can take with two babies shoved right up her ribcage.

'I am more nervous about afterwards, if I'm honest. How it will affect us. As a couple. It's been hard enough the past few years, just dealing with all my medical issues. And well, everyone says having twins is exhausting. And I hate the idea of...'

'What?'

'Something coming along and upsetting our little ecosystem. Does that sound odd? But throwing two babies into the mix – god knows how that will work out.'

'It'll be a big change,' Clara says. 'But you'll be fine. James adores you. He always has done. Ever since uni.'

She tails off, thinking of Richard. James's best friend. They never discuss him. What might have been.

'I know,' Lauren says. 'I'm very lucky.'

But it's too late. There are unspoken words in the air. Clara knows that for that brief second, before someone changes the subject, they are both thinking the same.

That Lauren is living the life that Clara might have lived.

If only.

July 2017

Benjamin

The nightmares are back.

He can't work out why, or where they have come from when he thought he had banished them for good, but each night it's the same. The tight sensation in his chest as though someone were choking him. Her face, those eyes he loved so much, staring at him huge and confused.

And her words to him.

What have you done?!

It's a question he's still trying to answer, all these years later.

He sits up in bed, panting, sweat pouring from his forehead. He's alone tonight, thankfully. Emily is back at her place. He hasn't told her the truth about him and he knows that it's wrong.

She is aware that he's been in prison, but not the details. And he knows he will have to sit her down eventually and explain it all to her. But when?

He climbs out of bed and pads down softly to the kitchen, pouring himself a cup of water and staring at the blinking clock on the oven: 3.23 a.m. He probably won't get back to sleep again, but that's OK. Experience has taught him you can survive on far less sleep than you realise.

He sits at the kitchen table and starts making some notes on his short film idea. He has been working part-time for a local charity, helping them to create videos about their mission and, while it's been rewarding, he's still working at the bar to pay the bills.

One day though, he will be working on feature films, he's sure of it. It will just take time, and persistence.

He thinks about Aiden, his unfailing dedication to football. It always surprises him how much his little boy has taught him about life. It's the gift you don't expect when you become a parent.

He makes notes until the sun comes up – drawing mind maps and scribbling any idea that comes into his head. It's all progress, even though it looks like an incomprehensible mess.

He thinks if he can tell his own story, through the medium of film, perhaps the nightmares will stop.

But it's more than that and he knows it. It's a way of reaching out to her, without actually reaching out to her.

His phone is sitting on the table beside him. He picks it up. Searches the internet for her name.

Clara Davies-Clark

She told him she hated her name – 'Ugh, it's so double-barrelled and wanky' – but he has always loved it. It suited her. It was distinctive. Unique.

Excessive. Like her.

And it makes stalking her online a lot easier.

She has an Instagram page now. That's new. It wasn't there the last time he looked her up. He taps on the link, heart thudding in his chest.

It takes a few seconds to load, but then, there she is. Her current life in curated snapshots. The photos on her page are mainly of nature and the outdoors, which surprises him: changing seasons on the Heath, carefully tended window boxes of colour, a wreath of dried flowers hanging on a smart front door, the occasional vase of dramatic blooms.

She always had an aesthetic eye. Something she inherited from her mother. He remembers the huge vase of lilies in the hallway of Clara's family home, the way every surface seemed to be dotted with beautiful, carefully chosen and placed *things*. He didn't really understand what made them so, but he knew they were tasteful. Impressive.

He clicks on one of the pictures that calls out to him: a giant oak tree silhouetted against the sun.

Lost amongst giants, the caption reads, followed by a string of star and leaf emojis.

Scattered in between the pictures of nature are a handful of selfies, mostly taken in the mirror, the phone itself throwing a shadow across her features. There's a photo of Clara with her arm around her sister Cecily at Christmas. They look happy together, and he's glad of it. Their relationship was so important to Clara, he knew, and he'd always hoped they'd grow together, not apart.

He finds himself holding his breath as he zooms in on Clara's face on his tiny screen. She looks thinner than he remembers. Rather than blossoming with age, it seems she has shrunk.

She isn't smiling in any of the images. Instead, she looks pensive and serious.

In spite of that, and the drawn expression on her face, she is still the most beautiful thing he has ever seen.

There are no photos of her husband. Benjamin knows who he is, though. One dark night a year or so ago, he drank half a bottle of whisky and read every single scrap of information he could find on Thom Beaumont, Jeweller to the Stars.

He taps on another image but a pop-up tells him that he needs the Instagram app in order to take a closer look. He puts down his phone. He's grateful for that message. It's a warning. *Too much of this is bad for you.*

He thinks about her last email to him, four whole years ago, the teasing way in which she invited him to visit her, and the cowardly way in which he simply didn't reply.

He had wanted to reply, so badly, but what could he say? *No, it's not a good idea*? She would have seen that as a challenge; an invitation to change his mind. And she would have felt rejected when she realised she couldn't.

He loved her enough to be the sensible one.

He hoped, on some level, his silence would have made sense to her. That she would have understood what it meant: that he wanted to come, but that he couldn't. That it would do them both more harm than good if he did. That he was ending it there, for both their sakes.

His eyes are damp. He sniffs, stands up and clears his throat, looking down at the notes in front of him.

He has been too introspective lately. It's Emily. He likes her. A lot. More than any of the handful of girls he's dated over the past ten years. But it scares him, the thought of her getting close. The thought of her finding out the truth about him, of trying to explain it all to her.

And the thought of having to tell her that he loves her, even though he's not sure he does.

At breakfast, Aiden brings up the invite to Coach Kenny's house again.

'Dad, you don't get it.' Aiden's voice is squeaky. 'It's part of the initiation. If I don't go, then I won't get into the county youth team. They'll give my place to someone else!'

Benjamin stares at his son, a memory surfacing. His own horrible initiation. He hid in the toilets afterwards and cried for his mam.

'What exactly happens at this initiation?'

'I dunno,' Aiden shrugs, as though his dad is an idiot. 'It's a secret. That's the whole point. You don't know until you get there.'

Benjamin sighs. It'll be something disgusting like drinking a cup of his teammates' spit. Or eating dog food. Or having a bucket of ice water thrown over him.

'Aid...'

'Please, Dad. You don't understand what this means to me. It's *everything*.'

The thing is, Benjamin does know. He understands exactly how Aiden feels, and he both wants to protect his son and also ensure he doesn't feel left out, like he did.

'Fine,' Benjamin says, against his better judgement. There's only a week left of the school year, at least. 'But you're not staying over. I know your coach lets some of the older boys crash at his house, but I'm not having it. You're far too young to be up all night drinking alcohol and playing god knows what on the Xbox.'

Aiden's eyes flash with excitement.

'Thank you, thank you, thank you!' he says. 'I'll make you proud, Dad. You won't regret it!'

July 2017

Clara

'Clara darling, you're fading away.'

Eleanor draws her close in a hug. Clara can smell the Chanel no.5 on her mother's skin, the Elnett in her hair. The smells of her childhood.

'I'm fine,' Clara says, taking her seat at the table opposite.

Eleanor pulls her phone out from her slim red handbag, looks at the screen and tuts.

'What?' Clara says, putting the napkin on her lap and looking down at the menu in front of her.

'Afternoon tea with my girls, what a treat,' Eleanor had said, when Clara had suggested it a few weeks ago. And now, here they are.

'Cecily's running late,' Eleanor says, tutting again. 'She said to start without her.'

'Oh, for god's sake,' Clara snaps, annoyed. 'She's so predictable.'

Clara is jealous of her sister.

Cecily doesn't remember much about being sick. And she doesn't know about the nights Clara sat at the top of the stairs when she should have been in bed, listening to her mother below as she wept with fear. The vacant, inattentive look in her father's eyes whenever Clara would ask him a question, the mumbled, inadequate reply he would give; or the way Eleanor pushed Clara away when she tried to comfort her, leaving her feeling even more confused than before.

Cecily doesn't remember what they all went through, because of, and for, her. She doesn't think of the scars they have been left with, too.

Instead, she treats it like a joke, an amusing anecdote to trot out at parties: 'Did you know, I nearly died when I was four? It's true!'

It's infuriating that someone who came so close to losing her *actual life* should now behave as though she has nothing to lose.

'Don't be mean, darling,' Eleanor says, waving her own napkin at Clara now. 'She's had a tough time of it.'

'She's had a tough time of it?' Clara says, seized by an unexpected rage. 'Yes, poor Cecily. Life's always been *so* difficult for her. Let's not upset precious, fragile Cecily!'

'Clara!' Eleanor's mouth forms a perfect oval.

'I'm sick of it. There are other people in this family too, you know. Not just Cece. And as for her having a tough time… how is that exactly? The last I heard she was living it up with her new boyfriend.'

'Clara, you know, she missed out on a huge part of her early childhood…'

'She has no memories of being sick. It's like she doesn't even believe it happened to her. She doesn't care that it was so traumatic for me I used to creep into her room at night for years after – *for years, Mum* – just to check she hadn't died in her sleep!'

'Clara,' Eleanor says, more gently this time. Her face has gone white, and now, of course, Clara feels guilty.

She takes a sip of her water.

'I'm sorry, Mum,' she says. 'But Cece isn't the only one who has had a tough time of it. Things haven't exactly been easy for me either. And sometimes it feels as though I'm the only one who remembers how scary it was. You all seem to have moved on, put it behind you. Pretending like it never happened.'

'You never put something like that behind you,' Eleanor says, sternly, after a heavy silence. 'But we didn't want to dwell on it. You were so little. We thought it was best as a family if we all looked forward.'

'But you *did* dwell on it. You do. You dwell on it all the time when you treat Cecily as though she's made of glass.'

Clara stops and bites her lip, wondering if she's gone too far. She knows her parents have always done their best. That's all any of us do: our best, with what we have.

'I had no idea about you going into her room to check on her… I didn't realise. You were so closed off, Clara. You didn't want to share anything with us.'

Eleanor is right, of course.

'I didn't know how to communicate what I was feeling. I was only six.'

Tears threaten then, because this has always been her problem, hasn't it? This is the root of it all. Her inability to communicate. Her fear of feeling, of *being*, too much.

'We should have tried harder to get through to you,' Eleanor says. 'I'm sorry Clara.'

Clara nods, looks away. It's no use now, really. Nothing to be done about it. But even so, she feels better for having finally said something. For forcing her mother to really listen.

The waiter sets down a cake stand in front of them, immaculate miniature pastries and scones ringing each level.

Clara has completely lost her appetite.

'Thank you,' Eleanor says to the waiter. Then she looks back at Clara.

'I'm worried about you, darling.'

'I'm sorry for snapping. I'm just a bit worn out,' Clara says. 'That's all. I've been working really hard lately. On my book. I think...'

She pauses, takes a deep breath.

Here, is something good. Here, is something she *can* share.

Eleanor's eyebrows rise. She has always been puzzled by her daughter's literary endeavours. Nerves, or snobbery, Clara isn't sure which. *It's a little bit gauche to write a novel, don't you think, darling? I hope it's not about us!*

'I think it might actually be ready,' Clara says.

'Oh, right,' Eleanor replies. 'For the publisher?'

Clara purses her lips, shakes her head.

'No Mum, I've told you, you can't just send it to a publisher. You have to have a literary agent first. They are the ones that submit it to publishers for you. It's really hard to get one, too. There's a lot of competition.'

Eleanor wrinkles her nose.

'Well, it is impressive. So long as you are happy. Grandpa would be very proud. He was such a big reader. And how is Thom? How did his recent exhibition go? We're so proud of him... Imagine, a son-in-law whose jewellery is worn to the BAFTAs!'

Clara zones out as her mother waxes lyrical about her perfect, wonderful husband. Who pretty much is perfect and wonderful, so she can't even be angry about it. Anyway, she's glad of the change of subject.

When she returns home later that afternoon, her perfect wonderful husband is sitting on the floor in the front room, the curtains drawn. She tiptoes in, confused as to why he's sitting in the dark.

'Are you OK?' she says, and his head snaps up. He had been looking at something on his phone. Even in the dull light, she can tell that his eyes are moist.

'Have you been crying?' she says, stunned.

'What?' he sniffs. 'No, of course not.'

'Is it your back? Is it bad today?'

He shakes his head. He doesn't say what she knows he is thinking: *it's always bad*. Despite the doctor finding no specific cause, Thom remains crippled by pain. He's been taking prescription painkillers, has seen four different physios, but some days it's so severe he can't even get out of bed.

'I just had a headache,' he says. 'Next door's building work… the drilling's been going on all day, and this is the only room I can hear myself think in.'

He gives a laugh. It's forced. Then he stands up, walks towards her and kisses her on the cheek.

'Hope you had a nice time with your mum,' he says. 'How was Cece?'

She looks at him carefully. What is he hiding?

'She didn't turn up,' Clara says.

'Oh dear, hope your mum wasn't too upset.'

'Some drama, I don't know. She was stuck all the way over the other side of town and didn't want to come out in the rain.'

Thom gives a knowing tilt of the head.

'Well, I'm sure your mum appreciated you making the effort. Let me get dinner on. Glass of wine?'

She follows him through to the kitchen and watches as he chops an onion. She stays silent, hoping it will force him to speak.

'Rory called,' he says, eventually. 'Abigail's pregnant again.'

Rory is Thom's best friend. And Abigail is the sort of wife she should be.

'Oh,' she says, allowing herself a minute. 'That's... good for them.'

Thom looks up at her. As he smiles, the wrinkles around his eyes deepen and she sees him as he is: a man in his thirties with sadness in his heart.

'Yes,' he says. 'They're thrilled. Rory really didn't want Margot to be an only child.'

She feels her body tense. They fall into silence again.

'How's Hamish?' she says, eventually. Clara rarely sees these people. They are Thom's friends and they don't often socialise with other couples. Everyone has got so much busier over the past few years. Children, careers...

But she knows the gossip. Hamish has just left his wife. Midlife crisis, Thom called it.

Thom rolls his eyes at the mention of Hamish. This is safer ground, she knows. Talking about this will make him angry, not sad.

'I don't know what to do with him,' he says, eventually. 'Claims he's in love. The girl's twenty-two for Christ's sake. It's embarrassing.'

Clara smiles.

'Ah well,' she says. 'I guess if he's happy...'

He looks at her crossly.

'I don't know if I'm the only one who took my marriage vows seriously, but sometimes it feels like it.'

She swallows. It's not a dig at her, she doesn't think. But she forgets how traditional he can be. How *good*.

She often wonders, if he was a bastard, whether things might be different.

After dinner, he puts a Bond film on and she decides to get an early night.

'It's a classic!' he says, his eyes wide. 'Admittedly not one of the best but... come on, you'll enjoy it.'

'I've seen it a dozen times,' she says. It's a lie. She's seen it once. Years ago, with Benjamin. They spent most of the film snogging, hands snaking underneath each other's clothes. 'And I'm a bit worn out after today. Mum. You know how much she tires me out.'

He nods.

''Night then,' he says, and turns back to the screen.

Upstairs, she sits in bed with her laptop on a pillow on her lap, working on her query letter to agents. Her writing has been the best source of therapy. She has worked like a demon for the past six months, imagining that the novel is a way of communicating her feelings to Benjamin. Because she can't actually reach out, not again. Not after last time, when he didn't reply.

Four whole years ago now.

Her heart is too fragile.

She runs her fingers over the trackpad on her laptop, and watches the words – so many words – scroll before her eyes. She has done this. She has created this. Whatever happens next, even if Benjamin never reads it – because, truthfully, the thought of him *actually* reading it terrifies her – whatever happens next, she has accomplished what she always wanted to.

She has written a novel, and she is proud of herself. And she knows that he would be, too.

July 2017

Benjamin

George is just serving their tea when Benjamin's phone rings. It's Aiden.

'Hey champ,' Benjamin says, surprised. It's only just gone 8 p.m. 'Everything all right?'

'Can you come and get me?' His son's voice sounds small, far away. 'Please, Dad.'

The initiation, Benjamin smiles to himself. Poor kid.

A rite of passage, but it doesn't make it any less shit.

'Of course,' Benjamin says, resisting a chuckle. 'I'm on my way.'

Coach Kenny lives just down the road from the training ground.

Kenny is a legend in the area, with a reputation as one of the top talent-spotters in the north east. Not the easiest of men to get on with, and definitely not known for his charm, but none of that matters when you have a track record like his.

He was also a fine player himself back in the day, before injury put paid to his career. But he turned to coaching, and never looked back.

Benjamin knows how lucky Aiden is to be in his team.

Benjamin has never been to Coach Kenny's house before, and he's surprised that it's this side of town.

When he was a kid, his mam didn't let him come down this way.

There's a rumbling noise as he pulls up outside the cramped red-brick terrace. He looks up to see a train trundling past on a bridge at the end of the street. Some of the houses have boarded-up windows.

Benjamin's jaw tenses as he knocks on the door. This wasn't what he was expecting. Aiden answers it almost instantly. He's pale, his eyes wide and he looks younger than when Benjamin last saw him, just this morning before school.

'You all right champ?' Benjamin asks again, but Aiden just shakes his head and pushes past him towards the car.

Benjamin peers into the house, briefly. It's dark inside, but he can hear the sound of a console game blaring from the front room – some kind of car race – and boys whooping with delight. In front of the tatty staircase is a green plastic recycling bin, filled with empty cans of beer.

He shakes his head.

Most of the lads in the team are fifteen or sixteen, but even so, they shouldn't be drinking on a school night. Or any night, really.

But Benjamin's club was just the same. He was so young that he can't even remember the first time he had a can of lager. It seemed normal at the time, but now he's a father himself, he realises how wrong it was.

Aiden is already strapped in the front seat when Benjamin sits down beside him.

'Don't you need to say goodbye?'

'Can we just go, Dad? Please.'

Benjamin frowns, starts the engine.

'Not the nicest of houses,' he says, mildly, glancing over at his son.

'He's just renting it for a bit,' Aiden says, his voice dull. 'While he gets his place done up. He's having a swimming pool put in.'

'Is that right?' Benjamin turns left at the end of the road and heads back towards their village. 'How did the initiation go?'

But Aiden doesn't reply. Instead, he turns his face away and stares out of the window.

Benjamin's heart breaks for him. He gets it. He was that sensitive kid too, once.

Alcohol helps, but Aiden's too young for that. Benjamin looks over at him again. He doesn't think he's been drinking, but he can't be sure.

Tomorrow, Benjamin will phone Aiden's coach and find out exactly what happened this evening.

When they get home, George asks Aiden if he's hungry.

'No. I had some pizza. Thanks, Grandad. I'm just going to go to bed.'

''Night son,' Benjamin says, ruffling his hair.

''Night Dad. 'Night Grandad.'

Benjamin turns back to George, and shrugs.

Aiden has training again the next day after school. But he is unusually quiet when Benjamin collects him.

His cheeks are red as he climbs into the car and pulls his seat belt on.

'All right?' Benjamin asks, glancing over at him.

But Aiden doesn't reply. He just turns and stares out of the window.

Hormones, thinks Benjamin as he pulls away. Or he's had a bad session. Perhaps his coach has told him off for something.

Once they're back at the house, Aiden gets out of the car without a word and goes up to his room. Benjamin finds George in the kitchen, preparing dinner.

'Did Aid say anything to you when he came in?' Benjamin asks.

'No, should he have done?'

'He's in a mood.'

At supper later, Aiden still doesn't speak. He eats his dinner – he has always finished his plate without complaint, and Benjamin is sure it's because of the way his mother used to leave him without food for hours – but then he stands up and announces he's tired.

It's 8.30 p.m.

'Right,' Benjamin says. 'Are you poorly?'

Aiden shakes his head.

'No, I just didn't sleep that well last night.'

'Aid, is there anything you want to tell me? About the initiation?'

Aiden's cheeks flush.

'No, don't be daft. 'Night Dad. 'Night Grandad.'

''Night son.'

In the night, Benjamin wakes up to the sound of someone using the bathroom. This isn't too unusual – his father has had issues with his prostate for years now but refuses to go and see anyone about it. But this time he hears something other than the toilet flushing.

Aiden is crying.

Benjamin sits up in bed, rubbing his eyes, and strains to listen. Is Aiden talking to someone on the phone? It doesn't sound like it.

All he can hear are soft sobs.

He gets out of bed and walks towards the bathroom. The door is closed but light seeps from under it.

He knocks gently.

'Aid,' he says, as softly as possible. He doesn't want to embarrass him by waking up George, too. 'Are you all right in there?'

But Aiden doesn't respond. The sobs grow heavier.

'Let me in,' he says. 'Whatever it is, I'm sure I can help.'

There's a silence and then the door unlocks. Benjamin turns the handle. His son is sitting on the floor, knees drawn up under his chin, a pile of damp toilet roll by his side.

He looks like he is seven years old again. It breaks Benjamin's heart, briefly, to realise that he will never be seven years old again. That his little boy has gone forever, and that this burgeoning man has replaced him.

'What's the matter?' he says. 'This isn't like you.'

His worry often comes out like this: accusatory. He's aware of it; the feeling that he can't cope if Aiden isn't OK. He has coped with a lot in his life, but Aiden not being OK is too much for him. He's not strong enough for it.

It's just his fear speaking but, instead of sounding sympathetic, he sounds as though he's reprimanding him.

This isn't like you = Pull yourself together.

'I mean… let me help,' he says, but it's too late.

Aiden looks up and meets him square in the eyes.

'I've made a decision,' Aiden says. 'I'm giving up footie.'

The words are so unexpected that Benjamin can't think how to respond.

'Wha... why?'

'I don't want to talk about it,' he says. 'I'm just not playing again. Ever.'

Benjamin sinks down onto the lino floor beside his son.

'Did something happen?' he says, eventually. 'At Coach Kenny's? Did something upset you?'

'It's a stupid career,' Aiden says, sniffing. 'Hardly anyone actually makes a decent living from it.'

'But...' Benjamin's mind is doing that thing again. Talking to him, trying to work out what's best to say next. 'You're good. You're really good. I called your coach earlier...'

'What?'

'I just wanted to check you were OK, after the initiation. I didn't like how upset you were when I picked you up from his house.'

Aiden stares at him.

'What did he say?'

'He said you're one of the best players in his squad.'

Aiden turns away.

'He's just blowing smoke,' he says. 'I'm no better than any of the others. And anyway, like you said, what if I get injured, and I've wasted all this time, all these hours, training, when I could have been having a life? Like my mates at school.'

'But you're better than them!' Benjamin says, shocked by the sudden rise of his own temper. 'For Christ's sake, Aiden, you have a gift. A talent. A skill. You can't just throw that away because of a what if!'

'You can't make me do it!' Aiden says, his voice rising, growing hysterical. 'Just because you fucked up your own life, that doesn't mean I have to live it for you!'

Benjamin takes a deep breath.

'I was never as good as you,' Benjamin says, staring at his

son. 'I never had your skills. It's nothing to do with me. I just would hate for you to throw away all these years of training. It's so rare, what you have. A proper talent. Most kids would kill for it.'

'Well, they can have it,' Aiden says, sharply. 'Because I'm done with it.'

He stands up, shoving the toilet paper into the loo.

'And whatever you say, you'll never change my mind.'

July 2017

Clara

You write well, but I'm afraid that the market for this kind of book is incredibly small, and therefore it's not something I would be able to take on.

Wishing you the best of luck in your writing.

Clara puts an X in the Rejection column of her spreadsheet. It's her first, and it's come so quickly, she's stunned.

She knows what her writing group would say – that it's not a bad rejection, that she shouldn't be disheartened. Any personal feedback should be considered a success.

But even so. She hadn't expected it to sting so much.

She closes the lid of her laptop and pads down the stairs. Thom is in the living room, watching the rugby.

'Are they winning?' she says, squinting at the score on the screen. Thom pauses the channel and looks up at her.

'Are you OK?' he says. 'You look sad.'

'I got a rejection,' she says. 'For the book.'

'On a Saturday?' he says, surprised.

She nods. It's lovely, how supportive Thom is, but at the same time she hates it. The fact that someone else knows about her ambition, her desire to have a book published. Now she's finally on submission to agents, it makes her feel exposed and vulnerable.

'I'm sorry,' he says. 'But that's normal, right? That girl in your group – the one that got the book deal – how many rejections did she get in the end?'

'Nineteen,' she replies.

'There you are then. One step closer to the yes.'

She smiles, for him.

'What would you like for supper?' she says. 'I think we have some chicken in the fridge…'

'We're meant to be going out for dinner, to celebrate my new commission. Remember? I did say. Yesterday.'

She's forgotten, of course.

'Oh god, sorry. It completely slipped my mind.'

'It's fine,' he says. 'I booked a table at the curry house.'

He turns back to the TV, shifting in his seat, a hand rubbing at the base of his spine. They have had three different sofas since his accident, but he is yet to find one comfortable.

'There's just half an hour left of this, then we'll go, yes? And we can drown your sorrows and celebrate at the same time?'

She nods. She feels like a small, useless child.

She can't forget the expression on his face when he told her about Rory and Abigail's new baby a few days earlier. The longing in his eyes, the way he swallowed it.

And his reaction when he found out Lauren was having twins. 'How amazing for them,' he said, as though he really meant it.

She knows what he wants. A family. A proper family. Someone to love him as much as he loves them.

That's all Thom has ever wanted. To be loved. *Really* loved.

And what does she want?

She wants to be nineteen again, lying on Hampstead Heath with the man who made her feel truly alive. Who looked at her in a way that made her feel deeply seen.

She goes back upstairs and stares at herself in the bathroom mirror. She can no longer find a trace of the girl she once was. The one who arrived at university filled with a nervous energy that felt like it held all the power in the world.

The energy has all been used up. And on what? On living this non-life, this pointless existence.

Her real life, the life she thought she'd lead, ended one night all those years ago – because of a miscommunication, because of youth, because of a gap between two people that was closing naturally (and closing so perfectly, that was the tragedy of it!) – but that didn't close fast enough.

She can't do it any more. It's not fair to Thom.

She ties her hair back into a ponytail and goes back downstairs.

'Thom,' she says, and he waves a hand behind his back, shushing her. She looks at the TV screen. The burly men roaring up and down the rugby pitch.

'Thom,' she says, again, louder this time.

'There's not long left,' he says, but he's still facing the screen.

She can't stand it. She can't stand it a second longer.

She marches towards him, picks up the remote and turns the television off.

'Thom,' she says again, as he stares at her in confusion. 'I think we should get a divorce.'

His eyebrows twist and then he laughs.

'I'm serious,' she says, the words tumbling out. 'I'm so sorry. But I can't do it any more. Knowing what you really want – the one thing you really want – is something I can never give you. It's not fair on you and it's not fair on me and I'm going to be the strong one here, the brave one, who finally says it out loud because otherwise we'll just carry on like this for the rest of our lives until we're dead. And one day you'll look back and wonder what happened to all the dreams you had and the vision of the life you wanted to live and how you ended up miserable and resentful instead, with a wife who failed you, and I don't want that to be my fault.'

She can hardly bear the sadness that passes over his eyes as he takes in her words. She knows he will feel as though she's abandoning him, just like his parents did.

She kneels before him and takes his head in her hands. She kisses his forehead, breathing in the comforting, familiar scent of his shampoo, and realises she is crying.

'I'm sorry, Thom,' she says, unable to stem the tide of tears. 'I'm sorry.'

He pushes her away, and stands, wincing with the pain in his back he always feels now. He shakes his head at her. Gives a confused laugh.

'I don't understand,' he says. 'Is there…'

She sees the possibility strike him, as painful as a knife to the chest.

'… someone else?'

'No,' she says, shaking her head. *Only the person that was always there.* 'No, no, no.'

'Then what?'

He's crying too, now, and she feels like she might vomit with the weight of it.

'I told you. I can't do it any more,' she says. 'I love you too much.'

He frowns then, a spark of anger rising.

'What are you talking about? I don't understand.'

'You want a baby,' she shouts, the release a relief. 'Just be honest! You want a baby, and I can't give you one because I can't... *you know*, and I'm wasting your time – wasting your life – and I can't... I can't cope with the guilt, the feeling that I'm letting you down all the time. It's exhausting.'

She closes her eyes.

'Is that how I've made you feel?' he says, through his tears. 'That you're letting me down?'

'No!' she says. 'No, it's how *I'm* making me feel.'

'I love you, Clara,' he says and his face is red with the effort of holding back his tears. Thom doesn't cry. He's not a crier. It's excruciating to watch him now. 'I love you and I love us. I love our life.'

'But you want a baby. Admit it.'

'I want you,' he says, his bottom lip trembling. 'That's all I want. We have a good life, don't we? Nobody's marriage is perfect. But we love each other. You're my best friend. For fuck's sake, Clara. Don't give up... don't give up on us.'

'You're my best friend, too,' she concedes.

'Well, then. And I'm not exactly a great catch, with my work and my stupid back.'

She sees now, perhaps for the first time, that he is vulnerable, too. That he also sees himself as second-rate, a disappointment.

'Your back isn't your fault.'

He takes a deep breath.

'And neither are your feelings about sex.'

The word is like a firecracker going off in their living room. She feels winded. All she can do is stare at him.

'I know something happened to you at university, Clara. Somebody took advantage of you, and it's not your fault. I know you don't want to talk about it, but I *know*. And do you think I don't care? Do you think I'm so selfish that I would rather be without you, just because of that?'

'No,' she says. 'I…'

'We're both damaged, aren't we? Me with my back. You with whatever it was that hurt you, all those years ago. Our life isn't perfect, but it's ours. And if you think I'd prefer to throw it away, just so that I can get laid twice a week with someone else, then you're wrong. You're completely wrong.'

July 2017

Benjamin

The next morning Aiden is still in his room at 10 a.m. Benjamin knocks softly on the door on three separate occasions but, when his knocks go unanswered, he decides not to disturb him.

'He'll come out when he's ready,' George says. He's out in the garden, pruning the roses that Benjamin's mother planted before she died.

'It's not like him,' Benjamin says.

'He'll have had a row with one of the other lads,' George replies, putting down his secateurs. 'It'll blow over.'

'I don't know,' he says. 'It felt like he meant it.'

'He's nearly a teenager,' George says. 'You don't remember what it's like, but I do.'

There's a sound from inside the house and George and Benjamin both turn towards it. Beyond the glazed sliding door they can see Aiden standing in the centre of the living room, in his pants.

Benjamin goes inside.

'Hello son,' he says. 'Are you feeling better? I'll get you some breakfast. Grandad's doing a barbecue for lunch seeing as it's nice.'

Aiden nods. His eyes are puffy, as though he's spent the night crying.

'Want a cuppa?'

He nods again and follows Benjamin through to the kitchen. They stand in silence as the kettle boils.

'Listen,' Benjamin says, eventually. 'I don't want to put any pressure on, you know. But if you want to talk about what happened, I'm here. I'm your dad. I know I'm not up to much but...'

He looks up at Aiden. His eyes are red again.

'You're the best dad there is,' Aiden says, sniffing. He rubs at his eyebrow. 'But I don't have anything to tell you. I've made my decision. I want to give up the training and concentrate on my schoolwork. I want to go to university like you and make something of my life.'

There's a painful pause as they both try to ignore the loaded meaning behind this last sentence. What has Benjamin made of his life, if not a total mess?

'Aid, that's grand but...'

'Dad, I said, I don't want to talk about it. It's done.'

'Well, it's not done,' Benjamin says, suddenly feeling that irrational parental anger rise – the feeling that comes from knowing you can't control, protect, cage the person who means more to you than anything. That you do actually have to just sit back and let them make their own mistakes. You have to let them mess up their own lives, even though it's agony. 'I mean, you made a promise. To the team. To your coach. I'm not sure you can just walk out on it all.'

'There's a hundred other lads want my place on that team,' Aiden says, his face darkening. 'He'll probably have a new boy in my spot by now anyway.'

He pauses, looking past Benjamin's head and into the

garden. Benjamin watches his face intently, thinking of how it's changed over the years. How he's lost the chubby, freckly baby look and how his face has lengthened, his eyes widened somehow, his jaw become more defined. But underneath the threat of adulthood he is still just a boy. His boy. And Benjamin can tell that he is on the verge of tears.

Something has happened to make him feel this way.

He tries a different tactic.

'OK,' he says. 'I'll let you quit. But first of all, you have to tell me why.'

Aiden opens his mouth and pauses. Then he shakes his head.

'Man, I told you! I just don't want to do it any more.'

The trouble is, Aiden is too much like Benjamin. And so, Benjamin knows that his son is doing exactly what he did, all those years ago. Taking a bad thing and burying it, somewhere deep inside himself, somewhere no one else can ever reach.

But Benjamin also knows that whatever it is, it will eat away at him. It will grow into a festering cancer, slowly turning him inside out.

He's meant to be going to see Emily's mother this afternoon. It's her birthday and Emily wanted to introduce them to each other. But he can't face it.

He texts her an apology. She's understanding – too understanding. He doesn't deserve her.

Instead, Benjamin goes for a long walk across the moors behind their house. Alone. The wind gets up later on and the sun disappears behind a cloud and he feels chilly, so he walks faster until he is marching, panting. Thinking of a way, any way, to break through Aiden's shell.

Trying to work out what it would have taken all those years

ago for him to have told Clara the truth: that he disappeared for three weeks because his mother was dying.

Why had it felt so difficult to tell her such a simple thing? What was it he was so afraid of?

The thought of being pitied. The thought of being seen differently. As a victim, rather than a hero.

He already saw himself as beneath his fellow students, inadequate by comparison. And this was another thing he didn't want to have stuck on him like a label.

The kid whose mother died of cancer when he was just nineteen. As fates go, it wasn't the worst. Some kids lose both parents before they turn nineteen. Aiden – for all intents and purposes – lost his mam at just seven. Benjamin had almost two decades with his mam. His wonderful mam, who meant the world to him.

So why did he hate the thought of talking about her? In prison, he spoke to a counsellor who said that maybe telling other people made it seem real. But that was bullshit. Because it was real every day to him. Every day that he woke up and remembered his mother was no longer there.

He remembers when he finally told Clara the truth. It was over the summer between their first and second years.

It was a Saturday and they were at their favourite place – Hampstead Heath – lying side by side in the sun.

'You never talk about your mother,' she said, and he immediately felt himself tensing.

'What do you want to know?'

'Well, I know that she's no longer with us,' she said, and he heard a tremble in her voice. She knew, instinctively, that it was unstable ground. She knew so much about him without him even having to say it. It was one of the things he loved about her.

'She was the best mam,' he said, because that was safest. To just focus on the positives.

'I know,' Clara said.

'How?'

'Because of the way you are. Because you can only be the way you are because someone really loved you.'

He considered this.

'People love you too, Clara,' he said. 'Your parents. Me.'

She took a deep breath.

'Yes,' she conceded. 'And *I* am the way I am, in spite of their love. But still. What happened to her? Why do you never talk about her?'

'Because...' he began. 'Because it's too sad and it hurts too much.'

He immediately regretted it. It felt like he had split himself open, and Clara, no matter how much she loved him, would inevitably want to poke around to see what was inside, no matter how sore it made him.

But she didn't say anything for a while.

Then: 'I'm sorry.'

'It's OK,' he said, the anxiety passing. 'She would have loved you. I told her about you, in fact, right before...'

It was a slip, a careless slip. Before he knew what was happening, Clara was up on her elbows.

'You told her about me?' she said, the confusion distorting her beautiful face. 'When? I thought... I thought she died years ago?'

He closed his eyes.

'Benjamin!' she squeaked. 'Talk to me. What the hell? When... when did she die?'

He opened his eyes and saw that she was crying. Her hand shook as she wiped away the tears from her nose.

'I'm sorry,' he said. 'She died in April. I didn't feel ready to...'

She pulled away from him.

'At Easter?' she said, frowning. 'When you disappeared?'

He nodded. 'She had been sick for a long time. Years.'

'Why the... why didn't you tell me?'

She was practically shouting at him now. He didn't understand the ferocity of the anger but, in a way, he was glad of it, because it stopped him having to think – or talk – about his own feelings, which were too painful and which he preferred to keep buried.

This was much better. He could do this. He could fight about this because it would be a welcome distraction.

'I just... we'd just met. I thought it was a bit too much to deal with, given we'd only been dating a few weeks.'

'It makes sense now!' Her voice was still raised and she was barely even looking at him. 'Your disappearing act! I thought... I don't know what I thought but why... why the hell didn't you say why you had to go home? I thought you'd got some other girlfriend or something – someone from home you had to finish with...'

'What?' he said, genuinely shocked. 'No, not at all. I told you...'

'But you were so weird when we met. You didn't want to sleep with me. I practically had to force you into it, and then you disappeared without a word and then when you came back everything was different.'

'I just liked you,' he said, quietly. 'And, well, it was difficult at home. With my dad. He wasn't good in the early days. He didn't cope well with losing her. Jesus. You thought I had another girlfriend? Really?'

'I don't know,' she said, miserably. 'It just didn't make sense.

But your mum – your mum was dying and you didn't tell me! What about the funeral? When was that?'

'While I was away,' he said. 'It all happened while I was away. I came back and I just wanted to put it all behind me. I'm sorry.'

He wasn't sure whether he was actually sorry, but he learnt a long time ago the power of those words to appease and to soothe.

She took a deep breath and her face softened.

'No,' she said. '*I'm* sorry. I'm sorry I never realised. I should have worked it out. I should have asked more questions.'

'Clara,' he said. 'What's done is done. And all I can say is thank you. For the last six months. Because you... you have been everything to me. I know, I'm awkward and I don't like talking about this stuff, but without you, I don't know what would have happened. How I would have dealt with everything. But you gave me something to look forward to. A reason to keep going. It felt...'

He paused, aware his cheeks were burning. It was like ripping himself raw. But it needed to be said. She deserved to hear it.

'It felt sometimes as though my mam had planned it somehow. Us meeting. That she was looking over us both, making sure I was OK. It was fate, wasn't it? We'd already seen each other once, and then we met again... I thought it was my mam's way of ensuring I'd be taken care of once she was gone. I know it sounds daft. But that's why I know that we'll love each other forever. And that I can cope with anything, so long as I have you.'

He felt winded after this speech, as though he'd run a mile at full speed.

He looked up at her, hoping to see understanding shining

back through her eyes, but there was something else there instead.

Something he couldn't interpret. Something that scared him.

Something that didn't make sense. He frowned, examined it more closely.

It looked like guilt.

July 2017

Clara

When she wakes up the next morning, it takes a few moments to figure out why her head is pounding. And then, of course, it all comes back. What she said.

They didn't make it out for the celebration dinner.

Thom is sitting up in the bed next to her now. He hands her a mug of tea.

'How are you feeling?' he says, softly.

'Awful,' she says. 'My head is killing me.'

A hangover from all the tears shed.

'Me too.'

He takes her hand, squeezes it between his.

'I've been awake all night. But I thought of something,' he says, his voice still gentle.

She takes a sip of her tea, enjoys the way it burns the insides of her cheeks.

'Yes?'

'What you said about children, yesterday. You never told me you wanted them,' he says. 'I didn't realise it was on your mind.'

Is that what she said? Does she want children?

The only time she's ever imagined it for herself was in the second year at university, when she and Benjamin discussed how many they would have, and what their names would be. It was such a vivid conversation, she found herself reliving it in her dreams, years later.

Somehow, it seemed unimaginable after that – the thought that she would have a child with anyone else.

But now she examines the possibility again. Having children. That's what people do, isn't it? They have children and then they don't have time to worry about their own selfish stupidity any more. It's altruism but not really. It's an escape. Nature's clever way of breaking up your life, so that it isn't one long monotonous slog of disappointment and failed goals.

Perhaps that's where she's been going wrong.

Thom is still speaking.

'I thought – well, we can go to a clinic.'

'Thom,' she says. 'That's a huge thing.'

'I know. But I didn't realise. Christ! I wish you had spoken to me about it before. I wish you had just trusted me.'

He looks at her, biting his lip. His eyebrows are lifted, as though he's trying to express something through them.

The promise that she can trust him.

He's trying, as he always does. He's trying so hard.

But his trying is so trying.

She understands now: she's a challenge to him, and perhaps that's why he stays. Because he still hasn't figured her out. He still hasn't solved the Puzzle of Her.

He has a new energy about him this morning, and she realises that what she did last night has upped the ante. Made her even more of a challenge.

Thom loves her more this morning than he did yesterday,

and it seems so ridiculous that the universe always so strongly objects to her ideas about how things should be that she decides, yet again, to give in to it.

'You know, you're a pretty amazing wife, the way you put up with me.'

'There's nothing to put up with,' she says, but then she thinks about his chronic pain, the fact it makes him grumpy and difficult. Constantly having to cancel plans because of debilitating flare-ups. No more long walks in Hyde Park. No more last-minute adventures. Just sitting around at home, getting older, waiting to die.

It *is* hard. Seeing him in so much agony and not being able to help.

They are co-dependent.

'Of course there is,' he says, as if reading her mind. 'I know what I'm like, Clara. With my back. And my stupid job. Flying all around the world and leaving you alone all the time. Coming home late when I get obsessed with a piece I'm making... not many wives would put up with that. I think sometimes you just need to give yourself more credit. You obsess about the things you don't do, rather than focusing on all the things you do. I love you, you know.'

She doesn't say it back to him, but instead she reaches out a hand and takes his again.

He has caught her, but it's OK. She's back in his safety net. She was never strong enough to break out of it.

He knows what's best for her. What's best for them both.

'OK. Let's go to a clinic,' she says. She tries to put the image of Benjamin out of her mind, the pathetic childish picture of the two kids they imagined they would have one day. A boy like him, and a girl like her.

It's time to grow up. To accept that her life, though not what she imagined, is rich, and worth living.

Her heart lifts a little. Perhaps this will be the answer, after all.

'Let's see if we can have a baby,' she says. 'Somehow.'

July 2017

Benjamin

It's been a fortnight now and, no matter how hard he has tried, he can't persuade Aiden to go back to football training.

An hour ago, Coach Kenny actually rang him.

'The other lads say he must be sick,' Coach Kenny said.

'I don't know what the issue is,' Benjamin replied. 'I can't get any sense out of him.'

'There are plenty of other boys that will fill his boots. You tell him that from me. I haven't got time to play games. If he's not back by the weekend, then he's out.'

'I'll talk to him again,' Benjamin said. 'I'm sorry.'

'I've done a lot for that lad.' Coach Kenny's voice was low, gnarly. 'This is not how I expect to be repaid.'

It sounded a bit like a threat. Benjamin hung up and went upstairs to Aiden's room.

He was lying on the bed, playing his Xbox.

'Turn it off, man,' Benjamin snaps.

Aiden rolled his eyes.

'That was your coach,' Benjamin said. 'He's not going to hold your place any longer. You have to be back at training on Saturday.'

Aiden blinked at him and then switched the game back on.

Benjamin took a deep breath. For a minute he felt like losing his temper. Properly shouting at his son. But something told him not to.

'Fine,' Benjamin said, picking up a plate full of toast crumbs from beside the bed. 'But quitting the team is a big decision. Just remember that. Once you make it, you can't go back.'

He closes the door behind him and pauses in the hall, wondering, agonising over as ever, whether or not he has done the right thing. Not for the first time, he wishes his mam was still alive. She would know what to do.

After a few minutes spent staring out of the small circular window at the top of the stairs, holding the plate with the crumbs on, he hears the sound of the Xbox being switched off. And then, his son's voice, low and furtive, on the phone to someone.

He freezes. He shouldn't be doing this. He shouldn't be eavesdropping, and yet it feels like child protection or something. Someone has done something to his son, and he needs to find out what it was.

'My dad just had a call from Coach,' Aiden is saying. Benjamin risks a step closer to the door.

'Nah, well he can forget it.'

There's another pause.

'It's not right. I don't like it. You don't have to... well, maybe I don't want it as much as you. All right? Maybe I just don't want it enough!'

It takes everything in Benjamin's power not to burst into the room and ask Aiden what he's talking about. But he resists.

And then an hour later, Aiden comes back down.

'I've made a decision,' he says. 'I'll go back to training.'

Benjamin tries to smile, but his face is stuck. This is good news, what they all wanted, but there's something in his son's eyes he doesn't like.

Resignation. Disappointment. Fear.

'Are you sure?'

'Yeah,' he says.

'Will you tell me now, then? What it was that was upsetting you?'

Aiden lingers in the doorway, cocks his head to one side. He opens his mouth as if to speak, closes it again.

'I just don't like all the drinking,' he says, eventually. 'It's stupid.'

Benjamin exhales. *Of course.*

'Look what it did to my mam. I don't understand why they all have to get so mortal all the time. Jonny was so out of it that night at Coach's, he wet himself. It's messed up.'

Benjamin closes his eyes. Aiden's only twelve. How could he have been so stupid, not to see the long shadow that Zoe's drinking would cast on his son?

'I get it,' he says, shaking his head at his own stupidity. 'I'm so sorry, champ.'

'It's moronic,' Aiden says, suddenly more animated than he has been in days. 'What's great about drinking so much you piss yourself? Or puke all over your shoes?'

He sounds like Clara. They were both right. And he's been blind to it. It was the same when he was a kid, so he just accepted it. The drinking culture came with the game.

But he should have said something to the coach. He should have protected his son.

'Nothing,' Benjamin replies. 'There's nothing great about it. You're completely right. I'll talk to your coach.'

He's so relieved that it's that. And not something else. Not something worse. His son is so clever. So sensible and strong.

'And is that it?'

'Yes. Will you drop me in the morning?'

'Of course,' Benjamin says, standing up and pulling his little boy – who suddenly seems anything but little – towards him in a hug. He's relieved, but at the same time a small voice whispers that Aiden is still keeping something from him. 'But only if you're sure. I don't want to put any pressure on you.'

'God,' Aiden says, pulling away and rolling his eyes. 'Make your mind up.'

And then he turns and goes into the garden, scooping up his ball and kneeing it in the air.

Benjamin goes to Emily's tiny flat on the seafront that evening. She's made an effort: cooked him dinner, got some beer in especially. She doesn't drink. She's the only northern woman he's ever met who doesn't. It's good for him, it makes him drink less.

He remembers the judge's words at his sentencing. Rather than excusing him, the fact he was drunk was taken as an aggravating factor. It was the reason his sentence was longer than it otherwise might have been.

'You're still worried about Aiden,' she says, as they finish their meals.

'I just don't think he's telling me everything. I get that he doesn't like the drinking culture...'

Emily gives him a look. Of course, she feels the same.

'But he's seen people pissed before, at the games. And he's never said anything about it. I'm worried that he's missing his mother. I mean, god, it's been more than four years since he saw her.'

'Has he ever mentioned her to you? Said he wants to reconnect?'

He shakes his head.

'No.'

'He's a canny lad. He'll tell you, if you don't push it. Give him a bit of space. He'll open up in the end. It's good that he decided to go back, anyway, isn't it? Shows it can't have been anything too serious?'

He frowns.

'Maybe. I guess. But he didn't exactly look happy about it.'

'It'll be the other lads. They can be brutal to anyone who goes against the grain. Has he been bullied before?'

'No,' he says. He thinks of Aiden's charm, the way he's carried himself through life so far with such poise, instinctively knowing how to behave to win people over. He has no idea where he gets that skill from. 'I don't think so anyway. He's never mentioned anything. He's always had tons of friends.'

Emily takes a sip of her water.

'Well, I suppose it's different with football, isn't it? They're all friends but they're also in competition with each other. Aren't they?'

'Yes. In a way. Although they're meant to be a team. I mean, that's a huge part of the whole sport.'

'Yes, but think about it. He's coming up for thirteen, right? All those hormones flying around?'

He smiles. She's trying, but it's not working. He knows his own son, more intimately than he knows anyone. He knows when something isn't right.

'Perhaps it's a girl?' she says, cutting through his thoughts. 'Perhaps he's met a girl and he wants to spend more time with her. Perhaps she's been having a go at him for neglecting her and putting football first?'

It's like a punch to the stomach, a reminder of how Clara used to accuse him of loving football more than he loved her. It was ridiculous and stupid, and, in a roundabout way, it led to the situation that took his life on a completely different trajectory.

For Aiden's sake, he hopes it isn't that.

'Would you like me to ask him?' Emily says. 'I can talk to him if you like? We get on really well. In fact, I was going to ask...'

Her cheeks turn pink and she takes another sip of her drink, then clears her throat.

'I thought, maybe, well, my contract is coming up on this place and I wondered if you both...'

He stares at her, nervous about what she'll say next.

'I know it's early days,' she continues, 'but you know how I feel about you, Benjamin. You know how much I love you. I wondered if perhaps it might be a good idea for us to...' She swallows. 'Get a place together? Somewhere bigger? Just the three of us? What do you think?'

He's so taken aback by this suggestion – one that on the surface is completely reasonable and understandable, but is also so far from anything he has ever considered.

'Forget it,' she says, seeing the look on his face. 'It doesn't matter. It's too soon, I get it. It's only cos of the flat thing... I have to say whether or not I want to stay for another year, but perhaps I'll ask my landlord if I could go on a rolling contract or something? I'm sure that would be fine.'

'No,' he says. She's wilting in front of him, visibly collapsing, and it's all his fault. Another heart broken by his inadequacy. 'No! I would like that. I just wasn't thinking, I'm sorry. You caught me by surprise. I just need to wrap my thick head around it.'

'Absolutely,' she says, perking up again. 'Absolutely. I don't want to put any pressure on you. Especially not with... well, your dad, too.'

His dad.

How could he do it? How could he go home tomorrow and tell his dad that he is moving out and taking Aiden with him? He might as well go home and shoot him in the head.

'It's just... my dad's very...'

How can he explain what it means for George to have a hand in raising his grandson, the purpose it gives to his days?

But more than that, Benjamin is worried about him, his frailty. George has been ageing – tiny microscopic shifts every day that will eventually lead to full-scale collapse. He cannot imagine losing his father. Not now. Not ever.

'He loves having Aid around. That's all. I just don't want to upset him.'

As always, he is damned. Doomed to upset one person or the other.

Rock and a hard place, his perpetual home.

'Of course,' she says. 'I wondered if perhaps he wanted a bit of peace in his old age, but of course.' She laughs, at herself. 'Stupid of me. Of course, he loves having you boys around.'

He knows George wouldn't want him to put his life on hold, and he knows that George likes Emily. But it feels like Benjamin's duty: to look after his father, who's alone and old, for the rest of George's life.

He has never thought about leaving. He knows George is happy to have them there, too. He has never once encouraged them to move out – not after Benjamin was promoted to manager at the bar, not even after he started picking up bits of freelance film work. But how can he ask Emily to continue in a relationship, when he has no intention of ever truly moving forward?

He can imagine now what George would say if he went home and told him that he was planning to move in with Emily, that he was taking Aiden with him.

He would smile and say, *Good idea, she's a lovely lass*, but he would also be sad, and he'd try to hide it.

'I'll think about it. It would be grand,' Benjamin says. 'But it's a big decision. Let's give it some more thought. Now, what film would you like to watch tonight?'

February 2018

Clara

She has defied the odds at the IVF clinic. Her consultant is baffled.

'I'm very sorry,' he says. 'These things are sadly not as clear-cut as we would like.'

Her eggs and his sperm do not want to mix. They have tried three rounds now. The first time, they did conventional IVF – and the sperm in the dish just swam around her egg, ignoring it. Almost as though they were repelled by it.

The second and third times they tried a more complicated procedure, where the very best sperm was chosen by experts, and then injected directly into the egg.

Forced in, like an invader.

Those eggs failed to develop, as though they had been poisoned.

If it wasn't so tragic, it would make her laugh.

'Of course, there's no reason why we can't try again, but I do understand that this will be a very disappointing result for you.'

She glances over at Thom. His mouth is set in a line, in the way it does when he receives information he doesn't like.

'What's the next step then?' he says, his voice flat.

'Well, as I said, we can try again, or perhaps we can investigate some other options?'

She zones out while the consultant discusses using donor eggs or sperm. She can only think that this is a sign.

That she and Thom are not meant to reproduce.

They were not meant to reproduce naturally, and they can't force it. They can't override the power of nature, no matter how much money or medical treatments they throw at the issue.

She's been talking to Lauren about it lately. Lauren with her six-month-old twins, who often calls her in tears, half-jokingly offering her one of them for free.

Solve both our problems in one go. How about it? You can have Sammy, the little shit! I gave birth to them so I deserve to keep the easy one.

But after six years, Lauren has run out of patience for her situation with Thom.

For Christ's sake Clara. Just leave him. I don't understand why you stay when you're clearly not happy.

Have you ever thought that the reason you don't want to have sex with him is because you don't actually fancy him?

As Thom kisses her on the cheek outside the IVF clinic and marches in the opposite direction, back to the Tube and his jewellery shop, she lingers for a while on the pavement.

She doesn't have a shift at the newspaper today. She should really go back home and work on her book, but the IVF stuff is hard to put away, and so she decides to head to the nearest coffee shop and really think about what she should do next.

'A latte please,' she says to the lady behind the counter. She eyes the cakes in their glass domes. 'And a carrot cake.'

She takes her coffee and cake to the last remaining table by the window and sits down, watching the world go by.

On the surface of it, she and Thom are good together. They rarely argue. They laugh, sometimes, about silly things on television. They talk about politics, and are broadly in agreement on all the main topics. Her family loves him. His family find her pleasant enough. They have the same taste in films. They both love being outdoors, walking for hours in Hyde Park when his pain isn't so bad, discussing the ins and outs of all the people they know.

She finds his work genuinely interesting, and he respects her opinion on his designs.

They are the best of friends. But he is not The One.

And she doesn't want to have a child with him. She knows that now, with a certainty that surprises her.

From nowhere, she starts to cry. Just gentle tears, an exhalation of the desperation she feels.

She misses Benjamin more than ever. It's a visceral ache, a physical pain. Yet it's been fifteen years since they were last together. It's insanity to long for him still.

She pulls out her phone and searches online for him, as she has done so many times, but there's nothing to be found.

Like an addict in search of a hit, she opens her old Hotmail account – one she hasn't used for years – and reads over their emails to each other. Back in the early days, when she had to queue for the computers in the university library in order to be able to send one.

There are hundreds. They sent each other emails every day for the entire time they were together. Even though they spent every night in each other's arms. Somehow, there was still so much to say.

Hers were great long diatribes. His were short and sweet and full of spelling mistakes.

She clicks on one at random.

I don't know where to go from here. Of course, I want to see you but I dont think its unreasonable to want to spend some time with my flatmates too. No, Tina won't be there. Shes gone home for the weekend. But even if she was going to be there, NOTHING HAPPENED. She's just a friend.

I don't know what to say. Im sorry that I like football. I'm sorry that i like watching it with my friends. Im sorry that you hate it so much.

I love you but this is tearing us apart.

YOUR

BE

Even though she has reread these emails from time to time over the years, it's a shock to read this one now and remember how unreasonable she was. How jealous and mistrustful.

But it wasn't just her insecurities that made her resent his time spent at the pub. It was the culture that surrounded it. The drinking until they couldn't stand up. The heckling and shouting and pissing in the street.

It is disgusting, animal behaviour. And it wasn't how she saw him. Her Benjamin.

When he was sober, he was like a different person, but he didn't seem to understand that. There were two sides to him: the wonderful, caring boy she fell in love with, and the drunk idiot she crossed the street to avoid. It was as though alcohol changed him into someone unrecognisable. Someone who couldn't control himself.

But it wasn't just him, and she knew it. Everyone did it, not just football fans. Everyone thought it was funny to down so many pints you found yourself vomiting into the gutter at 1 a.m. They were at university. They were having fun. It was part of the *experience*.

And she hadn't been immune to it herself. She had drunk until she puked with the rest of them. And when she did, he would take care of her. Not berate her.

So, she was a hypocrite.

She wonders what university life is like now. Do people still behave the same? Is drinking culture still ingrained into the experience as much as essays and lectures? She thinks about the zeitgeist obsession with wellness and hopes things have changed.

She clicks on her reply to that email.

I'm sorry that you don't love me more than you love getting pissed with your mates.

I would do anything for you. I would give up anything for you.

You are the most important thing to me.

I guess we are just different. I guess I just love you more than you love me. Not your fault. But lucky you, eh?

She closes her eyes, feeling her cheeks flush. God, she was so intense. She was so demanding and unwavering. She was so young.

And where had it come from? This deep-seated mistrust of him? From her stupid experience with Daniel?

From the fact that he had gone home when his mother was dying, and not told her what was happening?

Or from the knowledge that while he was there, she had slept with someone else? Pathetic one-upmanship that she would regret for the rest of her life.

Poor Benjamin. He never stood a chance.

February 2018

Benjamin

Benjamin is early to collect Aiden from training. He usually sits in the car, but today he decides to get out and watch as they finish up.

They are on the pitch, practising dribbling drills. It's raining and miserable. Benjamin pulls his hood up.

Coach Kenny is showing the boys how to dribble round the cones, keeping control of the ball at all times. The pitch is a sea of brown beneath their feet.

Benjamin remembers it well, feeling like he'd been marinated in mud and sweat by the end of a session.

One of the boys slips and falls and the coach rounds on him.

'Get up, you pussy!'

The boy rolls over.

'I can't hear you!' Kenny shouts.

He gets to his feet.

'Sorry Coach,' he mutters. Benjamin can see he's trying not to cry.

'Aye, sorry you are. Sorry you will be. Back to the start.'

The boy starts the exercise again, his cheeks puffed out and red.

Benjamin swallows. The beautiful game is as brutal as ever.

But then, life is brutal, and you need to be prepared for it. Benjamin's coach used to deck them if they did something wrong, and no one batted an eyelid. At least things have improved a little since then.

The coach blows his whistle and the boys stop and gather in a line. Muddy soldiers, red-cheeked and panting.

Benjamin looks at Aiden. His face is blank, staring at some indistinct spot in front of him.

Coach Kenny walks along the line, untucking shirts and even leaning down to pull up socks. He stops in front of the shortest boy. Benjamin hasn't seen him before. He looks so young. He's literally shaking in his boots.

Coach Kenny stands so close to him their noses almost touch.

'So, you want to play for England one day?'

'Aye Coach Kenny.'

'Better grow a pair then,' he says, looking down as he snaps the waistband of the boy's shorts.

Someone titters.

Gary, Aiden's mate, with the quick-fisted father. Though they haven't hung out much recently, Benjamin realises. He wonders what they've fallen out over. The parties at Coach's house, perhaps. Aiden told him that Gary goes to them regularly.

Benjamin still feels as though he never got to the bottom of what upset Aiden that evening.

Coach Kenny dismisses the boys with a wave of his hand, and the line breaks up.

Benjamin hangs back, watching, as the boys make their way to the concrete changing room. They're chatting happily, slapping each other on the back. One of the taller boys even puts his arm around the young lad Kenny made fun of.

But Aiden is left out of this camaraderie. He walks slowly

behind them all, his head down, and disappears into the changing room.

'Edwards?'

Benjamin looks up. Coach Kenny has spotted him and is now striding in his direction.

'Hi,' Benjamin says, as the coach swipes a forearm across his sweaty forehead.

'Problem?' Coach Kenny asks. He's panting slightly.

'I wanted to talk to you. About the parties at your place.'

He swallows, feeling ridiculously nervous. It's like he's twelve again himself, trying to stand up to his own coach.

'Specifically, the drinking.'

Coach Kenny's cheeks are covered with broken veins, his nose a patchwork of open pores. He lets out a great huff.

'The older ones get *one tin* if they've played well that day,' he says. 'One tin each. Put some hairs on their chests. It's nothing. Just a treat.'

'Aiden's only twelve.'

Benjamin tries to hold his nerve. He knows Kenny is lying – one can of lager wouldn't get a fifteen-year-old boy so drunk he wet himself.

'Aye, well that's as maybe. But he's only been to mine once, and he wasn't drinking, was he? So. There you go. Case closed, your honour.'

He gives a caustic laugh.

Benjamin frowns.

'You know, he's one of the best in the team,' Coach says. 'Just a shame he's so uptight.'

'He's a child,' Benjamin says firmly.

Coach Kenny holds his stare. 'Don't underestimate him.'

Benjamin's about to ask him what he means by this, when Gary appears.

'Ready, Coach?' Gary asks and the coach turns round.

'Aye,' he says, putting his arm around Gary as they walk away.

Benjamin stands there, watching as they leave together, Coach ruffling Gary's hair and laughing.

'Dad?'

Aiden is in front of him. Cross.

'What are you doing here? Why didn't you wait in the car?'

'I wanted to see how your training was going,' Benjamin says.

'It's fine. Howay man, let's go.'

Aiden stalks off ahead of him towards the small car park.

'Hey! How come Gary has gone off with the coach?' Benjamin asks, jogging to catch him up. 'Another party?'

Aiden shrugs.

As they drive home, Benjamin turns over what the coach said about Aiden being uptight.

'Coach Kenny's a bit of an arse, isn't he?' Benjamin asks, tentatively.

Aiden scoffs.

'He said you're one of the best in the team. But if football isn't making you happy...'

'Jesus Christ, not this again,' Aiden snaps.

'Son, all I'm saying is if it's making you unhappy.'

'*You're* making me unhappy! Training is fine. Football is fine. Just leave me be, man.'

Benjamin does as he's told. What else can he do?

Aiden and Benjamin's relationship has been strained for three months now. Ever since he broke up with Emily. Aiden still hasn't forgiven him.

Benjamin watches him as he eats his dinner too quickly, then picks up the empty plate and flings it in the sink.

'Oi,' he says, angrily. 'You'll sit down with us until your grandfather has finished eating.'

Aiden rolls his eyes and plucks an apple from the fruit bowl, rubbing it on his jumper.

George looks up from his meal.

'Training tonight?' he asks.

'Yes Grandad.'

'How's it going?'

Aiden shrugs.

'Fine.'

George nods, as though this answer isn't completely unsatisfactory, and continues eating. Benjamin feels the frustration building in his chest.

'Look, if you've got something to say to me Aiden, just say it,' he says. 'We all have to live together. I can't be doing with any more of this attitude.'

'I don't have anything to say,' Aiden says.

'I know you miss Emily,' Benjamin replies. 'I do too, but...'

'What?'

'It was complicated.'

Aiden scoffs.

'Like it was with my mam?'

Benjamin stares at him in surprise.

'That was different and you know it.'

'Whatever. I really don't care. You can end up a lonely old twat if you want.'

'I'll not have you speaking to me like that. Get to your room.'

Aiden stomps off without even looking back. Perhaps it was a deliberate provocation – he wanted to be sent away. Lately, it feels as though he'd rather do anything than sit and eat a meal with them.

'I've fucked it all up,' Benjamin says, pushing away the rest of his dinner and giving a great sigh.

George looks at him.

'No,' he says. 'You did what you thought was right with Emily. He'll come to understand in time.'

'Just like I did what I thought was right all those years ago?' George looks at him with pity. 'He's not been the same, Dad, not since he had that break from training. I don't know what it is. You should have seen how the other lads were with him today at the club. It's like he wasn't even there.'

'You've got to stop all this. It's his age. You're overthinking it.'

But Benjamin can't stop. Something is different in his son. And it's not just hormones. He's not even a teenager yet.

But rather than fight, he takes a deep breath. He tries to trust his father.

'I hope you're right, Dad. I really do.'

part four

April 2022

Clara

Clara stares at Benjamin on the television screen. For a few moments, she can't think how to react.

And then he's gone, the camera turned back to the reporter, who's reading out the number of the helpline that people can call if they're worried about a relative.

She wishes she could rewind the programme to see Benjamin again, but the camera moves back to the news studio. It'll be on a cycle – breaking news – and they'll show that footage again, she knows, but not for at least ten minutes.

She can't ring him now. Not knowing that he is there, in the thick of it, living a nightmare.

At least she now knows he's alive.

But what about his son, Aiden?

She had no idea he had a son.

It shouldn't be a surprise to her that Benjamin has kept him a secret, because that's what he does. Keeps secrets.

Does this mean he's happily married? Living a normal life?

What would his wife be like? Someone with a similar background? Someone like Tina, who loved football and didn't nag him, or ask him to choose between them?

Is that why he didn't want to meet up with her when she suggested it all those years ago?

She starts to cry but more with fury than sadness. Has she spent all these years dreaming of a future that she'll never have?

That's it, then. Game over.

She will crawl into her bed now, and then tomorrow morning she'll wake up and put her clothes back on and get the first train home to London.

And then, she'll do something about her life. Her shadow of a marriage.

And perhaps, she'll write another book. The sequel to her first, now long abandoned.

A book about how you try to move on, when you've wasted your life imagining that your first love felt the same way about you as you did about them.

June 2002

Benjamin

'I can't believe we only have a week left of university,' Clara says, pulling her T-shirt back on. Her cheeks are pink. They have just had sex, and now she is late for her last ever study group.

'It's insane,' he agrees, staring at the ceiling.

'I can't wait to get out of this city and start living my life, properly,' she says, leaning over him as he lies back on her bed. Her hair is long now – she hasn't had it cut for more than a year – and it falls in front of her face, obscuring her eyes.

He tucks it behind her ears.

'Won't you miss it,' he says, 'just a little bit?'

She shakes her head slowly. He pulls her back down on top of him.

'Won't you miss...' he says, kissing her, 'this?'

'You'll make me late,' she squeaks, batting him away. 'I'll see you tonight.'

And then she is gone, and he's alone in her room. Just him and Leonardo DiCaprio.

He's finding his final year tough.

He's never been the brightest of students. One of his teachers at school said he might be dyslexic but nothing was ever done about it.

The technical part of his course comes relatively easily to him, but explaining his methodology he finds difficult.

He had to write two long pieces for his final project, outlining the process behind the digital game he has produced, and it had been a struggle.

'Will you read it over for me?' he asks her that evening, when she's sitting on the floor, propped up against the side of her bed, making notes from yet another eighteenth-century novel. Her last piece of coursework – she's finished her exams. She works hard, and is on track for a First. He wonders, sometimes, what will happen if she doesn't get one. How she will cope.

Sometimes, she wakes in the night hyperventilating at the thought of getting her results. She puts so much pressure on herself.

Now, she turns to look at him. Her long hair is scraped up in a pile on top of her head and she's wearing her glasses. She hates her glasses, but they suit her.

'What?'

'My Production Project.'

He swallows.

She closes the book.

'Wow,' she says, smiling. 'Of course. I'd love to.'

'I know you have a lot on yourself,' he says, nodding at the huge ring binder of meticulous handwritten notes next to her. 'So, you know, only if you have time.'

'Of course,' she says, and she leans over and kisses him. 'Of course I have time. I mean, I've finished this really. I'm just going over it again.'

He's so relieved that he properly relaxes for the first time in weeks and, before he knows what's happening, their books are on the floor in a pile beside the bed and they are making love again, and he closes his eyes and tries to imagine anything in the world feeling better than this moment. It's impossible.

This is it. The pinnacle. Downhill only from here.

Afterwards, they lie together, and she giggles about how she's messed up his hair and he thinks about the future, how in just a few months he'll be going home to his dad, and she'll be going to London and they'll be apart.

He has to get a strong mark in his degree. He knows how competitive the good jobs in London are, and he needs to move down there as soon as possible after finishing.

Before she meets someone else. Someone better than him.

It's only a matter of time. He's seen the way other men look at her. She is a prize, even if she doesn't realise it.

'What do you think will happen?' he says, quietly, stroking her hair as she leans against him.

'With what?'

'Us.'

'What do you mean?' she says. Her voice is tinged with irritation.

'I'm worried I won't find a job easily,' he says. 'And you'll be down there, meeting people on your journalism course, and I'll be stuck in the north trying to get interviews for jobs five hours away, and...'

'You could move down with me,' she says. 'My parents wouldn't mind. I'm sure they wouldn't. And once my course is done, I'll get a job and a flat, and we can move in together.'

'I can't,' he says. 'I can't live with your parents. It's not standing on my own two feet. I have to make my own way.'

'Well, then, get a room in a house share or something. That's what most people do, isn't it?'

313

'But without a job, I won't be able to afford it. It's chicken and egg.'

She falls silent.

'Yes, but it will work out. I just know it will. You and me – it's fate. We'll make it work somehow.'

He smiles and kisses her again.

'I hope you're right CDC,' he says. 'Because I can't picture my life without you. I really can't.'

'Well that's good,' she says. 'Because you won't ever have to.'

One week later, his final project has been handed in, and England are in the quarter-finals of the World Cup.

They beat Argentina, which was a miracle in itself. He can't believe it. It feels like the perfect end to their university year. Could the three lions really go all the way?

Benjamin was first amused, and then saddened by how annoyed Clara was when England qualified for the quarter-finals.

'Can't you even get behind your national team?' he asked her, bewildered, and she shook her head stubbornly, like a toddler.

'It's not like they ever actually win anything,' she said, and her pessimism irritated him. 'And I hate the way it takes over the country. You never hear them reporting on the arts on the six o'clock news!'

'Clara, man.' He only called her Clara when he was annoyed with her. She narrowed her eyes. 'Where's your sense of patriotism?'

'Patriotism is the virtue of the vicious,' she snapped back at him. 'Oscar Wilde.'

He shook his head, tried to swallow the lump in his throat, and changed the subject.

Over the past year, they have come to a compromise. When there's a football match on, he leaves his phone at home, and she does whatever she has to do to distract herself while he's just a few streets away.

And then he calls her the next day, once he's sobered up, and they pretend nothing has happened. She asks no questions, tries not to imagine what he has got up to the night before.

He swears that he doesn't 'get up to' anything other than drinking with his friends, but even that, for some reason, she finds intolerable.

It makes him sad, but he has accepted it. And so what if Dave's girlfriend likes the football as much as he does, and comes out with them and drinks them all under the table? That just isn't Clara's thing. It doesn't mean there's anything inherently wrong with their relationship, does it?

He took her to a match once, at the start of their second year.

One of George's friends was bed-bound with flu, and offered up his season ticket. It seemed the perfect opportunity to take her to watch a game and introduce her to his father.

He wrapped his Newcastle City scarf around her neck before they left. She looked so cute – adorable, even – and he was so excited for them to meet.

He could tell by the way George looked at her that he was impressed, that he thought Benjamin had done well for himself. And she was polite and charming, if a little shy, with George. For a few brief moments outside the stadium, he was the happiest he'd been in years.

He squeezed her hand as they climbed the concrete steps together to their seats. It was a chilly day for September, and he was glad she had the scarf on. George had gone to sit in his friend's seat, a few rows behind.

But Benjamin's joy at having all the things that mattered to him the most come together was short-lived.

Clara hated it, remaining seated when the crowd roared to their feet in response to a goal. She wouldn't join in with the chants, even though he told her the words.

'It's too noisy,' she said at one point, tugging on his arm. 'That man behind keeps shoving me and screaming in my ear. I'm going to get a drink.'

She missed most of the match. She didn't like the way strangers tried to thump her on the back in celebration, the fact that the plastic seat was hard and unforgiving, and then she got upset when the goalkeeper was accidentally kicked in the face, leaving him with a bloody nose.

Afterwards, they met his father again outside.

'First time at a match, was it?' George asked her. 'What did you think?'

'It was certainly… memorable,' she said, giving an awkward smile. She was a pretty terrible liar, and George could see right through her.

'Ah you're alreet, pet. Benjamin's mam wasn't much of a fan either.'

She smiled properly at that.

'Maybe something just for the boys,' she said, and George gave her a nod of understanding. 'It was a bit raucous for me.'

'I'm sorry. I love you, but that was horrible!' she said, once George had left them to return home. Benjamin felt there was no come-back from that. 'Too much masculine energy in one place.'

After that, he gave up any hope of getting her to love – or even like – football.

No relationship is perfect, after all.

Today there is a double-header: England versus Brazil first up, then Germany versus the United States.

'I just can't believe you're going to a pub this early in the morning,' she says, sitting up in bed as he pulls his T-shirt over his head.

He's about to leave the small terraced house Clara has shared with Lauren for her third year to meet his friends at The Ram.

'Well, that's the problem with this World Cup being held in the Far East,' he says. 'The less-than-ideal time difference.'

The pubs have a special licence to open early to show the matches throughout the tournament. He can't believe he's going to the pub this early either – it's barely 7 a.m. – but it just makes it all the more exciting.

'But still, drinking at this time of the morning,' she says, curling a lip. 'It's gross.'

'I'll pace myself,' he says, winking at her. He can't be cross with her today – he's too happy. England might actually get through to the semis. It'll be epic.

'I hope you won't be upset if they lose,' she says, looking worried.

'It's a big deal,' he says, laughing. 'The World Cup only happens every four years, you know.'

'Right.'

'Clara.'

'I just don't understand why you have to watch the Germany match after too. Isn't one football match per day enough? You'll be paralytic by lunchtime.'

He shakes his head at her. He can feel his shoulders tensing, so instead he picks up the small cushion she keeps on her desk chair and lobs it at her.

'CDC,' he says, hoping the use of her nickname will placate her. 'You do know I love you more than I love football, don't you? And I love football a lot.'

She rolls her eyes, lies back on the bed.

'Whatever. It's fine. Let's not talk about it. You go, and have a nice time getting so drunk you end up pissing in your own front garden, and then tomorrow we'll move on with our lives like grown-ups.'

He takes a deep breath.

'Clara,' he says. 'I won't…'

'Won't what? Get drunk? Don't make promises you can't keep.' She pauses, considering it. 'You *won't* keep.'

He grinds his teeth together. Why does she have to do this, every time? Why do they always have to separate on such a horrible note?

'For Christ's sake. Me enjoying some drinks with my friends … it doesn't have to mean anything bad about us.'

As usual, he has tied himself up in words. He can't express himself properly, and it frustrates him. He turns away from her. He's tired of this. Of her jealousy, of the way she doesn't trust him. It poisons everything good that they do have. And even though he doesn't know much, he does know that most of what they have is good.

She gives a short exhalation – a sort of strange laugh – and stands up, pulling him towards her in a hug.

'I'm sorry,' she says, into his T-shirt. 'I am trying, I promise. I'll try harder.'

He pauses. It's still upsetting, he still wishes he could wind time back to yesterday, when they were lying on the bed together and he was thinking how perfect everything was.

'Would you like me to come back here afterwards?'

She stares at him.

'What?'

'Later on. I can come back here, if you like.'

'That's a terrible idea.'

He nods.

'But I can if you like.'

He understands now – a concession like that can mean so much to her. It doesn't make any sense to him, but it's not a lot to give.

She twists her lip, thinking about his suggestion.

'No, it's fine,' she says. 'Some of the girls I lived with in the first year are going out tonight anyway. To celebrate the end of exams. So I'll probably join them. Let's just leave it until tomorrow.'

He smiles. It's a relief – the thought of her enjoying her own night out. Not sitting at home getting angry and bitter, worrying about what he's doing.

'Great,' he says. 'I hope you have a good time. You deserve a night out. You've worked so hard this year. Time to let your hair down a bit.'

'It'll be awful,' she says, wrinkling her nose. 'They're going to that horrible club they all like – Options.'

'That's where we met!'

'Yeah, I know.'

'CDC,' he says. 'You might even enjoy yourself. You never know.'

He moves to kiss her but she turns her head, so he brushes her cheek lightly with his lips.

'I love you,' he says. 'And I'll see you tomorrow.'

'I love you too,' she says.

In later years, he will think about that conversation a lot. Their final goodbye.

What would he have said to her, if he had known that this was it? The last moment of purity, before everything was ruined.

June 2002

Clara

Lauren is watching the England match on the tiny TV in her bedroom. She calls across the landing as Clara is drying her hair to tell her the outcome.

'We lost!' Lauren says. 'Final score, 2–1 to Brazil. Why are England so crap!?'

Lauren doesn't really follow football but, earlier in the kitchen, she told Clara that she'd probably have the game on in the background: 'After all, it is *England* playing.'

'Shame,' Clara says to her, giving a faint smile. She takes a deep breath, thinks about what it means for her.

Benjamin will be devastated, but she's selfishly pleased that it means England's World Cup is over, and everyone can stop going on about it.

But she's also upset for him. She hates to think of him sad, or disappointed. She's been proven right about that stupid game, but there's no joy in the victory.

She's also worried. He'll drink himself into a stupor now, as he always does when Newcastle City lose a match.

She tries to put it out of her head. He'll be fine. This is what he signed up for when he decided to become a football fan. He will bounce back. She resolves to focus on her friends today. And think about Benjamin tomorrow.

She hasn't been out to a nightclub in months. She's spent her final year with her head deep in her books, or with Benjamin. She's a pariah among students.

It's time for her to have some fun.

Later, there's a knock on her bedroom door.

'Vodka Red Bull delivery!' Lauren calls. 'Oh, is that what you're wearing?'

Clara looks down at her outfit – boot-cut jeans and a flowery top from Oasis.

'What?'

'Well, I thought you might... you know. Tart it up a bit.'

Lauren is wearing a teeny tiny fitted black dress.

'Oh.'

'Don't you have a dress?'

She thinks.

'Yes,' she replies. 'I have the one I wore to my birthday dinner.'

'The red one? That's more like it,' Lauren says. 'Get your legs out for once.'

'Fine,' Clara replies, rolling her eyes. She takes a sip of the drink. 'Who's coming tonight then?'

'Everyone! Everyone from the old flat, plus the boys from upstairs. Richard will be there...'

Clara swallows. She has avoided him ever since first year, and in that time he has slept with and dated so many girls she has lost track.

'Right.'

'He still likes you, you know. And I know something happened with you two in first year...'

'Laur...'

'I know, I know, you've got your one true love in Benjamin.'

'I'd never cheat.'

'For god's sake, Clara. Who said anything about cheating? You do know you're only twenty-one? You don't have to be so grown-up and serious all the bloody time.'

Clara ignores that. She does have to. She doesn't have a choice. It's just who she is.

'Let me know when you're ready,' Lauren says, turning to leave the room. 'We're meeting the others in the Mulberry Tree for a drink first.'

'OK, give me a few more minutes.'

She changes quickly into the dress she bought for her twenty-first birthday meal. Benjamin took her to a swanky restaurant by the station. He ordered scallops thinking they were scampi, and when the two tiny pieces of seafood arrived, she couldn't stop giggling at his mistake. They both felt uncomfortable sitting there among all the middle-aged diners, who kept looking over at her tiny dress disapprovingly.

The dress is red velvet with spaghetti straps. She remembers the way Benjamin looked at her when she came down the stairs wearing it. She imagined it was similar to how film stars felt as they walked the red carpet, smiling at fans. A look of pure adoration.

She stares at herself in the mirror. Tonight, she doesn't feel like a film star. She feels tarty, overdressed. Her friends don't see her like this. At uni, she mostly wears Diesel jeans and T-shirts.

She hesitates for a few seconds, then grabs a black cardigan and shoves her feet into her strappy wedges. Sod it. It's literally her last night out. Who cares whether people think she's dressed like a slapper?

'Much better,' Lauren says when she comes into the front room. 'You look gorge. Here, let's have a picture, for posterity.'

She sets up her digital camera on the table in front of the window and turns on the timer. They take several shots before Lauren is happy with one.

When Clara looks at herself in the image, she's surprised by how thin she looks. She has lost weight again this year. The stress of exams. The fear of the future. She has wanted to be a real grown-up for so long, but, now that time is almost here, she's terrified of it.

'Off we go then,' Lauren says. 'Let's make it a night to remember!'

She's surprised by the size of the group in Options – people she hasn't seen since the first year. She can't really believe that this is it. That her university experience is almost over. She remembers being in sixth form, the hype and excitement they all felt about getting to leave home and do whatever the hell they wanted, and yet, what has she actually done? Barely anything really.

It's like she's slept through the whole thing. But it's been a comfortable, deep sleep. A sleep with Benjamin beside her.

She smiles. She's got more out of university than most people. She's got the love of her life.

They're all drinking Snakebite but she orders a Bacardi Breezer instead. She's still a lightweight, and it's been a while since she went out drinking.

'Cheers,' she says, wedging herself between Sinead and a girl she doesn't recognise.

'Hi,' the girl says. 'I'm Lucy.'

'Clara.'

'How do you know everyone?'

'Oh, I shared a flat with Lauren and Sinead in first year.'

'Oh that's right, you live with Lauren! Where's your boyfriend? Lauren told me you were glued at the hips.'

'He's out with his mates. They've been watching the football,' she says, feeling a bit stupid. Is that what they all think of her? Some sad sack who can't leave her boyfriend's side?

'Oh yeah, gutting isn't it? Well, cheers!'

'Cheers,' Clara replies, taking a sip of her drink.

She glances at everyone round the table. She recognises them all, vaguely. There's Rosie, the one with short blonde hair, who ended up in hospital a few months ago after taking a dodgy ecstasy tablet. Lauren went to visit her afterwards, then came home and told Clara how Rosie seemed to find the whole experience amusing, rather than traumatising.

She downs the rest of her drink and tries not to think of Benjamin, just a mile or so away, doing the same thing with his friends.

An hour later, she is four Bacardi Breezers down and feeling light-headed, when Richard slides into the seat next to her.

'Clara Davies-Clark,' he says, loudly. 'Long time, no fucking see.'

She bites her lip and nods at him. His temples are shiny with sweat.

'Here,' he says, putting a glass down in front of her. 'Drink something grown-up.'

'What is it?'

'Vodka and Coke.'

'I hate vodka.'

'Pathetic.' He rolls his eyes at her.

Out of the corner of her eye, she can see Rosie watching them. Something takes hold of her.

'Fine,' she says, and she downs the drink in one go, slamming it on the table. 'Happy now?'

He sits back in his seat, smiling. There is something predatory about the width of his smile. All those teeth.

'How are you?' he says, his face softening. 'Really? How are things in Clara's world?'

'Good,' she says. 'How about you?'

'Still with the boyfriend?'

She nods, looking away.

'How come he's not out tonight then?'

'The football,' she says, for the second time that night.

'That finished hours ago.'

'He'll be drowning his sorrows. Are you not a fan?'

'Not particularly, I'm a rugby man.'

She nods.

'Anyway,' she says. 'We don't do everything together.'

He takes a sip of his pint. His face falls.

'Ben-ja-min,' he says, quietly. 'He's a lucky guy.'

She doesn't know what to say to that so she just sits there, looking for an exit.

'What about you?' she says, when the silence has become awkward. 'How's things with you?'

He blinks at her. She feels something strange. Attraction. Is it the alcohol? Or the fact she's actually quite cross with Benjamin? Either way, it's nice to have the upper hand for once. Not that she would do anything. But a bit of harmless flirting – that's not against the law, is it?

'Good,' he says. 'Well, you know. It's a bit of a headfuck,

leaving uni. I've got a place on the PWC graduate scheme though. I have about a week off after we graduate and then I'm straight back to work again.'

She remembers reading about this. The £10,000 'golden hello' it offered.

'Wow,' she says. 'That's really competitive, right? Like, really hard to get a place on?'

He laughs.

'Can't be too hard, or they wouldn't have picked me.'

'Lauren told me you're really smart.'

'Oh, did she now?' Richard says, nudging her. 'So, does that mean you two have been talking about me? Should I be flattered or worried?'

'Neither,' she says, rolling her eyes at him. Is she... *flirting?*

'My round then, I guess?'

'Looks like it,' he says, finishing the end of his pint. 'Stella please.'

She waits at the bar, her heart hammering with the tension of something she doesn't quite understand. Is this why she never goes out?

Deep down, is she not as committed to Benjamin as she seems? Can't she trust herself to have a night out without doing something she might regret?

Or is it just the juvenile thought that for once she is doing something *he* might not like, while he goes off and gets off his face, even though he knows she hates it?

When she takes their drinks back to the table she's surprised to find that the others have all stood up and are now huddled in a big group by the window. Only Richard is still sitting at the table, looking over at her expectantly. She hands him his pint.

'Thank you,' he says, sitting back.

She sips her own drink.

'Well, this is nice, isn't it?' he says. 'I feel... I don't know, Clara. Just a bit sad about how everything worked out with us.'

'With us?'

'Look, I know there wasn't an *us*. I just mean, we could have been good friends. Don't you think? And after first year you sort of disappeared on us all.'

'I was concentrating on my course,' she says. 'It wasn't anything deliberate.'

'Really?'

Her cheeks are burning again.

'Really,' she says. Time to change the subject. 'How's your love life, anyway? Am I right in thinking something happened with Rosie?'

His eyebrows rise and he takes a deep breath. They both look over. Rosie is standing sideways to them, but it's clear she's watching them out of the corner of her eye.

'Rosie's great,' he says, eventually. 'Just not for me.'

'So you did sleep with her!' she says, batting him on the arm. 'I knew it! I could just tell.'

'Are you jealous?'

'No comment.'

What is she doing? It's a roller-coaster. Now she's on, she can't get off.

'You are. I can see! Clara. You're going red.'

He puts his arm over the back of the seat behind her and leans in close.

'I won't tell the boyfriend,' he whispers into her ear. His breath is warm on her cheek. He is wearing that same aftershave. It reminds her of the night they slept together.

She moves away, ever so slightly, and stares down at her drink.

'There's nothing to tell,' she says. Is she enjoying this? Or hating it? Why can't she be sure?

Then, she hears something. The tinny sound of her phone ringing in her handbag.

'Oh,' she says, in surprise. 'Hang on a second.'

She pulls it out of her bag, looks at the name calling, the small grey letters on the screen spelling out *Mr BE*.

Benjamin.

Why would he be calling her now?

'Are you going to get that?' Richard says, tilting his head slightly.

She looks back down at Benjamin's nickname. She thinks of him, standing in a crowded pub somewhere, hoping that she'll answer her phone.

She thinks of all the times over the past two years she has done the same, and he hasn't.

'No,' she says, putting the phone back in her bag. 'He can wait.'

June 2002

Benjamin

He is eight pints down. Or is it nine? He's not sure.

There's a TV on in the corner of the pub: the commentators are lamenting England's great defeat, along with the fact that their arch-rivals Germany are through to the semis and will probably fucking win now. Same old story.

Benjamin can't bear it.

Clara was right, all along. As she always has been. Football is stupid. This is a stupid way to spend a life. Devoted to a game that only ever seems to disappoint him. That promises so much and then snatches it away again.

He should say sorry to her. He should have gone out with her tonight. Sat by her side in the club with her friends and been the sort of boyfriend that she deserves.

Fucking football.

His head pounds.

On his way back from the toilet, he bumps into someone.

'Easy tiger,' a voice says.

He looks up. It's Tina. He can't remember the last time he saw her – they lost touch after he stopped working at Gordon's – but she looks exactly the same.

'Sorry,' he says.

'Pisshead,' she cackles. She's pretty far gone herself. She winks at him, gives his arm a squeeze. 'Benjamin Edwards. Well, well, well. I didn't realise you were here! You off to the bar?'

He nods, unthinking.

'Get me a whisky and Coke, would you?'

'Sure.'

He smiles at her and a thought flashes through his mind.

She liked him, once. She understands football. She doesn't overthink things. She doesn't try to attribute meaning to the meaningless.

Perhaps he should be with her.

What the fuck is he thinking like this for?

He slaps himself on the head and goes outside to get some fresh air.

It's a crisp night, the sun setting in the cloudless sky overhead. He's been out for hours, has completely lost track of time. And Clara is out there, somewhere, tonight. With her friends, having a good time.

He wants to be where she is. He doesn't want to be here, any more. With these people. He wants to be better than this.

He leans against a lamppost. He feels dizzy.

He hasn't told Clara what his tutor said yesterday. That his last piece of coursework was unsatisfactory. He'd missed a whole entire section. The tutor had asked him if it was a mistake, if he'd just forgotten to submit it. But no, he hadn't read the brief properly and he just hadn't done it.

He'd got into such a state with his Production Project that he'd completely forgotten about the final section of the module. Worse still, his tutor said there was no chance to resubmit it.

Things like that would never happen to Clara. Clara is a

winner. Built for success. Born into success and sure to continue being a success.

He isn't sure he'll ever be a success.

He takes his phone out and rings the only number he ever rings: hers. It rings and rings and rings and he frowns, confused, when eventually it switches to the generic voicemail message.

Where is she? She always answers. He can't remember another time when he has called her and she hasn't picked up.

His head is hurting. He puts the phone back in his pocket, stumbling again as he turns back towards the pub.

Drinks. He's meant to be getting drinks.

June 2002

Clara

The dance floor is a blur of faces and, as she spins and throws her arms around, she thinks: *why haven't I done this before?*

Why have I denied myself this? Pure, simple fun. *What was I so afraid of?*

They have gathered their handbags in a little pile, witches before a bonfire, and they take turns to strut around it, their faces beaming at one another, voices drowned out by the volume of the music, even though they are screaming the words to *Toca's Miracle*.

Her face is aching from smiling as she twirls and spins around on the spot. For once, she feels completely free. Free of any expectation, free of any sense of how she should be behaving. It's just her and the music, and these smiling, happy people she's friends with.

'More drinks?' she mouths at Lauren, who nods. James is behind Lauren, his arms around her waist, his mouth periodically buried in her neck, and Clara feels a rush of happiness for her friend.

Clara knows Lauren has loved James ever since they slept together in the first year, but they've both played the field since, tried to pretend they weren't actually interested each other. But Clara could see it.

Clara believes in The One. And James is Lauren's.

What a perfect ending it would be if they now got together. Right at the end of university. What a perfect, perfect finish to the experience.

She leans right over and shouts in Lauren's ear.

'I'm so happy for you! James is lovely!'

And Lauren smiles, wrinkling her nose and pushing her away with a laugh.

At the bar, Clara buys them both another vodka and Red Bull – she's lost track of how many drinks she's had now. But sod it. She's finished her degree, what does it matter? She can get as drunk as she likes, she can sleep all day tomorrow.

She takes the drinks back to the dance floor. Some of the girls have disappeared and there's someone new standing next to Lauren.

Richard.

He smiles at her as she hands Lauren her drink, and then he starts to dance next to her. It's funny, seeing a man dance. Most of the time they just stand there, rocking from side to side, but he really goes for it. He's good too, deft at flexing his body into different positions, keeping time with the music perfectly.

She briefly thinks of Benjamin. Has she ever seen him dance? No, of course not. He's too self-conscious. Plus, they never go anywhere. He doesn't like clubbing. He prefers sitting in the pub staring at football on the telly.

Well, it's his loss.

She starts to dance alongside Richard, allowing him to hold her hand and spin her under his arm. It's harmless fun. At one point he spins her over to James, who also twirls her underarm, and Lauren is smiling along the whole time. She has been so worried about her finals but, now, she feels free.

'Just need a wee,' she shouts to Lauren, who nods in response, and Clara pushes her way through the writhing bodies, the laser lights disorientating. For a second she thinks she can see Benjamin in the corner, and she remembers with a shock that this is where she met him two years ago, in the passage outside the toilets. She was sitting on the floor, crying, because everyone else had taken ecstasy and one of them had called her an uptight bitch, and she felt completely out of place and alone.

Have they all taken drugs tonight, too? She's not sure. She doesn't think so. But anyway, it doesn't matter because she is pissed.

She hops from one foot to another like a child as she waits in the queue for the ladies'.

'I love your dress,' a girl with spiky blonde hair says to her, stroking the red velvet. 'It's amazing.'

'Oh, thanks,' Clara replies, flushing slightly.

'You look well hot. Really.'

Clara doesn't know what to say to that.

When she finally gets into a toilet, there's no toilet roll and so she crouches over the seat and tries to aim as best she can, balancing with her elbows pressed against each side of the cubicle. She opens her handbag and finds a scrunched-up tissue at the bottom, blotted with lipstick, but that's all she has, so it will have to do. She pulls up her knickers and then she notices her phone.

A wave of dizziness overcomes her and she steadies herself. For a second or two, it feels as though the walls of the cubicle are closing in on her.

'God, I'm drunk,' she says, to no one, closing her eyes for a second.

She takes her phone out of her bag.

Four missed calls.

All from Benjamin.

'Good,' she says, to the grey screen. 'See how you like it!'

And then she cackles to herself, the whole time knowing that a small percentage of her – the good, decent part – is faking this nonchalance. That she knows it will have consequences – that the next day, she will be full of regret.

But she's done being the sensible one. She's done being the one trying to do the right thing.

Perhaps this will teach him. Perhaps he'll start to understand her point of view if he gets a taste of his own medicine.

The blonde girl with spiky hair is standing by the basins when she comes out, reapplying her lipstick. Clara glances over at her, admiring the way she perfectly traces the outline of her lips.

The girl spots Clara looking.

'Want some?' she says, holding out the lipstick. It's bright red. 'It's literally the same colour as your dress.'

'Oh,' Clara says, taking it from her. She has never worn red lipstick before – she usually sticks to pinks. 'Thanks.'

'Suits you,' the girl says, taking it back from her. 'Have a great night. You'll be fighting them off looking like that.'

June 2002

Benjamin

She's not picking up the phone. Why isn't she picking up the phone?

Donny sets another pint down in front of him.

'Put your phone away, you twat,' he says, taking it out of his hands. 'Or I'll confiscate it. Who you trying to ring now anyway?'

'Room for a little one?'

Benjamin looks up. His head is swimming. He has ordered more chips, his stomach rumbling. Tina sits down opposite him. He nods at her then looks over at Donny. Donny really fancies her, but she's not interested in him. She told Benjamin once that she thinks he looks like a fat bulldog.

'All right Tina,' Donny says, pulling her pork scratchings towards him, chubby fingers fumbling inside the packet.

Tina brings up the football again, although Benjamin would rather not talk about it. The same endless conversation going round in circles.

How could it have happened? David Seaman just GAVE Ronaldinho that last goal. We got cocky after Owen had scored after thirty minutes.

'It was all downhill after the equaliser,' Tina says. 'Beckham had a shite match.'

'And they only had ten men!' Donny says. 'We're a fucking disgrace.'

All the time he is thinking about Clara. Where is she? Why isn't she answering him?

He pulls his phone out again and stands up from the table, nearly falling over in the process.

'Careful,' Tina says. 'You're twatted.'

'I'm all right, leave me alone,' he slurs, and he stumbles towards the entrance of the pub.

He calls Clara again. It rings and rings and then he hears something – not her voice. But the sound of music playing. Thump-thump-thump.

He remembers. She's out with her friends.

'Hello!?' he says, leaning against a lamppost.

But the line goes dead. He rings again, but this time there's no answer.

Did she answer it by accident?

What is she doing?

Who is she with?

Has she realised that he is, in fact, a waste of space?

He's going to fail his degree. And then she'll see it.

He closes his eyes, his head rolling on his neck, feeling disconnected from the rest of his body. He's fucked everything.

He'll go to find her. That's what he'll do. She's always telling him he's not romantic enough. That he doesn't make any big gestures.

He'll go to find her in the club and tell her how much he loves her and tell her she was right about the football.

'Oi.'

He turns. Tina is there, holding out a pint. He takes it from her without thinking and downs half of it in one go.

'I'm a fucking mess, Tina,' he says, swiping his sleeve across his mouth, and she puts her arm around him.

'I know mate. I know,' she says. 'Man, you are drunk.'

She's staring at him strangely. And then, something is happening. Something that makes no sense.

She's kissing him, her hand on his bum.

'Fuck me Edwards, but even when you're off your face, you're hot,' she whispers when he breaks away.

He pushes her backwards, frowning. The rest of his pint slops to the floor.

'No,' he says. 'No... I'm with Clara.'

He closes his eyes again. He's dizzy, the ground moving beneath his feet.

'Sorry,' he says. 'Sorry Tina.'

He feels tired now. Perhaps he should just sit down, right here, and have a nap.

He puts his hand over his eyes. It feels as though he might actually fall asleep, right here, standing up. But then he hears something – a tinny tune he can't quite place – and he inhales sharply and his eyes spring back open.

He frowns again.

'It's all right Clara,' Tina is saying into his phone. 'I'm taking care of him for you.' She cackles again, snorting with amusement.

'What?' he says, confused.

Tina hands him something. His phone.

'Lighten up Benji Boy,' she says. 'What kind of girlfriend rings you when you're out with the boys? She needs to get back in her box.'

He looks at the phone. The call has disconnected.

'What did you do?' he says, raising his voice.

'Jesus,' Tina says, rolling her eyes and walking away.

He squeezes the phone. Stupid phone. He never wanted one in the first place. It was her idea to get one.

He rings Clara back, but this time the ringtone stops abruptly, as though she's deliberately cut him off.

He starts to write her a text message instead, but his eyes won't focus on the tiny screen properly, the letters blurring in front of him.

What did Tina say to Clara?

'Fuck this,' he says, to no one in particular, and then he turns and stumbles away from the pub, his feet taking him, somewhat unconsciously, in the direction of the city centre.

June 2002

Clara

She has been such an idiot. The stupidest, stupidest idiot.

She stands in the entrance to the club, staring down at the Nokia in her hand, as though it were the remains of a bomb that's just gone off. Blowing her to pieces.

I'm taking care of him for you, Clara.

Who is she? This woman, who has his phone?

Tina. It must have been. She knew her name.

A huge sob escapes and she clamps a hand over her own mouth, as though trying to keep her jaw from falling off. The pain radiates throughout her skull.

Benjamin. She has been wrong about him all along.

She closes her eyes, leans against the wall of the nightclub. People push past her, on their way in and out. It's as though she's not even there.

She doesn't know what to do. Should she go home? Just cry herself to sleep in bed? Should she try to find him, to confront him?

She wants to rip him to pieces. The intensity of her anger frightens her.

Or should she go back into the club and dance and try to forget?

Tears flow down her face. The last two and a half years of her life, it seems, have been a lie. A deception. A deceit.

Benjamin constantly insisted Tina and he were just friends, nothing more. He even said they'd lost touch! But Clara always knew Tina liked him. And this confirms it.

She has been a fool. She covers her face with her hands and sobs.

And then, someone is there, in front of her. A hand touches hers, gently, lifting it away from her face.

'Hey,' he says. 'What's the matter? Clara?'

Richard.

She shakes her head. She doesn't want to explain to him. It's all such a mess.

'Sweetheart,' Richard says, putting his arm around her. 'What is it?'

On some visceral level she knows he is too happy about this, about her misery. She knows it puts him at an advantage – opens the pitch for him to score.

On another level, she thinks perhaps this is how it's all meant to be. A lightning strike that splits her life forever. Before and After.

And now she's in the After, and in the After is Richard.

Richard, the sensible choice. The boy her parents would approve of. The boy who already has a good job lined up. The boy who would buy her a beautiful diamond ring and a home in West London. The boy who would fit the life she was born for.

He's the one she should be with. He was the one, all along, it seems.

But... Benjamin.

It's a knife to her heart.

The agony of it. How could he betray them – what they had – like this?

'What is it? Clara?' Richard says.

She can't speak, she just leans on his shoulder and sobs.

'Come on,' he says, gently, 'let's get you out of here.'

She allows him to steer her out of the club and into the cold night. She remembers the time that Benjamin did the same. The levity of that moment. The excitement.

And now there is nothing but heaviness. An ache in her soul, her legs like lead.

'You've had too much to drink,' Richard is saying. 'Happens to the best of us. I'll look after you.'

She lets him lead her up the road, towards the bus station.

'Wait,' she says. Her tears have dried up but her eyes feel heavy. 'Where are we going?'

'Don't worry,' he says. 'You know I've always liked you Clara. The truth is, the first time I saw you in that bar in our first year I knew we'd be good together. It's a shame it's taken us so long to work it out but better late than never...'

'Wait,' Clara says, but suddenly she feels his arm around her waist, pulling her tighter towards him, his body a solid mass at her side.

He slows his pace slightly. His breath is hot in her ear.

'You have no idea how sexy you look in that dress,' he whispers. 'Seriously. I can hardly contain myself. All the men in that club were looking at you tonight. All of them.'

Her eyelids flicker shut. She thinks of that time in her room, two years ago, the way he reacted when she kissed him, the way his hands were everywhere, octopus tentacles binding her to him, forcing her to go limp.

And then, he is kissing her again, this time his lips against her neck, sucking and twisting the flesh. She retches, opening her eyes, the pain in her head excruciating, and she can see that they have stopped on the main street, that he has pushed her up against the wall outside a shop. There are people everywhere, drunk revellers, walking down the road in front of her, ignoring them, thinking that what is happening is OK. Normal. Because it is. It's Friday night in one of the biggest university cities in the country, people will be behaving like this all over the city, and everyone will just see it as normal.

The brick wall is damp and cold against her back and his hands are under the hem of her dress now, squeezing the skin of her thighs as they make their way up to her knickers. She starts to cry again.

Benjamin.

How could he? How could he leave her to this?

For a few seconds she kisses Richard back. Angrily. She wants to hurt Benjamin and this is how she can do it. Richard reacts eagerly, pushing her harder against the brick wall, the skin on the back of her arms shredding against it.

It hurts.

And that's when she knows. It's all wrong. She doesn't want this. She doesn't want him. This boy, grabbing at her as though she is nothing.

'No,' she says, twisting her head away from his. 'You're hurting me. Get off!'

He stops, and she sees the rainbow of emotions move across his features: confusion, irritation, frustration and then something else. A moral struggle with himself.

'You little tease,' he says. His eyes are glinting. 'You want this. I know you do. You love playing these games, don't you? God, you make me so fucking hard.'

And then his head is back again, in that space between her neck and shoulder, his fingers digging into her bottom so aggressively that she can feel the flesh bruising.

'No,' she says, sobbing properly now. 'I don't want this. I don't want you!'

She shoves him harder this time and this time the look on his face is distinct. Anger.

'I don't want you!' she shouts. 'I'm with Benjamin. I love Benjamin!'

He is going to hit her, she's sure of it. She closes her eyes, lifting an arm in front of her face, and then, when she opens them again, Richard is gone.

And in front of her, she sees something that makes no sense.

As though she has conjured him with her words, Benjamin is there.

Her Benjamin, standing in front of her, panting and holding his fist. His eyes wide.

And then, on the pavement. Something else.

Spread-eagled and silent. His mouth open. Eyes shut.

Richard.

Richard, who just seconds ago had been so animated, such a force of energy, an unstoppable train.

Richard, now lying still; a line of something dark and ominous trailing out of his ear.

June 2002

Benjamin

Fate brought them together that first time. And now it has brought him to her again.

But this time it's wrong. All wrong. She's upset. There is someone there, doing something to her.

Hurting her.

It's an impulse, like gasping for breath when you surface from water.

He pulls the thing away from her, and his fist flies at its face. Once, then twice. Harder the second time. And now, whoever it was that was hurting her is lying on the ground and he has saved her and she is looking at him, one of the straps of her dress hanging down her arm, her face a smudged mess of tears and make-up, as though someone has rubbed a thumb over a painting while it was still drying.

'Clara,' he says. His brain scrambles to understand what has just happened. What he has just done.

She is safe, that's what matters.

She just looks at him.

'Are you OK?' he says. 'Did he hurt you?'

She shakes her head slowly from side to side, pushes her hair away from her face.

'Benjamin,' she says, her voice a whisper. 'What...'

They both turn to look at the body on the ground. And then, she reaches out and takes his hand, squeezing it, before kneeling down beside the person he has just punched.

'Shit,' he says.

His fist suddenly throbs with pain, like someone throwing a bucket of ice cold water over him, bringing him back to reality. To the reality of what he has done.

'Shit,' he says, again, kneeling beside Clara. 'Is he...'

There's blood staining the pavement. Benjamin's stomach churns. That's not right. That's not good.

'Richard,' Clara says, shaking the silent, still body in front of them. 'Wake up! Wake up!'

She looks up at him. She is terrified.

'Benjamin, what have you done?'

He takes his phone from his pocket, and, feeling more sober than he has ever felt in his life, he calls 999.

'Ambulance,' he says to the woman who answers. 'I've just... I hit someone and I think he's unconscious.'

June 2002

Clara

The police come and take them all away.

One car for her.

One car for him.

And an ambulance for Richard.

She stares, dazed, as they load him into the back of it. Listening to them muttering things she doesn't fully understand but that she knows are not good.

At the station, the police bring her a blanket and a cup of milky tea. She hates that she is wearing this stupid dress, a dress that seems to shout 'I deserved it', and she's grateful that she can cover herself with the blanket.

She has not been arrested, they explain, but she is a witness. What she tells them now is incredibly important.

So, she tells them the truth.

She explains what she remembers. That Richard didn't seem to understand the word 'No'. That Benjamin appeared from nowhere.

That he was trying to protect her.

Yes, he was her boyfriend.

No, he has never been aggressive before.

Yes, she has slept with Richard before. But once, a long time ago.

No, she wasn't encouraging him.

Yes, she did leave the club with him.

Yes, she was drunk. But it had only been a few drinks...

No, she and Benjamin hadn't had a row. Not really.

She cries when she sees how the line of questioning is going.

They have it all wrong. They think he's violent. Her lovely, gentle boyfriend.

Then, at 3.42 a.m. they come and tell her the worst.

Richard is dead.

Three words that shatter her life forever.

And then, more horror to follow it.

Benjamin has been charged with manslaughter.

part five

April 2022

Benjamin

'New casualty list,' a man in a hotel waistcoat shouts and the crowd of terrified relatives huddles around as he reads out the names. 'I have the new casualty list.'

Barbara Smith.

Patrick King.

Christopher Cooper.

Rebecca George.

Rahim Amer.

He strains as they read the list out again. But no. Aiden isn't on the list. He doesn't recognise any of these names.

He tries calling Aiden again, but his phone still goes to voicemail.

He sinks onto a sofa and starts to sob. Somehow, the horror of this day is not a surprise to him. Somehow, he always knew it was coming.

His day of reckoning.

'Who are you looking for?'

He turns to the voice, wiping his tears with his hand. A woman with cropped black hair and lined skin is staring at him.

'My son,' he says. 'I can't... he wouldn't normally sit that side of the stadium so he shouldn't have been near that exit but his phone is off and I don't... I can't understand why he's not answering.'

'How old is he?'

'Sixteen,' he says.

'I'm so sorry, love,' the woman says. It's then that he notices the cross around her neck. She takes it between her fingertips and gives it a squeeze. 'I'll pray for you. I'll pray for his safe return.'

He doesn't want to be rude so he smiles at her half-heartedly and nods, looking back down. It's enough to encourage her to leave, moving on to the next person.

He thought he had experienced hell that night, twenty years ago, when he sat in that prison cell, pinching his arm repeatedly, refusing to believe that the situation was real, that it wasn't something he could wake up from.

But no, this is the real hell. This.

It's his penance. All those years ago, he took away someone's son.

And now, someone might have taken away his.

April 2022

Clara

She makes herself a cup of tea using the kettle in the hotel room and sits there at the floor-to-ceiling window, looking out across the city, thinking about the last twenty years of her life.

She wishes she could make sense of it all. But it's all just a giant tangle in her head. A mess of feelings and confusion.

She remembers being in the police station that night, in that stupid red velvet dress, crying and staring into space as she tried to process what they were telling her. Trying to accept that her boyfriend, the gentle boy she had loved from the first second she looked into his eyes, had killed someone.

And it was all her fault.

He thought he had been protecting her. He hadn't realised his own strength – she remembers now the language they used at his sentencing. The way his lawyer had described his behaviour as instinctive.

Mr Edwards was trying to protect his girlfriend. He never intended to hurt Richard Claxton. He merely wanted to stop what he perceived as an assault on Miss Davies-Clark. Several witnesses to the event attested that it appeared Miss Davies-Clark was struggling to push Mr Claxton away from her.

Mr Edwards is deeply remorseful that his actions resulted in the death of Mr Claxton.

Benjamin had received three years in prison. The fact he was so drunk and that he had used undue force in his attempt to separate Richard and Clara were taken as aggravating factors. His lawyer was frustrated, said it was very bad luck, that he could so easily not have even been charged at all.

It was self-defence. Defence of the person, he said.

But the second punch, once Richard and Clara were separated, the CPS decided, was excessive. It was that second punch that resulted in Richard falling to the ground, hitting his head on the pavement. It was the second punch that got Benjamin charged.

She had gone to the sentencing, but she could barely look him in the eyes. Afterwards, she had written to him, but he had sent her only a short reply, telling her he was sorry and that he wanted her to move on with her life. To forget him.

Her parents were horrified, of course. Her mother was speechless for perhaps the first time in her life. The last few weeks in Newcastle were a blur. She got her degree, moved back home, and started her journalism course. Buried her head in the sand.

Her parents did their best to distract her, to convince her that she had no other choice than to move on, as he'd told her to.

'It's what he wants,' her mother said, as Clara cried into a sodden tissue. 'He doesn't want you sitting here, pining after him. Wasting your life. Wasting both of your lives.'

But Clara knew that, secretly, her parents were relieved. It was so ridiculous and awful and hackneyed, but the truth was simple: they were snobs.

She wrote to him again, in prison, asking if she could visit him. But he replied that no, he didn't want to see her. She remembers the letter word for word, even though she was so upset after she opened it that she threw it away.

Hi Clara

Thank you for your letter. I'm doing OK. It could be worse.

I think it's for the best you don't visit me. My lawyer told me something I hadn't known before. That you and Richard had slept together. Before. I have to say, when he told me, I was hurt and angry. I felt like a fool.

I understand now, why you didn't tell me at the time. But even so, I think it's best we don't see each other again.

It was good to get your letter, but I'll be honest, it was so painful. The thought of you and him... and then how it all turned out. I'm just about keeping my head above water here, and I want to look back on our time together with love. And so I think it's better – for us both, honestly – if we aren't in touch any longer.

I hope you have a wonderful life Clara. I'll always be grateful for meeting you.

B x

She could feel how much of his hurt and anger he was holding back through the words of the letter. It was all her fault.

She glances over at the television. As suspected, they are replaying the footage from earlier. She knows, seconds before he appears on screen, that his interview will be shown again next.

She turns the volume up on the television.

'Benjamin Edwards,' the reporter says. 'Please, tell us who it is you're looking for.'

'It's my son,' Benjamin says. 'My son Aiden. He was at the match and he's missing.'

She realises she can't leave now, not without knowing whether or not Aiden is OK.

And perhaps she can help with the search.

Clara is here and she has nothing to lose. She lost it all years ago, after all.

April 2022

Benjamin

It is only what he deserves. To experience this agony. After what he put Richard's family through.

They had forgiven him. While he was in prison, he wrote them a letter to apologise and, two months later, they replied. They said that they understood he had never meant to truly hurt Richard, and that they forgave him.

It made his guilt easier to bear but, as long as he lives, he'll never forget the look on Richard's mother's face at his sentencing. The grey beneath her eyes, the way her mouth was permanently turned down at the edges.

He did that to her. He took away her son. He changed the way in which she views the world forever.

She read out a victim impact statement at his sentencing. She was still angry with him, then. She talked about how clever Richard was. How funny and charming. How he had his whole life ahead of him. He had already lined up a job at a top accounting firm after graduation. He was head of the university rowing team. Under his leadership, they had won the Victor Ludorum just last year. He liked to sing, and was accomplished on the piano, too.

Richard's list of academic and sporting successes made the

whole thing even more unfair. Why was he the one that died? Why hadn't it been the other way round? Benjamin didn't have those gifts. This potential. This much to offer the world.

It made no sense that he was the one still living and breathing, while Gifted and Talented Richard lay cold in a grave.

There was more though. Mrs Claxton spoke of how kind her son was. How he would do anything to help anyone. How he was probably just taking care of Clara when he realised she was intoxicated and at risk. How popular he was with the opposite sex. Girls all loved him. They could see that he was a good one, apparently.

He had bristled at that part. The implication that Clara had done something wrong, by going out drinking that night. The suggestion that she was to blame.

He wished he could remember exactly what he had seen as he strolled up that busy street, looking for her. He'd been so drunk himself. But he knows, deep inside, that what he saw didn't look much like Richard was taking care of Clara.

And most importantly of all, he remembers Clara's voice, plaintive at first, then more forceful. A voice shouting 'NO'.

But he stayed silent as he listened to Richard's mother speak. There was no moral high ground left for him, a convicted killer. As his lawyer had said, he didn't have to punch Richard after he pulled him away from her. That was his choice. That was his Unlawful Act.

He didn't even risk a glance at Clara. The first and only time he looked, she had her face buried in a tissue.

He sat there and he listened as Richard's mother spoke of a life destroyed, and he accepted that he was the one who had destroyed it.

He accepted it all. But one thing he found difficult. It had come out in the investigation that Clara and Richard had 'been involved' before. He remembers his barrister telling him this news, the way he shook his head, his brow furrowed, saying it made things more complicated.

'He liked her,' Benjamin said. 'I knew that much but...'

'Apparently they slept together,' his barrister said, leafing through the notes in front of him. 'In April 2000.'

'But... we met in March,' he said, feeling stupid. And then he remembered. In April he was away, dealing with his mam's death.

While he was away, she had slept with Richard. She had never told him. And even though he understood why she might have done it – when he got back, she was so angry with him that he hadn't been in touch – the betrayal felt significant somehow. As though their relationship hadn't been this bright shiny thing of perfection after all.

The pain was excruciating, like being hit by a truck – but it was a good pain. It made it easier. It made it easier to move on.

After his barrister finished his mitigating statement, the judge handed him his sentence. Three years, to serve at least half in custody, the rest on licence. It seemed nothing, really. Three years of his life for the whole of someone else's.

But the judge recognised that of course, he had not intended to kill Richard. He had called an ambulance immediately, confessed when questioned. It was tragic and a lesson to all that such things are possible, and that lives can be ruined in an instant of unnecessary and mindless violence.

He found that description difficult to swallow. *Mindless violence.*

He was mindlessly violent.

But it hadn't felt mindless. It had felt instinctive.

He let it sit with him, tried to accept it as part of his identity.

He served just eighteen months in prison. When he got out,

George was waiting for him. And shortly after, he met Zoe in that pub, and his life took a whole different direction.

Somehow, though, it seems inevitable that it has led him here.

To this bland hotel lobby, where he waits to hear if his own son – the one good thing he's ever done – is alive or dead.

April 2022

Clara

She grabs her handbag from the bed and heads out of the hotel and into the night. It's cold now, the temperature dropped to single digits. She walks faster, raising her heart rate, until she builds up a bit of heat.

The stadium is just ahead of her, lit up by the blue beacons from the emergency services. There's a police cordon across the road that approaches the stadium, reporters dotted around, talking to their respective cameras.

She glances at them, remembers a time when she thought perhaps she'd make her career doing something like that. But no, when it came to it, she was too quiet. Didn't have the fire for it.

'I definitely see you as more of a backbencher,' her journalism tutor said. 'A sub-editor role would suit you nicely. But don't worry, they have all the power really...'

At the time, she was still traumatised, still trying to process what had happened to her, and she thought he might be right. The fire she had been born with had dampened, leaving behind only smoke.

'Excuse me,' she says to a policewoman standing in front of the cordon. 'Where do you go if you're missing someone?'

'Is it a relative?'

She swallows, considers the lie. Why is a blood relative considered more important than someone who has left their imprint on your soul?

'Yes.'

The policewoman looks at her, her face softening.

'If you head to the Crowne Plaza Hotel, just down the street and to the right, you'll find the Reception Centre. If you wait there, you'll be the first to hear of any news.'

'OK,' Clara says, nodding. 'Thank you.'

'You're welcome,' the policewoman says. 'I hope your loved one is found safe and sound.'

The sincerity of her words makes Clara start to cry. She hopes so too. She hopes so more than anything.

She trudges back past the reporters and down the crowded street. People have gathered in huddles, their hands covering their mouths, whispering to each other in shock and all staring at the stadium as though it was burning. Which she supposes it probably was, just a short while ago.

Eventually she sees the sign for the Crowne Plaza Hotel ahead, at the end of the street. There are more police here too, standing around outside, all bullet-proof vests, walkie-talkies and clipboards.

It feels as though she's on the set of a film. She's momentarily taken back to the time when Benjamin and she would spend every Friday night watching the latest blockbuster – back in the days when cinemas carried proper, big-budget blockbusters every week – and they'd share a box of Maltesers and talk about the film the whole way back to her tiny rented house.

She said that all the films with fire on their posters prioritised special effects over story, while he argued that people go to the cinema for special effects, not the story.

'But why can't you have both?' she said, and he nodded his head and they talked about the films – the rare ones – that did fit this criteria.

But this isn't a film. This is real life. She doesn't want the special effects. She wants the story. Girl meets Boy and all ends well.

She walks up to the hotel, swallowing the resurfacing nerves. He is most likely to be in here, now. Waiting for news of his son.

Will he even recognise her? Will he be alone or with Aiden's mother?

She's surprised that no one asks her who she is, or what she wants, and that she's able to simply push the revolving door and go through into the large lobby of the hotel.

The first thing she sees is that someone has set up a table at the back of the room, with water bottles lined up neatly and a coffee machine, looking too small for the space, in the corner. Someone has even thought to put biscuits out.

Her heart is pounding and she feels intense nausea as she scans the room, looking at all the people in there. They have one thing in common – a hollowed-out look on their faces – as though someone has literally sucked the life out of them. They are just shells. Zombies moving through the motions, disconnected from the situation to save themselves from collapsing entirely.

In one corner, a woman is sobbing loudly. She's the only one. Another woman has her arm around her and is whispering in her ear, urgently. Clara can't hear what she's saying but it sounds repetitive, like a chant almost. An incantation.

When they told her that Richard had died, her first reaction had been to laugh. It was a joke, surely.

'What? But Benjamin only hit him to get him off me,' she said. 'It wasn't hard!'

And then they explained; he had fallen and hit his head on the corner of the concrete pavement. 'Pavements are unforgiving,' the police officer had said, without much thought for Clara's feelings. The bleeding in his skull had been immense, there was nothing they could do to save him.

She has forgotten what happened after that. Blocked it out. The *trauma* that follows her around like a ghost, pressing on her chest whenever she thinks she might be able to breathe easily.

She looks again at the huddles of people in the room, her eyes flicking back and forth.

And then, she spies the lone figure, sitting with head bent low, over something small and black. A mobile phone. His hand, she sees, is shaking.

He runs it through his hair. Still curly, but darker than she remembers, the sides flecked with grey.

And then he looks up.

April 2022

11.59 p.m.

Benjamin

He closes his eyes. He is losing it now, well and truly, and it's terrifying.

His chest tightens. He's dying. A heart attack. It took his father, just a few months ago, and so it makes sense. That it's his time now.

He's having a heart attack and, at the same time, he is hallucinating. He had this thought, so long ago yet so vivid: the desire that Clara's face be the last thing he sees before he goes, and here she is, and it's all coming true.

Except... except her face is different somehow. He can't put his finger on it. She is the same, but not the same.

Her hair is shorter, cut into a neat shoulder-length bob. Some of it falls across her face. A side fringe.

She is still beautiful. The most beautiful girl he ever saw.

He closes his eyes, slowly, and reopens them. She's still there. Staring at him.

He can't see anything else. Just her eyes – lighter than the sky on a clear spring day. Looking right at him.

His chest tightens again, and he clutches it with his hand, his gaze momentarily dropping to his lap. When he glances up again, she's no longer there.

But it was nice, he thinks. To see her one last time.

'Benjamin.'

He hears her voice in his ear and he smiles. But then he feels it, a hand on his arm. He turns and she's beside him.

He stares at her for the longest time.

'I heard about your son. I'm so sorry,' she says. 'I'm so sorry that this has happened.'

He shakes his head, looks down at his hand. It doesn't make sense.

He can smell her – and despite it being twenty years since they last met, she smells the same.

'I expect it's a bit of a shock,' she is saying and he looks back up at her face. The same face, but different.

'I'm sorry, I know you'll probably think I'm completely crazy but I was at work and the reports came in about the explosion and I don't know... I knew that you went to every game and I just assumed you might be here and I was so worried about you. I didn't even think really – not at all – I just got on the train and came up here and it was like going back in time and I went to the bar you said you worked at when I last heard from you and the woman there gave me your number and I was going to ring you but I chickened out. But then I turned on the TV in the hotel room that Lauren had got me and there you were. On the television, talking about your son. And I couldn't bear to see you like that and I left and came here and I thought perhaps there was something I could do to help look for him... or perhaps, I don't know, perhaps you have help already. I'm sure his mother must be here somewhere and the last thing I want to do is upset anyone at all, in any way, but you know I'm here now so if I can make myself useful in any way then please do... please do just tell me because that's what I'm here for because well,

I've never forgiven myself and I want – no I need – to make it up to you somehow...'

She pauses, inhales a great gulp of air.

'You were like this the first time we met,' he says, and he takes her hand. It feels small and soft in his. 'Do you remember?'

She shakes her head.

'You were nervous, I think, and you didn't stop talking.'

'I'm nervous now,' she says.

He looks at her.

'It's nice to see you,' he says, and she smiles. 'It's been a long time.'

She nods.

'What can we do?' she says. 'About your son.' She pauses. 'Aiden.'

'He shouldn't be missing,' he says, looking down at her hand. 'He doesn't sit that side of the stadium, not usually, so he wouldn't be anywhere near that gate. But I'm worried because...'

He tails off. He hasn't told anyone this. About his deepest fear.

That something happened to Aiden at the football club, and that it changed him forever.

April 2022

Midnight

Clara

It's like no time has passed. Has it ever felt more natural to sit opposite someone? To be in their presence? She can't remember feeling this way with anyone else, ever. Her whole life.

He's in pain though. She can feel it.

At least this desperate situation means they can cut through all the bullshit – any sense of awkwardness – because there are bigger things at play here. Far more important things than social niceties or re-examining the past, what went wrong, how their insecurities and youth ruined the special thing they had.

'Why weren't you at the match?' she says, frowning. 'Why weren't you there together?'

He looks at her.

'I was working,' he says. 'I'm working in film now, and we had a weekend shoot. Couldn't get out of it.'

She laughs.

'So, you can miss a game, after all? And the world doesn't end?'

He nods, blinks. She shouldn't tease him. Not now.

'Listen. I'm going to ask that policewoman,' she says, standing up. 'It's ridiculous that there's no news yet. The explosion was hours ago.'

Benjamin just looks at her, his mouth open but remaining silent.

'Excuse me,' she says, tugging on the arm of the policewoman, who turns to her with that same sympathetic smile she received earlier, by the stadium cordon. 'But my friend, there. He's waiting for news of his son. Surely, you must have a clearer idea by now? Of all the casualties?'

'I'm so sorry,' the policewoman says. 'We're working really hard to inform relatives as soon as possible. Have we got all the details of the missing person? Description, where they were sitting at the match? Have you provided a photograph?'

She swallows. She doesn't know. But she assumes; he would have told them everything.

'Yes but... why can't we go to the hospital? Take a look at the people they've brought in? Wouldn't that just save everyone time?'

'I'm afraid it's better for you to stay here. The hospital teams will be very busy dealing with the injured,' the policewoman says. 'I'm sorry.'

Clara sees something else in her eyes – an attempt to communicate the unthinkable. *The reason you can't go to the hospital is because some of the people they have brought in are no longer recognisable.* Of course, they can't put the relatives through the trauma of trying to identify their loved ones through body parts.

She swallows. Tears spring to her eyes but she blinks them back. This is not her loss. It would be selfish to cry now. She needs to stay strong for him.

'She's going to let us know ASAP,' she says, smiling as she sits down beside Benjamin again. He's still staring down at his phone.

'My battery's nearly gone,' he says. 'I've been calling and calling him but his phone is switched off.'

'I'll get a charger,' she says, and she is up on her feet again. The sense of purpose is a life raft and she procures a charger from one of the receptionists working behind the main desk, and moves them to a sofa near a plug so that he can hold the phone while it charges. A small victory at least.

'Tell me about Aiden,' she says, taking his free hand again.

He looks up at her.

'He's amazing,' he says, his eyes lighting up. 'He's everything I'm not. Smart, kind, level-headed. He makes good decisions, good choices.'

'In that case, he's going to be fine,' she says. 'I just know it.'

'I've not done enough for him,' he says. 'I've let him down. There was something bugging him, I know it. Something on his mind, that he didn't want to share with me... I should have persisted.'

'He sounds like a normal teenage boy to me.' She tries to sound gentle.

'I don't know,' he says, his voice dropped to a whisper. 'Aiden's had a hard time over the past few years. He's in a youth football team. There's a lot of bullying... it's a high-pressure environment, you know. And lately he's been out a lot, and he hasn't been telling me where he's going and I...'

The anguish in Benjamin's face seizes her heart.

'What is it?' Clara presses.

'He's always been such a calm, thoughtful lad. But something's changed. There's a lad in his team that got dropped, Gary. They've started spending more time together, but I'm not sure he's a good influence. Aiden's been quieter than usual. Moody. Staying out late. Drinking too much. That kind of thing. I mean, sure, it's normal for his age, but it doesn't feel normal for *him*. I'm just worried he's been keeping something from me. Something big.'

He cradles his head in his hands.

'None of it makes sense.'

April 2022

Benjamin

He wishes he had Gary's phone number. Gary works at the stadium now, on one of the hot dog stands. He should have been right round the other side of the stadium this afternoon, away from the explosion.

Gary and Aiden were never that close, but when Gary got dropped from the team, Aiden reconnected with him. It seemed strange at the time and when Benjamin asked him about it, Aiden told him that Gary had been treated unfairly by Coach Kenny.

Benjamin remembers the heat of his anger as he said it, but Aiden didn't elaborate, despite Benjamin's probing.

They were once so close, but now it felt as though Aiden was keeping secrets from him.

Suddenly, Aiden and Gary were firm friends.

He didn't want to be *that* father, but he didn't like it. Gary was unpredictable, bad-news, the boy you didn't want your kid hanging around with. His father was arrested last year for beating up his mother, and he'd been kicked out of school for bringing drugs and a knife onto the premises.

But Aiden – his empathetic, thoughtful son – said none of it was Gary's fault.

374

'He deserves a break,' Aiden said. 'He's never had a single break in his life.'

How could Benjamin tell his son not to be kind? To cast aside someone in need?

But Aiden has been angrier lately. Aggressive, furious with the world about little things that never used to worry him. A reaction to George dying at the start of the year, Benjamin assumed. His way of processing grief.

And now, Aiden is missing.

He can't be thinking this, can he? He can't be thinking this about his son, his Aiden, the boy so sensitive he tried to save a butterfly with a broken wing when he was four.

He can't be thinking that this same boy would have somehow been involved in what happened today.

But he's heard about how young men become radicalised by things on the internet. Disenchanted with life, lured by the promise of being something special, of making their mark on the world.

And he can't stop thinking about the stuff he found in Aiden's bedroom the other week. Hair bleach. A packet of nails. A roll of electrical tape. All stuffed inside a dirty rucksack he had never seen before.

When Benjamin confronted him, Aiden said he'd found it in the park, and he'd brought it home meaning to throw it away but forgot. But he was shifty, refusing to look Benjamin in the eye.

And now, just a few weeks later, his son is missing, his phone is switched off, and someone has done exactly that – set off a bomb outside the stadium.

No. Not Aiden.

He's losing it.

It's just the terror of this situation. There's no way his boy would do something like that.

No *reason* that he would, either.

His phone starts to vibrate in his hand.

Benjamin and Clara both stare at it. It's a mobile number, one he doesn't have saved in his phone. Not Aiden, then.

'Hello?' he says, his voice a croak.

'Dad? It's me.'

And just like that, the world spins on its axis. He grips the side of the sofa, trying to steady himself. It's too much for his body to cope with; this avalanche of emotion.

The guilt – that he could have ever doubted his son – hits almost immediately after the relief that he's alive.

'Aid? Where are you? Are you OK? What's happened? Where have you been?'

He gasps for breath, the blood rushing around his head, drowning out his ability to hear or think straight.

'I'm fine. I'm just at the station. I'm sorry, I'm borrowing a stranger's phone so I can't be long. Mine died. I'll explain everything. Can you come and meet me? There's something I need to tell you.'

April 2022

Clara

She can tell it's Aiden from Benjamin's reaction.

Less than an hour ago she had no idea that Benjamin even had a son, but now she feels more relieved than she ever has to hear that this boy is OK.

She sits anxiously while he finishes the call.

'He's at the station,' he says to her. 'I don't know how or why or... fuck. He's got some explaining to do.'

And then he smiles. A great, gulping relief of a smile. She puts her arm around him and holds him as tight as she can.

'I'm so pleased,' she says. 'I'm so relieved.'

'We better go,' he says. 'If that's OK? I mean, of course, you don't have to come.'

'Are you serious? I'm not going to leave you now. Unless you want me to?'

He shakes his head.

'I can't believe he's OK,' he says, and then he starts to sob. 'Fucking hell. The man upstairs really has it in for me.'

They tell the lady with the clipboard not to worry, that their missing loved one has been in touch and is fine. Together, they leave the hotel lobby of despair.

She turns back for a second as they make their way through

377

the revolving doors. She wishes all the people in the room could get the same news that they've just received. Their heartbreak is almost palpable, filling the air like a fog.

The station isn't too far from the hotel. They make their way towards it in near-silence, punctuated by Benjamin's occasional exhalations of relief. Expletives, mostly. He never used to swear much, but what other words are there for situations like this? It needs a whole new language.

As they approach the station, the euphoria they both shared starts to dissipate, and she begins to feel nervous.

'Benjamin?' she says, cautiously.

'Yes?'

'What about... where is Aiden's mother? Do you need to tell her, too?'

He stops on the pavement and turns to her.

'His mother's gone.'

'Oh,' she says, her hand rising to her face. 'I'm so sorry.'

'She left when he was seven. We've never heard from her since.'

'That's horrible,' she says.

'He doesn't like talking about her,' Benjamin says. 'Under-standably. We've done all right, just the two of us. And my dad. Until recently. Bit of a weird setup, I guess. Three generations of men, living under one roof. But we've done all right.'

'Who was she?' she says. 'If you don't mind me asking?'

'She was someone I met,' he says, quietly. 'Just after I came off my licence... well she was just there. I mean, literally, there. I met her in a pub one night. I was so lonely back then. I was a mess.'

The tears burn her eyes.

'You should have called me then,' she says, angrily. 'I'm so cross that you didn't.'

'You deserved more,' he says, simply. 'I wanted you to have a good life. The life you should have always had.'

He stops in the street and their eyes lock again: hers full of tears, his hard with determination.

'Have you had a good life?' he says. 'Tell me.'

She looks away. What can she say? Now isn't the time for honesty.

'Yes,' she lies. 'I have.'

He smiles, a weight lifted.

The station is in sight now.

'What will you say to him?' she asks, the nerves returning. 'What will you say to him about me?'

'Whatever you like,' he says.

'Perhaps just that I'm an old friend?' she asks. 'For now?'

He nods.

'It'd be too complicated to try to explain anything else.'

'He knows about you,' he says. 'I told him. He knows what happened that night.'

'Oh.' She doesn't know what to say to that, how to react.

'But we can talk about it another time,' he says.

'Yes.'

'There he is,' he says.

She looks up. There's a boy standing under a lamppost, just in front of the taxi rank. For a second the silhouette of him chokes her breath, taking her back twenty years.

He is tall, slender, young. A mop of curly hair. The image of Benjamin, the boy she fell in love with.

April 2022

Benjamin

He runs towards his son without speaking, and pulls him into a bear hug.

'Thank god,' he says, sobbing onto Aiden's shoulder. 'Thank god you're OK.'

'I'm sorry, Dad,' Aiden says, and when they break apart Benjamin sees that he's crying too. His face looks younger than ever.

'What happened? Where the hell have you been?'

He stands back from his son and looks him up and down. He's wearing jeans and a T-shirt.

'Did you even go to the match?'

Aiden shakes his head. His face is swollen from crying, his eyes puffy and red.

'I couldn't do it, Dad,' he says, a mess of tears. 'I'm so sorry. I tried. I promise I tried, but I couldn't stop him. I tried really hard, but I just couldn't stop him.'

April 2022

Clara

It suddenly makes sense that she is here now. Because she needs to be the strong one. The sensible one. She can take care of him – of both of them – in a way she wanted to but wasn't able to do all those years ago.

She orders an Uber and wordlessly ushers them both into it.

'Where to?' she asks Benjamin. He is still shell-shocked but mumbles an address.

'Hi,' she says, leaning forward to Aiden. 'I'm Clara. I'm…'

'I know who you are,' he says, softly.

She sits back as though she's been slapped.

'Oh,' she says. 'I…'

'You're the reason my dad went to prison,' he adds simply, and suddenly her conviction that she's meant to be there disappears.

'Aiden, that's not true,' Benjamin says sharply.

'It was a long time ago,' is all she can manage.

'It's OK,' he says. 'I know it wasn't your fault.'

He sounds older than his sixteen years. There is something in his eyes that his father never had. Cynicism. Disgust. Disappointment. It makes her sad.

Their youth was a more innocent time.

'Clara happened to be in the city tonight,' Benjamin says. 'And when she heard about what happened she wanted to offer her support.'

'Sure,' Aiden says. 'I'm sorry. I'm sorry for worrying you both.'

'I saw your dad on the news,' she says, awkwardly. 'It was a real shock after all these years but... well, I just didn't want him to be alone.'

They pull up at the house. It's a modest cottage but she recognises the front door from pictures she saw in Benjamin's drawer when they were at university.

He still lives in the same house. She should be surprised, but somehow it makes perfect sense.

'We're going to sit down now and you're going to tell me everything,' Benjamin says, once they're inside. The digital clock on the oven tells her it's nearly 1 a.m., but it might as well be the middle of the day. She's never felt so awake.

'I'll make us all some tea, or something,' she says, and busies herself opening drawers trying to find mugs and teaspoons. Benjamin and Aiden go into the lounge.

She wonders if she should leave. But instead she takes them their tea and slips silently back into the kitchen, staring out of the front window at the small garden path, the road beyond.

There's a small corkboard stuck up next to the window, yellowing photographs pinned to it. A collage of grinning faces, old and young. She smiles as her eyes run over them.

A memory flashes into her mind. Something Benjamin said to her when they were lying together on Hampstead Heath all those years ago, staring up at the clouds moving slowly across the sky, thinking they had all the time in the world.

A simple life with people I love. That's all I've ever wanted.

April 2022

Benjamin

'Right,' he says, staring at his son. 'It's just you and me now. Tell me what's been going on, Aiden. I mean it this time.'

Aiden is gripping his knees with his hands, rocking back and forth.

'Whatever it is, we can deal with it. But you need to tell me what the hell is going on.'

'It's Gary,' Aiden says. His voice is so quiet, it's barely audible. 'I couldn't stop Gary.'

'What couldn't you stop Gary doing?' he says.

Aiden lets out an enormous choked cry, his face suddenly streaming.

'I'm so sorry, Dad,' he says, his whole body convulsing. 'I tried. So many times. I just wanted to help him. He sent me a message this morning, telling me he was going to kill himself. He'd threatened it before, but never gone through with it. But this time he sounded serious. He said he was going to walk into the sea and never come back.'

Aiden shakes his head, takes a deep breath.

'But it was just a trick, to get me out of Newcastle. Otherwise I would have been at the match today. I guess... he wanted to make sure I would be OK, because I was the only one who had any time for him lately. I should have called the police, but I thought if I could find him, I could talk him out of it. He's said stuff like this before, when he's had too much to drink, not thinking straight... he once said he wanted to jump off the Tyne Bridge, then another time he said he'd blow himself up. I thought he was just being a twat... but... then I found that stuff in his bag, the stuff you found in my room. I asked him what he thought he was playing at, but he didn't want to talk... he didn't want to listen.'

He takes his phone out of his pocket.

'I was in such a state earlier, I just left,' he says. 'I didn't realise my battery was so low. It died after I called Gary a few times.'

He plugs it in and turns it on. Then he taps the screen and holds the phone out.

It's a message from Gary.

Sayonara Edwards. I'm away to Northumberland. That village on Druridge Bay. Going to get an ice-cream and walk into the sea and never come back. Thanks for the laughs.

'We went on a drive there once,' Aiden explains. 'Just me, Gary, and Jonny from the team. He told me some stuff about his parents, and it was like he was just a little kid inside. I never thought he would do something like this... but he was so angry. At Coach. At what Coach did to him, throwing him off the team. And he was so bitter that Coach was now leading Newcastle City's youth team, that his career just went from strength to strength, after everything he put him through.'

'Slow down,' Benjamin says, gripping Aiden by the arms.

'And explain to me what you're saying. You're saying that Gary did this? Gary is responsible for the bomb at the stadium?'

Aiden nods, fresh tears spurting.

'I don't know,' he says. 'But I think…'

'Are you saying… Gary… blew himself up?'

Aiden nods, more slowly this time.

'I can't be sure,' he says, spluttering through the tears. 'But I think so, Dad. That's why he sent me miles across the country to try to find him. When I heard about the bomb, at the stadium, I realised – it was just his plan, to get me out of the way so that I was safe.'

'But why would Gary want to bomb the stadium?'

'He hates everything to do with Newcastle City now. He's eaten up with anger about it, about the fact that Coach Kenny gets to sit in the VIP area every week, while Gary has to work on the hot dog stand. That Coach Kenny still gets to be a big shot and that Gary is a nobody. You know what it's like, Dad. It's cut-throat, and the players that don't make the grade get tossed aside like rubbish. He felt betrayed by everyone, the whole football scene.'

Aiden pauses, takes a great gulp of air.

'But most of all he wanted revenge. He wanted Coach to pay for what he did to him.'

'But what did Coach do to him? Aiden! You have to tell me.'

'He raped him,' Aiden cries. 'He raped him, Dad. Every weekend for five years.'

April 2022

Clara

It strikes her that her life has been mostly mundane, but punctuated with occasional evenings of such insanity and drama that they somehow balance out all the groundhog days, when it felt like nothing happened, when nothing moved forward in any sense.

Tonight is one of those nights.

She's waiting inside a police station again, while Benjamin and Aiden tell the police what Aiden knows.

Finally, the adrenaline is wearing off and her eyelids begin to feel heavy. Soon the sun will come up. The start of a new day.

A day when everything is different, in every way.

part six

March 2023

Benjamin

It's Aiden's debut, and Benjamin can barely watch.

As he makes his way to his seat in the stands, he tells everyone who smiles at him that his son is Aiden Edwards. Midfielder. Yes, he'll be playing this afternoon. It's his first professional game for Newcastle City.

Even though he's alone, he feels the warmth from the people he tells; the way they slap him on the back and tell him how proud he must be.

And he thinks, yes, I am prouder than you could ever imagine.

If only George could be there too.

He swallows at the thought of his father. He misses him every day.

Even though Benjamin knew George was getting weaker, his death the January before last was still a massive shock. The only positive was that it was peaceful; a heart attack in his sleep. It was the way he deserved to go, an ending that suited him. No fuss or fanfare, just a quiet slipping away. Knowing that his job here, in this life, was done.

But even so, the hole he had left was larger than Benjamin or Aiden could have ever anticipated.

He's grateful that Aiden has picked himself up, proved himself to be stronger than Benjamin could imagine. He's been seeing a counsellor for the past year, and, perhaps most importantly of all, he's got back into the game.

Meanwhile, Coach Kenny is currently awaiting trial for child sex abuse.

Thanks to Aiden, several more victims have come forward and the police were able to charge him with multiple counts.

It seemed Kenny's modus operandi was to select the most vulnerable kids to groom, who were then discarded, just like Gary, when they got older.

Gary was never going to make it as a football player. Coach kept him on the team for his own twisted reasons, until he tired of him and moved on to his next victim.

Aiden felt lucky, he told Benjamin.

Coach Kenny never invited him back after he left the party early that night. He had ostracised him instead.

Lucky.

Benjamin could hardly bear it.

But of course, it made sense. The missing piece of the puzzle. How upset Aiden had been that night when he'd called, asking Benjamin to collect him from Kenny's house.

Despite being a young lad, enamoured with his coach, Aiden knew something strange was going on, even if he couldn't articulate what it was or why he felt that way.

It was only much later that Gary told Aiden the truth; that Kenny had been abusing him for years. Making him believe he was special, that he had potential, that he'd go far – only to drop him before he could play for the Newcastle City youth team.

Benjamin is deeply ashamed that he never suspected. He'd wondered if Coach Kenny had humiliated Aiden that night at the party – but never this. He had never imagined this.

Again, he had failed his son. But Aiden needed him to be strong, and so Benjamin stood by his side throughout the whole process. And now, hopefully, Coach Kenny will be locked away for a very long time.

But he doesn't want to think about that now. All that matters is the game.

The beautiful game.

They win the match. Afterwards, Benjamin is allowed to go and meet Aiden in the players' lounge. He's done his warm-down and is sitting, red-cheeked and smiling, a bottle of water in hand.

He stands up when Benjamin comes in.

'You were amazing,' he says, pulling him towards him and cradling the back of his head with his hand. 'I've never been more proud.'

'Thanks Dad,' he says. 'Did you hear the crowds? I was proper buzzing. Can't believe it, man. Can't believe I just did that.'

Benjamin takes a few steps back, shaking his head from side to side, taking in the magnificence of his son. What did he do to deserve this boy?

What did he do?

Later, Aiden goes out with his teammates to celebrate their win and Benjamin goes home, back to the cottage at 2 Heaton Way, and he calls Clara.

She squeals down the phone at him.

'I watched! He was incredible!' she says, and he can't help but laugh. This, the girl who once hated football with all her heart. She suddenly knows more than him – texting him her thoughts on the players throughout the week. 'The speed of him! I've never seen anyone run so fast. He really was the star of the match. You can see why they're calling him the lightning bolt.'

It's the best feeling in the world, hearing her say these words about his son.

'I'm made up for him,' he says. 'I really am. You should have seen his face. In the lounge afterwards. He was beaming. I only wish my dad could have been there. He would have been beside himself.'

'Aiden deserves to be happy,' she says. 'So much, after everything he's been through.'

'I really think he might…' he begins. Is it jinxing it? 'I really think he might make a career of this.'

'Of course he will,' she says. 'He's the lightning bolt!'

He smiles again. She sounds like that twenty-year-old from so long ago, who believed that the world is what you make it.

Yours for the taking. If only you have the courage to take it.

Of course, she was right all along.

May 2023

Clara

Clara sits on the small balcony at the back of her flat, looking out at the London rooftops. From this vantage point, she can see into almost all the gardens in the street and, while she speaks to Benjamin, she spies two cats, both curled up in the sun. One is fast asleep. The other is dreaming, its tail flicking in mid-air.

She has an orange lolly, a sunhat pulled low over her forehead.

She has lived here for the better part of a year now. The happiest year of her life.

It's just over a year since she returned home from Newcastle and told Thom the truth.

And this time, she refused to let him talk her out of it. She refused to let him speak until she had finished what she had to say.

She can't remember the exact words now, only the ferocity with which she delivered them.

And he could sense that something had changed in her, because he finally admitted what she had known all along. That he had been having an affair. For nearly a year.

'Natasha,' he said.

The name was like a needle on her skin. *Natasha.*

His friend Hamish's ex. But also…

'Not…' she said, the puzzle pieces clicking into place. She pictured herself holding her ring out, the sad look in the sub-editor's eyes as she complimented it.

Had she ever met Hamish's Natasha? She isn't sure. Perhaps not.

And somehow, it's not a shock. Perhaps deep down she had known, she had chosen not to see it. 'There was a new woman at the paper on Saturday – a freelance sub – she was called Natasha.'

'I'm so sorry. I tried to stop her,' he said, shaking his head.

'But how come she's a journalist too?'

'She's a friend of Chad's,' he said, looking down. 'That's how Hamish met her.'

'Small world,' Clara said, nodding.

'She was so angry with me. For not leaving you. But how could I leave you? You put up with me and my stupid back pain for years. I felt so guilty. I didn't know how to tell you.'

It's ironic and sadly predictable, Clara thinks, that once he began to see that osteopath and his back started feeling better, he had an affair.

'But, why come and get a shift at my paper? What did she think would happen?'

'I don't know what she was thinking,' Thom said. 'But she had wanted to meet you for ages. When you didn't come home that night, I thought something must have happened. That perhaps she'd told you.'

She shook her head.

'No,' she said. 'She was nice. She wanted us to have lunch together.'

Clara gives an involuntary laugh. But it doesn't matter any more.

'The truth is, we can't go on like this, Thom,' she said, quietly. 'You have to let me go.'

He nodded then, and she felt her heart lift with the relief.

'I let you down,' he said, rubbing his face with his hand. 'I failed you. I failed us both. I only wanted to make us happy. I tried so hard.'

He started to cry. She couldn't bear it.

'I tried so hard to get you to love yourself. I thought, if I loved you, if I proved to you just how much you deserved to be loved, that, eventually, you would start to believe it. I thought I could love you enough for both of us. But I let you down. And then... Natasha... we were both so lonely. So lost.'

'Please,' she said, welling up herself. She reached out and touched him lightly on the arm. 'It's OK. Thom, it's OK.'

'I'm so sorry,' he said, sniffing. 'Nothing worked. No matter how hard I tried.'

'That's because it wasn't meant to be,' she said, staring at him. 'It never was. And I had to love myself – that's not something you could do for me. But now... letting me go. That's how you'll make me happy. Please.'

And that was it. Her emancipation.

Why hadn't she thought to tell him that before?

She licks away the drips of melted lolly that have trickled down the stick and onto her fingertips.

On her wrist, she's wearing a thin white-gold bracelet. The tiny diamond star in its centre twinkles in the sunlight. She has kept it all these years, until the time felt right to wear it again.

Since she moved into this flat so many good things have happened.

For one: her second novel, *One Life*, has been picked up by a small but passionate publisher, scheduled for hardback release next year.

Even her mother was impressed at that.

And now, Benjamin's coming down for a visit in two days. It's been nearly a month since she last saw him. She's nervous, but at the same time she can't wait to see him.

To start talking to him. Properly.

They are just friends, but that's fine. She can see now that friendship is so much more valuable. There is so much pressure put on romantic love; a pressure that bends and distorts it into something harmful.

She has wrenched the One True Love Ideal from its pedestal. It's an illusion, a mirage, the stuff of films and fantasies. It is overrated.

Nothing is flawless.

What really matters are the people who care for you without any drama. The ones who will always be there. The ones who will love you when you're old and infirm. The ones who know how to make you smile when you're down. The ones who know when you want to be left alone, and equally know when what you need is a hug, a smile, a kind word... an invisible connection that can pass through any medium. The ones you can go years without speaking to, and then when you do, it's like no time has passed.

They don't have to be a boyfriend, or a wife, or a first love. They can be a father, an aunt, a grandparent. A friend.

But whoever they are, these are the people who truly shape our lives. Who leave their marks on our souls.

These, Clara realises, are the people who make life matter.

May 2023

Benjamin

They both found the one-year-anniversary of the explosion difficult. Benjamin was still tormented by the thought that he should have seen the signs. That he should have done more to investigate what was really going on when Aiden told him he wanted to quit the team, all those years ago. He was so caught up in his own head, thinking it was just about Zoe and her drinking, he couldn't see what was happening right in front of him.

But worst of all, he knows that Aiden still feels guilty that he wasn't able to stop Gary.

Survivor's guilt, the professionals call it. Benjamin knows it's more than that. Gary was Aiden's friend. They had grown up together, and then Gary had grown away from him, further and further, towards a place that was simply unreachable.

Aiden didn't want to talk about it, but he attended the memorial service at Newcastle Cathedral with Benjamin by his side.

Twenty people ultimately died in the attack, including Gary. Benjamin reads about them online. Each an individual. A life, stolen. The greatest of tragedies.

Twenty people killed. Hundreds more injured.

Mindless violence, Benjamin thinks. Except it's not. All violence has a root. A cause. A thread that can be traced back, offering lessons to be learnt. If only people would take the time to learn them.

The Lord Mayor thanked local people for the outpouring of love that followed the attack, stating that the city was stronger and more united than ever as a result. Benjamin hoped that was true.

Finally, the youth drinking culture has come under scrutiny. And this kind of child abuse, and the types of kids vulnerable to it, is now out in the open.

Several more boys have come forward with similar stories about their coaches. As hard as it is to stomach, as much as his heart breaks for each and every one of them, Benjamin thinks that the fact they're speaking up is a good thing.

What he knows for sure is that the ripple effect of Coach Kenny's behaviour will continue for years.

Aiden will never be the same again. And neither will he.

Benjamin doesn't know what the future will hold. As ever, he is cautious. He has been burnt so many times. And what he has with Clara now – a friendship that feels stronger than anything he has ever known – is too precious to risk.

'We need to get to know each other again,' she said to him on the phone a few days ago. 'The truth is, it's been a lifetime. We're different people now. The same, but different.'

She was right. But at least they have the rest of that lifetime. Who knows what might happen?

Aiden moved out of the cottage just over a month ago. Benjamin tried and failed to hide his tears as he helped him unpack his things.

'Don't be soft, Dad,' Aiden said. But Benjamin could tell he felt the same, and he drew his son towards him in a bear hug.

He's renting a flat in the city – in one of those shiny new skyscrapers just beyond the station. The view across Newcastle is magnificent. On match days, if the weather's right, you can practically see the players on the pitch from his living room window.

Aiden is his greatest achievement.

Somehow, he has passed down something – some of his hard-learnt wisdom – despite himself. Despite his ineptitude as a father: his inability to see things clearly, without the filter of his own childhood experiences clouding it all.

Benjamin hopes he hasn't pushed Aiden too much in his career. Sometimes, he worries he's used his son's success to compensate for his own failings.

He remembers the discussion with Clara, that warm July evening years ago by the Thames, when she said that she was writing a book about the pressure to conform as a teenager. She thought that it was just teenage girls who had it tough, but she was wrong. Teenage boys have their own pressures, they just manifest differently.

Aiden has taught Benjamin so much. And thankfully, against the odds, Aiden has turned out all right.

Benjamin is leaving for London today.

He packs his bag carefully: three clean T-shirts, another pair of jeans, a hoodie in case they go out for dinner and it gets chilly. His smartest pair of trousers, and his favourite shirt.

He hasn't told Clara about the interview. It's at one of London's most prestigious production companies, and he knows it's a long shot. More than a long shot.

And it would mean relocating. Leaving the city he has lived

in all his life, and moving down south. To the place that once held such fascination and terror for him. Leaving his son.

Making a home in the capital. Just twenty years later than planned.

He shrugs, folding the shirt carefully. What will be will be.

He checks through everything one last time. Then, once he's satisfied he has all he needs, he zips the bag up and heads for the station.

He knows that Clara will be waiting for him, on the platform at the other end.

Acknowledgements

I wasn't really meant to write this book. And for a long time, it was a secret project – nicknamed my "midlife crisis" book (I *may* have just had a significant birthday when I started to write it).

Perhaps it was the boredom of lockdown, perhaps it was entering my new decade, perhaps it was midlife nostalgia, but in 2021 I found myself thinking more and more about our early romantic relationships, and how they shape our lives. Suddenly, the character of Clara came to me: a woman my age who simply couldn't move past her first great love. Why not? What had happened in her first relationship that had scarred her so immeasurably? I was fascinated by her, and her story, and gradually as I started to write about her, she came to life.

But, as I said, I wasn't really meant to be writing this book. So, the biggest thank-you must go to Katherine Slee, who, during an offhand conversation, encouraged me to take a chance and write something out of my usual genre. Something just for me. Thank you, Katherine. I will forever be grateful – you have changed the course of my career with your words.

Heartfelt thanks to my parents and sister as always but most importantly a huge thank-you to my mum, who was the first person to read this book. She's a fierce critic and I vividly remember receiving the WhatsApp from her after she finished reading. It just said: 'Book is very good 👍'. It made me cry. Thank you, Mum, for always being honest with me.

My UK agent: Caroline Hardman, who is the smartest, most fearless woman in publishing. Thank you for your endless loyalty and wisdom and for loving this book. (Thank you too for being such excellent company!)

Thank you to everyone at Hardman & Swainson, especially Thérèse Coen, for getting behind this book and championing it to publishers across the world, and to Marc Simonsson for sharing it with Hollywood.

And a massive thank you to my US agent Sarah Levitt for making my biggest author dream come true by selling this book to St. Martin's Press in the US. I will never forget the day that email came in.

What can I say about my two amazing editors? I'm a writer but there aren't enough words. Thank you Rachel Faulkner-Willcocks and Sarah Cantin, you are both geniuses and I am in awe of your editing talents. Thank you Rachel for coming back to Caroline within three days to say you loved the book – and for your profound understanding of these characters. Thank you Sarah for your hugely insightful suggestions during the editing process, and for really making me laugh with some of your comments. Honestly it's the greatest privilege being edited by people at the top of their game, and I have learned so much from you both. You have elevated this book to a height I could only have dreamed of.

A huge thanks to everyone who has worked on this book at Head of Zeus: Jessie Price, Nina Elstad, Emma Rogers, Amy Watson, Jo Liddiard, Ana Carter, Paige Harris, Lottie Chase, Dan Groenewald, Nikky Ward, Christian Duck, Faith Stoddard, Yas Brown, Ayo Okojie, Kate Appleton and Bianca

Gillam. There are so many people working behind the scenes to bring novels to readers and I appreciate you all.

I am also very grateful to Graham Bartlett who provided me with invaluable legal advice, and my brother-in-law Wes for helping me to get inside the mindset of a dedicated football fan.

Thank you to all my writing friends – there are too many of you to mention individually and I live in fear of leaving someone out by mistake, but a special thanks to Rebecca Fleet, my oldest (sorry, *most long-standing*!) writing friend. We have been on this roller coaster together since the early days and I'm so happy we're still holding on.

I always say to people that this is not a love story, it's a story about first love. Ol, you may not have been my first love but you are my last. Thank you for your never-ending support and for the little family we have built together. It means more to me than anything.

Thank you Daphne, for making me happy every day (and for demanding that I spell out your name in my acknowledgements this time, so you can find it).

A simple life with people I love. That's all I've ever wanted.

Those are my favorite lines from this novel. They are Benjamin's words, but they are also mine. Daph and Ol: you two are my ultimate loves; you two are the people who make my simple life matter.

Author's Note

Dear Reader,

I have been fascinated by the topic of first love for a long time. It's such a formative experience that casts a lasting shadow on the rest of our lives, and it's been a real joy to explore it as a theme while writing *The One That Got Away*.

Clara and I have a lot in common. I was an insecure teenager; I didn't have the best time at university. I'd gone from being a big fish in a tiny pond (a very small secondary school) to being utterly lost at one of the biggest universities in the country. While I was there, I fell in love more intensely than I could have imagined possible. When university ended, we split up. My heart was broken. I remember those feelings so clearly; the pain that felt as though it might consume me, the feeling that I couldn't live without him, because he was everything to me.

These growing pains are something we all go through. What doesn't kill you makes you stronger, but it still hurts like hell.

Before we fall in love for the first time, we are 'baggage-free': open and trusting. Afterwards, whether we realise it or not, we are surrounded by invisible railings that were forged in the fire of our heartbreak.

For some people, the break-up fire burns more intensely than others. For these people, the railings are higher.

I wanted to examine the impact on two flawed, but very real people, when their first great love story ends in immense tragedy. How did this affect them? What impact did it have on the rest of their lives, and the lives of those around them? And most importantly of all, is there a way they can move on?

It made sense to me to set the early part of the novel at the turn of the Millennium – a time that I am very familiar with, as it was when I too headed off to university. A time before social media and smart phones, but a time when attitudes towards women were worse, in many ways, than they are today. Lads' mags were big business, 'ladette' culture was in its element, female celebrities were objectified across traditional media and there was very much a feeling that if you received an unwanted advance from a man, it was probably because you were in some way, 'asking for it'.

Consent wasn't something that was talked about it – I'm not sure I was even aware of the concept at the time. If you got yourself into a compromising situation then, well, really you only had yourself to blame. You shouldn't have worn such a short skirt. You were leading him on. You drank too much.

This environment is the crucible within which Benjamin and Clara's attitudes towards dating are formed. This backdrop, along with their youth, family histories and differing insecurities, leave them poorly equipped to deal with the challenges they face while negotiating their relationship. They both make a lot of mistakes, but I hope you can understand *why* they make them, and, in your hearts, find some sympathy for them both.

21 is still so very young and tender, even though at that age we think we know it all.

I think it's important not to shy away from the darker areas of modern society in fiction. I was 20 years old when 9/11 happened, and I was actually in London at work on the day of the July 2005 bombings. The threat of terrorism has been a constant throughout my adult life. When major events occur close to home, we understandably worry that loved ones might have been caught up in them. For Clara, this worry is the catalyst that finally propels her to seek the resolution with Benjamin she so needs. These horrific events really pull focus towards what – and who – matter to us most in life.

For those of you who are familiar with the North East, I wanted to confirm that yes, Newcastle City is a made-up football team – not a mistake. I am superstitious, and would never want to set a bomb off in a real location in one of my novels. Thus, I invented the location of Vintage Park stadium, and the fictionalized football team Newcastle City, for the purposes of this story.

Looking back, I feel a great affection for 21-year-old me, who was so hard on herself, who thought she had ruined her own life. In *The One That Got Away*, Clara makes a lot of mistakes. I did too. I forgive her, and I forgive me.

First love is magical, devastating, all-consuming, exhausting, and often bittersweet. When it ends, it's hard to imagine that you will ever love again. But you will, and we do.

As I've grown older, I've come to value a different kind of love. Your last love: one that is equally fascinating and special. But I will always look back on my first love with immense fondness. I hope you do too, and I hope you were moved by Clara and Benjamin's story.

Charlotte x

About the Author

CHARLOTTE RIXON is the pen name of Charlotte Duckworth, *USA Today* bestselling author of suspense fiction published by Quercus. Charlotte studied Classics at Leeds University and went on to gain a PGDip in Screenwriting. She worked for many years as a magazine journalist, and is a graduate of the Faber Academy 'Writing A Novel' course.